Firebird 1

EDITOR: T. J. BINDING

Firebird 1

Writing Today

PENGUIN BOOKS / ALLEN LANE

Penguin Books Ltd, Harmondsworth, Middlesex, England
Penguin Books, 625 Madison Avenue, New York, New York 10022, U.S.A.
Penguin Books Australia Ltd, Ringwood, Victoria, Australia
Penguin Books Canada Ltd, 2801 John Street, Markham, Ontario, Canada L3R 1B4
Penguin Books (N.Z.) Ltd, 182–190 Wairau Road, Auckland 10, New Zealand

This selection first published 1982
Published simultaneously by Allen Lane

Made and printed in Great Britain by
Hazell, Watson and Viney Ltd, Aylesbury, Bucks.
Set in Sabon with Gill display by MS Filmsetting Ltd, Frome, Somerset
Designed by Peter Ward

Paperback ISBN 0 14 00 6206 8
Hardback ISBN 0 7139 1492 0

CONTENTS

Ron Butlin

SCENES
FROM
AN
OPERA

RON BUTLIN was born in 1949 in Edinburgh where he still lives. At present he is writer-in-residence at Edinburgh University. He has published two collections of poems, *Stretto* (1976) and *Creatures Tamed By Cruelty* (1979) and a third, *The Exquisite Instrument*, will be published in 1982. He was awarded a writer's bursary by the Scottish Arts Council in 1977.

There is a flight of stairs leading up to the next floor. Mitchell lives under these stairs. He crouches there to cook and lies full length to sleep. He has been living here for two years. He bothers nobody and nobody bothers him – some of the friendlier residents even bid him good day as they pass. One morning he found a pail and mop beside him when he woke up. 'A strange gift,' he thought to himself – the pail and mop being completely new – then he realized what was expected of him in return for his lodgings, and that day and twice a week from then on, he cleaned the stairs.

Occasionally people left food out for him, but not now. The main door was locked three days ago and a list of the residents' names was pasted up on each floor. He is on the list as 'Cleaner – third floor'. Already some of the names are stroked out. No one enters or leaves the building. There is a notice which says that anyone seen climbing out of the windows will be shot on sight.

He is getting very hungry. He spends the afternoons seated on the window-sill at the end of the corridor, looking down into the street. But nothing happens or it happens too quickly: a window smashes, a building collapses or somebody is killed. There is the occasional explosion or burst of gunfire but it is always over too soon to see exactly what is happening. He has not had a cigarette since yesterday and there is a rumour that the drinking-water is poisoned.

It is late afternoon. Mitchell is looking out of the window and seems to be swaying slightly. Perhaps he is singing into himself 'Im Mohrenland gefangen war' from Mozart's *The Seraglio*. He understudied the part of Pedrillo when he was training to be an opera singer – four completely wasted years as it turned out. He climbs off the window-sill, walks over to one of the flats and rings the bell.

Nothing happens and so he knocks. The door seems to be made of heavy wood. It appears solid and is painted a very bright green. It is being opened slowly. Mitchell stands up straight. A woman appears who could be Blondin out of *The Seraglio*.

'Yes?' she begins. Then she recognizes him. 'Oh! it's you.'

'Who is it?' a voice asks from backstage. Blondin steps back into the flat.

'The cleaner,' she replies, waiting for Mitchell to develop the situation. By gesturing he tries to tell her that he is hungry and also that he would appreciate a cigarette.

'What does he want?' the voice comes again. A deep voice. Osmin's.

'Just a minute,' she says and closes the door. Mitchell stands and waits. There is a burst of machine-gun fire from outside, and people shouting. But he doesn't go to the window; he waits.

Several moments pass and he is still standing outside the flat. It is almost dark now and the lights on the stair have not been working for the last few days. Someone is coming along the corridor. Mitchell walks beside him trying to tell him that he is hungry.

'Aren't we all,' the man remarks and goes into a flat further down the corridor. Mitchell walks a few steps and then sits down on the floor, his back against the wall. He seems to be quite dejected. A moment later the man comes out of his flat and calls to Mitchell, then throws him a couple of cigarettes. He doesn't wait to be thanked but goes back inside again. There is a loud explosion from nearby that makes the whole building shake. Mitchell goes over to the window where he smokes one of the cigarettes while looking down into the street. When it is finished he feels his way to his bed under the stairs and then lies in the darkness staring at nothing until he falls asleep.

It is morning. Mitchell is drinking some of the water that is rumoured to be poisoned. He was awakened during the night by someone hammering on the street-door to get in, then the hammering stopped and he went back to sleep. When he got up he tried a few doors but no one answered. Some more of the names on the list are stroked out. They will have died. Perhaps it is not the water as there seems to be quite a few old people living here. Once all the names in a flat are stroked out, then it will be empty and Mitchell will be able to break in and secure it for himself.

He knocks on the door of the man who gave him the cigarette last night. He is invited in. This is the first time that he has been inside one of the flats. The man tells him that he shares it with his wife and her mother; they have no children. He says that they would die – he seems to mean the children. His mother-in-law is very fat and appears to be completely deaf. He says that she never moves from her chair and that she'll never die. He adds that unfortunately his wife loves her, otherwise he'd have killed her years ago.

In this scene there is clothing hanging everywhere. There is a radio on the sideboard. It is tuned into a foreign station and so perhaps the mother-in-law is not deaf but just does not understand English. Three tables are set round her heaped with objects to fill up her day. A television is facing her across the room. There is a programme about underwater life and the sound is turned down. The atmosphere is stifling.

She speaks to Mitchell but he doesn't understand a word she says. Her voice is a pleasant mellow contralto. Then she turns slightly and spits into a small basin on one of the tables beside her. She begins rummaging about in the articles on the table – magazines, pens, cigarettes, a whistle, some sewing – and she beckons him to come closer. There is quite a growth of hair on her chin and upper lip. She smells very unpleasant especially when her movements disturb her clothing. Possibly she isn't so much fat as very swollen and in great pain all the time.

At last she finds what she has been looking for – a piece of cake which she offers to Mitchell. Her son-in-law tries to interfere but she glares at him and he does nothing. As Mitchell eats it her face relaxes into a smile. However he seems afraid that she will want to pat or fondle him perhaps, and he gradually moves away. The cake must have made him thirsty because he seems to be asking them for something to drink when the building is shaken by an explosion. The windows rattle and one of the panes cracks right across.

A woman's voice, an alto, comes from a room off-stage. She is calling for the man, Robert. He goes to her, leaving Mitchell and the fat woman together. She smiles broadly, then points firstly to the window and then to the room into which Robert has gone. She is talking very excitedly.

Mitchell doesn't understand a word of it of course – then suddenly she breaks off to spit into the basin again. He goes over to a sink in the corner of the room for a cup of water. The woman shouts to him – she is probably warning him about the water being poisoned; her daughter must have told her about it. He pays no attention.

Robert comes back out of the room and asks Mitchell his name. He tries to say it. Sometimes he can almost manage something, but not today. Robert gives him a paper and pencil. He writes very casually though his hand seems to be trembling – 'Mitchell'. First name? Robert demands – and Mitchell begins to write but the pencil breaks. For some reason Robert takes offence at such clumsiness and, completely ignoring Mitchell's attempt to sound out his name, states curtly that *his* name is Sinclair. His wife would like a word. He indicates that Mitchell should follow him.

The bedroom is tastelessly furnished from budget catalogues. The curtains are drawn. Very harsh lighting comes from a coiled silvery object which stands on the bedside table. Robert's wife looks very weak.

'My husband ...' she begins and then stops. 'He can *hear*, can't he?' she asks in an aside.

'I think so; yes, he can,' comes the reply after a moment's pause.

'My husband ...' she begins once more then trails off again. She picks up a reel of cotton from the folds of the bedspread and begins snapping pieces of thread.

'I shall come straight to the point,' she declares firmly and sits up in bed. 'You are the cleaner and you say that your name is Mitchell?' Then without waiting for a reply she continues.

'Well then, Mitchell.' Her voice has suddenly become contemptuous in tone. 'Why aren't you out fighting? Don't you care that they might break in here and murder us all? Do you wish me and my mother dead?' She has a very harsh voice. Mitchell shakes his head, he seems very embarrassed. She must be very ill to speak like this. Mitchell glances over to her husband with a look of understanding and pity. Robert glares back at him.

She continues snapping thread in silence for a moment. Then she begins again.

'My husband has to stay here to look after my mother and myself. But you – you've no family, have you? No one depends on you for anything, do they? So don't act so selfishly!' She falls back against the pillows quite exhausted with her performance.

Robert goes to her side. He gives her something to drink and then sits on the bed taking her hand in his. He kisses her gently on the forehead then turns to face Mitchell.

'Don't just stand there. Aren't you ashamed of yourself?' he says. His wife smiles, then, holding on to her husband, raises herself up again.

'Why don't you *do* something for once, something amusing?' she sneers. 'Make us all feel good for a change. I'm in bed. I'm dying. Amuse me, come on.' She begins pointing at Mitchell and shouting. 'Come on you bastard, you creeping little bastard, amuse me – do something to cheer me up.'

And when she sees Mitchell going at this point she begins screaming the crudest obscenities after him. Her husband joins in. Mitchell rushes through the kitchen where the fat woman immediately starts in counterpoint to her daughter and son-in-law. Her entry is perfect and her contralto soothing. She blows him a kiss and he gives her a wave as he goes out the door.

The corridor looks chilly after the closeness of the flat. Mitchell goes to look at the list again. Some of the names have been crossed out in red, some in blue – so different people must mark off who'd died. Then if it is the people in the flats who mark off their own dead, it surely follows that there will never be a flat with everyone's name stroked out – for the last person can hardly be expected to cross off his own name. Mitchell must realize this now.

There may be a flat empty at this moment; all he need do is look for the flats with only one name left and try them. He is scanning the list eagerly and notes that there are two flats worth trying on this floor. The first is three doors along.

He tries it. He rings the bell. He rings it again. What if no one answers? It is possible he will have to break the door down. Break the lock maybe. There was a time when you could force your way in with a piece of plastic – but people have better locks nowadays, more's the pity for him. Or he could drive wedges into the top and bottom of the door – then the tensions will build up between the door, the frame and the lock until the weakest part gives way. Noisy, but no one here would pay the slightest attention.

He is about to knock on the door for one last time when a voice asks who's there. He doesn't move. The voice asks again and again gets no reply. The door remains shut. The owner must be standing still and listening closely. Mitchell walks quietly round to the next flat. He rings the bell and waits.

There is no reply. He rings again and again there is no reply. He knocks loudly and still there is no reply. It must be empty and so he will break in.

There are two locks on the door, large ones. He steps back then slams his shoulder against the panel. He hurts his shoulder. He steps back again and then kicks it twice, hurting each foot in turn. He decides to rest. Perhaps he should wait until someone else dies – someone with smaller locks. What he needs is a tool of some sort – an axe, a crowbar. Perhaps he could borrow one, but it seems unlikely. He sits down opposite and stares at the door.

A few moments pass and then he notices a small window set above the lintel. This must be to let light into the hallway. Not a big window certainly – but if he managed to smash it and climb in without bleeding to death, then he wouldn't need to bother with the door. There does not seem to be very much in the way of handy props with which to break the glass, but there is a fire-extinguisher further down the hall. He goes to pick it up.

Fighting has begun again outside – machine-gun and mortar fire. Bullets hit the main door downstairs and echo loudly. Then someone begins hammering loudly, begging to be let in. There is another burst of gunfire against the door followed by a scream. Quickly Mitchell hurls the fire-extinguisher through the window, clambers on to the lintel and squeezes past the broken glass. He jumps down on to the floor.

The flat is in darkness. He gropes his way along the passage and into one of the rooms. The furniture is large and old, but looks quite comfortable. It is a bedroom and there are two bodies – a man on the bed and a woman on the floor. Mitchell opens the window very cautiously, then drags them both over and pushes them out. As each one falls to the ground there is a burst of gunfire. He closes the window and then goes to look round his flat.

After a meal of corned beef and pineapple slices he settles down to watch television, having placed a bottle of sherry and a packet of cream crackers within reach. There is a schools programme about transportation; a consumer phone-in; and then, to his delight, a filmed performance of Mozart's *Seraglio*. He relaxes into his chair and dips a cracker into his cup of sherry.

During the rather laboured finale to Act 2 the doorbell rings. He ignores it. It rings again and again he ignores it. Suddenly there is a gunshot and the door is forced in. A chorus of soldiers enter and begin shouting in a foreign language. Mitchell tries to show them that he cannot speak. One of them is impatient and shoots at the TV screen. There is silence. Then he points the gun at Mitchell.

At this point another soldier enters and the chorus stands to attention. He must be an officer.

'We are soldiers of the army of liberation. Until everything is over you must remain indoors.' The officer has a good voice with only the slightest trace of accent. He glances quickly round the kitchen and then looks into the hall.

'You have room for four soldiers,' he states. Mitchell nods in agreement. Four soldiers are picked to remain and one of them, Mamk, is placed in charge. The rest leave.

Mitchell and the soldiers sit down to finish the sherry. An enormous slab of cooking chocolate is produced and shared out. By way of introduction each of them points to himself and says his name. Mitchell writes down the name 'Donaldson' – which is the name on the door. He can't help laughing at the sounds they make when trying to say his name. Soon the soldiers join in laughing as well, and then everyone shakes hands and another bottle of sherry is opened.

There is a ring at the doorbell. Mitchell gets up to answer it but one of the soldiers motions him back to his seat and answers it himself. He returns with Robert, the man who invited Mitchell into his flat. Robert is crying. He is given a solo in which he says that soldiers forced their way into his flat and then raped his wife. When he tried to stop them they threatened to shoot him. What could he do? Then he says that his mother-in-law was a collaborator and he has killed her. He begins acting out the events he is describing. He shows everyone some blood on his clothes and then brings out a knife. At this, one of the soldiers shoots him. He falls to the floor. Mamk and another soldier drag the body out into the hall.

It is evening a few days later. Mitchell is sleeping on a couch in front of the stove. Mamk returns with some food and wakes him. He is starting to prepare the evening meal when Mamk indicates that he has a surprise for him. When the other soldiers return, he tells him, they will be bringing a woman. They have brought women back before, but this time the woman will be for Mitchell.

And a few moments later the other soldiers enter with Robert's wife. She seems very ill, perhaps even dying; she is still wearing her nightdress. They put her in the bedroom and then go through one at a time until it is Mitchell's turn.

He enters the bedroom where Robert's wife is lying on the bed. She seems hardly aware that there is someone else in the room. Mitchell stands and looks at her. After a few moments he goes and sits on the edge of the bed. Still she seems unaware of what is happening. He takes her hand, and when he kisses it she looks at him in disgust then turns her face away. She does not seem to recognize him. He kisses her hand again, then suddenly grabs her shoulders and, twisting her round, kisses her very roughly on the lips. She doesn't struggle; she makes no response at all. He lets go and she falls back on the bed and lies still. Her nightdress is up round her waist and Mitchell smoothes it down gently. His hand rests on her knee for a moment. Then he takes it away and appears to be about to stand up when the soldiers rush into the room.

They begin shouting at him and pushing him against her. They are joking and angry at the same time. They sing a robust comic quartet – each taking a verse, telling and acting out what he'd done with her; the chorus is an unexpectedly gentle lyric in praise of women and love. At the same time, they are forcibly undressing Mitchell and one of them rips open the front of the woman's nightgown.

Having stripped him naked they stand Mitchell on his feet and they wait. Robert's wife has been made to sit up in bed; her face is quite expressionless. Mitchell just stands there and then Mamk points a gun at him. This makes the other soldiers laugh. Mitchell still doesn't move and Mamk suddenly fires past him shattering one of the window-panes. It seems as if Mitchell hardly notices the shot for he remains standing exactly where he is. But the woman gets up off the bed and is coming towards him. She is terrified. She takes him in her arms. The soldiers give her a loud cheer.

Mitchell seems almost unaware that she is holding him. She presses herself against him; she says that the soldiers may kill them if nothing happens. She keeps shouting at him, asking if he understands. He gives no response. Desperately she begins caressing him and saying things to get him excited. She says that her name is Sandra but she will be whoever he wants. Finally she says that they should pretend. Then she lies down pulling him on top of her, and she begins to moan gently.

It is a week later. Mitchell is standing at the sink washing dishes. Sandra is looking out of the window. The kitchen is as before, except there is a blackboard set up on the mantlepiece. On it are four columns of chalk marks. The dishwater looks slightly greenish; it must be poisoned. He goes over to Sandra and puts his arm round her. She says that as the streets are so full of tanks perhaps the rumours are true – and the soldiers are really going to leave in the next few days. They kiss.

She goes over to the blackboard. She calls them bastards because even when they've won they're still killing people. Even when they've won they're still playing it like a game and keeping scores. And tomorrow, with any luck, they will go away. And what would be done with the blackboard – just wipe it clean again? She is getting very angry and it looks as if she is about to pick up the blackboard when Mitchell grabs her and holds her still. Gradually she calms down. She agrees that would have been a very stupid thing to do. Only a few more days, she says, maybe even tomorrow.

Mitchell is looking at the blackboard. His arms are folded and he is staring hard. All at once he smiles, and then laughs. Sandra looks at him in amazement. He seems really excited. He is waving his arms about and now he has turned her round to face the blackboard. Then he goes over to it and rubs out two of the marks on two of the columns. He turns to Sandra looking very pleased with himself.

Sandra doesn't understand. Mitchell is desperate to tell her what he thinks will happen now, and so he does a charade. He pretends he is each soldier in turn. The first one comes in, chalks up his day's score and then adds it all up to himself. The next soldier does the same. But when the other two add their scores up they see the totals are one less than they should be. They check them again. Then they accuse the first two, who deny everything. None of them suspects Mitchell – why should they? A fight starts and eventually they shoot each other.

Sandra agrees that it will probably work. She adds that just to be on the safe side perhaps they should go into her flat until it is all over. They leave.

After a few moments the soldiers enter and the finale begins.

A. S. Byatt

THE
JULY
GHOST

'I think I must move out of where I'm living,' he said. 'I have this problem with my landlady.'

He picked a long, bright hair off the back of her dress, so deftly that the act seemed simply considerate. He had been skilful at balancing glass, plate and cutlery, too. He had a look of dignified misery, like a dejected hawk. She was interested.

'What sort of problem? Amatory, financial, or domestic?'

'None of those, really. Well, not financial.'

He turned the hair on his finger, examining it intently, not meeting her eye.

'Not financial. Can you tell me? I might know somewhere you could stay. I know a lot of people.'

'You would.' He smiled shyly. 'It's not an easy problem to describe. There's just the two of us. I occupy the attics. Mostly.'

He came to a stop. He was obviously reserved and secretive. But he was telling her something. This is usually attractive.

'Mostly?' Encouraging him.

'Oh, it's not like *that*. Well, not ... Shall we sit down?'

They moved across the party, which was a big party, on a hot day. He stopped and found a bottle and filled her glass. He had not needed to ask what she was drinking. They sat side by side on a sofa: he admired the brilliant poppies bold on her emerald dress, and her pretty sandals. She had come to London for the summer to work in the British Museum. She could really have managed with microfilm in Tucson for what little manuscript research was needed, but there was a dragging love affair to end. There is an age at which, however desperately happy one is in stolen moments, days, or weekends with one's married professor, one either prises him loose or cuts and runs. She had had a stab at both, and now considered she had successfully cut and run. So it was nice to be immediately appreciated. Problems are capable of solution. She said as much to him, turning her soft face to his ravaged one, swinging the long bright hair. It had begun a year ago, he told her in a rush, at another party actually; he had met this woman, the landlady in question, and had made, not immediately, a kind of *faux pas*, he now saw, and she had been very decent, all things considered, and so ...

He had said, 'I think I must move out of where I'm living.' He had been quite wild, had nearly not come to the party, but could not go on drinking alone. The woman had considered him coolly and asked, 'Why?' One could not, he said, go on in a place where one had once been blissfully happy, and was now miserable, however convenient the place. Convenient, that was, for work, and friends, and things that seemed, as he mentioned them, ashy and insubstantial compared to the memory and the hope of opening the door and finding Anne outside it, laughing and breathless, waiting to be told what he had read, or thought, or eaten, or felt that day. Someone I loved left, he told the woman. Reticent on that occasion too, he bit back the flurry of sentences about the total unexpectedness of it, the arriving back and finding only an envelope on a clean table, and spaces in the bookshelves, the record stack, the kitchen cupboard. It must have been planned for weeks, she must have been thinking it out while he rolled on her, while she poured wine for him, while ... No, no. Vituperation is undignified and in this case what he felt was lower and worse than rage: just pure, child-like loss. 'One ought not to mind places,' he said to the woman. 'But one does,' she had said. 'I know.'

She had suggested to him that he could come and be her lodger, then; she had, she said, a lot of spare space going to waste, and her husband wasn't there much. 'We've not had a lot to say to each other, lately.' He could be quite self-contained, there was a kitchen and a bathroom in the attics; she wouldn't bother him. There was a large garden. It was possibly this that decided him: it was very hot, central London, the time of year when a man feels he would give anything to live in a room opening on to grass and trees, not a high flat in a dusty street. And if Anne came back, the door would be locked and mortice-locked. He could stop thinking about Anne coming back. That was a decisive move: Anne thought he wasn't decisive. He would live without Anne.

For some weeks after he moved in he had seen very little of the woman. They met on the stairs, and once she came up, on a hot Sunday, to tell him he must feel free to use the garden. He had offered to do some weeding and mowing and she had accepted. That was the weekend her husband came back, driving furiously up to the front door, running in, and calling in the empty hall, 'Imogen, Imogen!' To which she had replied, uncharacteristically by screaming hysterically. There was nothing in her husband, Noel's, appearance to warrant this reaction; their lodger, peering over the banister at the sound, had seen their upturned faces in the stairwell and watched hers settle into its usual prim and placid expression as he did so. Seeing Noel, a balding, fluffy-templed, stooping thirty-five or so, shabby corduroy suit, cotton polo neck, he realized he was now able to guess her age, as he had not been. She was a very neat woman, faded blond, her hair in a knot on the back of her head, her legs long and slender, her eyes downcast. Mild was not quite the right word for her, though. She explained then that she had screamed because Noel had come home unexpectedly and startled her: she was sorry. It seemed a reasonable explanation. The extraordinary vehemence of the screaming was probably an echo in the stairwell. Noel seemed wholly downcast by it, all the same.

He had kept out of the way, that weekend, taking the stairs two at a time and lightly, feeling a little aggrieved, looking out of his kitchen window into the lovely, overgrown garden, that they were lurking indoors, wasting all the summer sun. At Sunday lunch-time he had heard the husband, Noel, shouting on the stairs.

'I can't go on, if you go on like that. I've done my best, I've tried to get through. Nothing will shift you, will it, you won't *try*, will you, you just go on and on. Well, I have my life to live, you can't throw a life away . . . can you?'

He had crept out again on to the dark upper landing and seen her standing, half-way down the stairs, quite still, watching Noel wave his arms and roar, or almost roar, with a look of impassive patience, as though this nuisance must pass off. Noel swallowed and gasped; he turned his face up to her and said plaintively,

'You do see I can't stand it? I'll be in touch, shall I? You must want ... you must need ... you must ...'

She didn't speak.

'If you need anything, you know where to get me.'

'Yes.'

'Oh, well ...' said Noel, and went to the door. She watched him, from the stairs, until it was shut, and then came up again, step by step, as though it was an effort, a little, and went on coming, past her bedroom, to his landing, to come in and ask him, entirely naturally, please to use the garden if he wanted to, and please not to mind marital rows. She was sure he understood ... things were difficult ... Noel wouldn't be back for some time. He was a journalist: his work took him away a lot. Just as well. She committed herself to that 'just as well'. She was a very economical speaker.

So he took to sitting in the garden. It was a lovely place: a huge, hidden, walled south London garden, with old fruit trees at the end, a wildly waving disorderly buddleia, curving beds full of old roses, and a lawn of overgrown, dense rye-grass. Over the wall at the foot was the Common, with a footpath running behind all the gardens. She came out to the shed and helped him to assemble and oil the lawnmower, standing on the little path under the apple branches while he cut an experimental serpentine across her hay. Over the wall came the high sound of children's voices, and the thunk and thud of a football. He asked her how to raise the blades: he was not mechanically minded.

'The children get quite noisy,' she said. 'And dogs. I hope they don't bother you. There aren't many safe places for children, round here.'

He replied truthfully that he never heard sounds that didn't concern him, when he was concentrating. When he'd got the lawn into shape, he was going to sit on it and do a lot of reading, try to get his mind in trim again, to write a paper on Hardy's poems, on their curiously archaic vocabulary.

'It isn't very far to the road on the other side, really,' she said. 'It just seems to be. The Common is an illusion of space, really. Just a spur of brambles and gorse-bushes and bits of football pitch between two fast four-laned main roads. I hate London commons.'

'There's a lovely smell, though, from the gorse and the wet grass. It's a pleasant illusion.'

'No illusions are pleasant,' she said, decisively, and went in. He wondered what she did with her time: apart from little shopping expeditions she seemed to be always in the house. He was sure that when he'd met her she'd been introduced as having some profession: vaguely literary, vaguely academic, like everyone he knew. Perhaps she wrote poetry in her north-facing living-room. He had no idea what it would be like. Women generally wrote emotional poetry, much nicer than men, as Kingsley Amis has stated, but she seemed, despite her placid stillness, too spare and too fierce – grim? – for that. He remembered the screaming. Perhaps she wrote Plath-like chants of violence. He didn't think that quite fitted the bill, either. Perhaps she was a freelance radio journalist. He didn't bother to ask anyone who might be a common acquaintance. During the whole year, he explained to the American at the party, he hadn't actually *discussed* her with anyone. Of course he wouldn't, she agreed vaguely and warmly. She knew he wouldn't. He didn't see why he shouldn't, in fact, but went on, for the time, with his narrative.

They had got to know each other a little better over the next few weeks, at least on the level of borrowing tea, or even sharing pots of it. The weather had got hotter. He had found an old-fashioned deck-chair, with faded striped canvas, in the shed, and had brushed it over and brought it out on to his mown lawn, where he sat writing a little, reading a little, getting up and pulling up a tuft of couch grass. He had been wrong about the children not bothering him: there was a succession of incursions by all sizes of children looking for all sizes of balls, which bounced to his feet, or crashed in the shrubs, or vanished in the herbaceous border, black and white footballs, beach-balls with concentric circles of primary colours, acid yellow tennis balls. The children came over the wall: black faces, brown faces, floppy long hair, shaven heads, respectable dotted sun-hats and camouflaged cotton army hats from Milletts. They came over easily, as though they were used to it, sandals, training shoes, a few bare toes, grubby sunburned legs, cotton skirts, jeans, football shorts. Sometimes, perched on the top, they saw him and gestured at the balls; one or two asked permission. Sometimes he threw a ball back, but was apt to knock down a few knobby little unripe apples or pears. There was a gate in the wall, under the fringing trees, which he once tried to open, spending time on rusty bolts only to discover that the lock was new and secure, and the key not in it.

The boy sitting in the tree did not seem to be looking for a ball. He was in a fork of the tree nearest the gate, swinging his legs, doing something to a knot in a frayed end of rope that was attached to the branch he sat on. He wore blue jeans and training shoes, and a brilliant tee shirt, striped in the colours of the spectrum, arranged in the right order, which the man on the grass found visually pleasing. He had rather long blond hair, falling over his eyes, so that his face was obscured.

'Hey, you. Do you think you ought to be up there? It might not be safe.'

The boy looked up, grinned, and vanished monkey-like over the wall. He had a nice, frank grin, friendly, not cheeky.

He was there again, the next day, leaning back in the crook of the tree, arms crossed. He had on the same shirt and jeans. The man watched him, expecting him to move again, but he sat, immobile, smiling down pleasantly, and then staring up at the sky. The man read a little, looked up, saw him still there, and said,

'Have you lost anything?'

The child did not reply: after a moment he climbed down a little, swung along the branch hand over hand, dropped to the ground, raised an arm in salute, and was up over the usual route over the wall.

Two days later he was lying on his stomach on the edge of the lawn, out of the shade, this time in a white tee shirt with a pattern of blue ships and water-lines on it, his bare feet and legs stretched in the sun. He was chewing a grass stem, and studying the earth, as though watching for insects. The man said 'Hi, there,' and the boy looked up, met his look with intensely blue eyes under long lashes, smiled with the same complete warmth and openness, and returned his look to the earth.

He felt reluctant to inform on the boy, who seemed so harmless and considerate: but when he met him walking out of the kitchen door, spoke to him, and got no answer but the gentle smile before the boy ran off towards the wall, he wondered if he should speak to his landlady. So he asked her, did she mind the children coming in the garden. She said no, children must look for balls, that was part of being children. He persisted – they sat there, too, and he had met one coming out of the house. He hadn't seemed to be doing any harm, the boy, but you couldn't tell. He thought she should know.

He was probably a friend of her son's, she said. She looked at him kindly and explained. Her son had run off the Common with some other children, two years ago, in the summer, in July, and had been killed on the road. More or less instantly, she had added drily, as though calculating that just *enough* information would preclude the need for further questions. He said he was sorry, very sorry, feeling to blame, which was ridiculous, and a little injured, because he had not known about her son, and might inadvertently have made a fool of himself with some casual reference whose ignorance would be embarrassing.

What was the boy like, she said. The one in the house? 'I don't – talk to his friends. I find it painful. It could be Timmy, or Martin. They might have lost something, or want...'

He described the boy. Blond, about ten at a guess, he was not very good at children's ages, very blue eyes, slightly built, with a rainbow-striped tee shirt and blue jeans, mostly though not always – oh, and those football practice shoes, black and green. And the other tee shirt, with the ships and wavy lines. And an extraordinarily nice smile. A really *warm* smile. A nice-looking boy.

He was used to her being silent. But this silence went on and on and on. She was just staring into the garden. After a time, she said, in her precise conversational tone,

'The only thing I want, the only thing I want at all in this world, is to see that boy.'

She stared at the garden and he stared with her, until the grass began to dance with empty light, and the edges of the shrubbery wavered. For a brief moment he shared the strain of not seeing the boy. Then she gave a little sigh, sat down, neatly as always, and passed out at his feet.

After this she became, for her, voluble. He didn't move her after she fainted, but sat patiently by her, until she stirred and sat up; then he fetched her some water, and would have gone away, but she talked.

'I'm too rational to see ghosts, I'm not someone who would see anything there was to see, I don't believe in an after-life, I don't see how anyone can, I always found a kind of satisfaction for myself in the idea that one just came to an end, to a sliced-off stop. But that was myself; I didn't think *he* – not *he* – I thought ghosts were – what people *wanted* to see, or were afraid to see ... and after he died, the best hope I had, it sounds silly, was that I would go mad enough so that instead of waiting every day for him to come home from school and rattle the letter-box I might actually have the illusion of seeing or hearing him come in. Because I can't stop my body and mind waiting, every day, every day, I can't let go. And his bedroom, sometimes at night I go in, I think I might just for a moment forget he *wasn't* in there sleeping, I think I would pay almost anything – anything at all – for a moment of seeing him like I used to. In his pyjamas, with his – his – his hair ... ruffled, and, his ... you said, his ... that *smile*.

'When it happened, they got Noel, and Noel came in and shouted my name, like he did the other day, that's why I screamed, because it – seemed the same – and then they said, he is dead, and I thought coolly, *is* dead, that will go on and on and on till the end of time, it's a continuous present tense, one thinks the most ridiculous things, there I was thinking about grammar, the verb to be, when it ends to be dead ... And then I came out into the garden, and I half saw, in my mind's eye, a kind of ghost of his face, just the eyes and hair, coming towards me – like every day waiting for him to come home, the way you think of your son, with such pleasure, when he's – not there – and I – I thought – no, I won't *see* him, because he is dead, and I won't dream about him because he is dead, I'll be rational and practical and continue to live because one must, and there was Noel...

'I got it wrong, you see, I was so *sensible*, and then I was so shocked because I couldn't get to want anything – I couldn't *talk* to Noel – I – I – made Noel take away, destroy, all the photos, I – didn't dream, you can will not to dream, I didn't ... visit a grave, flowers, there isn't any point. I was so sensible. Only my body wouldn't stop waiting and all it wants is to – to see that boy. *That* boy. That boy you – saw.'

He did not say that he might have seen another boy, maybe even a boy who had been given the tee shirts and jeans afterwards. He did not say, though the idea crossed his mind, that maybe what he had seen was some kind of impression from her terrible desire to see a boy where nothing was. The boy had had nothing terrible, no aura of pain about him: he had been, his memory insisted, such a pleasant, courteous, self-contained boy, with his own purposes. And in fact the woman herself almost immediately raised the possibility that what he had seen was what she desired to see, a kind of mix-up of radio waves, like when you overheard police messages on the radio, or got BBC 1 on a switch that said ITV. She was thinking fast, and went on almost immediately to say that perhaps his sense of loss, his loss of Anne, which was what had led her to feel she could bear his presence in her house, was what had brought them – dare she say – near enough, for their wavelengths to mingle, perhaps, had made him susceptible ... You mean, he had said, we are a kind of emotional vacuum, between us, that must be filled. Something like that, she had said, and had added, 'But I don't believe in ghosts.'

Anne, he thought, could not be a ghost, because she was elsewhere, with someone else, doing for someone else those little things she had done so gaily for him, tasty little suppers, bits of research, a sudden vase of unusual flowers, a new bold shirt, unlike his own cautious taste, but suiting him, suiting him. In a sense, Anne was worse lost because voluntarily absent, an absence that could not be loved because love was at an end, for Anne.

'I don't suppose you will, now,' the woman was saying. 'I think talking would probably stop any – mixing of messages, if that's what it is, don't you? But – if – *if* he comes again' – and here for the first time her eyes were full of tears – 'if – you must promise, you will *tell* me, you must promise.'

He had promised, easily enough, because he was fairly sure she was right, the boy would not be seen again. But the next day he was on the lawn, nearer than ever, sitting on the grass beside the deck-chair, his arms clasping his bent, warm brown knees, the thick, pale hair glittering in the sun. He was wearing a football shirt, this time, Chelsea's colours. Sitting down in the deck-chair, the man could have put out a hand and touched him, but did not: it was not, it seemed, a possible gesture to make. But the boy looked up and smiled, with a pleasant complicity, as though they now understood each other very well. The man tried speech: he said, 'It's nice to see you again,' and the boy nodded acknowledgement of this remark, without speaking himself. This was the beginning of communication between them, or what the man supposed to be communication. He did not think of fetching the woman. He became aware that he was in some strange way *enjoying the boy's company*. His pleasant stillness – and he sat there all morning, occasionally lying back on the grass, occasionally staring thoughtfully at the house – was calming and comfortable. The man did quite a lot of work – wrote about three reasonable pages on Hardy's original air-blue gown – and looked up now and then to make sure the boy was still there and happy.

He went to report to the woman – as he had after all promised to do – that evening. She had obviously been waiting and hoping – her unnatural calm had given way to agitated pacing, and her eyes were dark and deeper in. At this point in the story he found in himself a necessity to bowdlerize for the sympathetic American, as he had indeed already begun to do. He had mentioned only a child who had 'seemed like' the woman's lost son, and he now ceased to mention the child at all, as an actor in the story, with the result that what the American woman heard was a tale of how he, the man, had become increasingly involved in the woman's solitary grief, how their two losses had become a kind of *folie à deux* from which he could not extricate himself. What follows is not what he told the American girl, though it may be clear at which points the bowdlerized version coincided with what he really believed to have happened. There was a sense he could not at first analyse that it was improper to talk about the boy – not because he might not be believed; that did not come into it; but because something dreadful might happen.

'He sat on the lawn all morning. In a football shirt.'

'Chelsea?'

'Chelsea.'

'What did he do? Does he look happy? Did he speak?' Her desire to know was terrible.

'He doesn't speak. He didn't move much. He seemed – very calm. He stayed a long time.'

'This is terrible. This is ludicrous. There *is no boy*.'

'No. But I saw him.'

'Why you?'

'I don't know.' A pause. 'I do *like* him.'

'He is – was – a most likeable boy.'

Some days later he saw the boy running along the landing in the evening, wearing what might have been pyjamas, in peacock towelling, or might have been a track suit. Pyjamas, the woman stated confidently, when he told her: his new pyjamas. With white ribbed cuffs, weren't they? and a white polo neck? He corroborated this, watching her cry – she cried more easily now – finding her anxiety and disturbance very hard to bear. But it never occurred to him that it was possible to break his promise to tell her when he saw the boy. That was another curious imperative from some undefined authority.

They discussed clothes. If there were ghosts, how could they appear in clothes long burned, or rotted, or worn away by other people? You could imagine, they agreed, that something of a person might linger – as the Tibetans and others believe the soul lingers near the body before setting out on its long journey. But clothes? And in this case so many clothes? I must be seeing your memories, he told her, and she nodded fiercely, compressing her lips, agreeing that this was likely, adding, 'I am too rational to go mad, so I seem to be putting it on you.'

He tried a joke. 'That isn't very kind to me, to infer that madness comes more easily to me.'

'No, sensitivity. I am insensible. I was always a bit like that, and this made it worse. I am the *last* person to see any ghost that was trying to haunt me.'

'We agreed it was your memories I saw.'

'Yes. We agreed. That's rational. As rational as we can be, considering.'

All the same, the brilliance of the boy's blue regard, his gravely smiling salutation in the garden next morning, did not seem like anyone's tortured memories of earlier happiness. The man spoke to him directly then:

'Is there anything I can *do* for you? Anything you want? Can I help you?'

The boy seemed to puzzle about this for a while, inclining his head as though hearing was difficult. Then he nodded, quickly and perhaps urgently, turned, and ran into the house, looking back to make sure he was followed. The man entered the living-room through the french windows, behind the running boy, who stopped for a moment in the centre of the room, with the man blinking behind him at the sudden transition from sunlight to comparative dark. The woman was sitting in an armchair, looking at nothing there. She often sat like that. She looked up, across the boy, at the man, and the boy, his face for the first time anxious, met the man's eyes again, asking, before he went out into the house.

'What is it? What is it? Have you seen him again? Why are you...?'

'He came in here. He went – out through the door.'

'I didn't see him.'

'No.'

'Did he – oh, this is so *silly* – did he see me?'

He could not remember. He told the only truth he knew.

'He brought me in here.'

'Oh, what can I do, what am I going to *do*? If I killed myself – I have thought of that – but the idea that I should be with him is an illusion I ... this silly situation is the nearest I shall ever get. To him. He was *in here with me*?'

'Yes.'

And she was crying again. Out in the garden he could see the boy, swinging agile on the apple branch.

He was not quite sure, looking back, when he had thought he had realized what the boy had wanted him to do. This was also, at the party, his worst piece of what he called bowdlerization, though in some sense it was clearly the opposite of bowdlerization. He told the American girl that he had come to the conclusion that it was the woman herself who had wanted it, though there was in fact, throughout, no sign of her wanting anything except to see the boy, as she said. The boy, bolder and more frequent, had appeared several nights running on the landing, wandering in and out of bathrooms and bedrooms, restlessly, a little agitated, questing almost, until it had 'come to' the man that what he required was to be re-engendered, for him, the man, to give to his mother another child, into which he could peacefully vanish. The idea was so clear that it was like another imperative, though he did not have the courage to ask the child to confirm it. Possibly this was out of delicacy – the child was too young to be talked to about sex. Possibly there were other reasons. Possibly he was mistaken: the situation was making him hysterical, he felt action of some kind was required and must be possible. He could not spend the rest of the summer, the rest of his life, describing non-existent tee shirts and blond smiles.

He could think of no sensible way of embarking on his venture, so in the end simply walked into her bedroom one night. She was lying there, reading; when she saw him her instinctive gesture was to hide, not her

bare arms and throat, but her book. She seemed, in fact, quite un-
surprised to see his pyjamaed figure, and, after she had recovered her
coolness, brought out the book definitely and laid it on the bedspread.

'My new taste in illegitimate literature. I keep them in a box under the
bed.'

*Ena Twigg, Medium. The Infinite Hive. The Spirit World. Is There
Life After Death?*

'Pathetic,' she proffered.

He sat down delicately on the bed.

'Please, don't grieve so. Please, let yourself be comforted. Please...'

He put an arm round her. She shuddered. He pulled her closer. He
asked why she had had only the one son, and she seemed to understand
the purport of his question, for she tried, angular and chilly, to lean on
him a little, she became apparently compliant. 'No real reason,' she
assured him, no material reason. Just her husband's profession and lack
of inclination: that covered it.

'Perhaps,' he suggested, 'if she would be comforted a little, perhaps
she could hope, perhaps ...'

For comfort then, she said, dolefully, and lay back, pushing Ena Twigg
off the bed with one fierce gesture, then lying placidly. He got in beside
her, put his arms round her, kissed her cold cheek, thought of Anne, of
what was never to be again. Come on, he said to the woman, you must
live, you must try to live, let us hold each other for comfort.

She hissed at him 'Don't *talk*' between clenched teeth, so he stroked her
lightly, over her nightdress, breasts and buttocks and long stiff legs,
composed like an effigy on an Elizabethan tomb. She allowed this,
trembling slightly, and then trembling violently: he took this to be a sign
of some mixture of pleasure and pain, of the return of life to stone. He
put a hand between her legs and she moved them heavily apart; he
heaved himself over her and pushed, unsuccessfully. She was contorted
and locked tight: frigid, he thought grimly, was not the word. *Rigor
mortis*, his mind said to him, before she began to scream.

He was ridiculously cross about this. He jumped away and said quite
rudely 'Shut up,' and then ungraciously 'I'm sorry.' She stopped
screaming as suddenly as she had begun and made one of her painstaking
economical explanations.

'Sex and death don't go. I can't afford to let go of my grip on myself. I
hoped. What you hoped. It was a bad idea. I apologize.'

'Oh, never mind,' he said and rushed out again on to the landing, feeling foolish and almost in tears for warm, lovely Anne.

The child was on the landing, waiting. When the man saw him, he looked questioning, and then turned his face against the wall and leant there, rigid, his shoulders hunched, his hair hiding his expression. There was a similarity between woman and child. The man felt, for the first time, almost uncharitable towards the boy, and then felt something else.

'Look, I'm sorry. I tried. I did try. Please turn round.'

Uncompromising, rigid, clenched back view.

'Oh well,' said the man, and went into his bedroom.

So now, he said to the American woman at the party, I feel a fool, I feel embarrassed, I feel we are hurting, not helping each other, I feel it isn't a refuge. Of course you feel that, she said, of course you're right – it was temporarily necessary, it helped both of you, but you've got to live your life. Yes, he said, I've done my best, I've tried to get through, I have my life to live. Look, she said, I want to help, I really do, I have these wonderful friends I'm renting this flat from, why don't you come, just for a few days, just for a break, why don't you? They're real sympathetic people, you'd like them, I like them, you could get your emotions kind of straightened out. She'd probably be glad to see the back of you, she must feel as bad as you do, she's got to relate to her situation in her own way in the end. We all have.

He said he would think about it. He knew he had elected to tell the sympathetic American because he had sensed she would be – would offer – a way out. He had to get out. He took her home from the party and went back to his house and landlady without seeing her into her flat. They both knew that this reticence was promising – that he hadn't come in then, because he meant to come later. Her warmth and readiness were like sunshine, she was open. He did not know what to say to the woman.

In fact, she made it easy for him: she asked, briskly, if he now found it perhaps uncomfortable to stay, and he replied that he had felt he should move on, he was of so little use ... Very well, she had agreed, and had added crisply that it had to be better for everyone if 'all this' came to an end. He remembered the firmness with which she had told him that no illusions were pleasant. She was strong: too strong for her own good. It would take years to wear away that stony, closed, simply surviving insensibility. It was not his job. He would go. All the same, he felt bad.

He got out his suitcases and put some things in them. He went down to the garden, nervously, and put away the deck-chair. The garden was empty. There were no voices over the wall. The silence was thick and deadening. He wondered, knowing he would not see the boy again, if anyone else would do so, or if, now he was gone, no one would describe a tee shirt, a sandal, a smile, seen, remembered, or desired. He went slowly up to his room again.

The boy was sitting on his suitcase, arms crossed, face frowning and serious. He held the man's look for a long moment, and then the man went and sat on his bed. The boy continued to sit. The man found himself speaking.

'You do see I have to go? I've tried to get through. I can't get through. I'm no use to you, am I?'

The boy remained immobile, his head on one side, considering. The man stood up and walked towards him.

'Please. Let me go. What are we, in this house? A man and a woman and a child, and none of us can get through. You can't want that?'

He went as close as he dared. He had, he thought, the intention of putting his hand on or through the child. But could not bring himself to feel there was no boy. So he stood, and repeated,

'I can't get through. Do you want me to stay?'

Upon which, as he stood helplessly there, the boy turned on him again the brilliant, open, confiding, beautiful desired smile.

Angela Carter

PETER
AND
THE
WOLF

At length the grandeur of the mountains becomes monotonous; with familiarity, the landscape ceases to provoke awe and wonder. Above a certain line, no trees grow. Shadows of clouds move across the bare alps as freely as the clouds themselves move across the sky. All is vast, barren, unprofitable, unkind.

A girl from a village on the lower slopes left her widowed mother to marry a man who lived up in the empty places. Soon she was pregnant. In October, there was a severe storm. The old woman knew her daughter was near her time and waited for a message but none arrived. After the storm passed off, the old woman went up to see for herself, taking her grown son with her because she was afraid.

From a long way off, they saw no smoke rising from the chimney. Solitude swelled around them. The open door banged backwards and forwards on its hinges. Solitude engulfed them. There were traces of wolf-dung on the floor so they knew wolves had been in the house but had left the corpse of the young mother alone although of her baby nothing was left except some mess that showed it had been born. Nor was there a trace of the son-in-law but a gnawed foot in a boot.

They wrapped the dead body in a quilt and took it home with them. Now it was late. The howling of the wolves excoriated the approaching silence of the night.

Then winter came with icy blasts, when everyone stays indoors and stokes the fire. The old woman's son married the blacksmith's daughter and she moved in with them. The snow melted and it was spring. By the next Christmas, there was a bouncing grandson. Time passed. More children came.

The summer that the eldest grandson, Peter, reached the age of seven, he was old enough to go up the mountain with his father, as the men did every year, to feed the goats on the young grass. There Peter sat in the clean, new sunlight, plaiting straw for baskets, contented as could be until he saw the thing he had been taught most to fear advancing silently along the lea of an outcrop of rock. Then another wolf, following the first one.

If they had not been the first wolves he had ever seen, the boy would not have looked at them so closely, their plush, grey pelts, of which the hairs are tipped with white, giving them a ghostly look, as if their edges were disappearing; their sprightly, plumey tails; their sharp, inquiring masks that reflect an intelligence which, however acute, is not our way of dealing with the world.

Because Peter did not turn and run but, instead, looked, he saw that the third one was a prodigy, a marvel, a naked one, going on all fours, as they did, but hairless as regards the body although it had a brown mane around its head like a pony.

He was so fascinated by the sight of this bald wolf that he would have lost his flock, perhaps himself been eaten and certainly been beaten to the bone for negligence had not the goats themselves raised their heads, snuffed danger and run off, bleating and whinnying, so that the men came, firing guns, making hullabaloo, scaring the wolves away.

His father was too angry to listen to what Peter said. He cuffed Peter round the head and sent him home in disgrace. His mother was feeding this year's baby. His grandmother sat at the table, shelling peas into a pot.

'There was a little girl with the wolves, granny,' said Peter. Why was he so sure it had been a little girl? Perhaps because her hair was so long, so long and lively. 'A little girl about my age, from her size,' he said.

His grandmother threw a flat pod out of the door so the chickens could peck it up.

'I saw a little girl with the wolves,' he said.

His grandmother tipped water into the pot, heaved up from the table and suspended the pot of peas on the hook over the fire. There wasn't time, that night, but, next morning, very early, she herself took the boy up the mountain.

'Tell your father what you told me.'

They went to look at the wolves' tracks. On a bit of dampish ground they found a print, not like that of a dog's pad, much less like that of a child's footprint, yet Peter worried and puzzled over it until he made sense of it.

'She was running on all fours with her arse stuck up in the air ... therefore ... she'd put all her weight on the ball of her foot, wouldn't she? And splay out her toes, see ... like that.'

He went barefoot in summer, like all the village children; he inserted the ball of his own foot in the print, to show his father what kind of mark it would make if he, too, always ran on all fours.

'No use for a heel, if you run that way. So she doesn't leave a heel-print. Stands to reason.'

His father nodded a slow acknowledgement of Peter's powers of deduction.

They soon found her. She was asleep. Her spine had grown so supple she could curl into a perfect C. She woke up when she heard them and ran, but somebody caught her with a sliding noose at the end of a rope; the noose over her head jerked tight so that she fell to the ground with her eyes popping and rolling. A big, grey, angry bitch appeared out of nowhere but Peter's father blasted it to bits with his shotgun. The girl would have choked if the old woman hadn't taken her head on her lap and pulled the knot loose. The girl bit the grandmother's hand.

The girl scratched, fought and bit until the men tied her wrists and ankles together with twine and slung her from a pole to carry her back to the village. Then she went limp. She didn't scream or shout, she didn't seem to be able to, she made only a few dull, guttural sounds in the back of her throat, and, though she did not seem to know how to cry, water trickled out of the corners of her eyes.

How burned she was by the weather! Bright brown all over; and how filthy she was! Caked and mired with mud and dirt. And every inch of her chestnut hide was scored and scabbed with dozens of scars of sharp abrasions of rock and thorn. Her hair dragged on the ground as they carried her along; it was stuck with burrs and you could not see what colour it might be, it was so dirty. She was dreadfully verminous. She stank. She was so thin that all her ribs stuck out. The fine, plump, potato-fed boy was far bigger than she, although she was a year or so older.

Solemn with curiosity, he trotted behind her. Granny stumped alongside with her bitten hand wrapped up in her apron. When they dumped the girl on the earth floor of her grandmother's house, the boy secretly poked at her left buttock with his forefinger, out of curiosity, to see what she felt like. She felt warm but hard as wood. She did not so much as twitch when he touched her. She had given up the struggle; she lay trussed on the floor and pretended to be dead.

Granny's house had the one large room which, in winter, they shared with the goats. As soon as it caught a whiff of her, the big tabby mouser let out a hiss like a pricked balloon and bounded up the ladder that went to the hayloft above. Soup smoked on the fire and the table was laid. It was now about supper-time but still quite light; night comes late on the summer mountain.

'Untie her,' said the grandmother.

Her son wasn't willing at first but the old woman would not be denied, so he got the breadknife and cut the rope round the girl's ankles. All she did was kick a bit but, when he cut the rope round her wrists, it was as if he had let a fiend loose. The onlookers ran out of the door, the rest of the family ran for the ladder to the hayloft but granny and Peter both made for the door, to pull it to and shoot the bolt, so that she could not get out.

The trapped one knocked round the room. Bang – over went the table. Crash, tinkle – the supper dishes smashed. Bang, crash, tinkle – the dresser fell forward in a hard white hail of broken crockery. Over went the meal barrel and she coughed, she sneezed like a child sneezes, no different, and then she bounced around on fear-stiffened legs in a white cloud until the flour settled on everything like a magic powder that made everything strange.

She started to make little rushes, now here, now there, snapping and yelping and tossing her bewildered head.

She never rose up on two legs; she crouched, all the time, on her hands and tiptoes, yet it was not quite like crouching, for you could see how all fours came naturally to her as though she had made a different pact with gravity than we have, and you could see, too, how strong the muscles in her thighs had grown on the mountain, how taut the twanging arches of her feet, and that indeed, she only used her heels when she sat back on her haunches. She growled; now and then she coughed out those intolerable, thick grunts of distress. All you could see of her rolling eyes were the whites, which were the bluish, glaring white of snow.

Several times, her bowels opened, apparently involuntarily, and soon the kitchen smelled like a privy yet even her excrement was different to ours, the refuse of raw, strange, unguessable, wicked feeding, shit of a wolf.

Oh, horror!

She bumped into the hearth, knocked over the pan hanging from the hook and the spilled contents put out the fire. Hot soup scalded her forelegs. Shock of pain. Squatting on her hindquarters, holding the hurt paw dangling piteously before her from its wrist, she howled, she howled, she howled, high, sobbing arcs that seemed to pierce the roof.

Even the old woman, who had contracted with herself to love the child of her dead daughter, was frightened when she heard the girl howl.

Peter's heart gave a hop, a skip, so that he had a sensation of falling; he was not conscious of his own fear because he could not take his eyes off the sight of the crevice of her girl child's sex, that was perfectly visible to him as she sat there square on the base of her spine. The night was now as dark as, at this season, it would go – which is to say, not very dark; a white thread of moon hung in the blond sky at the top of the chimney so that it was neither dark nor light indoors yet the boy could see her intimacy clearly, as if by its own phosphoresence. It exercised an absolute fascination upon him. Everything. He could see everything.

Her lips opened up as she howled so that she offered him, without her own intention or volition, a view of a set of Chinese boxes of whorled flesh that seemed to open one upon another into herself, drawing him into an inner, secret place in which destination perpetually receded before him, his first, devastating, vertiginous intimation of infinity, as if, in the luminous, ambiguous dusk of the night/not-night of the northern uplands, she showed him the gnawed fruit of the tree of knowledge, although she herself did not know what 'knowledge' was.

She howled.

And went on howling until, from the mountain, first singly, then in a complex polyphony, answered at last voices in the same language.

She continued to howl, though now with a less tragic resonance.

Soon it was impossible for the occupants of the house to deny to themselves that the wolves were descending on the village in a pack.

Then she was consoled, sank down, laid her head on her forepaws so that her hair trailed in the cooling soup and so closed up her forbidden book without the least notion she had ever opened it or that it was banned. The household gun hung on a nail over the fireplace where Peter's father had put it when he came in but when the man set his foot on the top rung of the ladder in order to come down for his weapon, the girl jumped up, snarling and showing her long, yellow canines.

The howling outside was now mixed with the agitated dismay of the domestic beasts. All the other villagers were well locked up at home.

The wolves were at the door.

The boy took hold of his grandmother's uninjured hand. First the old woman would not budge but he gave her a good tug and she came to herself. The girl raised her head suspiciously but let them by. The boy pushed his grandmother up the ladder in front of him and drew it up behind them. He was full of nervous dread. He would have given anything to turn time back, so that he might have run, shouting a warning, when he first caught sight of the wolves, and never seen her.

The door shook as the wolves outside jumped up at it and the screws that held the socket of the bolt to the frame cracked, squeaked and started to give. The girl jumped up, at that, and began to make excited little sallies back and forth in front of the door. The screws tore out of the frame quite soon. The pack tumbled over one another to get inside.

Dissonance. Terror. The clamour within the house was that of all the winds of winter trapped in a box. That which they feared most, outside, was now indoors with them. The baby in the hayloft whimpered and its mother crushed it to her breast as if the wolves might snatch this one away, too; but the rescue party had arrived only in order to collect their fosterling.

They left behind a riotous stench in the house, and white tracks of flour everywhere. The broken door creaked backwards and forwards on its hinges. Black sticks of dead wood from the extinguished fire scattered the floor.

Peter thought the old woman would cry, now, but she seemed unmoved. When all was safe, they came down the ladder one by one and, as if released from a spell of silence, all burst into excited speech at once except for the mute old woman and the boy. Although it was well past midnight, the daughter-in-law went to the well for water to scrub the wild smell out of the house. The broken things were cleared up and thrown away. Peter's father nailed the table and the dresser back together. The neighbours came out of their houses, full of amazement; the wolves had not taken so much as a chicken from the hen-coops, not snatched even a single egg.

People brought beer into the starlight, and schnapps made from potatoes, and snacks, because the excitement had made them hungry. That terrible night ended up in one big party but the grandmother would eat or drink nothing and went to bed as soon as her house was clean.

Next day, she went to the graveyard and sat for a while beside her daughter's grave but she did not pray. Then she came home and started chopping cabbage for the evening meal but had to leave off because her bitten hand was festering.

That winter, during the leisure imposed by the snow, after his grandmother's death, Peter asked the village priest to teach him to read the Bible. The priest gladly complied; Peter was the first of his flock who had ever expressed any interest in literacy.

Now the boy became amazingly pious, so much so that his family were startled and impressed. The younger children teased him and called him 'Saint Peter' but that did not stop him sneaking off to church to pray whenever he had a spare moment. In Lent, he fasted to the bone. On Good Friday, he lashed himself. It was as if he blamed himself for the death of the old lady, as if he believed he had brought into the house the fatal infection that had taken her out of it. He was consumed by an imperious passion for atonement. Each night, he pored over his book by the flimsy candlelight, looking for a clue to grace, until his mother shooed him off to sleep.

But, as if to spite the four angels he nightly invoked to protect his bed, the nightmare regularly disordered his sleeps. He tossed and turned on the rustling straw pallet he shared with two little ones. He grew up haggard.

Delighted with Peter's precocious intelligence, the priest started to teach him Latin; Peter visited the priest as his duties with the herd permitted. When he was fourteen, the priest told his parents that Peter should now go to the seminary in the town in the valley where the boy would learn to become a priest himself. Rich in sons, they spared one to

God, since he had become a stranger to them. After the goats came down from the high pasture for the winter, Peter set off. It was October.

At the end of his first day's travel, he reached a river that flowed from the mountain into the valley. The nights were already chilly; he lit himself a fire, prayed, ate the bread and cheese his mother had packed for him and slept as well as he could. In spite of his eagerness to plunge into the white world of penance and devotion that awaited him, he was anxious and troubled for reasons he could not explain to himself.

In the first light, the light that no more than clarifies darkness like egg shells dropped in cloudy liquid, he went down to the river to drink and to wash his face. It was so still he could have been the one thing living.

Her forearms, her loins and her legs were thick with hair and the hair on her head hung round her face in such a way that you could hardly make out her features. She crouched on the other side of the river. She was lapping up water so full of mauve light that it looked as if she were drinking up the dawn as fast as it appeared yet all the same the air grew pale while he was looking at her.

Solitude and silence; all still.

She could never have acknowledged that the reflection beneath her in the river was that of herself. She did not know she had a face; she had never known she had a face and so her face itself was the mirror of a different kind of consciousness than ours is, just as her nakedness, without innocence or display, was that of our first parents, before the Fall, and if she was hairy as Magdalen in the wilderness, she need never fear to lose her soul since she had never got one.

Language crumbled into dust under the weight of her speechlessness.

A pair of cubs rolled out of the bushes, cuffing one another. She did not pay them any heed.

The boy began to tremble and shake. His skin strangely prickled. He felt he had been made of snow and now might melt. He mumbled something, or sobbed.

She cocked her head at the vague, river-washed sound and the cubs heard it too, left off tumbling and ran to burrow their scared heads in her side. But she decided, after a moment, there was no danger and lowered her muzzle, again, to the surface of the water that took hold of her hair and spread it out around her head.

When she finished her drink, she backed a few paces, shaking her wet pelt. The little cubs fastened their mouths on her dangling breasts.

Peter could not help it, he burst out crying. He had not cried since his grandmother's funeral. Tears rolled down his face and splashed on the grass. He blundered forward a few steps into the river with his arms held open, intending to cross over to the other side to join her, impelled by the access of an almost visionary ecstasy to see her so complete, so private. But his cousin took fright at the sudden movement, wrenched her teats away from the cubs and ran off. The squeaking cubs scampered behind. She ran on hands and feet as if that were the only way to run, towards the high ground, into the bright maze of the uncompleted dawn.

When the boy recovered himself, he dried his tears on his sleeve, took off his soaked boots and dried his feet and legs on the tail of his shirt. Then he ate something from his pack, he scarcely knew what, and continued on the way to the town; but what would he do at the seminary, now? Now he knew there was nothing to be afraid of.

He pissed against a tree and, for the first time in his life, took a good, long, unembarrassed look at his prick. He laughed out loud. Had he truly thought this sturdily sprouting young fellow would lie still under a surplice?

He experienced the vertigo of freedom.

He carried his boots slung over his shoulder by the laces. They seemed a great burden. He debated with himself whether or not to throw them away but, when he came to a road, he put them on, although they were still damp, because bare feet can't cope with hard roads.

The birds woke up and sang. The cool, rational sun surprised him; morning had broken on his exhilaration and the mountain now lay behind him. He looked over his shoulder and saw how, with distance, the mountain began to acquire a flat, two-dimensional look. It was already turning into a picture of itself, into the postcard hastily bought as a souvenir of childhood at a railway station or a border post, the newspaper cutting, the snapshot he would show in strange towns, strange cities, other countries he could not, at this moment, imagine, whose names he did not yet know: 'That was where I spent my childhood. Imagine!'

He turned and stared at the mountain for a long time. He had lived in it for fourteen years but he had never seen it before as it might look to someone who had not known it as almost part of the self. The simplicity of the mountain, its magnificence. Its indifference. As he said goodbye to it, he saw it turn into so much scenery, into the wonderful backcloth for an old country tale, of a child suckled by wolves, perhaps, or of wolves nursed by a woman.

Then he determinedly set his face towards the town and tramped onwards.

'If I look back again,' he thought with a last gasp of superstitious terror, 'I shall turn into a pillar of salt.'

Jack Debney

AT
VASSILIOU'S

JACK DEBNEY was born in 1941 in Cheshire. He was brought up in Grimsby and studied English at Leeds University from 1959 until 1962. He then became a lecturer in English at the University of Alexandria from 1963 until 1966 when he moved to live in Athens, returning to England in 1968 to take an MA at Warwick University. Since 1970 he has been a Lektor in the Englisches Seminar at Marburg, West Germany. *At Vassiliou's* belongs to a sequence of stories set in Egypt in the sixties, other parts of which have recently been published by *Stand* and *New Edinburgh Review*. Jack Debney is, at present, at work on a novel and a belated doctorate.

M r Fox flicked over the pages of the *Journal d'Egypte* impatiently. 'Nothing but propaganda,' he said. He read from an article about the building of the High Dam to show me what he meant. I listened to his thin, griping, world-weary voice with its self-conscious nasal attempts at Frenchness and felt bored. I looked out of the window at the people walking slowly along by the sea wall. Mr Fox started to translate as though French was an arcane language and only he held the key to it, and my boredom changed to annoyance.

After he'd finished, he summoned Samir, the boot-boy, over with a commanding gesture full of tired disdain; having his shoes cleaned was obviously a contemptible ritual that had somehow to be borne. Samir crouched down by his box and, taking no notice of him beyond putting his right shoe up to be cleaned first, Mr Fox told me the correct price to be paid to boot-blacks.

'Don't give them more than two piastres. That's enough and they know it, but they'll try to get more out of you because you're a European and new here, too.'

Samir tapped the box with the back of his brush and Mr Fox put his left shoe up and his right one down. Samir grinned at him ingratiatingly. I ate some *soudani*, salted peanuts, and drank some beer which, thankfully, was still cold. When Stella beer got warm it tasted soapy, and I felt queasy already. I should have stayed at home, not come out here. I felt in my pocket to check if I had my Entero-Vioform with me. I'd taken two at breakfast and wondered if I should have another now.

Samir spat on Mr Fox's shoes and wiped them vigorously with an old cloth. Fox leaned down and paid him, and Samir, after thanking him, pointed inquiringly at my shoes. Samir was about fifteen, quite tall and thick-set, and already had a moustache, but there was something childish about him that seemed at odds with this and his man's body. He repelled me and, afraid that my dislike of him might become evident if I didn't let him clean my shoes, I put them on the box too, alternately, Samir tapping rhythmically at each change, looking up at me and grinning. I smiled faintly back. Mr Fox went on lecturing me, but I hardly listened to what he said. Then Samir gave a final flourish with his cloth over my shoes and beat a tattoo on the box with his brush. Fox watched carefully as I handed over two piastres and sardonically as the boy, apparently puzzled, as though there'd been some mistake, held up five fingers to me, almost apologetically. Fox's thin brown face twitched with pleasurable irritation.

'You see what I mean,' he said. 'He's stupid, but not too stupid to try it on.' He shouted at the still crouching Samir, '*Le! Le! Aitneen piastre* – good – *kwise! Bas, bas, walléd! Emshi!*'

The tiny ancient waiter whom Mr Fox had nicknamed Old Father Time hurried over, flicked his napkin at Samir's head and quavered something to him in Arabic. Samir got up, saluted us and shambled over to the entrance where he took up his post to watch for possible customers.

Old Father Time asked for our orders.

'Don't have the *gandoufli*,' Mr Fox said.

'The what?'

'The *gandoufli* – poor men's oysters. Just typhoid traps. They say if you sprinkle lemon over them they're safe. Superstitious nonsense. And beware of the *rizza*.'

'What are they?'

'They look a bit like hedgehogs – prickly outsides. But inside they're wet and orange-coloured. Some people like them, but I find them revolting. And I know for a fact that they're dangerous.'

'What would you recommend then, Mr Fox?' I asked.

'The *crevettes* – good and safe.'

After the order had been given and the *suffraggi* had brought us another bottle of Stella, Mr Fox began telling me more about what I should and shouldn't eat in Alexandria, the constant war against typhoid.

'But I've had shots against typhoid and cholera.'

He smiled knowingly. 'I shouldn't trust them too much if I were you,' he said. 'I've had typhoid twice and both times I thought I was well protected.' He shooed a fly away from his beer. 'These are the gentlemen to be cautious of – cleaning their feet in your food after paddling in all sorts of disgusting muck.' I remembered the cow's carcass I'd seen hanging outside a butcher's shop, the mass of flies that buzzed and crawled on it. But then if the meat was cooked properly it'd be all right, wouldn't it? Salads. But make sure they're washed. Don't eat them in restaurants in the summer.

'I woke up with such a headache I couldn't move,' Mr Fox recounted. 'This was the first typhoid I had, years ago now. Luckily the servant called the doctor straight away. I was in bed three weeks. Couldn't eat anything but yoghurt all that time, because of the pustules in the intestines, you see. If they burst you're done for – got to eat something soft and smooth like yoghurt that slides by them.'

After a pause he asked me, 'Did you say you were lodging with a Greek family?'

'Yes – in *sidi* Gaber.'

'How much do you pay?'

'Twenty-five pounds a month.'

'Twenty-five pounds! Far too much, far too much.'

'But I get everything I want. I'm looked after very well.'

'The Greeks, by and large, are crooks. And when they know you know that, then you can deal with them. Otherwise ...' His voice tailed off as the *suffraggi* placed the knives and forks on the table. Mr Fox watched, tensed, like a pernickety overseer. I felt a sharp pain high up in my stomach and I pressed my hand on it. The pain sank towards the navel and then subsided.

'Still,' Fox continued, 'if you like it with your Greek family ...'

I felt angry and wished that the lunch was over. For the first time since arriving in Egypt a couple of months before I began to believe I belonged to something there. The Greeks, *my* Greeks, had been unfairly attacked and I ought to defend them.

'The people I live with have shown me a damn sight more kindness than anybody else in this place!'

My anger pleased Mr Fox. It was as though, after a little goading, he'd drawn first blood and was satisfied. He poured me a glass of beer and said dreamily, mildly, 'Yes? Well ... that's good then.'

The *crevettes* arrived. I felt I'd somehow been cheated of my right to defend the Greeks properly and kept a sullen silence as I ate. Mr Fox didn't seem to notice. He concentrated on getting the most out of his food, searching and scraping the *crevettes* for the last particle of flesh. When he'd finished he turned his chair inwards slightly for a better view of the room. It was filling up now – mainly Egyptian families on holiday from Cairo and Upper Egypt, but here and there a few Europeans.

'Now for something interesting,' he said, picking his yellowed front teeth with his fingernails. 'Old Vassiliou's mid-day meal. Quite a ritual. Watch this, Mr Skaife. Unforgettable.'

I moved my chair round and looked where Mr Fox directed me. Vassiliou was sitting behind his desk at the far side of the restaurant, in the darkest, coolest part near the marble-topped counter. Some canaries chirped nearby in their cage which hung close to the ceiling. Before the desk stood Old Father Time quavering over a disputed bill. Vassiliou stared at him balefully, his bloated face working in absolute distrust as he checked the figures.

A few feet away from him, two Greek women in black, one in late middle age and the other at least in her eighties, were setting a small table with great care. They stroked the cloth smooth and placed Vassiliou's cutlery in a parallel position to the one he had at the desk so that, whilst eating, he could still survey the room. The two women went down the corridor behind the counter to the kitchen and brought back bread, a carafe of water and a glass. Then the older woman fetched his soup – carrying it high, staring at it as if she were able to neutralize the slight trembling of her hands by the steadiness of her eye. A little of the soup lapped on to her thumb as she put the bowl down on the table.

Now old Vassiliou had to be moved. The women put their hands under his shoulders and heaved. And he tried to heave himself with them. His face lolled forward, pop-eyed and mottled red-purple not only with the effort he was making but also with rage and humiliation at not being able to fend for himself. At last they got him up and he was half-pushed, half-carried the few perilous feet to the table. The women stood on either side of him, their hands bracing his shaking arms, as he lowered himself slowly into his chair.

'The same performance at the same time every day,' Mr Fox said. 'The great journey to the dining-table. I don't know why he doesn't eat at the desk and have done with it, but no – evidently he doesn't find it proper to do so.'

I drank the rest of my beer. It had got warm and tasted foul. I could feel it churning around in my stomach and expected the pain back again. But it didn't come – at least not in such a localized and concentrated form. Now the sense of unease, of being awry, was more diffuse.

I swallowed a couple of Entero-Vioform, although I feared it was too late for them to have any effect, and watched the younger woman tie a big napkin around Vassiliou's neck. When she'd finished he bent his head to the spoon, which he'd raised uncertainly a few inches from the bowl, and started supping at the soup. The older woman appeared from the kitchen carrying some chops on a massive blue and white plate. Vassiliou made a gesture of impatience as though she'd brought them too soon and was trying to hurry him. Unperturbed, she set the plate by him and went back into the kitchen again. This time she brought a dish of potatoes and another of vegetables.

'Vassiliou's devoted sister,' said Mr Fox. 'Older even than Father Time.'

'And the other woman's his wife?'

'Yes. They all came from Smyrna after the trouble in '22.'

The two women moved about Vassiliou with an odd sympathy set on their faces. It didn't strike me as anything put on, a mask meant to conceal irritation or emptiness, rather that the sympathy had become formalized over the years, part of the ritual Fox had referred to.

'Of course, Vassiliou's gaga. Very different from when I first knew him. He was very sharp then, in his own Greek way. A sort of amiable cunning, you know.'

He clapped his hands and a *suffraggi* hurried over. '*Aitneen* Stella, *min fadlak,*' Mr Fox ordered. I wanted to say, 'No more for me, thank you,' but out of timidity and pride I didn't, even though I felt bad. And when the beer came Mr Fox filled my glass again, insistently, and I thanked him, trying to sound sincere.

'My God!' he said. 'If you saw my father – what a contrast to that pathetic old heap over there! My father must be at least as old, probably older. Yes ... yes ...' He paused a moment, calculating, staring hard at Vassiliou's table where Vassiliou's wife was cutting up his meat for him.

His sister sat on a nearby chair watching the procedure calmly. 'A good few years older. And he looks over twenty years younger. As spry as they come. Last summer, when I was back home for a few weeks' leave, we went on a walking tour of North Wales together. Hiking boots, full packs, camping out, the lot. Up in the mountains every day. Marvellous, the vigour he has! I couldn't keep up with him, I can tell you.'

Mr Fox's voice changed as he talked about his father. It became animated, affectionate, almost resonant. I was surprised. I began to think that I might be able to like him after all.

He finished his beer and lit a cigarette. Then he shifted position and gazed out of the window at the Corniche. 'Of course, my father was in the army for most of his life. Still helps him – the discipline and training, all the things that are sneered at nowadays. He was a brigadier in the end. Served in India mainly, but he was in this area, too, in the First World War. Rode with Allenby into Jerusalem. And he knew T. E. Lawrence. Lawrence talks about him in *Seven Pillars*. He says my father was one of the few men in Cairo he could trust.'

'Was he with Lawrence? – in the desert, I mean.'

'No. Lawrence wanted him and the old man was all for going, but Allenby wouldn't wear it. He relied on my father too much, you see.' The cigarette with its growing head of ash drooped from Mr Fox's mouth as he paused, then waggled up and down again as he resumed speaking. 'In fact, I was talking to my father about Lawrence when we walked up Cader Idris. He said that all this filth they were putting out about him now – homosexuality, masochism, whatever – was all wicked nonsense, simply anti-British propaganda. He said Lawrence was the finest man he ever knew – a fine officer, a fine scholar, and a fine gentleman.' He turned and looked at me sternly. The ash-head fell on to the table, but he didn't notice it.

'I haven't seen the film they've made yet. But I read Richard Aldington's book and, well, it seems quite convincing, really.'

'Convincing!' Mr Fox snapped. 'I suppose you would think it was convincing!' He snatched the half-smoked cigarette out of his mouth and stubbed it angrily into the ashtray. 'This debunking or whatever you call it is very fashionable these days. First cousin to the kitchen sink and all that sordid rubbish!'

I said nothing, determined not to lose my temper again. I ignored him

and watched Vassiliou's sister clear away the dirty plates from the table
and bring Vassiliou's *crème caramel*. While he ate it, messily, his wife
wiped his chin several times with the napkin. She did it slowly and
gravely, no sign of repulsion on her face at all. At last he grew tired of her
constant tending and pushed her hand away angrily.

'I'm an anachronism, I know,' said Mr Fox, his voice faded again now,
'but I don't care. I know what a gentleman is. The idea hasn't been
debunked' – he emphasized the word with great distaste – 'for me. I still
honour and treasure it.'

Some more beer arrived. Fox filled his glass and left mine alone this
time. I looked at him. The usual guarded expression had gone. His face
had hardened into a grandiose pose, as formal as that of a stone hero. He
seemed to think himself, for the moment at least, the last gallant defender
of an old, noble ideal, a kind of latter-day Sir Bedivere.

A voice above us began chattering lugubriously: 'It's all right, Mr Fox,
really, all right. I wouldn't have dreamt of asking you ... troubling you at
such an awful time as this. I know how you feel, but one's got to go on.
Got to! Look at me. That little matter ... don't worry about it, please.
We'll discuss it some other time. I only mentioned it because, well ...
things are not easy these days. Believe me, I didn't realize. It wasn't until
after you'd gone last night that what you said really sunk in. I must have
appeared callous. I'm sorry – I'd been drinking, I wasn't myself. It didn't
sink in, Mr Fox! I can't tell you how sorry I am ...'

I looked up and saw a tall, stooped figure swaying over the end of the
table. His long horse-face was pulled inadvertently into a cartoon of grief
and condolence as he spoke. I turned to Fox, hoping for some
explanation, and was just in time to catch a shiftiness pass from eyes to
mouth, cracking the stone pose. For a few seconds he seemed like a man
in a trap, wondering desperately how to get out of it; then his face closed
again. He still looked decidedly unheroic yet ready, in his own way, to do
battle.

'That's all right, de Basra,' he said, trying to adopt the mournful tone
of the other man and sound gently forgiving too.

'You're not angry with me?'

'No, no, of course not.'

'Do you mind if I sit down for a minute or so? I feel faint. The heat and
the humidity are terrible today.'

'Not at all.' Mr Fox motioned him to an empty chair, but I saw, by the slight hesitations before he replied, that he very much wanted de Basra to go away.

His recent belligerence towards me apparently forgotten, Mr Fox introduced us. 'Mr de Basra, this is Mr Skaife, the new man at the Faculty. Mr Skaife, Mr de Basra, a prominent local businessman.'

'I was. Until they took everything away from me.'

Samir came up and began to unsling his kit, but de Basra, without looking at him, waved him away, casually and decisively but somehow despondently too.

'How long have you been in Alexandria, Mr Skaife?' Mr de Basra asked me.

'Two months.'

'It's not an easy time for an Englishman in Egypt, but still – easier for you than for me. If things get even worse, you can always leave, go back home. My home's here and they're making it more and more difficult for me to live in it.'

His large, brown eyes stared at me pathetically, watering with rheum or tears, perhaps both. His eyes must have given an appealing quality to his face once, but now they were bleary, the whites yellowish. I noticed how sunken his cheeks were, the grey stubble on them. Altogether he looked hungover and spent.

He stared down at the table silently and then, willing himself out of his sad reverie, addressed Fox: 'But what are my troubles compared with yours?' Fox, who was smoking another cigarette and watching him warily, grunted ambiguously. I wondered what his troubles were, but doubted if he'd confide them to a debunker like me.

The *suffraggi* brought us some more beer and another glass. Mr de Basra motioned him to fill the three glasses and then raised his, his hand shaking a little. 'Cheers! Chin-chin!' he shouted frantically and forced himself to laugh. The sour smell I'd been vaguely aware of grew stronger as he opened his mouth wide. De Basra had halitosis, too. The smell was like a mixture of stale garlic and old greens rotting fast in hot weather, and it stood firmly before my nose. What was left of my stomach gave a lurch, but the danger passed and I was safe for a while yet.

Suddenly there was an awful, rasping, croaking sound. Mr Fox spluttered over his cigarette and coughed. 'Not this ghastly sod again!'

'Oh yes,' Mr de Basra said. 'Vassiliou's favourite for some reason. This is one of the few places where he's let in.'

I saw a very dark, simian-featured man, in a dirty tattered shirt and pair of trousers, standing in the middle of the restaurant nuzzling a battered old violin into the right position against his shoulder. He drew a few more croaks with his bow and then, satisfied that the violin was tuned properly, started scraping his way through an Arabic song. Vassiliou calmly watched from his dinner table, drinking Turkish coffee and eating small cubes of *loukoumi.* He seemed not to mind the violinist who was playing with shrieking fervour now, eyes closed, oblivious to everybody, bending and straightening his thin body as though in ecstasy. He was barefoot and I noticed that each of his big toes had a thick toenail that curved up a bit. They looked like small yellow horns. I stared at them, partly because I was fascinated by them, but also because I couldn't bear looking at the man's enraptured, deluded face.

Most of the people in the restaurant seemed as tolerant of him as Vassiliou and his wife and sister, who stared at the tattered man in the middle of the floor as though simply using him to focus on something inward and quite different. Some of the customers grinned and joked about him mildly, but the only person who was really amused was Samir. He squatted by the entrance, clutching his genitals through his *galabeya,* bellowing with laughter.

The violinist had brought a small boy with him to collect the money. I saw him now for the first time, a few tables away from ours, holding out an old tin. He was a timid, unhappy-looking boy of about ten or so. There was a long, raw-red sore on his right temple, and his short, frizzy hair grew in clumps so that on some parts of his head he was almost bald. He looked ill-fed and ill-cared for. When he came up to us, held out the tin in front of him and murmured for money, he stared down at it rather as Mr de Basra had stared down at the table. I could tell he felt humiliated by what he was doing. The violinist believed he was creating beautiful music which people appreciated and paid for, but his boy knew that they gave to him as they might to any other beggar.

Mr de Basra put three piastres in the tin and looked up with his large, tearful-rheumy eyes, smiling at the boy, trying to make him smile back. But he simply said, '*Shukran, ya bey,*' in a soft, weak voice and, eyes still on the tin, waited for Mr Fox and myself to contribute something. Fox clicked his tongue impatiently as though, once more, for the umpteenth time, his good nature was being taken advantage of, and gave two piastres. I gave the same. The boy thanked us, as though he were apologizing to us, and went on to the next table. 'Poor little fellow,' sighed Mr de Basra. A fly was crawling over the cloth towards a beer bottle and I waved it away.

The violinist had come to a stop but after a short pause the scraping began again, with redoubled force as this was obviously meant to be a cheery, sprightly piece. I watched the horned feet tapping out the rhythm and the tattered body weaving from side to side. Mr Fox, who'd been looking out of the window, snapped his head back, uncontrollably incensed. 'Oh, for Christ's sake, piss off!' he shouted into the room, but the wan, weary voice didn't carry far – only some people at the next table tittered appreciatively. Mr de Basra started as if Fox had meant him. A reflective look came into his lugubrious face, and then fondness and sympathy. He leant over to Fox and stroked his lean brown forearm. 'Yes, you must let it out,' he said. 'It's the best way in the end. Perhaps a bit embarrassing at the time, to an Englishman, always cool, calm and collected, eh?' He laughed hollowly. 'But believe me, my old friend, there are occasions when this English reserve is not the best thing. Weep! Go on, weep!' As though he were going to demonstrate his own advice, Mr de Basra's raddled eyes filled to overflowing and his voice trembled. The sour breath butted me across the face and I leant back to try to escape it. Mr Fox sucked at his cigarette vehemently, his lips thinned almost to nothing. He looked nonplussed at Mr de Basra for a moment and then nodded absently.

The violinist's boy had now reached Vassiliou's table. The old man struggled up in his chair and tried to put his hand in his trousers pocket. His wife guided it down, whilst he half-allowed her and half-attempted to push her away. Face contorted with the effort, he finally got a few coins out of his pocket and managed to put them into the tin. His sister gave the boy a piece of *loukoumi*, dropping it into his outstretched palm as though she were frightened of even the slightest contact with his skin. But there was nothing of this in her face – just a slightly distant expression of kindness as she watched the boy put the sweet in his mouth and begin chewing. She dipped her head delicately in acknowledgement as he thanked her before passing on to the remaining tables.

'It wasn't always like this,' Mr de Basra was saying. 'I mean, in the old days I could have given you the money and not thought twice about it . . .'

The *suffraggi* brought more beer and *soudani*, and also some thin strips of carrot in a glass. Mr de Basra began munching at one of them. He waved the stub of it at Mr Fox as he continued talking.

'Your dreadful news drove everything else out of your mind . . . even though it is quite a while now since I first asked you. But enough of that. In a time of grief like this . . . I understand, Mr Fox.'

'Thank you, Mr de Basra, most kind. I wish everybody showed the same consideration. When I've . . . I'll do what I can.'

'Yes, yes, that goes without saying. But please don't worry about it now.'

The violinist finished his strident jig and made his bows. To Vassiliou he bowed more deeply than to the customers, accepting the deference as no more and no less than his due. The violinist and his boy then left the restaurant, passing Samir who had ceased laughing. Instead he watched them gape-mouthed with dull apprehension as if there were something horrible about them that he was just beginning to guess at.

Mr de Basra ate another piece of carrot, finished his beer and rose. 'Unfortunately I have to dash off now. Must just have a quick word with Vassiliou first,' he said.

Mr Fox looked alarmed. He made to fill de Basra's glass, but he put his hand flat across the top of it. 'No, no, thank you. I feel quite sleepy already.'

'But please . . .'

'No, thank you.'

'A little.'

'No, thank you. Very kind of you, but I must go.'

Mr de Basra shook hands with me. 'Very glad to have met you, Mr Skaife. I hope you enjoy Alexandria, although I'm sorry to say it's nothing like it was. Ah – the good old days, eh?' He smiled wistfully, shook hands with Fox, too, commiserated with him once more, and then went over to Vassiliou's table.

I wondered whether Fox would tell me what his tragedy was if I asked him. And I wondered why he was so anxious to prevent de Basra from talking to Vassiliou. But I could feel my bowels beginning to dissolve and to discover Fox's secrets suddenly didn't seem very urgent.

'Don't take too much notice of what de Basra says, Mr Skaife. He's a hopeless drunkard. Gets very maudlin. He might refuse another drink here, but that's a blind. Common enough trick amongst alcoholics. He'll go home now and drink himself silly for the rest of the day.'

The canaries abruptly broke into frenzied song and then were as abruptly silent again. Almost directly beneath their cage, Mr de Basra was talking to Vassiliou and his wife and sister.

'But I don't blame him,' Mr Fox said. 'I'd do the same if I'd been treated as he has.'

'What do you mean?'

'He's a Jew and you can imagine how Jews are treated here now. And his business was nationalized in '61. He also lost some land he had.'

The two women were staring at Mr Fox in shocked compassion. Even Vassiliou tried to compose his unwieldy features into the correct expression. But Fox didn't see this and, staring down at his glass, went on. 'De Basra is a broken man. I'm sorry for him, but I'm afraid I have to tell you that you mustn't trust him. He lies terribly – doesn't know he's doing it, of course. Believes it all himself.'

I looked out of the window. The violinist and his boy were on the other side of the Corniche, by the sea wall, counting the money in the tin.

'Then there's his wife. His ex-wife rather. As soon as the going got rough she left him – somehow persuading the poor soft fool to pay her handsomely for doing so. They got divorced, and she turned Moslem and married a general.'

The violinist started striding swiftly along the Corniche, but the boy lagged behind him, hanging his head and dawdling almost to a standstill. He was being defiant in his own timid, dejected way. The violinist stopped and looked back at him.

'Once it was a profitable thing to marry a rich Jew – now it's a general in the glorious Egyptian army instead.' Mr Fox laughed wearily.

When the boy came level, the violinist put his arm around him and started to pet him. He stroked his shoulder, the upper part of his arm, laid his hand on his cheek, and all the time he was telling him something, but I couldn't even guess what because the dark face was expressionless. The boy shifted his feet a little and went on staring at the pavement, whilst the stroking moved to his uneven hair.

'She's a whore, a blowsy old whore!' Mr Fox said, almost gleefully.

And the violinist took his hand away and walked off very fast up the Corniche as before. This disturbed me. It was as though the allotted period of comfort was over, it was simply a set restorative – like the clumps of grass the *gharry* drivers threw down for their thin, dilapidated horses in the same place at the same time every day. The violinist strode out of sight, the boy still lagging behind him, but not dawdling now, following him however slowly.

'Still, that's what they like around here,' mused Mr Fox. 'Depilated cunts and fat arses.'

The *suffraggi* opened another bottle of Stella and filled our glasses. I stared at the cold glass and felt the sweat form on my forehead and upper lip. The pain in my bowels was there all the time now, and I knew that I couldn't hope for a false alarm. It was going to happen; I just had to wait, perhaps an hour, perhaps much less. I sipped at the beer, pretending to be all right, simply not thirsty, then put it down again.

Mr de Basra waved to us, smiling encouragingly as he walked from Vassiliou's table to the entrance where grinning Samir snapped to attention, parade-rigid, as he left. Mr Fox was silent. He seemed worried, occasionally glancing quickly and rather furtively at Vassiliou. Then, as nothing happened, he relaxed a little. I didn't attempt to talk to him. His cigarette gathered its precarious head of ash and I sweated, my shirt sticking to my back, and tried without success to keep the pain at bay.

Suddenly there was a commotion from Vassiliou's table. The old man was trying to lever himself up out of his chair. His wife and sister protested and tried to make him stay where he was, but he shouted at them angrily; they gave way and helped him up. He started in our direction, very slowly, unsurely, his feet shuffling and slurring in their big carpet slippers. The two women offered to assist him but he refused. It was important that he make this journey alone. Old Father Time paused in his work, watching Vassiliou anxiously as he neared our table. In spite of the heat and the humidity Vassiliou wore a waistcoat and dark jacket which made him seem even squatter, laden with thick clothes and excess flesh. But as I looked at his face, the jowl-wattles shaking with strain over his collar, his mouth pressed inwards, quivering a little, I was surprised to see that he wasn't sweating at all. I envied him this at least.

He reached our table and paused to get his breath before he spoke. His wife and sister were regarding us with a grave, sorrowful expression, completely in keeping with their sombre clothes. And people at the tables adjacent to ours glanced at us and whispered, sensing drama. Fox tried to appear at ease, unconcerned, but it was too studied to be convincing. A breeze blew in the smell of the sea and I wished that I was out there, strolling along the Corniche. Vassiliou's presence, close to, oppressed me. I was ashamed of myself for fearing some kind of scene in which I'd be involved.

Vassiliou stuck out his hand – Fox shook it and then motioned to the place where Mr de Basra had been sitting. But Vassiliou took no notice. His mouth worked furiously, loosening, twisting, and his eyes stared away above our heads at nothing.

'All my sadnesses, Mr Fox,' he said at last.

Out of the corner of my eye I saw Vassiliou's wife move over to the desk to deal with a bill that Old Father Time had brought her there.

'Thank you, thank you,' Fox said hastily as though to head Vassiliou off. But he continued resolutely.

'To lose *un père, c'est mal, très mal et triste.*'

'*Oui – oui,* I . . .'

'You will be desolated, Mr Fox. Desolated! Losing the *père* is the worst from losing the *mère.*'

'*Oui – merci bien – pour* . . .'

Vassiliou snorted with the exertion of what he'd been saying and balanced himself less precariously, feet wide apart, hand resting against the table.

'Mr de Basra told us and we are sad for you.'

'Thank you . . .'

Vassiliou's wife and sister came up cautiously, murmured condolences, shook Fox's hand gently and then retreated back to their chairs. Vassiliou, his huge red face both compassionate and imperative, stood where he was, trying to master himself for the rest of his speech.

'But remember, Mr Fox – *le bon Dieu,* the *Theos,* is always watching – He has your father and He will have you!'

Fox looked guilty and alarmed. The fear of a scene left me and I wanted to laugh. But I kept my face straight. I began to realize what the whole business was about. Fox had spun de Basra a story about his father's death in order to avoid paying back some money he owed him. It must have been easy to exploit Mr de Basra's tender heart and tearful eyes. Now the story had rebounded upon Fox. I wished I could enjoy his come-uppance, but the urge to laugh disappeared as quickly as it had come and I just felt ill and depressed. The brigadier on his walking tour of North Wales sounding off about Lawrence! What a cheap, stupid trick. Then I remembered Fox's voice when he had been talking about his

father, how it had changed, and I wasn't so sure. Perhaps he'd been trying
to keep his father alive, near, to refuse to believe that he was dead. But
Fox's obvious guilt – that should give me the answer. I looked at him.
The thin, brown face was closed again; I couldn't read it at all.

Vassiliou thrust out his jaw and, with an immense effort, stilled the
quivering of his lips and jowls. He looked dignified, prophetic.

'*Le bon Dieu* will have us all!' he thundered.

As though on mocking cue, primed by some malign agency, the skirl of
bagpipes came from the Corniche. Startled, I glanced out of the window
and saw a man wearing a faded tam-o'-shanter crossing the road towards
us. For a moment I thought it was the violinist returning to continue his
performance in a different guise. Then I saw that the bagpiper, although
similar in build, was less tattered and had a lighter complexion. I looked
back at Vassiliou. He was outraged. His mouth puckered uncontrollably
and his shaking red wattles began to turn purple.

The piper stopped beneath our window and smiled up at me. He
started to play a spirited version of 'Colonel Bogey'. I couldn't help
laughing this time. And Fox, far from being offended, his grief insulted,
was sniggering behind his cigarette – more at Vassiliou's rage, it seemed
to me, than at the piper.

Vassiliou pushed himself away from the table and lurched to the
window, bellowing furiously at the piper in Arabic and Greek. The thin
skirling continued unabated. Vassiliou, in frustration, kicked his feet up
somehow – it was almost like a dance step – and fell against the window
sill. His huge arse stuck out as though poised to blast a devastating fart
through the room and, chin resting on his hand which clutched the sill, he
stared out wild-eyed and panting at his enemy. Some of his customers
adjusted him into a standing position and his wife and sister helped him
slowly back to his chair behind the small dining-table. The purple in his
face faded to red, but he didn't go into battle again. He sprawled in his
chair, silent, abstracted, seemingly defeated, and left it to his wife to drive
the piper away.

She came over to the window and screamed out impressively but the
piping went on, faster and more insolent than before. Old Father Time
was mobilized – to no avail; his weak, querulous voice was lost in the
jeering music. Laughing, Mr Fox and I showered the tam-o'-shanter with
piastres and gradually 'Colonel Bogey' whined to a close. Fox's unusual
generosity surprised me until I realized how grateful he must be to the

piper for saving him from any further embarrassment at the hands of Vassiliou, and also how much he enjoyed seeing the old man humiliated.

The bagpiper acknowledged us by saluting us smartly. He was completely still for about thirty seconds, then he relaxed and smiled again. 'Bless you, captain and colonel!' he said and made off down the Corniche, in the direction that the violinist and his boy had gone.

'He used to be a batman in a Scottish regiment here and they taught him to play the pipes,' said Mr Fox. 'One of the less intolerable scavengers.' He chuckled. 'He even wears that damn Scottish cap like a soldier's beret!'

Things calmed down. Mme Vassiliou and her sister-in-law put Vassiliou back at his desk and he resumed work. Mr Fox went on drinking and smoking. The *suffraggi* brought us two more bottles of Stella and Fox poured a token drop into the top of my glass. I was too ill even to sip at the beer now – my glass stayed full. But he didn't seem to think it strange and didn't ask me if anything was the matter. His eyes had taken on a glazed look; his movements were slow and deliberate. Should I try to get the truth out of him once and for all? Perhaps, being drunk, he wouldn't be able to guard himself as carefully as he normally did. But I had the odd idea that if I accused Fox of lying to Mr de Basra he'd just frown at me with offended self-righteousness and then, lighting a new cigarette, would turn away to stare out of the window, silently contemptuous of me, as though I'd said something so vulgar, so below the belt, it didn't deserve any answer at all. Or perhaps he'd be surprised at my literal-mindedness, having himself long since accepted de Basra and Vassiliou simply as performers, with as much right to their scripts as he had to his. Sweating badly, hunched against the table, I didn't attempt to find out. I looked down at the warm, soapy beer in the glass, at the tall, green bottles, and waited for the final alarm signs in my bowels.

After a long silence, Fox began to talk. It was mainly a series of complaints – about the school where he worked, particularly the villainy of the headmaster; about Abdel Nasser; about the dishonesty of the Egyptians and the insulting way Europeans were treated by them. And then, as a contrast, he described some friends of his, aristocrats of Turkish descent, charming, courteous, civilized people; they and their kind were the natural leaders of the country, but they had been dispossessed, robbed blind, by Nasser. The Egyptians would regret the day when they chose to follow him. Old King Fouad, and even Farouk at the beginning, were better patriots than Nasser would ever be.

The thin voice droned contentedly on and on, its long dirge of wrong and decline. 'Spies everywhere, Mr Skaife. You've got to be very careful what you say and to whom ... That's the only efficient thing in this country ... spying, informing ... the picture is built up ... flies ... files on every foreigner ... the truth. Friend of mine ... when you come to my flat you must ring three times ... Three, three times ... one short, one long, one short. Everybody who comes has a code, even the servant. Don't let anyone in otherwise ...' His head nodded on to his chest and he dozed for a few seconds. 'Whores everywhere, too ... some of them more dangerous than the spies. You must be careful, Mr Skaife.'

'Typhoid from the food, clap from the whores, eh Mr Fox?'

His cigarette was burning dangerously close to his lips. Eyes closed he jerked up and pushed it out a little with his tongue.

'But I know a good place ... off Rue Talaat Harb ... girls clean there ... I'm known ... could get a reduction for you ...'

The fire crawled up to him again. This time his lips loosened and the cigarette fell on to his hand. I leant over the table quickly, knocking over a bottle, spilling its dregs on the cloth, and brushed the cigarette stub away to the floor. Mr Fox slumped forward, head on arms, asleep at last.

It was the middle of the afternoon now and Vassiliou's was almost empty; most people had gone home to rest. I wiped my upper lip with my forefinger and looked at the thick line of sweat there. Some children's shrill voices, raised in joy or anger, I couldn't tell which, were carried in from the beach. Fox started to snore. I felt feverish, hot and yet cold, too, my body was trembling, my rectum was on fire; I knew I must go to the lavatory immediately. The moment at last. But where was the lavatory? I looked at the counter. Old Father Time was sleeping behind it – I could just see the top of his head. Whom to ask? Vassiliou was still sitting at his desk, although his wife and sister had gone to their quarters at the back somewhere. But Vassiliou was glowering before him at nothing, maybe remembering the bagpiper or some other, more distant cause of fury. Even Samir was asleep, slumped on the floor by the entrance, his head on his knees. Well, wake one of them up – you must. No time to be reticent now. I heard a radio from the back, suddenly loud, playing a sentimental Greek song. Then the sound was cut off as a door closed. Fortunately, the *suffraggi* who had been serving us appeared and stood by the counter. I signalled him over urgently and got up. The Arabic word for lavatory? *Dortmaya*? I tried it on him, but he didn't understand. I began to panic – I only had a couple of minutes at the very most. Toilet, *merros, lavabo, pissoir*, '*Ana mish fairhim*, mister.' Fox stirred a little and champed peevishly, his face cagey even in sleep. Wake him up and get him to ask. '*Dortmaya*!' Bending my knees and leaning forward, I pointed to my arse and scrubbed it with imaginary paper. The *suffraggi* laughed at my dumb-show and pointed to the corridor, motioning me to go right down it. He patted me gently and sympathetically on the back and went off to the entrance where he kicked Samir awake.

I walked slowly across the restaurant; decorum, decorum till the very end. Old Vassiliou was leaning back in his chair now, looking up at his canaries. He fumbled in his waistcoat pocket and brought out a whistle on which he chirruped up to them. They were motionless, alert, for a moment or two and then they dashed frantically from their perches to the bars of the cage and back again, over and over, chirruping in reply. Vassiliou watched and smiled a broad smile of happiness and well-being that I'd never seen on him before. As I went by him, he wrenched his false teeth out of his mouth and put them in a glass of water which stood on his desk. He took a sip, the teeth, ancient and stained, chinking against the side of the glass. Throwing away the last remnants of dignity, I broke into a run, past the kitchen where the cooks and the *suffraggis*, resting and eating, looked up at me in astonishment, past several closed rooms, to the battered, dingy-looking lavatory at the end of the corridor. As I flung the door open and made my way into the dark hole, gasping at the thick stench of shit and piss, I heard Vassiliou whistling to his canaries again and the flood of chirruping that answered him, the bird claws rattling the bars, and then, as I kicked the door shut, tugged my trousers down and squatted, I heard a hoarse, bellowing sound – which might have been the old man laughing.

Douglas Dunn

THE
CANOES

DOUGLAS DUNN was born in Scotland in 1942. He lives in Hull and Dundee. His most recent book of verse is *St Kilda's Parliament*. His stories have appeared in *Encounter*, *London Magazine*, *Punch* and the *New Yorker*.

Peter and Rosalind Barker began their holiday on Loch Arn on an evening in the first week of August. We were standing by the rail of what is known in our village of Locharnhead as the Promenade – a name that does no more than repeat the intent of the old Duke, who paid for its construction many years ago as a means of employing our fathers. It is just a widening of the pavement by the side of the road that runs along the head of Loch Arn and then peters out in an unpaved track a mile farther on. We have ten yards of Promenade, and that is not much of a walk. Our fathers used to lean on a low stone wall there. Now, as the old Duke considered this wall a symbol of our fathers' idleness, the job of knocking it down for good wages was meant to be significant. As a boy, I remember the old Duke's rage when, within a day of the work's completion, as he found our fathers loafing on the splendid new barrier they had just built, he craned from the window of his big car and cursed them to lean perpetually on a hot rail by the hearths of damnation. On summer evenings, therefore, we stand where our fathers stood, and one or two very old men sometimes stand beside their sons. For the most part we keep our mouths shut and enjoy the mild breeze that whispers across the water.

The Barkers looked a prosperous young couple. Mr Barker could have been no more than thirty years of age; his wife might have been a year or two younger. Their skins were already tanned, which I thought strange for two people at the start of their holiday. Mrs Barker wore a broad red ribbon in her fair hair, and I was pleased to see that her husband was not the sort of young man whose hair hides his ears and touches his shoulders. They both wore those modern clothes that, in my opinion, look so good on young, slender, healthy men and women. And I noticed that they wore those useful shoes that have no laces but can just be kicked off without your stooping to struggle with ill-tied knots as the blood rushes to your head.

Mr Barker parked his car in the place provided by the County Council, adjacent to the jetty. The jetty was paid for by the old Duke. It is announced as Strictly Private Property on a wooden notice board, though few people here can be bothered to read notices. The paint has long since peeled from it, and its message is rewritten in the badly formed letters of the new Duke's son's factor. Perhaps more would be done for the attractions of Locharnhead, which stands in need of a coat of paint throughout, if it was not the sort of place you can only get back from by returning along the arduous way you came.

Our eyes swung genially to the left to inspect the new arrivals – all, that is, except those of Martin MacEacharn, who is so dull of wit he proclaims himself bored with the examination of tourists. They are a kind of sport with the rest of us. Much amusement has been given to us by campers and hikers and cyclists in their strange garbs and various lengths of shorts and sizes of boots. We tell them they cannot light fires and pitch their tents where they are permitted to do so; and we tell them they may light fires and pitch tents to their hearts' desire where gamekeepers and bailiffs are guaranteed to descend on them once it is dark and there will be inconvenience in finding a legal spot for the night.

Young Gregor remarked enviously on the couple's motorcar. It was low to the ground, green, sleek, and new, and obviously capable of a fair rate of knots. Magee, whose father was an Irishman, ambled over towards Mr and Mrs Barker, pretending he was too shy to speak to them. They were admiring the fine view of the long loch from the jetty. Mr Barker had his arm around his wife's shoulders and was pointing to various phenomena of loveliness in the scenery. They are a familiar sight to us, these couples, who look and behave as if they feel themselves to have arrived in a timeless paradise of water and landscape and courteous strangers in old-fashioned clothes. On fine summer evenings the stillness of the water may be impressed on all your senses to the abandonment of everything else. Our dusks are noted far and wide and remembered by all who have witnessed them. On Loch Arn at dusk the islands become a mist of suggestions. There are old songs that say if only you could go back to them once more, all would be well with you for ever.

Mr Barker noticed Magee beside him and said, 'Good evening,' which Magee acknowledged with his shy smile and slow, soft voice. 'You'll be looking for me, perhaps,' Magee said. All of us leaning on the rail of the Promenade – Muir, Munro, Young Gregor, MacMurdo, MacEacharn, and myself – nodded to each other. When the couple saw us, we all nodded a polite and silent good evening to them, which we believe is necessary, for they have heard of our courtesy, our soft-spoken and excellent good manners and clear speech. All except Martin MacEacharn extended them the thousand welcomes; he was undoubtedly thinking too hard in his miserable way about the Hotel bar behind us and for which he had no money to quench his thirst.

'If you're the boatman, then, yes, you're the man we're waiting for,' said Mr Barker to Magee. My, but he had a bright way of saying it, too, though we all thought that a couple who possessed two long kayak canoes on the trailer behind their motorcar had no need of a boatman. He towered over Magee, who is short, wizened, bowlegged, and thin, though his shoulders are broad. Mrs Barker, too, was a good half foot taller than him.

'Well, I think I can just about more or less manage it,' said Magee, with a quick look at his watch, which has not worked in years. 'Yes,' he said, for he must always be repeating himself, 'just about. Just about, if we're handy-dandy.'

'Handy-dandy?' said MacMurdo with contempt. 'Where does he pick them up, for goodness' sake?'

Magee, as we all knew, was desperate for a bit of money, but a lethargic disregard of time is obligatory in these parts. Or that, at least, is the legend. What I will say is that if Magee is late for his dinner by so much as half a minute, his wife will scatter it, and probably Magee as well, before her chickens. Social security keeps him and the rest of us alive, and I have yet to see a man late for his money. If it ever came to the attention of the clerk that Donal Magee turns a bob or two with his boat, then he would be in deeper water than the depths of Loch Arn, some of which, they say, are very deep.

It soon became clear why the Barkers couldn't paddle themselves out to Incharn. Gear and suitcases are awkward to transport by canoe. Magee, a lazy man, turned round to us with a silent beckoning. He was asking us to lend him a hand but was frightened to say so aloud for fear that our refusals might ruin the atmosphere of traditional, selfless welcoming he had created with such skill and patience. We turned away with the precision of a chorus line it was once my good fortune to see in one of these American musical films – all, that is, except Martin MacEacharn, who wasn't looking.

Once Magee had loaded his boat and tied the canoes to its stern, the flotilla set off in the dusk like a mother duck followed by two chicks. I treated them to one of my lugubrious waves, which I am so good at that no one else is allowed to make one while I am there. How many times, after all, have the holiday types said to us, 'We will remember you for ever'? It is a fine thing, to be remembered.

Incharn is a small and beautiful island. That, at any rate, is how I remember it, for I have not stepped ashore there since I was a boy. A school friend of mine, Murray Mackenzie, lived on Incharn with his mother and father. Only one house stands there among the trees, with a clearing front and back, between the low knolls at each side of the small island. When the Mackenzies left for Glasgow, or whatever town in the south it was, Murray was given a good send-off at school. We had ginger ale, sandwiches, and paper streamers. The minister of the time presented him with a Holy Bible, in which we all inscribed our names in their Gaelic forms.

For a good few years the house lay empty. None of the Duke's men were inclined to live there and put up with rowing back and forth on the loch to get to work and come home from it. A childless couple took its tenancy. The man was a forester, and every day he rowed his boat to a little landing stage by the loch side and then followed the steep track over the hill. But his wife was visited by another boat, at whose oars sat Muir's elder brother, a self-confident and boastful lad who had spent four years at sea with the P & O Steam Navigation Company. Still, the poor woman must have been lonely on Incharn, all by herself most of the day, and she would have grown sick of it, especially in winter, waiting for her man to row back in the early dark; and it would have been worse if there had been a wind blowing or a bad snow. Muir's elder brother went back to sea without so much as a farewell to his fancy woman, and he has never been heard of since. She was found by her husband, standing up to her middle in the waters by the pebble beach, shivering and weeping but unable to take that last step – and one more step would have been enough, for it shelves quickly to the depths. They, too, left soon after that, and the island and its house lay empty. To row past it used to give me the shudders. I was a young man then, and had been away, and would go away again.

For a number of years the house has been rented in the summer months. The Duke's factor will accept only those who are highly recommended by the solicitor in London who handles the Duke's English business.

Magee and his hirers were soon no longer visible to the naked eye. We lounged by the rail, which has been rubbed by our hands and elbows to a dull shine. Muir, I think, remembers his lost brother when he looks towards Incharn, though he is too sullen to say so.

'Another couple to Incharn, then,' said Munro. 'Now, there's been more folk through the door of that house in a couple of years than there have been kin of mine through the door of my mother's house.' He always calls his house his mother's. She has been dead for twenty years; but we are born in houses, as well as of mothers.

'It's a sad thing that no one will lend a man the price of a pint of beer,' said MacEacharn.

'If we wait for Magee returning,' said the cool, calculating, and thirsty MacMurdo, 'then we'll have the price of several apiece. A twenty-minute drag over the loch is worth a pound or two.'

'Aye,' said Young Gregor, 'and don't forget the twenty minutes back.'

Eyes tried to focus on Incharn as its form vanished into the dusk. Lips were wetted by tongues as we imagined the pints of beer to which Magee might treat us on his return if we behaved nicely towards him or threatened him with violence. But Magee was in one of his funny moods. He is not the man to stand up to a woman like his wife. Munro has said, 'I'm glad I am married to the woman who accepted my proposal, but I'm doubly thankful I'm not married as much as all *that.*'

Magee did not come back but illustrated once again how he has inherited from his father an aptitude for the evasion of responsibilities.

He beached his boat a few hundred yards to the right of us, where there is a spit of sand, and then went home in the dark with his money, hoping perhaps to buy a few hours of peace and quiet through giving his wife a cut of his boatman's fee.

That Magee had been well paid is a matter of which I am certain. A couple of nights after the arrival of Mr and Mrs Barker, I had nothing to do, and Magee agreed that I go with himself and another English couple to Inverela, where there is another house on the new Duke's son's estates. It stands by the loch side and cannot be reached by road unless you park a mile from it and then walk along a narrow track. To go by boat is only sensible.

'Well, well, then,' Magee began as we were taking our leave of the Englishman on Inverela's tiny landing stage. His wife, by the way, was running around cooing about how wonderful it was, but we took no notice of that. 'I hope the weather stays fine and the loch remains as calm as a looking glass all the while you are here.' Highly impressed by this eloquent desire for their comforts, the Englishman gestured for his wife to come over and hear this, because it was obvious that Magee was far from finished. 'And may there be no drop of rain, except perhaps once or twice in the night, to make your mornings fresh and to keep the leaves as green as you wish to see them.' They settled back before this recitation. 'And may your sleep be undisturbed and tranquil and you have no reminder whatsoever of the cares of the world, which I am told are the very devil outwith of Loch Arn. And, to translate from our Gaelic' – of which Magee knows one curse, two toasts, and a farewell – 'may your bannocks never freeze over or your hair fall out, and may you never forget to salt your potatoes.'

I imagined how that couple would say to each other, as soon as our backs were turned, that it was true after all: the people here speak better English than the English. In that matter, the explanation is to be found in the care with which our kinsmen of long ago, in their clachans by the shores of Loch Arn, set about forgetting their original tongue so that their children, and their children's children, and all their posterity, would converse in translation.

As Magee stepped into his boat, it was in the way of a man who expects to be paid nothing at all for his trouble. His grateful employer was shuffling in his jacket for money – a sight studiously avoided by

Magee's little blue eyes, which are too close together. The Englishman
had a look of prosperity about him and a willingness to be forthcoming.
'Ah ... ah ...' The Englishman was a bit embarrassed. 'How much do I
owe you?'

Now, there can be a long and historical answer to that one, but Magee
thought for a moment with one hand on his chin while with the other
hand he removed his hat and began scratching his head. 'How ... how
much would you say it was worth?'

'Would a fiver do?' said the Englishman. His wife nudged him. Magee,
like myself, was quick to notice that this woman, in a hat of unduly wide
brim – dressed, it seemed to me, for a safari – was a touch on the over-
paying side of humanity.

I was all for putting an end to Magee's playacting and stretching my
own hand out to receive the note. But Magee began ponderously
calculating: 'Now, then ... It is thirty minutes out, after the ten minutes
it took to get you aboard, and unloading you took another ten minutes,
while it will take us another thirty to get back home ...'

That was a fine stroke of obscurity, for the man was nudged once more
by his grinning wife, and he produced another fiver. I can remember
when two fivers together was more than the government gave you for
having no job. Magee looked at the notes as if insulted. 'Now, that seems
a lot to a man like myself ... sir,' he said. 'How does the seven pounds
strike you ... sir? You see, it's the fair price.'

'A bit of a problem there,' said the gent. 'I haven't a single note on me.'

'Then, in that case,' said Magee, a bit too quickly, 'I'll take the ten
pounds and I'll see you when you come to Locharnhead.'

'How will we get there?' asked the woman, who was already blinking
in a soft hail of midges.

'By that boat there,' said Magee, who pointed to a beached rowing
boat that belonged to the house. 'Or you may walk by the track, on your
right.'

'Ah. I see. Yes, indeed. On the right, you say?'

'On the right, sir. But you will be quicker by the loch.'

I remember it took the Englishman four hours to row to Locharnhead
the following day, for that canny son of an Irishman had been to Inverela
that morning to hide one of the oars. Magee did well with a sort of
contract for their subsequent transportation.

'Ten pounds for a night's work, Magee,' I said on our return voyage.

'Is it not a liberty to take so large a sum, even from an Englishman who looks as though he can well afford it?'

'Do you want a drink?' he asked. 'Or do you want a *good* drink?'

'You know me,' I said.

'Then hold your hush and don't whine at me for a hypocrite. Because daylight robbery is exactly what it is, and you and the rest of them will sup on the benefit of it. Though I'll tell you true enough that if he didn't look such a pig of a rich man in his pink shirt and white breeks, I'd have let him off with the three pounds the factor says is the fixed charge to Inverela.'

We passed Incharn on the return trip in the late dusk. I waved to its holiday tenants, who had lit a fire on the beach. That couple we'd just left at Inverela could not be imagined lighting a bonfire. I had a feeling the Barkers would have been glad of our company if we had called on them for a few moments, but the thirsty lads, we knew, would be waiting for us on the Promenade, and with me in the boat Magee would have no chance of getting up to his tricks. In the light of their bonfire Mr and Mrs Barker looked like people of the far long ago, when, we are told, there was great happiness and heroism in the world. Or it may just have been the way they carried their youthfulness that led me to think so.

'Now, I hope you didn't fleece that nice couple of the Barkers there.'

'What kind of a thief do you take me to be? I asked for the factor's fixed charge, and they were kind enough to pass me a fiver.'

'Aye, well, there will be no more work for you out of that pair. These two are water babies.'

A day or two later I was walking on the hill. My old pal Red Alistair was, I knew, reluctantly laying down a drain on the Duke's lower pastures – the one he was meant to do the year before but didn't get around to finishing. He is called Red on account of the political pamphlets he inherited from his father. He is annoyed by the nickname, being twice the Tory even than the new Duke's son, and he keeps his legacy of pamphlets in deference to his father's memory. As I was looking for Red Alistair, I found the minister scrutinizing the loch through his spy-glass.

'Now, there's a sight I've never seen on the loch before,' he said. 'There are two canoes on it today.'

He gave me his glass and I had a clear view of Mr and Mrs Barker in single line ahead. They wore yellow waterproof jackets and sensible life jackets as well, which was a relief to me.

'Is there any chance of that becoming popular?' I asked the minister, after I had told him who the two canoeists were and what nice people they had turned out to be.

'You should ask that of Young Gregor. He's the boy who's daft on boats round here, though if he ever opens that marina he does nothing but talk about, we will become a laughing-stock for our broken craft, and make no mistake.'

He was as disappointed in Young Gregor as we all were. 'Go, for God's sake, to a southern city,' we urged the boy. 'There's nothing here but old men and the bed-and-breakfast trade.' Lack of capital was what he complained of – that and the poor show of enthusiasm he received from the manager of the Bank, which comes twice a week to Locharnhead in a caravan escorted by a police car.

'These canoes can fairly shift some,' said the minister. 'My, if I was young, I'd be inclined to try my hand at that. What an emblem of youth is there before our eyes.'

'We should encourage Young Gregor in it,' I suggested. 'These craft appear to have no engines at all.'

'That boy will break my heart. Is there nothing that can be found for him to do?'

'Can you imagine any woman from round here sporting about on the water like that?'

'Our women are not so much bad-natured as unpredictable,' he decided. 'By and large, though, it might be the bad nature you cannot predict. But we have known great joys in our time. There is no sweeter thing in this life than an harmonious domesticity. You know, I even miss the bad nature of my late wife.' He paused as he peered through his telescope. 'They are a tall couple, these English Barkers.'

'They tell me she is called Rosalind.'

'Now, that is a name from Shakespeare, I believe.'

'Then it's a fair English name,' I remember saying, 'for a young woman as handsome as Mrs Barker and with a true demeanour to go with it.'

'It makes a change from Morag, or Fiona, I'll say that much,' said the minister.

For many more minutes we stood there on the hill, exchanging the spy-glass as we watched the two canoes.

'What time is it?' asked the minister.

'I think it must be Thursday, for I saw the women waiting on the fishmonger's van.

Mr and Mrs Barker visited the Hotel bar in the early part of some evenings for a drink and a bite to eat. While they were inside, we took the opportunity of examining their Eskimo craft – not, of course, that there is much to look at in a kayak canoe. I studied them longer than the others had the patience for. A jaunt in one of them would have been very satisfying. To have asked Mr Barker might have been thought a bit eccentric of me, though I doubt if he would have taken it as an impertinence. Their canoes had a very modern look to them, as, indeed, had that bright and lively couple with their air of freedom.

'Aye,' said MacMurdo, who joined me on the jetty, 'that must be a fine and healthy outdoor sport for them – the sort of thing that could set you up for the winter and keep you well.' MacMurdo, fresh-faced as he is for his years, is housebound for three months of the calendar with the sniffles. When the Barkers came back, we stood to one side and said our soft 'Good evening' together, which they returned. Then we watched them slip into their canoes and paddle away into the early dusk.

'It's the best time of all to be on the water,' said MacMurdo. 'Just look at the beauty of it over there. The whole world is getting itself ready to settle down for the night.'

'Do you think he'd mind if I asked him – I mean, if he'd let me take his canoe out for a few minutes?'

'What's so special about one of these canoes?'

'They strike me for one thing as an exciting little sort of a craft, that's what. Now, look there, and see how close you would be to the water.'

'A man of your age ... A boat like that is for young things.'

'It would be interesting to *me*.'

A man like myself might be expected to resent these folk who come up from the south like the swallows to take their ease on a country that has brought me no prosperity. All the same, no one can tell me better than I tell myself I am as lazy as any man born. Part of my trouble is that I have become content enough on plain victuals in modest quantities and two packets of Players a week. What jobs I've done in other parts than this one did not contribute much to my happiness. But there are things I've seen, and people I've met, I would not do without if I had my chance again. When the mobile library, which is a wonderful thing, calls at Locharnhead, I am the first man aboard and the last man out. That is not hard, as the only other reader in our community, apart from the youngest MacMurdo when he's at home, is Mrs Carmichael, wife of our stingy publican and the Hotel's cook. By the way, I once ate a large dinner there. It was not worth the money, and Magee and the rest of them watched me through the window for all five courses, screwing up their faces and licking their chops in an ironic manner. MacEacharn, I noticed, was there, too, but that obstinate man wasn't even looking.

But for all the large contrast between myself and the likes of Mr and Mrs Barker, it made me mellow and marvellously sad to watch them paddle in the still waters of Loch Arn at dusk, going towards Incharn, where the Mackenzies once lived, and that unhappy couple who followed them.

Incharn, as I have said, is a beautiful island. A good number of trees grow there, and on the side you cannot see from the head of the loch there is low ground and a growth of reeds of which nesting swans and waterfowl are appreciative. This is the most beautiful side of all, though you can only see it properly from the water, which means that it has been observed by few people. Facing Locharnhead, the beach is of fine pebbles, and it slopes quickly into the water. Crab apples grew there when my friend Mackenzie lived on it, and that bitter fruit made grand jelly in his mother's big copper pan. They had a black-leaded stove of great size, which Mrs Mackenzie kept as spotlessly black as a Seaforth's boots, and we were famous for the spit and polish. Mrs Mackenzie would do her washing in a wooden tub on the beach, and her suds floated and spread as Murray and I threw stones at the scattering patches of foam. People on holiday do no washing at all, I'm told. Sometimes I felt like telling Mr and Mrs Barker about Incharn, but I never got round to it. They might have been interested. Magee has been known to tell those he ferries to the island of the tragedy that befell there. In his story, the woman drowned herself, and her demented husband first slew her lover with his bare hands and then committed his own life to the chill waters, but it was not that way. For all I know, the Barkers heard that story from Magee; but if they did, they were too happy to pay it any heed.

At night you can see the small lights of the cottage if its blinds or curtains are not drawn. In our famous dusks and sunsettings, the lights seem to spread in the open and watery mist, and they float above the island like benedictions. A man can look towards Incharn and feel drawn towards it. Muir's brother may have felt that, too, for whether the beauty of a place discriminates among those who are to be compelled by it is not a subtlety I am prepared to go into. Incharn draws a charitable thought from me, at any rate. But then I was always a bachelor, though not because I wanted to be one; and so I am always glad of something that holds disgruntlements at bay. All winter long I look forward to the holiday couples. It would please me more if Mr and Mrs Barker were to come back, with their frail canoes, and the way they splashed each other with water off their paddles, and capsized and rolled over under the water and came back up again as my heart beat with admiration for them – and, above all, the way they just followed each other about on the still water.

Alasdair Gray

THE
COMEDY
OF
THE
WHITE
DOG

ALASDAIR GRAY was born in Glasgow in 1934 and lives there mainly by painting portraits and mural decorations. In 1981 he published his first novel *Lanark*. He has written for television, radio and the theatre and is just now completing a new novel, *1982, Janine*.

On a sunny afternoon two men went by car into the suburbs to the house of a girl called Nan. Neither was much older than twenty years. One of them, Kenneth, was self-confident and well dressed and his friends thought him very witty. He owned and drove the car. The other, Gordon, was more quiet. His clothes were as good as Kenneth's but he inhabited them less easily. He had never been to this girl's house before and felt nervous. An expensive bunch of flowers lay on his lap.

Kenneth stopped the car before a broad-fronted bungalow with a badly kept lawn. The two men had walked half-way up the path to the door when Kenneth stopped and pointed to a dog which lay basking in the grass. It was a small white sturdy dog with a blunt pinkish muzzle and a stumpy tail; it lay with its legs stuck out at right angles to its body, its eyes were shut tight and its mouth open in a grin through which the tongue lolled. Kenneth and Gordon laughed, and Gordon said, 'What's so funny about him?'

Kenneth said, 'He looks like a toy dog knocked over on its side.'

'Is he asleep?'

'Don't fool yourself. He hears every word we say.'

The dog opened its eyes, sneezed and got up. It came over to Gordon and grinned up at him, but evaded his hand when he bent down to pat it and trotted up the path and touched the front door with its nose. The door opened and the dog disappeared into a dark hall. Kenneth and Gordon stood on the front step stamping their feet on the mat and clearing their throats. Sounds of female voices and clattering plates came from nearby and the noise of a wireless from elsewhere. Kenneth shouted, 'Ahoi!', and Nan came out of a side door. She was a pleasant-faced blonde who would have seemed plump if her waist, wrists and ankles had not been slender. She wore an apron over a blue frock and held a moist plate in one hand. Kenneth said jocularly, 'The dog opened the door to us.'

'Did he? That was wicked of him. Hullo Gordon, why, what nice flowers. You're always kind to me. Leave them on the hall-stand and I'll put them in water.'

'What sort of dog is he?' said Gordon.

'I'm not sure, but when we were on holiday up at Ardnamurchan the local inhabitants mistook him for a pig.'

A woman's voice shouted 'Nan! The cake!'

'Oh, I'll have to rush now, I've a cake to ice. Take Gordon into the living-room, Kenneth; the others haven't arrived yet so you'll have to entertain each other. Pour yourselves a drink if you like.'

The living-room was at the back of the house. The curtains, wallpaper and carpets had bright patterns that didn't harmonize. There was an assortment of chairs and the white dog lay on the most comfortable. There was a big very solid oval table, and a grand piano with two bottles of cider and several tumblers on it.

'I see we're not going to have an orgy anyway,' said Gordon, pouring cider into a tumbler.

'No no. It's going to be a nice little family party,' said Kenneth, seating himself at the piano and starting to play. He played badly but with confidence, attempting the best-known bits of works by Beethoven and Schumann. If he particularly enjoyed a phrase he repeated it until it bored him, if he made a passage illegible with too many discords he repeated it until it improved. Gordon stood with the tumbler in his hand looking out of the window. It opened on a long narrow lawn which sloped down between hedges to a shrubbery.

'Are you in love with Nan?' said Kenneth, still playing.

'Yes. Mind you, I don't know her well,' said Gordon.

'Hm. She's too matronly for me.'

'I don't think she's matronly.'

'What do you like about her?'

'Most things. I like her calmness. She's got a very calm sort of beauty.'

Kenneth stopped playing and sat looking thoughtful. Voices and clattering dishes could be heard from the kitchen, a telephone was ringing and the noise of a wireless still came loudly from somewhere. Kenneth said, 'She's not calm when she's at home. They're all very nice folk, pleasant and sincere I mean, but you'll find all the women of this family – Nan, her mother and grandmother and aunt – all talk too loudly at the same time. It's never quiet in this house. Either the wireless is on loudly, or the gramophone, or both. I've been to one or two parties here. There are never many guests but I've always felt there are other parties going on in rooms of the house I don't know about. Do you want to marry Nan?'

'Of course: I told you I loved her.'

Kenneth laughed and swung from side to side on the piano stool, making it squeak. He said, 'Don't mistake me – there's nothing disorderly about the house. Nobody drinks anything stronger than cider. Nan's father and brothers are so quiet as to be socially non-existent. You only see them at mealtimes and not always then. In fact I'm not sure how many brothers she has, or how large this family is. What are you grinning at?'

'I wish I could talk like you,' said Gordon. 'You've told me nothing surprising about Nan's family yet you've made it seem downright sinister.'

Kenneth began to fumble out the tune of 'The Lark in the Clear Air'.

'Anyway,' he said, 'You won't get a chance to be alone with her, which is what you most want, I suppose.'

Nan came in and said 'Gibson and Clare will be here in half an hour ... er ... Would you like to have tea in the garden? It's a good day for it. Mum doesn't like the idea much.'

'I think it's a fine idea,' said Kenneth.

'Oh, good. Perhaps you'll help us with the table?'

Gordon and Kenneth took the legs off the table, carried the pieces on to the back lawn and reassembled it, then put chairs round it and helped to set it. While they did so Nan's mother, a small gay woman, kept running out and shouting useless directions: 'Put that cake in the middle, Gordon!

No, nearer the top! Did ye need to plant the table so far from the house? You've given yourself a lot of useless work. Well, well, it's a nice day. Where's my dog? Where's my dog? Aha, there he is below the table! Come out, ye bizum! No, don't tease him, Kenneth! You'll only drive him made.'

Gibson and Clare arrived. Gibson was a short thickly built man whose chin always looked swarthy. At first sight he gave a wrong impression of strength and silence for he was asthmatic and this made his movements slow and deliberate. Though not older than Gordon or Kenneth his hair was getting thin. As soon as he felt at ease in a company he would talk expertly about books, art, politics and anything that was not direct experience. Clare, his girl-friend, was nearly six feet tall and beautiful in a consciously chaste way. Her voice was high-pitched, pure and clear, and she listened to conversation with large wide-open eyes and lustrous lips slightly parted. Her favourite joke was to suspect an indecency in an ordinary remark and to publicize it with a little exclamation and giggle. Kenneth had nicknamed the two Intellect and Spirit. He said there seemed nothing animal between them.

The tea was a pleasant one. Only Nan, her four guests and the dog were present, though Nan's mother often ran out with a fresh pot of tea or plate of food. The sun was bright, a slight breeze kept the air from being too warm, and Kenneth amused the company by talking about the dog.

'There's something heraldic about him,' he said. 'It's easy to imagine him with another head where his tail is. Look, he's getting excitable! He wants to sit on a chair! Oh, I hope he doesn't choose mine.'

The dog had been trotting round the table in a wide circle, now it came towards Kenneth, wagging its tail and grinning. Kenneth grabbed a plate of meringues and got down under the table with them.

'These at least he shall not have!' he cried in a muffled trembling voice. The others laughed, left their chairs and finished the meal sitting on the grass. All but Gordon felt that pleasant drunkenness which comes from being happy in company. Kenneth crawled about the lawn on his knees with a sugar bowl in his hand and when he came to a daisy peered at it benevolently and dropped a small heap of sugar into the flower. Gibson crawled after him adding drops from the milk jug. Clare sat with the dog on her lap and pretended to cut it up with a knife and fork. Actually she stroked and tickled its stomach gently with the edge of the knife and murmured baby-talk: 'Will I be cruel and eat oo up doggie? No no no doggie, oo is too sweet a doggie to eat up.'

Nan had taken needles and wool from her apron pocket and was quietly knitting and smiling to herself. Gordon lay nearby pretending to sunbathe. He was worried. He really did not know Nan well. He had only seen her at the homes of friends and had not even spoken to her much. His invitation to the party had been a surprise. Nan did not know him as well as several other people she might have invited. He had assumed she knew what he felt for her and was giving him a chance to know her better, yet since his arrival she had not paid him any special attention. Now she sat placidly knitting, sometimes glancing sideways at Clare with a slight ironic smile; yet he believed he saw in her manner a secretive awareness of him lying apart and wanting her.

'Ach, the bitch,' he thought, 'she's sure of me. She thinks she can hurt me all she likes. Well, she's wrong.' He got up, went to the table and started piling the plates together.

'I'll take these indoors,' he said.

'Oh, don't bother,' said Nan, smiling at him lazily.

'Someone will have to shift them,' said Gordon sternly.

He took several journeys to carry the table things into the kitchen. It was cool and dim indoors. Nan's father and three of her silent brothers were eating a meal at the kitchen table. They nodded to him. The mother was nowhere to be seen but he heard her voice among several shrill female voices in some other room. Gordon brought in the last table things and put them on the drying board of the sink, then stood awkwardly watching the four eaters. They were large men with stolid, clumsily moulded faces. Some lines on the father's face were deeply cut, otherwise he looked very like his sons. He said to Gordon, 'A warm evening.'

'Yes, I prefer it indoors.'

'Would you like a look at the library?'

'Er, yes thanks, yes I would.'

The father got up and led Gordon across the hall and down a short passage, opened a door and stood by to let Gordon through. The library had old glass-fronted bookcases on each wall. Between the bookcases hung framed autographed photographs of Havelock Ellis, H. G. Wells and D. H. Lawrence. There was a leather-covered armchair and a round tin labelled 'Edinburgh Rock' on a low table beside it.

'You've a lot of books,' said Gordon, looking round.

'The wife's people were great readers,' said Nan's father. 'Can I leave you now?'

'Oh yes. Oh yes.'

The father left. Gordon took a book at random from a shelf, sat down and turned the pages casually. It was a history of marine engineering. The library was on the opposite side of the hall from the living-room, but its window also looked on to the back garden and sometimes Gordon heard an occasional shout or laugh or bark from those on the lawn. He told himself grimly, 'I'm giving her a chance. If she wants me she can come to me here. In fact if she has ordinary politeness and decency she'll be bound to look for me soon.' He imagined the things she might say and the things he would say back. Sometimes he consoled himself with a piece of rock from the tin.

Suddenly the door sprang open with a click and he saw coming through it towards him, not Nan, but the dog. It stopped in front of him and grinned up into his face. 'What do you want?' said Gordon irritably. The dog wagged its tail. Gordon threw a bit of rock which it caught neatly in its jaws, then trotted out through the door. Gordon got up, slammed the door and sat down. A little later the door opened and the dog entered again. 'Ye brute!' said Gordon. 'Right, here's your sweet; the last you'll get from me.' He escorted the dog to the door, closed it carefully then pulled the handle hard. The lock held the door tight shut. There was a key in it which he turned to make doubly certain then went back to the chair and the book. After a while it struck him that with the door locked Nan wouldn't get in if she came to him. He glanced uneasily up. The door was open and the dog stood before him grinning with what seemed, to his stupefied eyes, triumphant amusement. For a moment Gordon was too surprised to move. He noticed that the animal was grinning with its mouth *shut*, a thing he had never seen a dog do before. He raised the book as if to throw it. 'Grrr, get out!' he yelled.

The dog turned jauntily and trotted away. After thinking carefully Gordon decided some joker must be opening the door from outside to let the dog in. It was the sort of pointless joke Kenneth was fond of. He listened carefully and heard from the lawn the voice of Kenneth and the barking of the dog. He decided to leave the door open.

Later he found it too dark to see the page of the book clearly and put it down. The noises from the lawn had subtly altered. The laughter and shouting were now not continuous. There were periods of silence disturbed by the occasional shuffle of running feet and the hard breathing of somebody pursued, then he would hear a half-cry or scream that did not sound altogether in fun. Gordon went to the window. Something strange was happening on the darkened lawn. Nan was nowhere to be seen. Kenneth, Gibson and Clare were huddled together on the bare table-top, Clare kneeling, Kenneth and Gibson crouching half-erect. The white dog danced in a circle round the table among overturned chairs. Its activity and size seemed to have increased with the darkness. It glimmered like a sheet in the dusk, its white needle-teeth glittered in the silently laughing jaws, it was about the size of a small lion. Gibson was occupied in a strange way, searching his pockets for objects and hurling them at the shrubbery at the far end of the garden. The white dog would run, leap, catch these in its mouth while they were in the air, then return and deposit them under the table. It looked like a game and had possibly begun as one, but obviously Gibson was continuing in an effort to get the dog as far away as possible. Gordon suddenly discovered Nan was beside him, watching, her hands clenched against her mouth.

Gibson seemed to run out of things to throw. Gordon saw him expostulate precariously for a moment with Kenneth, demanding (it appeared) his fountain pen. Kenneth kept shaking his head. He was plainly not as frightened as Gibson or Clare, but a faint embarrassed smile on his face suggested that he was abashed by some monstrous possibility. Gibson put a hand to his mouth, withdrew something, then seemed to reason with Kenneth, who at last shrugged and took it with a distaste which suggested it was a plate of false teeth. Kenneth stood upright and, balancing himself with difficulty, hurled the object at the shrubbery. It was a good throw. The white dog catapulted after it and at once the three jumped from the table and ran to the house, Kenneth going to the right, Gibson and Clare to the left. The dog swerved in an abrupt arc and hurled towards the left. He overtook Clare and snapped the hem of her dress. She stumbled and fell. Gibson and Kenneth disappeared from sight and two doors were slammed in different parts of the house. Clare lay on the lawn, her knees drawn up almost to her chin, her clasped hands pressed between her thighs and her eyes shut. The dog stood over her, grinning happily, then gathered some of the clothing round her waist into its mouth and trotted with her into the bushes of the shrubbery.

Gordon looked at Nan. She had bowed her face into her hands and was shuddering with sobs. He put an arm round her waist, she laid her face against his chest and said in a muffled voice, 'Take me away with you.'

'Are you sure of what you're saying?'

'Take me away, Gordon.'

'What about Clare?'

Nan laughed vindictively. 'Clare isn't the one to pity.'

'Yes, but that dog!'

Nan cried out, *'Do you want me or not?'*

As they went through the dark hall the kitchen door opened. Nan's mother looked out then shut it quickly. In the front garden they met Kenneth and Gibson, both shamefaced and subdued. Kenneth said, 'Hullo. We were just coming to look for you.'

Gordon said, 'Nan's coming home with me.'

Kenneth said, 'Oh good.'

They stood for a moment in silence, none of the men looking at each other, then Gibson said, 'I suppose I'd better wait for Clare.' The absence of teeth made him sound senile. Nan cried out. 'She won't want *you* now! She won't want *you* now!' and started weeping again.

'I'll wait all the same,' Gibson muttered. He turned his back on them. 'How long do you think she'll be?' he asked. Nobody answered.

The drive back into the city was quiet. Gordon sat with Nan in the back seat, his arm around her waist, her mourning face against his shoulder. He felt strangely careless and happy. Once Kenneth said, 'An odd sort of evening.' He seemed half willing to discuss it but nobody encouraged him. He put off Gordon and Nan at the close-mouth of the tenement where Gordon lived. They went upstairs to the top landing, Gordon unlocked a door and they crossed a small lobby into a very untidy room. Gordon said, 'I'll sleep on the sofa here. The bedroom's through that door.'

Nan sat on the sofa, smiled sadly and said, 'So I'm not to sleep with you.'

'Not yet. I want you too much to take advantage of a passing mood.'

'You think this is a passing mood.'

'It might be. If it's not I'll see about getting a marriage licence. Are you over eighteen?'

'Yes.'

'That's good. Er ... do you mind me wanting to marry you, Nan?'

Nan got up, embraced him and put her tear-dirty cheek against his. She laughed and said, 'You're very conventional.'

'There's no substitute for legality,' said Gordon, rubbing his brow against hers.

'There's no substitute for impulse,' Nan whispered.

'We'll try and combine the two,' said Gordon. The pressure of her body started to excite him so he moved apart from her and started making a bed on the sofa.

'If you're willing, tomorrow I'll get a licence.'

He had just settled comfortably on the sofa when Nan came to the bedroom door and said, 'Gordon, promise you won't ask me about him.'

'About who?'

'You can't have forgotten him.'

'The dog? Yes, I had forgotten the dog. All right, I won't ask ... You're sure nothing serious has happened to Clare?'

'Ask her when you see her next!' Nan cried, and slammed the bedroom door.

Next day Gordon bought a marriage licence and engagement ring and arranged the wedding for a fortnight later. The next two weeks were among the happiest in his life. During the day he worked as an engineering draughtsman. When he came home from work Nan had a good meal ready for him and the apartment clean and tidy. After the meal they would go walking or visit a film show or friends, and later on they would make rather clumsy love, for Gordon was inexperienced and got his most genuine pleasure by keeping the love-making inside definite limits. He wasn't worried much by memories of the white dog. He prided himself on being thoroughly rational and thought it irrational to feel curious about mysteries. He always refused to discuss things like dreams, ghosts, flying-saucers, and religion. 'It doesn't matter if these things are true or not,' he said. 'They are irrelevant to the rules that we have to live by. Mysteries only happen when people try to understand something irrelevant.'

Somebody once pointed out to him that the creation of life was a mystery. 'I know,' he said, 'and it's irrelevant. Why should I worry about how life occurred? If I know how it is just now I know enough.'

This attitude allowed him to dismiss his memories of the white dog as irrelevant, especially when he learned that Clare seemed to have come to no harm. She had broken with Gibson and now went about a lot with Kenneth.

One day Nan said, 'Isn't tomorrow the day before the wedding?'

'Yes, what about it?'

'A man and woman aren't supposed to see each other the night before their wedding.'

'I didn't know that.'

'And I thought you were conventional.'

'I know what's legal. I don't much care about conventions.'

'Well, women care more about conventions than they do about laws.'

'Does that mean you want me to spend tomorrow night in a hotel?'

'It's the proper thing, Gordon.'

'You weren't so proper on the night I brought you here.'

Nan said quietly, 'It's not fair to remind me of that night.'

'I'm sorry,' said Gordon. 'No, it's not fair. I'll go to a hotel.'

Next evening he booked a room in a hotel and then, since it was only ten o'clock, went to a coffee bar where he thought he might see some friends. Inside Clare and Kenneth were sitting at a table with a lean young man whom Gordon had not seen before. Clare smiled and beckoned. She had lost her former self-conscious grace and looked an adult, very attractive girl. As Gordon approached Kenneth stopped talking to the stranger, stood up, gripped Gordon's hand and shook it with unnecessary enthusiasm.

'Gordon! Gordon!' said Kenneth. 'You must meet Mr McIver. (Clare and I are just leaving.) Mr McIver, this is the man I told you about, the only man in Scotland who can help you. Goodnight! Goodnight! Clare and I mustn't intrude on your conversation. You have a lot to discuss.'

He rushed out pulling Clare after him and chuckling. Gordon and the stranger looked at each other with embarrassment.

'Won't you sit down?' said Mr McIver, in a polite North American voice. Gordon sat down and said, 'Are you from the States, Mr McIver?'

'No, from Canada. I'm visiting Europe on a scholarship. I'm collecting material for my thesis upon the white dog. Your friend tells me you are an authority on the subject.'

Gordon said abruptly, 'What has Kenneth told you about the dog?'

'Nothing. But he said you could tell me a great deal.'

'He was joking.'

'I'm sorry to hear that.'

Gordon stood up to go, sat down again, hesitated and said, 'What is this white dog?'

McIver answered in the tone of someone starting a lecture: 'Well-known references to the white dog occur in Ovid's *Metamorphoses*, in Chaucer's unfinished 'Cook's Tale', in the picaresque novels of the Basque poet Jose Mompou, and in your Scottish Border Ballads. Nonetheless, the white dog is the most neglected of European archetypes, and for that reason perhaps, one of the most significant. I can only account for this neglect by assuming a subconscious resistance in the minds of previous students of folk-lore, a resistance deriving from the fact that the white dog is the west-European equivalent of the Oedipus myth.'

'That's all just words,' said Gordon, 'What does the dog *do*?'

'Well, he's usually associated with sexually frigid women. Sometimes it is suggested they are frigid because they have been dedicated to the love of the dog from birth...'

'Dedicated by who?'

'In certain romance legends by the priest at the baptismal font, with or without the consent of the girl's parents. More often the frigidity is the result of the girl's choice. A girl meets an old woman in a lonely place who gives her various gifts, withholding one on which the girl's heart is set. The price of the gift is that she consents to marry the old woman's son. If she accepts the gift (it is usually an object of no value) she becomes frigid until the white dog claims her. The old woman is the dog's mother. In these versions of the legend the dog is regarded as a malignant spirit.'

'How can he be other than malignant?'

'In Sicily the dog is thought of as a benefactor of frigid or sterile women. If the dog can be induced to sleep with such a woman and she submits to him she will become capable of normal fruitful intercourse. There is always a condition attached to this. The dog must always be, to a certain extent, the husband of the woman. Even if she marries a human man the dog can claim her whenever he wants.'

'Oh God,' said Gordon.

'There's nothing horrible about it,' said McIver. 'In one of Jose Mompou's novels the hero encounters a brigand chieftain whose wife is also married to the dog. The dog and the chieftain are friends, the dog accepts the status of pet in the household, sleeping by the fire, licking the plates clean et cetera, even though he is the ghostly husband of several girls in the district. By his patronage of the house in this ostensibly servile capacity he brings the brigand luck. His presence is not at all resented, even though he sometimes sleeps with the brigand's daughters. To have been loved by the dog makes a woman more attractive to normal men, you see, and the dog is never jealous. When one of his women marries he only sleeps with her often enough to assert his claim on her.'

'How often is that?'

'Once a year. He sleeps with her on the night before the wedding and on each anniversary of that night. Say, how are you feeling? You look terrible.'

Gordon went into the street too full of horror and doubt to think clearly. 'To be compared with a *dog*! To be measured against a dog! Oh no, God, Nan wouldn't do that! No, it would be wicked, Nan isn't so wicked!'

He found he was gibbering these words and running as fast as possible home. He stopped, looked at his watch then forced himself to walk slowly. He arrived home about midnight, went through the close to the back court and looked up at the bedroom window. The light was out. He tiptoed upstairs and paused at the front door. The door looked so much the same as usual that he felt nothing wrong could be behind it, he could still return to the hotel; but while he considered this his hand was stealthily putting the key in the lock. He went softly into the living-room, hesitated outside the bedroom door, then opened it quickly. He heard a gasp and Nan shrieked 'Gordon!'

'Yes,' said Gordon.

'Don't put the light on!'

He switched the light on. Nan sat up in bed blinking at him fearfully, her hands pressed protectively on a mound between her legs under the tumbled bedclothes. Gordon stepped forward, gripped the edge of the bedclothes and tugged. 'Let go!' he said. She stared at him, her face white with terror, and whispered 'Go away!' He struck her face and she fell back on the pillows; he snatched away the bedclothes and the white dog sprang from between the sheets and danced on them, grinning. Gordon grabbed at the beast's throat, with an easy squirming movement it evaded his hand then bit it. Gordon felt the small needle teeth sink between his finger-bones and suddenly became icy cold. He sat on the edge of the bed and stared at the numb bitten hand still gripped between the dog's grinning jaws: its pink little eyes seemed to wink at him. With a great yell he seized the beast's hind leg with his free hand, sprang up and swung its whole body against the wall. Nan screamed. He felt its head crush with the impact, swung and battered it twice more on the wall leaving a jammy red stain each time, then flung the body into a corner and sat down on the edge of the bed and stared at his bitten hand. The sharp little teeth seemed to have gone in without piercing any veins or arteries for the only mark on the skin was a V-shaped line of grey punctures. He stared across at the smash-headed carcass. He found it hard to believe he had killed it. *Could* such a creature be killed? He got to his feet with difficulty, for he felt unwell, and went to the thing. It was certainly dead. He opened the window, picked the dog up by the tail and flung it down into the back court, then went over to the bed where Nan lay gazing at him with horror. He began to undress as well as he could without the use of the numbed right hand.

'So, my dear,' he muttered, 'You prefer convention.'

She cried out, 'You shouldn't have come back tonight! We would all have been happy if you hadn't come back tonight!'

'Just so,' said Gordon, getting in bed with her.

'Don't touch me!'

'Oh yes, I'll touch you.'

Towards morning Gordon woke feeling wonderfully happy. Nan's arms clasped him yet he felt more free than ever before. With a little gleeful yelp he sprang from the nest of warmth made by her body and skipped upon the quilt. Nan opened her eyes lazily to him then sat up and kissed his muzzle. He looked at her with jovial contempt, then jumped on to the floor and trotted out of the house, the shut doors springing open at the touch of his nose. He ran downstairs into the sunlit street, his mouth hanging open in a grin of sheer gaiety. He would never again be bound by dull laws.

Graham Greene

ON
THE
WAY
BACK:

a work not in progress

In memory of my friend Omar Torrijos

I

She felt the unprofessional shyness that she always experienced, with
a sense of inadequacy, before an interview – she lacked, as she
well knew, the brazen front of the traditional male reporter, but
not, or so at this time she still believed, his cynicism – she could be as
cynical as any man and with reason.

She found herself now surrounded in the small courtyard of a white
suburban villa with half-Indian faces. The men all carried revolvers on
their belts and one had a walkie-talk which he kept pressed closely to his
ear as though he were waiting with the intensity of a priest for one of his
Indian gods to proclaim something. The men are as strange to me, she
thought, as the Indians must have seemed to Columbus five centuries ago.
The camouflage of their uniforms was like painted designs on naked skin.
She said, 'I don't speak Spanish,' as Columbus might have said, 'I don't
speak Indian.' She then tried them with French – that was no good – and
after that with English, which had been her mother's tongue, but that was
no good either. 'I am Marie-Claire Duval. I have an appointment with the
General.'

One of the men – an officer – laughed, and at his laugh she wanted to
walk straight out of the courtyard, to make her way back to the pseudo-
luxury of her hotel, to the half-finished airport, to take the whole dreary
way back to Paris. Fear always made her angry. She said, 'Go and tell the

General that I am here,' but, of course, no one would understand what she was saying.

One soldier sat on a bench cleaning his automatic. He was stubby and grey-haired. He wore his uniform with the stripes of a serjeant carelessly as though it was just a raincoat which he had huddled on against the thin vagrant rain which was blowing up now from the Pacific. She watched him closely as he cleaned his gun, but he didn't laugh, while the man with the walkie-talk continued to listen to his god and paid her no attention at all.

'Gringo,' the officer said.

'I am not a gringo. I am French,' but of course she knew by this time that he didn't understand any word she said – except gringo. He accused her again with his mocking smile – or so she believed because she didn't speak Spanish. All women, he seemed to be saying to her, were inferior if they hadn't a protector and she was more inferior than most because she spoke no Spanish.

'The General,' she repeated, 'the General,' knowing that she pronounced the word all wrong for a Spaniard, and she fished out of the poor memory she always had for foreign names that of the General's adviser who had made this appointment for her, 'Señor Martinez,' wondering all the time whether the name was right – perhaps it was Rodriguez or Gonzalez or Fernandez.

The serjeant snapped back the chamber of his automatic and spoke to her in almost perfect English from his bench. 'You're Mademoiselle Duval?' he asked.

'Madame Duval,' she said.

'Oh, you're married then?'

'Yes.'

'Well, it doesn't much matter,' he said, and he set his safety catch.

'It does to me.'

'I wasn't thinking of you,' he said. He got up and spoke to the officer. Although by his stripes he was only a serjeant, he had a kind of unmilitary authority about him. She found his manner a little insolent, but he was equally insolent to the officer. He swung his automatic to indicate the door of the small unimportant suburban house. 'You can go in,' he said. 'The General will see you.'

'Is Señor Martinez here – to translate?'

'No. The General wants me to translate. He wants to see you alone.'

'Then how can you translate?'

His smile, she noticed, after all was quite free from insolence in spite of the words he used. 'Ah, but here we say to a girl, "Come with me to be alone."'

She was stopped short again just inside a little hall which contained a bad picture, an occasional table, a nude statue of the late Victorian kind and a life-size china dog, by a soldier who pointed at the tape recorder which was slung over her shoulder.

'Yes,' the serjeant said, 'it would be better if you left that on the table.'

'It's only a recorder. I never learned shorthand. Does it look like a bomb?'

'No. All the same – it would be better. Please.'

She laid it down. She thought, I'll have to trust to my memory, my damnable memory, the memory I hate. 'After all,' she said, 'if I am an assassin you have your gun.'

'A gun is no defence,' he told her.

2

It was more than a month since the editor had invited her to lunch at Fouquet's. She had never met him, but he sent her a neat and courteous letter stamped out in a type which resembled book printing, praising an interview which she had published in another journal. Perhaps the letter read a little condescendingly, as though he were conscious of controlling a review of a higher intellectual grading than the one in which she wrote. It would certainly pay less, always the sign of quality. She accepted his invitation because the morning it arrived she had had one more 'final' quarrel with her husband – the fourth in four years. The first two had been the least damaging – jealousy after all is a form of love; the third was a furious quarrel with all the pain of broken promises, but the fourth was the worst, without love or anger, with just the irritated tiredness that comes from a repeated grievance, from the conviction that the man one lives with is unchangeable, and the sad knowledge that she didn't care much anyway any more. This one *was* the final quarrel she thought. All that was left for her now was the packing of suitcases. Thank God there were no children to consider.

She came into Fouquet's ten minutes late. She had been kept waiting in restaurants far too often to be punctual. She asked the waiter for

Monsieur Jacques Durand's table and saw a man rise to greet her. He was tall and lean and very good-looking – in that he reminded her of her husband. Good looks could be as nauseating as chocolate truffle. He would have had an air of almost overpowering distinction if his greying hair had been a little less well waved over his ears, though the ears, she admitted, were the right masculine size. (She disliked small ears.) She would have taken him for a diplomat if she had not known him to be the editor of that distinguished left-wing weekly which she had seldom read, not being in sympathy with its tendency towards modish politics. Many men who at first sight seem dead come alive in their eyes: but in his case it was the eyes which were the deadest part of him, in spite of their condescending gallantry: only in the gestures of his elegant carcass as he seated her beside him and handed her the menu did he come to a sort of life – a seductive life but a seduction which expressed itself only with words.

He suggested that it would be best if they took the turbot, and when she agreed he told her again in exactly the same phrases that he had used in the letter, how much pleasure her last interview had given him, so perhaps the words really were his and not his secretary's – he would hardly have learnt her words by heart. He added, 'The turbot here is very good.'

'Thank you. It's very kind of you.'

'I've been noticing your work for a long time now, Madame Duval. You get below the surface. Your interviews are not dictated by your victims.'

'I use a tape recorder,' she said.

'I didn't mean literally.' He crackled his toast melba. 'For a long time now, you know,' – his vocabulary seemed limited, perhaps by the rules of journalistic protocol – 'I have thought of you as one of us.' Obviously he meant the statement to be a compliment and he paused, probably waiting for her to repeat 'Thank you'. She wondered how long it would be before he began to talk real business. The suitcases were yawning emptily on her bed. She wanted to fill them before her husband returned – it was unlikely, but not impossible, that he would return before dinner.

'Do you know Spanish?' Monsieur Durand asked.

'French and English are my only languages.'

'Not German? Your interview with Helmut Schmidt was beautiful – and so destructive.'

'He speaks English well.'

'I doubt if the General does.' He fell silent over his turbot. It was very good turbot, one of Fouquet's specialities. She thought, 'If I can get out of the apartment before Jean returns it will save a lot of argument.' Argument could be left later to the two *avocats*. There would have to be, she supposed, a meeting of *conciliation* – the thought bored her profoundly. She wanted as quickly as possible to wipe the whole slate clean.

'The situation in Jamaica is another subject I have in mind. You could pick up Jamaica on your way out. You said you speak English, didn't you? A rather more sympathetic approach perhaps to Manley than you are used to. He's one of us, even though for the moment he's "out". The General, I think could be a subject in your usual style. Suitable for your brand of irony. As you can imagine we don't much care for generals – especially Latin-American generals.'

She asked, 'You mean you want to send me somewhere?'

'Well, yes. You are a very attractive woman. And by all accounts the General likes attractive women.'

'Doesn't Manley?' she asked.

'I wish you spoke a little Spanish. You have such a valuable knack of asking the right personal question. Politics, we believe, should never make dull reading. You are not under contract, are you?'

'No, but what General? You don't want me to go to Chile, do you?'

'We are getting a little tired of Chile. I doubt if even you could be very fresh on the subject of Pinochet – and would he receive you? The advantage of a really small republic is that it can be covered – in depth mind you – in a matter of weeks. We can regard it as a microcosm of Latin-America. The conflict with the United States, of course, is more in the open there – because of the bases.'

She looked at her watch. She was wondering if she could get all she wanted for the moment into two suitcases – to go where? 'What bases?' She would not leave a note because it could be used by lawyers.

'The American, of course.'

'You want me to interview the President? Of what republic?'

'Not the President. The General. The President doesn't really count. The General is chief of the revolution.' He poured her out another half-glass of wine. She had only ordered a small carafe. 'You see we are a little bit suspicious of the General. It's true that he has visited Fidel, and that he met Tito at Colombo. But we wonder whether his socialism is not rather skin-deep. He is no Marxist certainly. Your method with Schmidt would suit him admirably. And perhaps on the way there or back a sympathetic portrait of Manley in Jamaica. We feel quite happy about Manley.'

She was still not sure what country it was he wanted her to visit. Geography was not her strong point. Perhaps he *had* mentioned the name, but if he had it had dropped out of sight into the empty suitcases. Anyway it didn't really matter: anywhere was preferable at the moment to Paris. She said, 'When is it you want me to go?'

'As soon as possible. You see there may be a crisis in the next few months, and if that happens ... you might find yourself only writing the General's obituary.'

'A dead General, I suppose, would certainly not be a socialist good enough for you.'

His laugh, if it could really be called a laugh, was like the scraping of a dry throat, and his eyes, which were now fixed on the menu, the turbot having been meticulously finished, showed no sign that a joke, like an angel, had passed quietly overhead and vanished. 'Oh, as I said, we are rather doubtful about his kind of socialism. May I suggest a little cheese?'

3

'You might find yourself writing his obituary' – the phrase spoken two weeks ago by a modish left-wing editor over the Fouquet menu – came immediately back to Marie-Claire's mind when she encountered the tired and doom-laden eyes of the General. Death was the accepted premature end, she had always understood, for generals in Latin-America; the alternative might of course be Miami, but she couldn't see the man before her in Miami, sharing that city with the ex-President of the Republic and the ex-President's wife and his brother-in-law and cousin. Miami was known here, she had already learnt that, as 'The Valley of the Fallen'. The General was dressed in pyjamas and bedroom slippers and his hair was tousled in a boyish way, but no boy would have had eyes so laden with the future. He spoke to her in Spanish and the serjeant translated with correct though rather stiff English.

'The General says you are very welcome in the Republic. He does not know the paper for which you write, but Mr Martinez has told him that it is very well known in France for its liberal views.'

Marie-Claire believed in provocation; Helmut Schmidt had responded promptly with anger and pride, to her first questions, he had given himself away to the merciless tape, but the tape this time had been left behind in the recorder. She said, 'No, not liberal – left-wing. Would it be true to say that the General is much criticized for moving so very reluctantly towards socialism?'

She watched the serjeant closely as he translated, trying to attach a meaning to the Latin-sounding words, and his eyes twinkled back at her as though he were amused at the question and perhaps approved it.

'My General says he is going where his people tell him to go.'

'Or is it the Americans who tell him?'

'My General says that naturally he has to take the Americans into account, that is politics in a country as small as ours, but he need not accept their views. He suggests that you must be tired of standing: you should make yourself comfortable in the armchair.'

Marie-Claire sat down. She felt the General had scored over Helmut Schmidt – and over herself too. She hadn't yet had time to think of her next question – she had expected the General to leave a door open for her to make a quick impromptu question, but he seemed to have closed all doors firmly in her face. There was a long and awkward pause; she was relieved when the General spoke again.

'My General says that he hopes Señor Martinez is helping you in every way he can.'

'Señor Martinez has very kindly lent me his own car, but the chauffeur speaks only Spanish which makes it difficult for me.'

The two of them began to discuss together what she had said at some length. The General slipped off one shoe and stroked his left sole.

'My General says you may dismiss the car and the chauffeur. He has given me orders to look after you – Serjeant Gurdián is my name. I am to take you wherever you may wish to go.'

'Señor Martinez asked me in his letter to make out a programme for him to approve.' Again there was a consultation.

'My General says it is best for you not to have a programme. A programme kills.'

The tired and brooding eyes watched her with what she took to be amusement like those of a chess player who knows that he has made a surprise move and disconcerted his opponent.

'My General says that even a political programme kills. Your editor ought to know that.'

'Señor Martinez thought that I should visit . . .'

'My General says you should always do the opposite of whatever Señor Martinez advises.'

'But I was told that he was Chief Adviser to the General.'

The serjeant shrugged his shoulders and smiled too. 'My General says that while, of course, it is *his* duty to listen to his advisers, it is not *your* duty.'

The General began to talk in a low voice to the serjeant. Marie-Claire had an impression that the interview was slipping disastrously out of her hands. When she had abandoned the recorder she had abandoned her best weapon.

'My General wants to know if your editor is a Marxist.'

'Oh, he supports the Marxists – in a way, but he would never admit to being one himself. Before the war people used to call his type a fellow-traveller. The Communist Party is legal here, isn't it?'

'Yes, it is quite legal to be a Communist. But we have no parties.'

'Not even one?'

'Not one. A man can think what he likes. Is that true in a party?'

She said – and she meant it to be an insult – for in her experience it was only when a man became angry that he told the truth – even Schmidt had told a few truths – 'Is your General a fellow-traveller like my editor?'

The General gave her an encouraging smile, and for a moment he looked a little less tired, a little more interested. 'My General says the Communists are for a while travelling on the same train as he is. So are the socialists. But it is he who is driving the train. It is he who will decide at what station to stop, and not his passengers.'

'Passengers usually have tickets for certain destinations.'

'My General says he will be able to explain more easily to you when you have seen something of his country. My General would like before you return to Europe to see for once his country through your eyes. A stranger's eyes. He says they are very beautiful ones.'

So the editor was right, she thought, he likes women, he finds women easy, power is an obvious aphrodisiac . . . Charm too can be an aphrodisiac, Jean had plenty of charm, he had exuded charm with the skill of a politician, but she was finished with charm and aphrodisiacs. She said, 'Now that the General has power, I suppose he finds women easy to come by.' Serjeant Gurdián smiled. He didn't translate.

'I suppose he enjoys his power,' she said. She nearly added, 'And his women.'

She tried a question which she had sometimes found worked surprisingly well. 'What does he dream of? At night I mean. Does he dream of women?' She continued with mockery, 'Or does he dream of the terms he is going to make with the gringos?' The tired and wounded eyes looked at the wall behind her. She could even understand the single phrase he spoke in reply to her question. '*El muerte.*'

'He dreams of death,' the serjeant translated unnecessarily, and I could build an article on that, she thought with self-hatred.

Helen Harris

DREAMING
BACKWATERS

HELEN HARRIS was born in 1955. She read French and Russian at Oxford and then spent a year in Paris. She now lives in London. Her stories have appeared in a number of magazines and she is now working on her first novel.

Randolph Wheat, fifty-one, who wore steel-rimmed glasses and whose favourite colour was blue, wondered when a familiar expression of his wife's, 'Darling, I am yours forever', had begun to sound like a threat. She used it as an entreaty: 'If you could reach down the disinfectant, honey, I am yours forever,' or as a reward: 'Darling, these are the best scrambled eggs I ever tasted, I am yours forever.' He was sure that, once, the cadence of it had made him love her more. In the beginning, she had charmed him by a number of her habits, which had gradually stopped seeming uniquely delightful, one by one. He no longer heard now her characteristic way of saying, 'Pardon me?', twisting her chubby neck, which had once invariably aroused him to surprising sexual excitement. And a pensive gesture with her forefinger, propping her right temple, was such a predictable response to any challenging suggestion that he did not register it.

But Randolph was a reasonable man; he knew that initial infatuation could not be expected to last forever and, to a certain extent, he was mentally prepared for a tailing-off. He knew he might well feel boredom or disillusionment after an established period. When they came, he recognized them sensibly and made a praiseworthy effort to overcome them. He was sure that he himself must also have lost some of his appeal with the years. But this sinking, this dread when Elyse said, 'Darling, I am yours forever,' was outside his area of preparation. It was, he told himself, biological. Naturally, he considered consulting Dr Stein. But the idea of sitting in that green surgery and attempting to verbalize his malaise to the busy doctor was preposterous. He preferred to suppress the sinister feeling, even though suppression was not a positive move, and concentrate on other things.

They went to Europe. Elyse said it to him on the Champs Elysées and on the Rhine cruise. If she says it in Venice, he caught himself imagining . . . Venice was to be the highlight of the trip for him. They had studied the guidebooks together beforehand, and the Swiss Alps were her favourite spot and Venice was his. They went to the Swiss Alps first – their tour had begun with Belgium and then Holland's Water Wonderland – and Elyse loved it; the bright little chalets with their delicate wooden balconies, the pretty music of cow bells from the fields and, high up in the sky, that snow, all pure and clean, even though in the valleys it was a warm summer day. Men in national costume came and yodelled right outside their hotel the day they arrived and, in the evening, there was a fondue party in the timbered dining room. After the party, they were both very happy. It felt as though nothing could ever go wrong between them. They lay under their hilarious Swiss eiderdown and recalled all the best bits of the trip so far. They led each other on to relish and exaggerate. Randolph remembered 'Paris by Night', their evening ride on a *bateau mouche*. There had been music and he had taken Elyse onto the dance floor as they sailed past Notre Dame cathedral. Elyse reminded him of the beautiful little Dutch toytown where they had been served cheese by smiling peasant girls in clogs. In a rare flurry of affection, they both swore they had never had so much fun.

From Switzerland, they went to Italy. Straight away, you could tell the difference. The roads were rougher and the towns shabbier and less well kept. As befitted the country with about the lowest average income in Europe, their hotel room was not as pleasant as that in the snug Swiss Hotel Post. From their bedroom window, they could see a man in a vest reading his newspaper in bed on the other side of the narrow street. Although they found these primitive aspects picturesque, some things upset them; around the road works, and there were certainly an awful lot of road works, dangerous little black lanterns with live flames in them stood burning in the road. The sanitation left a great deal to be desired. But they enjoyed the antipasto and the lasagne verde they were served for dinner and, continuing a habit they had taken up in France, they drank wine.

Their second night, they arrived in Venice. Elyse might have overdone the lasagne verde, because she was miserably unwell and stayed in their hotel room, which was tall, narrow and green like a fish tank, while Randolph went out for his first evening stroll through Venice alone. He felt a little guilty about leaving Elyse but, he reasoned, no one likes to be watched vomiting. What was worse, he felt pleased to be meeting Venice alone. Not that Elyse had in any way upset him of late; she had not used that phrase, for instance, since the Bierfest. But more and more, as they travelled through Europe, Randolph had found himself wanting to be a real traveller, finding out about these places on his own, instead of one of a bunch of loud-voiced but cowardly tourists. Opposite their hotel was a tasteful gift shop and he promised himself that, on the way back, he would buy some sort of present for Elyse.

His attraction to Venice had different origins. In part, he supposed it was professional; swimming pools were his line of business and the mechanics of Venice fascinated him. But there was a less prosaic attraction as well. In the same way as Elyse had been taken by the Swiss Alps because they seemed so gratifyingly to respond to a facet of her personality, so, Randolph imagined, Venice would evoke some latent poetic part of him. He feared he would be especially intolerant of silly superficialities there. The words of one of the guidebooks appealed to him: 'Venice,' it said, 'is not a city for the hasty holiday-maker or the tripper beloved of gaudy bazaars. Through her canals and dreaming backwaters, there glides a subtle, sorrowful mood, more suited to the solitary spirit and the brooding soul.'

The dark street bent and at its end there was a hump-backed bridge. A muffled lady passed him on the bridge, with a muzzled chihuahua on a leash. The two of them clattered over the polished cobbles extraordinarily loudly in the stillness. Randolph stayed on the bridge and listened to their clatter move away into the labyrinth of unlit streets, turning right and left, until somewhere they found the centre and their noise vanished. He followed the street past a square church, which he would have liked to visit, but an enormous padlock hung on its doors. Twice, the street opened without explanation into a square weakly lit by a pale blue lamp. There seemed no reason for these squares; no statues or trees and benches. They were like defeated gaps in a jigsaw puzzle. Randolph walked around the sides each time; he would have felt brashly conspicuous if he had crossed the middle. He went quietly beside the facades of the shuttered houses; close rectangles spotted with stone animals and rotting heads. Their pointed windows, so near together, seemed to him wise and secretive. Then the street widened conclusively and something like a hill ahead of him turned out to be a steep bridge. In the dusk, he could just make out its peaked ridge and knew it was the Rialto. In front of him, the Grand Canal spread out superbly and washed at the pavement.

He returned to the hotel to find Elyse sleeping soundly, curled to the wall, with her buttocks rising out of her seersucker nightdress. He had a shower, cleaned his teeth, and then read a little in the guidebook by the light of the mauve glass bedside lamp.

In the morning, there was the excursion programme. Elyse had got over her upset and chattered happily as she prepared her equipment. 'I suppose it might have been that mortadella. I've always been funny about that shade of pink. Or it could have been the aubergine; I never really understood exactly what aubergines are.'

They joined the party assembling in the foyer – 'Buon giorno!' they all cried, 'buon giorno!' – and were led out to a hired motor launch. This morning's visit was to 'Grand Canal, St Mark's Square, St Mark's Basilica and Doges' Palace'.

It was a brilliant morning. The sun glanced off the bobbing water and spread bright, flickering patterns of light across the old facades. The palaces along the Grand Canal seemed to be buckling and swaying; Venice was an imaginary city and, at any moment, they might all give way.

Their party clicked cameras. On the left was the Ca' d'Oro and on the right, the Accademia. As their motor launch came round the last bend and slowed up to moor beside the Piazza San Marco, the vista ahead of them was so beautiful it would have been most appropriate to weep. But, instead, a jovial voice cried out, 'Oh boy, can you be seasick on a canal?'

As the morning progressed, Randolph felt gloom close in around him. They were herded in numbered groups through the famous items of their programme. He was no nearer the dreaming backwaters than he had been at home. Elyse noticed and finally asked him if he hadn't got a touch of stomach trouble too. He was mortified to hear himself snap back at her.

The afternoon was intended for shopping along the Mercerie. There was no way Elyse would let him miss that. Holding tight onto her handbag with one hand and Randolph's right arm with the other, she veered eagerly from one display to the next, her face enthralled by the gilded leather and the bulbous glass.

In the evening, for a certain supplement, there was the 'Gondola Serenade'. Beforehand, Randolph slipped away from the group on a pretext of buying extra film, and went back to walk on the Riva degli Schiavoni. Although it was noisy and crowded with evening strollers, still it felt a wildly different place on his own. Some wonderful ships and yachts had moored alongside it and he allowed himself for a minute the easy fantasy of sailing away on one of them. He watched the pink lagoon and knew again how delightful Venice would be if he could only encounter it alone.

Elyse snuggled against him as the prow of their gondola clove the black water. The serenade was rhythmic and guttural; to his ears, somehow lewd. Randolph had been afraid that Elyse would choose this of all moments to pronounce the dismal phrase, but she concentrated on not toppling, avoiding splashes and catching every cadence of the schmaltzy songs. The banks slid by them, rigid and remote.

That night, Randolph thought of staying behind in Venice; a stupid idea, which he knew he could not carry out. Elyse would naturally be heartbroken and, without the concessionary group rate, a hotel room would be beyond his means. He dreamt about a palazzo in which he had a room above the water, high-ceilinged and solemn, with long windows which he threw open to the rippling morning.

'Darling,' Elyse woke him, 'our smalls still aren't dry in this damp bathroom.'

They only had three nights in Venice. Their last day was to be spent on a boat trip to the islands of Murano, Burano and Torcello in the lagoon, followed by an afternoon at the Accademia picture gallery, with the option of leisure for the unartistic. The following morning, a coach was due to collect them at eight fifteen from the Piazzale Roma and drive them via an especially scenic route to Florence.

Randolph braced himself for that day. He spent it in sullen suspense, with Elyse at his side ready to detonate his resentment with her words at any minute. She had taken to interspersing her talk with Italian words, after which she trilled with laughter. '*Caro*,' she said to him, 'don't you think a *gelato* would be *molto* welcome?' In the afternoon she chose leisure and Randolph, with the deepest deceit of which he was capable, said he would take a look at the Accademia. Elyse would go shopping with her friend Rowene and, like a thief, Randolph hurried down the stairs and out into the street he had walked the first evening. He had Venice to himself until seven.

In the church of the Frari, he wondered if he was making the best use of his time. He went back outside and consulted his map. Then he set off in the direction of the Fenice Theatre; he walked briskly and didn't dawdle. He took a peep at the Accademia on the way, just in case he was questioned. After a while, he felt rather footsore and decided to sit down and order a drink. Although it was mid afternoon, he chose a large glass of beer. He sat tentatively in the little café and looked around him at the décor and at the other customers. Outside, a large cat sprawled on a paving stone, scratched and stood up, lay down again and then scratched and got up. The barman pointed it out to Randolph and laughed. 'Fleas,' he said and pretended to scratch. Randolph grinned at him, an excessive, insecure grin. He even thought of photographing the cat out of courtesy. When he left, he put a generous tip by his glass. He wandered towards St Mark's Square with an eye on his watch. However much he tried not to think about it, he was conscious of the limit to his independent afternoon.

He returned to the hotel at a quarter to seven. When he realized that he had actually come back too early, that he had voluntarily surrendered a quarter of an hour of his freedom, he suddenly felt wretched. He could almost have cried. He plunged onto his bed and covered his face with his hands. Elyse was not as prompt. When he eventually heard the bedroom door open, it was nearly half past seven. Randolph anticipated her greeting. He rolled over on the bed and spread his arms. 'Darling,' he intoned theatrically, 'I am yours forever.' And Elyse, standing in the doorway with the enamelled cuff-links she had bought for him clutched in her hand, gazed down at him and slowly beamed with joy.

Dermot Healy

FIRST
SNOW
OF
THE
YEAR

DERMOT HEALY was born in Finea, County Westmeath, Ireland, in 1947. He has lived in Cavan and Dublin, and now lives in London. He has published poetry and prose in various periodicals and his work was featured in *Best Irish Short Stories* (edited by David Marcus), and two other anthologies of recent Irish writing, *Paddy No More* and *A Soft Day*. He has received two Hennessy Literary Awards, in 1974 and 1976. He has two books forthcoming, *Banished Misfortune*, a collection of short stories, and a novel, *Fighting with Shadows* (both will be published by Allison & Busby/Irish Writers' Co-operative in 1982).

For a few bewildering seconds, Jim Philips, on the day of his retirement, queried late-morning sounds he had not heard in years. His spirit complained of a slight guilty headache from oversleeping. Then his solitary sense of freedom began. He looked with leisure at the low pink boards that ran the length of the ceiling, yellowing at the fireplace, brightening by the window.

Light was hammering on the broken shutter.

Shadows darted across the mildewed embroidery of dogs and flowers.

He cleared his womanless bed with a light heart, glad to have outgrown the ache in his smothered loins, outlived his job that he might die in a time of his own making. He nimbly laid his drinking clothes before last night's fire, coaxed first with paraffin, then whiskey. He hung his postman's uniform in the closet under the stairs.

He buttoned himself up for the air.

The ground was rock-hard and early frost had frozen the colours about the bog. The valley across which he had been a messenger for thirty years lay stretched out below him in a state of moral predictability. He saw John and Margaret Cawley, the gipsies, stealing through the yellow gorse with rotten turf. Their children moved from clownish tree to clownish tree out of the wind.

He shattered the surface water of the well and, from where Jim stood, the earth was on its side, reflected in every piece of ice, the wind sounding through the gulleys and drains like a concert flute. The bitter cold cleared his scalp and breath as he walked back. Young Phildy was standing under the gable. He felt a kind of fatalism seeing Phildy there, out of the wind looking at the earth, humourless and uncertain. Phildy threw in some frost-flecked sods of turf for the old man and then waited about impatiently till they were ready to go down.

Phildy stood under the gable again, surly-looking, but of sudden times, nearly by inspiration, his tall frame would relax, his face ruffle with silent laughter.

The bell sounded.

'What are you thinking about?' asked Jim.

'Nothing. There's no change.'

'We'll look down from the hill.'

Phildy did not answer, but mumbled, with a hint of anger was it, in his voice.

They came to the edge of a small mossy clearing and looked towards the funeral. Jim dropped to his knee. The children of Liz's relations tottered among the appealing shapes of stone and foreign marble, flowers under glass, and when the priest stooped to say the final prayers the mourners turned left and studied Stagg's grave, the hunger-striker who had died in England. Owen Beirne, the son of the dead woman, and his jovial uncles delivered Liz on their shoulders and light as mercury she was lowered down cautiously with leather straps.

The long-jawed undertaker paid out the clay with jerky fingers into the son's palm.

Snow began amid the hand-shaking.

Helen stood with Phildy's child away from the mourners like a stranger. Owen Beirne's woman now, she once was Phildy's. Phildy moved toward her as Jim Philips joined the throng by the grave. Phildy said to himself, 'Not to be possessed, not that.' Phildy said to himself, 'I have no desire ever to lie in her bed again.' Helen looked closely at him, the child leaped into his arms. They swung round and round, and when they stopped Phildy said to her, 'If you have a baby by that bastard, I'll come and cut it out of your stomach.'

The dreadful shapes of the parish surrounded them with guilt and terror. She turned her head.

Phildy moved off with Jim by the History Road, through land killed over, by the Four Altars of stone, past the secluded oak trees that shelter

the unfrightened children who died before Christ, a flowerless limbo for
the unbaptized in the corner of a field, over the bridge where REMEMBER
STAGG was written in coarse white lettering, past the American cars and
the hikers sitting smoking in a ditch.

'What did he say?' asked Owen, taking Helen by the hand and then the
elbow.

'He said he would kill me,' she replied.

'Wait at the house for me,' he said.

Phildy and Jim walked into the dim light of O'Grady's public house. 'I
have been considering what you might call a new theory,' said Devine,
the second-hand watch-man, his shiny waistcoat and nose covered with
snuff, 'I have read recently that turf, mind you, if properly compressed
could provide a queer cheap and powerful source of power. And I mean
well beyond the briquette stage.'

'This round is on me,' said O'Grady without enthusiasm. In honour of
Jim Philips, postman, recently retired. O'Grady set up an electric kettle
on a stout crate and dropped a measure of cloves and sugar into each
glass. His wife was throwing darts with the boys in the bar. The light was
right for drinking by. Elephants from a circus roared from a nearby town.
The radio said – 'Walton's, your weekly reminder of the grace and
beauties that lie – '

'I'll have a woman above in the house in no time, true as God,' spoke
Jim.

'Smell that,' said Phildy.

Phildy went into the lounge and took a cue off one of the young lads
playing there. He missed an easy ball. He broke up the pool game for no
good reason. He turned one of the young fellow's arms behind his back.
He pulled him to him. 'What were you saying?' he asked. The young
fellow looked him in the eye. Phildy left two shillings on the table.

He strolled back to the men.

' – when that fellow was a child,' continued Jim, 'along with his
brother I used push them happily along in a tub down a sheugh off the
mountain, and every time I was ready to quit, your man there, Phildy,
would pipe up "Ah, just once more." Back up again and start all over.
Well, I pushed till night fell and now they've grown and taken all my
demesne and I wouldn't say a word against their father.'

Their thoughts faded into the interior.

In a field over from there a circle gambling formed around a penny or a

bird, a cock crowed by the wheel of a wagon, the sixth bird lost an eye
and a wing was slung in a ditch and the handler picked blood and
feathers out of the mouth of the seventh and breathed life back into him,
sucked at his beak and rubbed his chin murmuring along the back of the
fighter, while the trainer stood away from the fight another tossing bag in
his hand ready with the oiling tape, the washer and the weights. The men
stood with the weight of their feet on their money.

'I saw them go by this morning,' O'Grady whispered.

'Did you now,' said Jim.

'I did. Dowds did the burying.'

'Was it now.'

'Dowds it was.'

'Driving like a ginnet he was.'

'Is that a fact.'

'That'll do,' said Devine.

Owen Beirne watched the sparse mourners leave through the falling
snow. It must have been years since any of them had laid eyes on her, yet
the old came here faithfully from their rooms in a vast acreage of wind
and cold. Uncle James sneezed and sneezed. Helen, who had nursed his
mother up to the day she died, had left dispiritedly, as if she had never
once visited misfortune, nor taken old men dispassionately out of their
rheumy beds to insert a catheter. Holding their shoddy under-garments.
Weeding them of fading hair from armpit and groin. She was terrified for
her child and herself. Of other minds speaking with her eyes, her tongue.

His mourning uncles talked of going up the village.

Their families had gone ahead in near ecstasy.

'A man can best fix the orifices of the world,' said Devine.

'Helen pressed with her thumbs to see the cat's eye of death,'
whispered the barman, 'powdered and combed Liz to a child.'

'Jesus Christ, stop the sound of that man's voice,' raised Phildy.

'You're the beast of the mirage, boy,' advised Jim.

'Now Phildy, take it easy,' said O'Grady.

'Will you stop talking,' cried Phildy. His intestines shivered and grew
weighty. He saw Owen withdraw from Helen, coursing his penis through
her hands. His blood no longer went freely between the isolated and
unbalanced part of himself. His white Christian bones grew rigid.

'As bad as '47,' said Jim when after the first skirmish the void began,
and the door opened into the pub to admit Mr O'Dowd, undertaker,

grocery-cum-pub owner. He kicked back with his boots as he surveyed
the company. Jerky movements fretted around his temple and fingers.

'The worst,' he said.

'— ah, but not interrupting you there,' said the watch-man, as he
looked into the distance, studs rattling, 'but that '47 blizzard wasn't so
bad in the morning, but by evening it would smother a body. For I lay in
my bed that night without an ounce of sleep, thinking myself grown to a
statue, and the following morning I lay on and on thinking it was dark,
and get up I did eventually, pushed open the door after a long harangue,
and lo and behold you, it was bright ...'

'There is no mystery to the whore,' said Phildy.

Owen Beirne sat in an empty pub at the back of a grocery among the
tinned beans, Chef bottles of sauce, Saxo packets of salt, where every
time someone entered to do their shopping a crisp otherworld bell rang.
The soft smell of flour and more bitter odour of rotting vegetables hung
in the air. A rich woman delayed over the trade names of certain goods
till he hated the living sight of her. A child with his mother's face smiled
at him from the woman's pram. The smell of the flour seemed to come
from his own living flesh. In that acute silence which the spirit of the dead
make their own. And at last his mourning uncles arrived and they talked
and talked, the first drink was for sorrow and the second for joy. Owen
carried Uncle Festy, a disturbing old villain, to his Ford van. An
explosion in a nearby river rocked the street. The other relations left,
speaking with great understanding and humour. His uncles' empty
glasses filled the wooden counter. There was nowhere on that counter he
could rest his hand with the fingers spread, nor know what should be
darkened and what brightened. Thinking of Helen was the last cheerful
thing in the world. 'Man to man,' Uncle Festy said as he lowered him into
the driver's seat. The children were singing in the back. 'Remember
Frank Stagg,' said he. And lastly, 'Take your own road, no matter what,'
said he and his eyes watering.

'And I opened the door and looked out and lo and behold you, it was
bright,' the watch-man Devine continued, 'so bright that it would dazzle
your eyes ... and I stood at the door and I called, and I went up the low
hill from the door and I called and called ... the sister within shouting at
the greyhound like a woman tormented ... and I thought all my beasts
were dead, taken from me during the night ... when, Lord save me, out
of the drifts by the galvanize shed they came, one by one, struggling up

towards me like the newborn . . . and I fed them like a man whose wits had got the better of him . . . nudging and poking at my chest . . . Lord, wasn't I the happy man when they came up striking out of the snow and took the hay without a word.'

'For one bright sovereign sold my life away,' a cockfighter was singing. Trucks lumbered into the council yard across the valley. The roads were quick as lightning.

The great juggernauts moved out of the milk factory and turned their dipped lights on to the white plains. Mrs O'Grady, the publican's wife, looked like she might live forever.

'"Throw the clay on top of me," wailed the sergeant, climbing on top of his dead wife's coffin, and then he turned round and married another.'

Stones were hurled across the polythene to keep the peat dry.

And the sea drove shells into the cairn, sounding in Owen's ears as he rode a stolen bike crazily down the hill from the village, swerving in the torrents of snow. The white of the road curved into a single turning tyre. The colours on every side gathered into a frenzied shape, time slowed down to the independent moment. Helen, so delicate a thing, trussed up in the snow beside the grave. The begging trees on the mountain crisp as a child's brain. Owen feared the men looking for him. Those that tormented Helen. And that moment he heard the chisels at work undoing the image of his mother, he flew up the rafters to see. First they shaped those perfect eyes, then gouged them out. Circled and released the breasts with care, and when he looked back they were gone. The cheeks. The back of the head. The builder held his cheek to the small lift of the stomach. Then suddenly butted his head into the interior and the whole figure gave way. When he looked back, the builder was gone. Owen freewheeled on, till, at Edmonstown Cross, he went into a ditch with awkward attempts to save himself. As the wheels hit the grass margin deep down, he was carried round and round on his back a few yards up the road.

Phildy on his way back from O'Grady's had seen the final impact. He stood silently watching from the far side of the road where everything was normal, not moving, blindfolded. With him stood two other young witnesses, dressed in great gaberdines and boots, their hair pommaded beneath woollen caps. A snowdrift in a sheugh had nearly covered Owen, he surrendered gladly to the shock of the fall, lay quiet, swallowed blood from a cut on his lip. He gathered the feeling of pain back into his bones.

He raised himself onto his elbows, moaning, onto his knees and stayed there a while till gradually he focused on the dark figures silhouetted against the snow-tipped, serrated evergreens. As he watched, a figure would appear and disappear, stepping forward, stepping backward. Owen called across. 'Let it be now, just yourself and myself.' The man standing kicked him on the bottom of the spine. 'That's for Helen,' Phildy said. The others hammered into his face with the violent devotion of the obsessed. Then Phildy pulled the others off Owen and they went up toward Monestrevin, their anger anaesthetized by nature for a time. 'Come back and fight, you cunts!' Owen shouted after the retreating ghosts. He gathered himself and roared helplessly. 'One at a time,' he shouted after them.

'And a few days later,' Devine went on, 'I took the gun and went down to Lough Gara and I shot some wild ducks, the urchin that I was, 'cause there wasn't a bit of food in the house . . . not a bit . . . Sure there was no eating in them . . . and that mad creature of a spaniel I had rose the poor things, and up they got fighting their cause.'

'Yes,' said Jim Philips, 'and the trams, what with the drifts of '47, stopped that day in Brighton.'

The undertaker hammered his heels and buttoned his coat up tightly about him. 'Two hot whiskeys for the gentlemen,' he asked, 'and a small brandy for myself.'

Owen's feet dragged through the silence like many people walking. While the studs of the watch-man's boots clinked in the yard, and the postman thought of the turf in above, it was to fall into Helen's arms Owen desired. He ran this way and that, terrified of the long drop into the bogholes, his senses failed him, he could make nothing of this white silence where the particles of the mind were dispersed so quietly. He had never known this blind panic before. He stood for a long time trying to get his bearings, but the light was the same everywhere, not the separate light towards which the individual can turn, shining in his own beauty, but dispersed so freely that a great weary record of endless detail began.

'I would not want to be struggling with a woman as to my worth. Not that thing.'

'Nor be a woman mending my ways for others, that little pleasure come of it.'

'A new frustration cannot enter the world,' said the undertaker resignedly.

'The kali.'

'The auld culcannon.'

'A skillet full of kali, with the onions and the homemade butter.'

'That's the stuff.'

'And the boxty.'

'The boxty. Ah, man dear.'

'And the potato cake.'

'Stop! Stop!'

It stopped snowing, the brittle stars came out. Would the dead forgive him if his hands had wandered over Helen's face in the darkness of the mourning house, touching and parting flesh here, and folding his body around her against death. The canoe to the sea. He walked across a new planet, journeying inwards, without thought of his fellows. There were so many clear stars that he found the gravel track on the far side of the bog as in a dream, all beaten up and restored, like the others of his tribe. He ran forward through the shells of snow-filled houses where the elders had lived it all. Through deserted kitchens, middens, bedrooms with nothing to be seen, hearths filled with torn fishing nets, old potato gardens drilled hard with the frost, turf stiff with snow. He came to Phildy's house, plastered with gravel and ivy, the laughter of the men echoed back from the trees. Sparks flew from the chimney. The abandoned pram on the path filled with berries. He came to his own house. There was no one there. Owen did not search long but followed the horses' path up to the rocks. He crossed the rocks. The stars so low he could have blown them out. Helen was sitting in the gipsy tent babysitting, looking after little Barney and Roger. Her own child asleep between them. The parents were over the road drinking, 'Sh,' she said. He came in and sat beside her. They sat in utter silence. When the children woke, she spoke in gipsy talk to reassure them. He filled the stove with timber and turf, snow dripped from the black canvas. He lay his head on her shoulder and they kissed in a direct trusting manner. Soon John Cawley and Margaret Cawley came over the rocks singing dead verse.

Desmond Hogan
THOUGHTS

She came from a place not far from where Daniel O Connell, the Liberator, was born. O Connell was Ireland's leading pacifist. In the late eighteenth and early nineteenth centuries his family defied the British penal laws, sending their children to school in France, building handsome buildings from lime and cows' blood, storing the beeves in autumn for a winter of resplendent fires and feasting in the shadow of a valley far from London, far from the nucleus of an empire which had distorted a country's sense of nationhood for over one hundred and fifty years. Gráinne's family owned huge meringue hotels now, palm trees outside them and verandas overlooking a mild sea with its currents sweeping from the Caribbean. This was the warmest part of Ireland, where primroses grew in winter and where it was not uncommon to see a rhododendron bush open in March. Gráinne grew up here, only child of a rich family, much given to walks, to meditations on primroses and rhododendron bushes, a child of solitude in her vestigial white blouses, a party to all things growing and all things moist. She had a host of relatives who were nuns in France and when she was fifteen was sent to a convent in Paris where she completed her secondary education. She then attended the Sorbonne, living all the time with an order of nuns who had head-dresses like windshields, raised above them, warning all who came near them of the strange and ancient conglomeration of principles which comprised their order.

Eugene was sixteen when he met Gráinne, the winter of 1967. She was teaching French for a year in the small town where he lived, recovering from a shattered love affair. He started going to her for French lessons and that brought the two of them together. She lived in a room overlooking a river. He lived up the road. Ostensibly they met for French lessons but little French was spoken, few if any lessons transacted. There were more important things to talk about.

This was a town on your way west in Ireland. Midland flat but unrelenting in Atlantic rain. The town was notable for its many statues of Mary, a uniquely devout statue of Mary outside the convent. What really brought Gráinne to this town Eugene never knew but she didn't seem too happy here, smoking, relaying gossip about nuns. What was distinctive about Gráinne was her face, alive and clear like the interior of a sea-shell, her legs, bountiful under a mini skirt, and her hair, brown-blond, a little bucket of it nearly unkempt, not quite. But it was her clown's mouth that really distinguished her as though it was going to utter a cry at any time. There were no cries, restrained laughter. The rain came and the winter and they got to know one another really well.

She told him about Paris, her student days, the coffee shops, the bistros, the casual wine, the casual decorum, scarves, baggy jumpers, cigarettes in the fingers and eyes on the boulevard. She never ceased being conscious of her Irishness on the streets of Paris, that she was from a place, that Daniel O Connell, her neighbour, had come here during the French Revolution and witnessed the violence of the Revolution and vowed himself for life to peaceful means. More than anything she remembered the sea, the colours in the bays in Kerry where water shimmers and where the bellies of sand were visible, all glad, magical, elusive colours. She never forgot the underside of her nation in Paris; the Kerry storytellers, the Kerry farmers, the widows staring from cottages towards the Atlantic and ultimately towards Boston. She had a cherished upbringing and he wondered what brought her here to this town, gales, wet empty streets and then she answered that question without him asking.

She told him about the affair she had which scarred her innocence, one which issued from one of those cafés in Paris, meeting an Austrian writer who liked men, liked women. She painted a most extravagant picture of him as she stood against a winter night, trains going by outside – distantly – and geese clanking over a river slashed with the sky's last light. Her boyfriend had been a little pale, the intoxicated colour of men who are sensual but think too much; he'd had lots of hair like herself, multi-layered blond hair. Eugene imagined a head of rich shades, the peroxide of a female film star, the pale of a young boy's hair, curls on a swab of country butter. And after that she gave him dark glasses, a red jacket, scarves, hankerchiefs, all kinds of hankerchiefs, some black and white dotted.

She had him sitting in cafés, dreaming of his novels, emerging, only half-emerging from an unclear background: Vienna. He'd had two books published and at first they'd just talked, she the Irish girl and he inquisitive because many Irish people had gone to Austria and distilled a sense of their country, the Wild Geese, soldiers from Ireland who fled the Jacobean wars to take up arms in Europe. She was different then, she said, bony even. Now she was fatter. She wore ribbons then. She was more doll-like. Gabriel had besieged her every defence right from the beginning, his mixture of things, colour, more interestingly a mixture of faith and despair, masculinity and femininity. She'd relinquished not just virginity at eighteen but remorse. She'd been absorbed from a convent of nuns into a world of spiritual nomads. Gráinne Dempsey had been drawn away from her Irish background and her Irish memories into a world of artists and writers like a changling in Irish legend, the child stolen by the fairies and replaced by one of them. She was nurtured on art and the gossip it generated. She came close to her lover's masterpieces; inspected them once or twice but couldn't read them because they were in German.

Gabriel had been moody, violent, equally sensitive, brooding, bountiful in his generosity. But above all theirs hadn't been a sexual relationship Gráinne affirmed, but spiritual, a kind of elevating of things into a vision. Mutually looking at Rodin's sculpture 'La Pensée', a woman's head in deep thought, Gráinne had been struck by its marble, its totality, the way it expressed the coming together of things, adolescence and adulthood, a moment when one was self-aware and self-welcoming.

Gabriel had been older than her, of course, otherwise it would not have totally convinced – but the shackles of age were easily shed. Gabriel approached, shedding some light in the empty rooms of her life, the remembered attics from hotels in Kerry. She offered him something; she was scarecrow to him, a western scarecrow. She approached him from the west, the sea, and renewed something in him, faith in words, with her vocabulary of icons. Gráinne was full of an exciting vocabulary he said, bearing the little messages, the little phrasings from a Gaelic past. They touched; they briefed one another in their individual pain but ultimately she failed to perform a miracle, to totally incandesce as a kind of Irish ghost, a fairy, a changeling, a being from the light and sea of Kerry. She was ordinary like all the other girls so he faded into the romanticism of other flesh, male and female. She finished at the Sorbonne, returned to Ireland but not before she became a kind of druid of sex, making love in all crevices, all corners, to American GIs, Japanese tourists; to expurgate her pain she became for a night or two in Montmartre, drinking white wine mixed with blackberry juice, a prostitute.

Eugene could see why she came here, to this penitential windswept town, to attone, to narrow her scope and make amends, become ordinary again. But he was so full with her life he told her about his, his upbringing, lonely, his friends, few but always working class and ultimately separated from him by very middle-class parents. The previous summer, alone in this town of tennis-playing young people he'd taken an overdose. No one had known. He'd woken on floor under a naked bulb buzzing with flies at five in the morning. Then he'd met her. This was it, the gang plank. Both met in this town. They had winter nights together. She missed them she said, the photographs on the jackets of French and German books. She had him, Eugene McMurrough.

Nuns crawled like black snakes. The rains grew thicker, cry of geese more unrelenting. Eugene stared into another year. There was a play in town, by his namesake, – Eugene O Neill, *Long Day's Journey into Night*. The main part was played by a bank manager's wife who'd go every week to the tinkers' encampment with boxes of chocolates. The parish priest nearly drank himself to death that winter; a farmer's wife walked into the flood waters; usual occurrences. Eugene protested a lot, member of every political organization he could think of, Anti-Apartheid, Irish Voice of Vietnam, Amnesty, Peace Pledge Union, writing away to people in Dublin or London for badges, protesting alone on hurling fields against the Vietnam war. Gráinne went home at Christmas, returned in the New Year, refurbished. She spoke of swans on the sea waters of Kerry. She spoke of seeing a Hollywood film-star in the rain in her village. She spoke of change within herself. She too stared into a new year.

They met and talked and she smoked. She took his hand sometimes, fidgeting with her ring at the same time. Her body had shrunken. This was all too much for her, this town, the nuns. She should be off – on a magic carpet – back to Paris.

'O God,' she cried, 'where are they, the painters, the writers, the musicians, more than anything the young, the young in spirit?'

She couldn't so well have returned to a life of prostitution in town so she began having an affair with an engineer who worked in Bord na Móna, the Irish peat industry. They went to dances, to the hotel. She paradoxically wore black now. On Sundays she went to the mental hospital grounds to see him play rugby, voices rising and bulls of men converging on tiny balls. This was her allocation, standing on the side of a rugby pitch, with the other carnally inviting ladies of town, teachers, bank assistants. This was middle-class Ireland. Mental hospital patients stared from behind iron bars.

'O God,' Gráinne cried one night, 'I've given myself to that brute.'

Proust, George Sand, Colette, Camus, de Beauvoir, Sagan, Fournier, Lamartine; she repeated their names, French writers, old and modern, like the names of friends as trains swept into the night, aureoles of gold. And the names of Gaelic writers. Eoghan Ruadh O Súilleabháin, Aoghán O Ruhaille, Eibblín Dubh ní Chonaill. It was her mantra, the voices of literature, French and Irish. All through this period Gráinne went to Mass, Holy Communion. You had to do such things in this society. She was leaving she said, going. But the floods grew higher and she was like one of those mental hospital patients behind iron bars. Her face became thin and papier-mâché-like. Her eyes grew large, looming even, and her mouth grew longer, more tragic, a clown's mouth. And Eugene saw her, making love, floors in Paris, her removed bi-sexual lover. He wanted to believe everything she said. Sometimes he doubted but what one could not easily dispense with was an image, an inspiration, Rodin's 'La Pensée' – 'The Thought' – self-confrontation, the tentative approach to a work of art which for one moment objectifies our life, arrests its flow, creating something, wonder in the eyes, remorse in the heart, sublimation at the highest level. Gráinne Dempsey saw herself through that sculpture, a young Irish girl in Paris, scarf tied out like a mad, ecstatic flag, the tricolour at home on a day of political parades, maiden speeches or bishop's blessings.

She perceived herself at her height, a cross between fact and fiction, in celebration.

Now she had different surroundings but no less intact in another way, wet streets, left-over cinema posters. At night she walked the wet streets, alone, without her rugby player. Watching from his window Eugene saw a brunt of loneliness descend on her and sharpen her face. No doorbells to ring. Just a lonely room to return to, her books ...

She gave little speeches now about books, lectures. Eugene learnt a lot about various authors, their habits, what brand of tea Colette liked. Gráinne had these facts at the tips of her fingers but sometimes even that stopped, the rush of words, and she'd look all of a sudden despairing, as though a bomb was dropping on to her, slowly but insipidly, breaking her defences.

She became more determined on her small town life, going to more than her quota of rugby matches, a daily communicant at Mass. With Eugene, though, she'd still wander over the debris of the past but it was becoming fainter and it was as though she wanted to grab something of it before it faded away, so she moved closer to him, holding his hand as before, but this time differently, with more playfulness, the amber stone on her ring glinting and her face vague, a study in lack of concentration.

Sometimes it was as though she was going to launch into predictions about his future. Thankfully she refrained, spoke about the sea, her love of it. One evening she went so far as to suggest they jump into her Mini and head off to Kerry. He pointed out to her that after all he was a student, and was expected home. That alarmed her. She looked at the disarray of French grammar books and remembered the purpose of their meetings. But it was too late and she launched into them again, the names of French writers as if they would add up to something for him.

Spring came, an affront, cherry blossoms in outlying regions of town, and Gráinne noticeably found it difficult accustoming herself to renewed light. She took to wearing dark glasses. She wrote a letter with him to the Soviet president about the treatment of some political prisoner and she marched on the hurling pitch with him in protest against the war in Vietnam but these manifestations of spirit apart she crumbled a little, losing faith in herself, her own ability to cope with this environment. She could be seen everywhere with her male friend and early one week she returned from Kerry to tell Eugene she was pregnant.

Paris was erupting in a riot of colour but it seemed very far away now, another world. As students rushed about Paris in protest against old forms Gráinne Dempsey marched up the aisle in church, chiffon scarf tied out in double wings, to receive Communion.

What would she do? Have an abortion she said. Like any good Catholic Irish teacher. She lay on a couch, legs in the air, smoking a cigarette. Eugene was due to go to France on a student exchange scheme but he volunteered to run away and join her in London. No she said. Gerry was going with her. Anyway no use dragging you into it she said.

He watched her lead the convent girls on the Corpus Christi procession. There was a deluge of flags out in town, papal flags, Irish flags; bushels of lilac on the fronts of grocery shops and pictures of a very demented-looking Sacred Heart everywhere, the Sacred Heart grabbing his breast which shed a few sparse drops of blood like tomato juice. Gráinne led her fold, in dark glasses, a spy.

She watched his every movement, a silent effigy on a couch, and suddenly she spoke – making a pronouncement: 'I came back to be mediocre again, to re-establish that part of myself. Now look at me. Having an abortion with a man who sweats too much.' She spoke with so much authority that Eugene looked at her. He was moved by her and without warning she was in his arms, weeping, feeling the width and breadth of his shoulders as he conquered her waist, a little package in a pink blouse.

'Do not forget to go to see Rodin's "La Pensée",' she said, as if making her last will and testament.

The sycamore blossomed and the oak; the limestone town looked its best. Miss Dempsey went away one day, skidaddling off to Kerry, thence to London, to be replaced in Eugene's life by a big, fat French student who ate lollipops all the time.

Gráinne wrote to him in Paris that summer.

16 Bolingbroke Road,
London W14
10 August 1968

Dear Eugene,

Had my abortion. It was like a butterfly slipping away. It's very hot here, scorching. The dustbins are overflowing. Gerry's out getting groceries. I'm alone here, thinking what Daniel O Connell said. 'The freedom of Ireland is not worth the shedding of a single drop of blood.' I feel I've killed something for Ireland, the baby within me. There's a space within me that they can't fill, the nuns, the schoolgirls, the statues of Mary. It will go on and on, gathering force like a huge wave. I wish you were here. I know you'd understand but even you couldn't stop it. I've murdered a part of myself and buried it under the floor of a classroom.

Lots of kisses,
Gráinne

He went to see Rodin's 'La Pensée'. In a wet and grey summer in Paris, staying in a suburb, factories nearby emitting flames that burnt into the mind, it was the highlight, this wonder of marble. Looking at it he confronted some extraordinary fragment of himself, a boy in a white jersey and tweed tie who had complimented a girl in a white blouse and chiffon scarf in Ireland in May. He wondered if it had been real, her affair in Paris, but knew that it didn't matter because they'd been real, they'd touched, his head had sunk into hers and their mutual tremor would shake their lives, going on and on when guns raged in another part of Ireland and footsteps inevitably led away from a country which caused so much pain and so much affliction.

When he returned to Ireland that autumn she was nowhere to be seen. Her boyfriend was back, excelling himself on the local rugby team. It rained a lot, Peter Sarstedt sang 'Where do you go to, my lovely?' from the local café and her ghost walked, a girl on a wet street past the solitary neon of the café. He wondered what had happened to her. Had she died from the after-effects of abortion? Had she gone back to Paris as she said she might? In either case he was determined on going on, the shadow of a Rodin sculpture inside, the knowledge gained from art that life is worth holding on to, that if you keep fighting it will come, freedom. Gráinne had given him his first lessons in freedom. It was up to him to go on, rung by rung until he met someone or something that touched him again as deeply as Rodin's 'La Pensée'.

Years later he met that person. A journalist from London he walked up a pathway on the outskirts of Cork city to interview a marine biologist about a marine biology project in West Cork. The pathway led to a white house which was identical to the illimitable miles of white houses which swept around him. She answered the door, half fearfully, Gráinne Dempsey, her face sunken in.

She'd gone back to Paris as she said she would but found the streets forever led home, to a point of negation, to a small town in Ireland.

She showed him in now. Around her fashion magazines lay on tables. His first impulse was to embrace her but he was restrained by the look on her face. Gráinne Dempsey, wife of a marine biologist, looked at him and he saw himself for the first time in years, in a makeshift collection of clothes, black suit, pink shirt, white socks, still trying even as she tried, her face white and sunken now but her eyes still burning and alive, repeating themselves over and over in his mind just as the white houses repeated themselves, over and over again, until they reached the sea.

James Kelman

NOT
NOT
WHILE
THE
GIRO

say not talkin about
not analysin nuthin
is if not not
– Tom Leonard, 'Breathe deep, and regular with it'

JAMES KELMAN is a citizen of Glasgow.

of tea so I can really enjoy this 2nd last smoke which will be very very strong which is of course why I drink tea with it in a sense to counteract the harm it must do my inners. Not that tea cures cancer poisoning or even guards against nicotine – helps unclog my mouth a little. Maybe it doesnt. My mouth tastes bad. Hot and kind of squelchy. I am smoking too much old tobacco. 2nd hand tobacco is stiff, is burnt ochre in colour and you really shudder before spluttering on the 1st drag. But this is supposed to relieve the craving for longer periods. Maybe it does. It makes no difference anyway, you still smoke them 1 after the other because what happens if you suddenly come into a few quid or fresh tobacco – you cant smoke 2nd hand stuff with the cashinhand and there isnt much chance of donating it to fucking charity. So you smoke rapidly. I do – even with fresh tobacco.

But though the tea is gone I can still enjoy the long smoke. A simple enjoyment, and without guilt. I am wasting time. I am to perambulate to a distant broo. I shall go. I always go. No excuse now it has gone. And it may be my day for the spotcheck at the counter. Rain pours heavily. My coat is in the fashion of yesteryear but I am wearing it. How comes this coat to be with me yet. Not a question although it bears reflecting upon at some later date. Women may have something to do with it. Probably not, that cannot be correct. Anyway, it has nothing to do with anything.

I set myself small tasks, ordeals; for instance: Come on ya bastard ye and smoke your last, then see how your so-called will fucking power stands up. Eh! Naw, you wont do that. Of course I wont, but such thoughts often occur. I may or may not smoke it. And if it does come down to will power how the hell can I honestly say I have any – when circumstances are as they are. Could begin smacking of self pity shortly if this last continues. No, yesteryear's coat is not my style. Imitation Crombies are unbecoming these days, particularly the kind with narrow lapels. This shrewd man I occasionally have dealings with refused said coat on the grounds of said lapels rendering the coat an undesired object by those who frequent said man's premises. Yet I would have reckoned most purchasers of 2nd hand clothing to be wholly unaware of fashions current or olden. But I have faith in him. He does fine. Pawnshops could be nationalized. What a shock for the smalltrader. What next that's what we'd like to know, the corner bloody shop I suppose. Here that's not my line of thought at all. Honest to god, right hand up that the relative strength of the freethinkers is neither here nor there. All we ask is to play up and play the game. Come on you lot, shake hands etcetera. Jesus what is this at all. Fuck all to do with perambulations to the broo.

Last smoke between my lips, right then. Fire flicked off, the last colour gone from the bar. Bastarn rain. The Imitation Crombie. And when I look at myself in the mirror I can at least blow smoke in my face. Also desperately needing a pish. Been holding it in for ages by the feel of things. Urinary infections too, they are caused by failing to empty the bladder completely ie cutting a long pish short and not what's the word – flicking the chopper up and down to get rid of the drips. Particularly if one chances to be uncircumcised. Not at all.

In fact I live in a single bedsitter with sole use of confined kitchenette whose shelves are presently idle. My complexion could be termed grey. As though he hadnt washed for a month your worship. Teeth not so good. Beard a 6 dayer and of all unwashed colours. Shoes suede and stained by dripping. Dripping! The jeans could be fashionable without the Imitation Crombie. Last smoke finished already by christ. Smile. Yes. Hullo. Walk to door. Back to collect the sign-on card from its safe place. I shall be striding through a downpour.

Back from the broo and debating whether I am a headcase after all and this has nothing to do with my ambling in the rain. A neighbour has left a child by my side and gone off to the laundrette. An 18 month child and frankly an imposition. I am not overly fond of children. And this one is totally indifferent to me. The yes I delivered to the neighbour was typically false. She knew fine well but paid no attention. Perhaps she dislikes me intensely. Her husband and I detest each other. In my opinion his thoughts are irrelevant yet he persists in attempting to gain my heed. He fails. My eyes glaze but he seems unaware. But his wife appreciates my position and this is important since I can perhaps sleep with her if she sides with me or has any thoughts on the subject of him in relation to me or vice versa. Hell of a boring. I am not particularly attracted to her. A massive woman. I don't care. My vanities lie in other fields. Though at 30 years of age one's hand is insufficient and to be honest again my hand is more or less unused in regard to sexual relief. I rely on the odd wet dream, the odd chance acquaintance, male or female it makes no difference yet either has advantages.

Today the streets were crowded as was the broo. Many elderly women were out shopping and why they viewed me with suspicion is beyond me. I am the kind of fellow who gets belted by umbrellas for the barging of so-called 'infirm' pensioners while boarding omnibuses. Nonsense. I am polite. It is possible the Imitation Crombie brushes their shoulders or something in passing but the coat is far too wide for me and if it bumps against anything is liable to cave in rather than knock a body flying. Then again, I rarely wear the garment on buses. Perhaps they think I'm trying to lift their purses or provisions. You never know. If an orange for example dropped from a bag and rolled in my direction I would be reluctant to hand it back to its rightful owner. I steal. In supermarkets I lift flat items such as cheese and other articles. Last week, having allowed the father of the screaming infant to buy me beer in return for my ear, I got a large ashtray and two pint glasses and would have got more but that I lacked the Imitation Crombie. I do not get captured. I got shoved into jail a long time ago but not for stealing cheese. Much worse. Although I am an obviously suspicious character I never get searched. No more.

My shoes lie by the fire, my socks lie on its top. Steam rises. Stomach rumbles. I shall dine with the parents. No scruples on this kind of poncing. This angers the father as does my inability to aquire paid employment. He believes I am not trying, maintains there must be something. And while the mother accepts the prevailing situation she is apt to point out my previous job experience. I have worked at many things. I seldom stay for any length of time in a job because I cannot. Possibly I am a hopeless case.

I talk not at all, am confined to quarters, have no friends. I often refer to persons as friends in order to beg more easily from said persons in order that I may be the less guilty. Not that guilt affects me. It affects my landlord. He climbs the stairs whenever he is unwelcome elsewhere. He is a nyaff, yet often threatens to remove me from the premises under the misapprehension I would not resort to violence. He mentions the mother of this infant in lewd terms but I shall have none of it. Maybe he is a secret child molester. I might spread rumours to pass the time. But no, the infant is too wee. Perhaps I am a latent molester for even considering that. Below me dwells the Mrs Soinson, she has no children and appears unaware of my existence. I have thought of bumping into her and saying, Can I watch your television.

Aye, of course I'll keep the kid for another bastarn half hour. Good christ this is pathetic. The damn parent has to go further messages. Too wet to trail one's offspring. I could hardly reply for rage and noises from the belly and sweet odours from the room of a certain new tenant whom I have yet to clap eyes upon though I hear she is a young lady, a student no doubt, with middle class admirers or fervent working class ones or even upper class yacht drivers. I cannot be expected to compete with that sort of opposition. I shall probably flash her a weary kind of ironic grin that will strike her to the very marrow and gain all her pity/sympathy/respect for a brave but misguided soul. What sort of pish is this at all. Fuck sake I refuse to contemplate further on it although I only got lost in some train of thought and never for one moment contemplated a bastarn thing. I day dream frequently.

This infant sleeps on the floor in an awkward position and could conceivably suffocate but I wont rouse her. The worst could not happen with me here. Scream the fucking place down if I woke her up.

I am fed up with this business. Always my own fault with the terrible false yesses I toss around at random. Why can I not give an honest no like other people. The same last time. I watched the infant all Friday night while the parents were off for a few jars to some pub uptown where this country & western songster performs to astonishing acclaim. Now why songster and not singer. Anyway, they returned home with a ½ bottle of whisky and a couple of cans of lager so it wasnt too bad. This country & western stuff isnt as awful as people say yet there are too many tales of lost loves and horses for my liking although I admit to enjoying a good weepy now and then unless recovering from a hangover in which case – in which case ... Christ, I may imagine things more than most but surely the mother – whom for the sake of identity I'll hereon refer to as Greta. And I might as well call him Percy since it is the worst I can think of at present – displayed her thigh on purpose. This is a genuine question. If I decide on some sort of action I must be absolutely sure of my ground, not be misled into thinking one thing to be true when in fact the other thing is the case. What. O jesus I have too many problems to concentrate on last week and the rest of it. Who the hell cares. I do. I do, I wish to screw her, be with her in bed for a lengthy period.

Oxtail soup and insufficient bread which lay on a cracked plate. Brought on a tray. Maybe she cant trust herself alone with me. Hard to believe she returned to lunch off similar fare below. I cant help feeling nobody would offer someone soup under the title of 'lunch' without prior explanation. Tea did of course follow but no further bread. I did not borrow from her. I wanted to. I should have. It was necessary. I somehow expected her to realise my plight and suggest I accept a minor sum to tide me over, but no. I once tried old Percy for a fiver on his wages day. He looked at me as if I was daft. Five quid. A miserable five. Lend money and lose friends was his comment. Friends by christ.

Sucked my thumb to taste the nicotine. A salty sandish flavour. Perhaps not. In the good old days I could have raked the coal embers for cigarette ends. Wet pavements. I am in a bad way – even saying I am in a bad way. 3.30 in the afternoon this approximate Thursday. I have until Saturday morning to starve to death though I wont. I shall make it no bother. The postman comes at 8.20–7.50 on Saturdays but the bastarn postoffice opens not until 9.00 and often 9.05 though they disagree about it.

I refuse to remain here this evening. I will go beg in some pub where folk know me. In the past I have starved till the day before payday then tapped a handful on the strength of it and ... christ in the early days I got a tenner once or twice and blew the lot and by the time I had repayed this and reached the Saturday late night I was left with thirty bob to get me through the rest of the week ie the following 7 days. Bad bad. Waking in the morning and trying to slip back into slumber blotting out the harsh truth but it never works and there you are wide awake and aware and jesus it is bad. Suicide can be contemplated. Alright. I might have contemplated it. Or maybe I only imagined it, I mean seriously considered it. Or even simply and without the seriously. In other words I didnt contemplate suicide at all. I probably regarded the circumstances as being ideal. Yet in my opinion

No more of this shite. But borrowing large sums knowing they have to be repaid and the effects etc must have something to do with the deathwish. I refuse to discuss it. A naïve position. And how could I starve to death in two days, particularly having recently lunched upon oxtail soup. People last for weeks so long as water is available.

Why am I against action. I was late to sign-on this morning though prepared for hours beforehand. Waken early these days or sometimes late. If I had ten pence I would enter supermarkets and steal flat items. And talking about water, I can make tea, one cup of which gives the idea of soup because of the tea bag's encrustation viz crumbs of old food, ooze, hair, dandruff and dust. Maybe the new girl shall come borrow sugar from me. And then what will transpire. If

Had to go for a slash there and action: the thing being held between middle finger and thumb with the index slightly bent at the first joint so that the outside, including the nail, lay along it; a pleasant, natural grip. If I had held the index a fraction more bent I would have soaked the linoleum to the side of the pot. And the crux is of course that the act is natural. I have never set out to pish in that manner. It simply happens. Everyman the same I suppose with minute adjustments here and there according to differing chopper measurements. Yet surely the length of finger will vary in relation. Logical thought at last. Coherence is attainable as far as the learned Hamish Smith of Esher Suffolk would have us believe. I am no Englishman. I am for nationalization on a national scale and if you are a smalltrader well

No point journeying forth before opening time.

It is possible I might eat with them as a last resort and perhaps watch television although in view of the oxtail soup a deal to hope for. But I would far rather be abroad in a tavern in earnest conversation with keen people over the state of nations, and I vow to listen. No day dreaming or vacant gazing right hand up and honest to god. Nor shall I inadvertently yawn hugely. But my condition is such company is imperative. I can no longer remain with myself. And that includes Percy, Greta and the infant, let us say Gloria – all three of whom I shall term the Nulties. The Nulties are a brave little unit gallantly making their way through a harsh uncaring world. They married in late life and having endeavoured for a little one were overwhelmed by their success. The infant Gloria is considered not a bad looking child though personally her looks dont appeal. She has a very tiny nose, pointed ears, receding hair. Also she shits over everything. Mainly diarrhoea that has an amazingly syrupy smell. Like many mothers Greta doesnt always realise the smell exists while on the other hand is absolutely aware so that she begins apologizing left right and centre. Yet if everybody resembles me no wonder she forgets the bastarn smell because I for the sake of decency am liable to reply: What smell?

Greta is a busy mum with scarce the time for outside interests. There is nothing or perhaps a lot to say about Percy but it is hell of a boring. The point is that one of these days he shall awaken to an empty house. The woman will have upped and gone and with any sense will have neglected to uplift the infant. Trouble with many mothers is their falling for the propaganda dished out concerning them ie and their offspring – *Woman's Own* and that kind of shite. Most men fall for it too. But I am being sidetracked by gibberish. No, I fail to fit into their cosy scene for various reasons the most obvious of which is 3's a crowd and that's that for the time being.

But dear god I cannot eat with them tonight. They skimp on grub. One Saturday (and the straits must have been beyond desperation if Saturday it truly was) they sat me down and we set to on a plate of toast and tinned spaghetti. For the evening repast! My christ. But what I said was, Toast and spaghetti, great stuff. Now how can I tell such untruths and is it any wonder that I'm fucking languishing. No, definitely not. I deserve all of it. Imitation tomato sauce on my chin. And after the meal we turn to the telly over a digestive smoke and pitcher of coffee essence & recently boiled water; and gape our way to the Late Weather. I could make the poor old Nulties even worse by saying they stand for God Save The

Queen Of The Great English Speakers but they dont to my knowledge —
it is possible they wait till I have departed upstairs.

I have no wish to continue a life of the Nulties.

Something must be done. A decisive course of action. Tramping around
pubs in the offchance of bumping into wealthy acquaintants is a
depressing affair. And as far as I remember none of mine are wealthy and
even then it is never a doddle to beg from acquaintances — hard enough
with friends. Of which I no longer have. No fucking wonder. But old
friends I no longer see can no longer be termed friends and since they are
obliged to be something I describe them as acquaintances. In fact every
last individual I recollect at a given moment is logically entitled to be
termed acquaintance. And yet

Why the lies. Concerning the tapping of a few bob; I find it easy. Never in
the least embarrassed though occasionally I have recourse to the
expression of such in order to be adduced ethical or something. I am a
natural born beggar. Yes. Honest. A natural born beggar. I should take
permanently to the road.

The pubs I tramp are those used by former colleagues, fellow employees
of the many firms which have in the past employed me for mutual profit.
My christ. Only when skint and totally out of the game do I consider the
tramp. Yet apparently my company is not anathema. Eccentric but not
unlikeable. A healthy respect is perhaps accorded one. Untrue. I am
treated in the manner of a sick younger brother. It is my absolute lack of
interest in any subject that may arise in their conversation that appeals to
them. I dislike debates, confessions and New Year resolutions. I answer
only in monosyllables, even when women are present. Still Waters Run
Deep is the adage I expect them to use of me. But there are no grounds for
complaint. Neither from them nor from me. All I ask is the free bevy, the
smoke, the heat. It could embarrass somebody less sensitive than myself.
What was that. No, there are weightier problems. The bathwater has
been running. Is the new girl about to dip a daintily naked toe. Maybe it
is Mrs Soinson. Or Greta. And the infant Gloria. And Percy by christ. But
no, Percy showers in the work to save the ten pence meter money. Petty
petty petty. I dont bathe at all. I have what might be described as an
alloverbodywash here in the kitchenette sink. I do every part of my
surface bar certain sections of my lower to middle back which are

impossible to reach without one of those long stemmed brushes I often saw years ago in amazing American Movies.

Incredible. Someone decides to bathe in a bath and so the rest of us are forced to run the risk of bladder infection. Nobody chapped my door. How do they know I didnt need to go. So inconsiderate for fuck sake that's really bad. Too much tea right enough, that's the problem.

No, Greta probably entertains no thoughts at all of being in bed with me. I once contemplated the possibility of Percy entertaining such notions. But I must immediately confess to this strong dislike as mutual. And he is most unattractive. And whereas almost any woman is attractive and desirable only a slender few men are. I dont of course mean slenderly proportioned men, in fact – what is this at all. I dont want to sleep with men right hand up and honest to god I dont. Why such strenuous denials my good fellow. No reason. Oho. Honest. Okay then. It's a meal I need, a few pints, a smoke, open air and outlook, the secure abode. Concerted energy, decisive course of action. Satisfyingly gainful employment. Money. A decidable and complete system of logic. Ungibberishness. So many needs and the nonexistent funds. I must leave these square quarters of mine this very night. I must worm my way into company, any company, and the more ingratiatingly the better.

Having dug out a pair of uncracked socks I have often made the normal ablutions and left these quarters with or without the Imitation Crombie. Beginning in a pub near the city centre I find nobody. Now to start a quest such as this in a fashion such as this is fucking awful. Not uncommon nevertheless yet this same pub is always the first pub and must always be the first pub in this the quest.

Utter rubbish. How in the name of christ can one possibly consider suicide when one's giro arrives in two days' time. Two days. But it is still Thursday. Thursday. Surely midnight has passed and so technically it is tomorrow morning, the next day – Friday. Friday morning. O jesus and tomorrow the world. Amen. Giro tomorrow. In a bad way, no. Certainly not. Who are you kidding. I have to sleep. Tomorrow ie tonight is Friday's sleep. But two sleeps equal two days. What am I facing here. And so what. I wish

To hell with that for a game.

But I did move recently. I sought out my fellows. Did I really though. As a crux this could be imperative, analogous to the deathwish. Even considering the possibility sheds doubt. Not necessarily. In fact I dont believe it for a single solitary minute. I did want to get in with a crowd though, surely to christ. Maybe I wasnt trying hard enough. But I honestly required company. Perhaps they had altered their drinking habits. Because of me. In the name of fuck all they had to do was humiliate me – not that I would have been bothered by it but at least it could have allayed their feelings – as if some sort of showdown had taken place. But to actually change their pub. Well well well. Perhaps they sensed I was setting out on a tramp and remained indoors with shutters drawn, lights extinguished. My christ I'm predictable. Three pubs I went to and I gave up. Always been the same: I lack follow through. Ach.

Can I really say I enjoy life with money. When I have it I throw it away. Only relax when skint. When skint I am a hulk – husk. No sidesteps from the issue. I do not want money ergo I do not want to be happy. The current me is my heart's desire. Surely not. Yet it appears the case. I am always needing money and I am always getting rid of it. This must be hammered home to me. Not even a question of wrecking my life, just that I am content to wallow. Nay, enjoy. I should commit suicide. Unconsecrated ground shall be my eternal resting spot. But why commit suicide if enjoying oneself. Come out of hiding Hamish Smith. Esher Suffolk cannot hold you.

Next time the landlord shows up I shall drygulch him; stab him to death and steal his lot. Stab him to death. Sick to the teeth of day dreams. As if I could stab the nyaff. Maybe I could pick a fight with him and smash in his skull with a broken wine bottle and crash, blood and brains and wine over my wrist and clenched fist. The deathwish after all. Albeit murder. Sounds more rational that ie why destroy one's own life if enjoyable. No reason at all. Is there a question. None whatsoever, in fact I might be onto something deep here but too late to pursue it, too late. Yet it could be a revelation of an extraordinary nature. But previously of course been exhausted by the learned Smith of Esher decades since and nowadays taken for granted – not even a topic on an inferior year's O-level examination paper.

He isnt even a landlord. I refer to him as such but in reality he is only the bastarn agent. I dont know who the actual landlord really is. It might be Winsom Properties. A trust that is. I dont like this kind of thing either. I prefer to know names.

Hell with them and their fucking shutters and lights out.

It isnt as bad as all that; here I am and it is now the short a.m.'s. The short a.m.'s. I await the water boiling for a final cup of tea. Probably only drink the stuff in order to pish. Does offer a singular relief. And simply strolling to the kitchenette and preparing this tea: the gushing tap, the kettle, gather the tea-bag from the crumb strewn shelf – all of this is motion.

My head gets thick.

One of the chief characteristics of my early, mid and late adolescence was the catastrophic form of the erotic content. Catastrophic in the sense that that which I did have was totally, well, not quite, fantasy. Is the lack by implication of an unnatural variety. Whether it is something to do with me or not – I mean whether or not it is catastrophic is nothing to do with me I mean, not at all. No

Mr Smith, where are you. No, I cannot be bothered considering the early years. Who cares. Me of course it was fucking lousy. I masturbated frequently. My imagination was/is such I always had fresh stores of fantasies. No wish to imply I still masturbate; nowadays for example I encounter difficulties in sustaining an erection unless another person happens to be in the immediate vicinity. Even first thing in the morning. This is all bastarn lies. Why in the name of fuck do I continue. What is it with me at all. Something must have upset me recently. Erotic content by christ. Why am I wiped out. Eh. Utterly skint. Why is this always as usual. Why I do even

Certain clerks behind the counter.

I mend fuses for people, oddjobs and that kind of bla for associates of the nyaff viz tenants. I am expected to do it. I allow my – I fall behind with the fucking rent. Terrible situation. I have to keep on his right side. Anyway, I dont mind the oddjobs. It gets you out and about.

I used to give him openings for a life of Mrs Soinson but all he could ever manage was, Fussy Old Biddy. And neither he nor she is Irish. I cant figure the woman out myself. Apart from her I might be the longest tenant in the premises. And when the nyaff knows so little you can be sure nobody else knows a thing. She must mend her own fuses. I havent even seen inside her room – or rooms. It is highly possible that she actually fails to see me when we pass on the staircase. The nyaff regards her in awe. Is she a blacksheep outcast of an influential family closely connected to Winsom Properties. When he first became agent around here I think he looked upon her as easy meat whatever the hell that might mean as far as a nyaff is concerned. She cant be more than fifty years of age, carries herself well and seems an obvious widow. But I dispute that. A man probably wronged her many years ago. Jilted. With her beautiful sixteen year old younger sister beside her as bridesmaid, an engagement ring on her finger just decorously biding her time till this marriage of her big sister is out the way so she can step in and get married to her own youthful admirer, and on the other side of poor old Mrs Soinson stood her widower father or should I say sat since he would have been an invalid and in his carriage only waiting his eldest daughter's betrothal to be over and done with so he can join his dearly departed who died in childbirth (the beautiful sixteen year old's) up there in heaven. And ever since that day Mrs Soinson has remained a spinster, virginal, the dutiful but pathetic aunt – a role which she hates but accepts for her parents' memory. Or she could have looked after the aged father till it was too late and for some reason, on the day he died, vowed to stay a single lady since nobody could take the place of the departed dad and took on the title of Mistress to ward off would-be suitors, although of course you do find men more willing to entertain a single Mrs as opposed to a single Miss which is why I agree with Women's Liberation. Mirs should be the title of both married and single women.

In the name of god.

Taking everything into consideration the time may be approaching when I shall begin regular, paid, fulltime employment. My lot is severely trying. For an approximate age I have been receiving money from the state. I am obliged to cease this malingering and earn an honest penny. Having lived in this fashion for so long I am well nigh unemployable and if I were an Industrial Magnate or Captain of Industry I would certainly entertain doubts as to my capacity for toil. I am an idle goodfornothing. A neerdowell, the workhouse is too good for the likes of me. I own up. I am incompatible with this Great British Society. My production rate is less than atrocious. An honest labouring job is outwith my grasp. Wielding a shabby brush is not to be my lot. No more setting forth on bitter mornings just at the break of dawn through slimy backstreet alleys, the treacherous urban undergrowth, trudging the meanest cobbled streets and hideously misshapen pathways of this grey with a heart of gold city. Where is that godforsaken factory. Let me at it. A trier. I would say so Your Magnateship. And was Never Say Die the type of adage one could apply to the wretch. I believe so Your Industrialness.

Fuck off.

Often I sit by the window in order to sort myself out – a group therapy within, and I am content with a behaviourist approach, none of that pie in the sky metaphysics here if you dont mind. I quick-fire trip questions at myself which demand immediate answers and sometimes elongated thought out ones. So far I have been unsuccessful, and the most honest thing to say is that it is unintentionally on purpose, a very deeply structured item. Choosing this window for instance only reinforces the point. I am way way on top, high above the street. And though the outlook is unopen considerable activity takes place directly below. In future I may dabble in psychiatry – get a book out the library on the subject and stick in, go to nightschool and obtain the necessary qualifications for minor university acceptance whose exams I shall scrape through, industrious but lacking the spark of genius, and eventually make it into a general sanatorium leading a life of devotion to the mental health of mankind. I would really enjoy the work. I would like to organize beneficial group therapies and the rest of it. Daily discussions. Saving young men and women from all sorts of breakdowns. And you would definitely have to be alert working beside the average headbanger or disturbed soul who are in reality the sane and we the insane according to the learned H. S. of Esher S. But though I appear to jest I give plenty of thought to the subject. At least once during their days everybody has considered themselves mad or at least well on the road but fortunately from listening to the BBC they realise that if they really were mad they would never for one moment consider it as a possible description of their condition. So then ... But sometimes they almost have to when reading a book by an enlightened foreigner or watching a meaty play or documentary or something – I mean later, when lying in bed with the lights out for example with the wife sound asleep and eight and a half months pregnant maybe and suddenly he advances and accidentally bumps her shoulder all ready with some shite about, O sorry if I disturbed you, tossing and turning etc, couldnt sleep after that bla bla bla we were watching and that. And then it dawns on him, this, the awful truth, he is off his head or at best has this astonishingly bad memory – a memory which under the circumstance may actually be at worst. And that foreigner is no comfort once she will have returned to slumber and you are on your own, alone I mean in the middle of the night, the darkest recesses, dan d ran dan. But it must happen. What must fucking happen.

The postoffice may be seeking reliable men. Perhaps I shall fail their medical. That goes for the fireservice. But Her Majesty's. The Army Navy Air Force and Constabulary. Public Transport. I shall inform the Nulties. But each a creditable occupation and eager to take on such as myself. Security. I shall apply. The Military Life would suit me. Uplift the responsibility, the decision making, temptations, choice. A sound bank account at the wind up – not a vast sum of course but enough to set me up as a tobacconist cum newsagent in a small way, nothing fancy, just to eke out the pension.

But there should be direction at thirty years of age. A knowing where I'm going. Alright Sir Hamish we cant all be Charles Clore or Grace Darling but at least we damn well have a go and dont give in. Okay we may realise what it is all about and to hell with their christianity, ethics, the whole shebang and advertising but do we give in. Do we Give Up The Ghost. Throw in the Literal Towel. No sirree by god we dont. Do you for one moment think we believe someone should starve to death while another feeds his dog on the best steak and chips, of course not, we none of us have outmoded beliefs but do we

I cannot place a finger somewhere. The bastarn rain is the cause. It pours, steadily for a time then heavier. Of course the fucking gutter has rotted and the constant torrent drops just above the fucking window. That bastard of a landlord gets nothing done, too busy peeping through keyholes at poor old Mrs Soinson. I am fed up with it. Weather been terrible for years. No wonder people look the way they do. Who can blame them. Christ it is really bad. Depresses everything. They cant even chatter about it, the weather, it is so fucking consistent. Recently I went for a short jaunt in the disagreeable countryside. Fortunately I got soaked through. The cattle ignored the rain. The few motor cars around splished past squirting oily mud onto the Imitation Crombie. I kept slipping into marshy bogs from where I shrieked at various objects while seated in the saturated grass. It wasnt boring. Of yore, on country rambles, I would doze in some deserted field with the sun beating etc the hum of grasshoppers chirp. I never sleep in a field where cattle graze lest I get nibbled. The countryside and I are incompatible. Yet I used to like the place. Everybody maintains they like the countryside but I refuse to accept this. It is absurd. Just scared. To admit they are feart and hate the very idea of journeying through pastureland or craggyland. Jesus christ. I dont mind small streams burning through arableland. Hardy fishermen with waders knee-deep in lonely inshore waters earn my absolute indifference. Not exactly. Not sympathy, nor pity, nor respect, envy, hate. Contempt. Not at all. But I hero-worship lighthousemen. No. Envy is closer. Or maybe jealousy. And anyway, all men are nowadays created equal. But whenever I have had money in the past I have enjoyed the downpour. If on the road to somewhere the rain is fine. A set purpose. Even the cinema. Coat collar turned up. Street lights reflecting on puddles. Arriving with wind flushed complexion and rubbing your damp hands and parking the arse on a convenient convector heater. But without the money. Still not too bad perhaps.

According to the mirror I have been going about with a thoughtful expression on one's countenance. I appear to have become aware of myself in relation to the field by which I mean the external world. In relation to this field I am in full knowledge of my position. And this has nothing to do with steak and chips

Comfortable degrees of security are not to be scoffed at. I doff the cap to those who attain it the bastards. Seriously, I am fed up with being fed up. What I do wish

I shall not entertain day dreams

I shall not fantasize

I shall endeavour to make things work

I shall tramp the mean streets in search of menial posts or skilled ones. Everywhere I shall go, from Shetland Oilrigs to Bearsden Gardening

Jobs. To Gloucestershire. I would go to Gloucestershire. Would I fuck. To hell with them and their cricket and cheese. I refuse to go there. I may emigrate to distant horizons. A prime disadvantage might be language. O jesus I am curtailed to The Great Englishes. Dear god Australia and New Zealand. Well then, America or Canada.

Christ sake all I ask is regular giros and punctual counter clerks.

Ach well son, cheer up. So quiet in this dump. Some kind of tune was droning around a while back. I was sitting clapping hands to the rhythm and considering moving about on the floor. I dream of playing the banjo. Even the guitar, just being able to strum but with a passable voice and dropping into a party and playing a song, couple of women at the feet keeping time and slowly sipping from a tall glass, 4 in the a.m.'s with whisky on the shelf and plenty smokes. That is it now, that is definitely that.

black and white consumer and producer parasite thief come on shake hands you lot

Well throw yourself out the fucking window then. Throw myself out fuck all window ya fucking bastard ye – do what you like but here I am, no suicide no malnutrition no nothing, I am getting to fuck out of it. A temporary highly paid job, save a right few quid and then off on one's travels. Things will be done. Action immediate. Of the Pioneering Stock would you say. Of that ilk most certainly Your Worship. And were the audience Clambering to their Feet. I should think so Your Grace.

The fact is I am a late starter. I am

I shouldnt be bothering about money anyway. The creditors have probably forgotten all about my existence. No point in worrying about anything other than current arrears. The old me would not require funds. A red & white polkadot hanky, a stout sapling rod, the hearty whistle and hi yo silver for the short ride to the outskirts of town, Carlisle and points south.

It is all a load of shite. I often plan things out then before the last minute do something mindblowingly ridiculous to ensure the plan's failure. If I decided to clear the arrears and get a few quid together, follow up with

a symbolic burning of the Imitation Crombie and in short make preparations to mend my ways I could conceivably enlist in the majestic Navy to
spite myself – or even fork out a couple of month's rent in advance for
this dump simply to sit back and enjoy my next step from a safe distance
and all the time guffawing in the background good christ I am
schizophrenic, I never thought I acted in that manner yet I must admit it
sounds like me, worse than I imagined, bad, bad. Perhaps I could use the
cash to pay for an extended stay in a private nursing home geared to the
needs of the Unabletocope. But can it be schizophrenia if I can identify it
by myself. Doubtful. However I regard

I was of the opinion certain items in regard to my future had been
resolved. Cynical of self, this is the problem. Each time I make a firm
resolution I scoff. Yes. I sneer. Well well well what a shite. That really
does Take the Biscuit. And the bastarn milklorries will be crashing about
shortly. Captains of Industry should create situations for my ilk. I could
be the Works Philosopher. With my own wee room to the left of the
Personnel Block. Dissidents would be sent to me during teabreak.
Militancy could be cut by 90%. Yet no Works Philosopher would be
classed as staff, instead stamping in and out like the rest of the troops just
in case he might aspire to reclassification within Personnel. Ach,
gibberish. And yet fine. That would be another one out the road and then
they could promote the Dissident in Chief up to Works Philosopher and
so on. And they would stick it, they would not be obliged to seek out
Square Quarters whose shelves are crumb strewn.

I shall have it to grips soon. Tomorrow or who knows. After all, I am but
thirty, hardly matured. But fuck me I'm getting hell of a hairy these days.
Maybe visit the barber in the near future, Saturday for instance, who
knows what's in store. Only waiting for my passion to find an object and
let itself go. Yes, who can tell what's in store, that's the great thing about
life. Always one more Fish in the Sea and Iron in the Fire. This is the great
thing about life, the uncertainty and the bla

Jesus what will I do, save up for a new life, the mending of the ways, pay
off arrears, knock the door of accredited creditors, yes, I can still decide
what to do about things concerning myself and even others if only in
regard to me at least it is still indirectly to do with them and yet it isnt

indirect at all because it is logically bound to be direct if it is anything and obviously it is something and must therefore be directly since I am involved and if they are well

well well, who can tell what the fuck this is about. I am chucking it all in. My brain cannot cope by itself. Gets carried away for the sake of thought no matter whether it be sense or not, no, that's the last fucking thing ever considered. Which presents problems. I really do have a hard time knowing where I am going. For if going, where. Nowhere and somewhere. Children and hot meals. Home and security and the neighbours in for a quiet drink at the weekend. Tumbling on carpets with the kids and television sets and golf and even heated discussions in jocular mood while the wives gossip ben in the kitchen and

Now then, here I am in curiously meagre surroundings living the life of a hapless pauper, my pieces of miserable silver supplied gratis by the browbeaten taxpayer. The past ramblings concerning outer change were pure invention. Comments made upon one's total inadequacy were made in earnest albeit with a touch of pride. Even the hearty Greta is abused by me at least in regard to grub and smokes. And all for what. Ah, an ugly sight. But it has to be admitted that with a rumbling stomach I have often refused grub, preferring a lonely smoke and the possible mystery of, Has he eaten somewhere else. And if so with whom. But for all anybody knows I have several trunks packed full of clothes. Nobody knows a thing about me apart from a couple of clerks. I could be a Man About Town. They probably nudge each other and refer to me as a bit of a lad. I might start humping a large suitcase plastered with illegible labels. Save up and buy a suit in the modern mode. Get my coat dyed, even stick to the symbolic burning. Yet I could flog it. A shrewd man I occasionally have dealings with once refused it. But I asked a Big price. Shoes too I need. Presently I have what can be described as Bumpers. With leather efforts and the new rig-out I could go anywhere. I can be a Computer Programmer. But they're supposed to reach their peak at twenty one years of age. Still and all the sex potency peak is sixteen years of bastarn age. Ach. I dare say sex plays more of a role in my life than grub. If both were in abundance my problems could only increase. Yet one's mental capacities would be bound to make more use of the potential without problems at the fundamental level. Jesus my mind would blow up if unharnessed.

But

the plan. From now on I do not cash giros. I sleep in on Saturday mornings and so too late for the postoffice's 1 p.m. closure. By the time Monday morning arrives I shall have it alright and if I can stretch out and grab at next Saturday then the pathway shall have been erected, I shall have won through.

Recently I lived in seclusion. I existed for a considerable period on a tiny islet not far from Toay. Sheep and swooping gulls for companions. The land and the sea. After dark the inner recesses. Self knowledge and acceptance of the awareness. Swam in rockpools. No trees of course. None. Sheer drops from mountainous regions, bird shit and that of sheep, goats perhaps in that terrain. No sign of man or woman. The sun always far in the sky but no clouds. Not tanned. Weatherbeaten. Hair matted but by salt water. Food requires no mention. Swirling eddies within the standing rocks and nicotine wool stuck to the jagged edges, the droppings of the gulls.

Since I shall have nothing to look forwards to on Saturday mornings I must reach a state of neither up nor down. Always the same. That will be miserable I presume but considering my heart's desire is to be miserable (this seems well ironed out) then with uncashed giros reaching for the ceiling I can be indefinitely miserable. Total misery. However, to retain misery I may be obliged to get out and about in order not to be always miserable since – or should I say pleasure is imperative if perfect misery is the goal and therefore a basic condition of my perpetual misery is the occasional jaunt abroad in quest of joy. Now we're getting somewhere Hamish, arise and get your purple sash. And since ambling round pubs only depresses me I must seek out other means of entertainment or risk desisting a description of myself as wretch. And setbacks and kicksin-theteeth are out of the question. Masochism then. Can this be the

Obviously I am just in the middle of a nervous breakdown, even saying it. But for christ sake saving a year's uncashed giros is impossible because the bastards render them uncashable after a six month period.

Walking from Lands End to John O'Groats would be the ideal in fact because for one thing it would tax my resistance to the utmost. Slogging on day in day out. Have to be during the summer. I dislike the cold water and I would be stopping off for a swim. Yet this not knowing how long it takes the average walker – well, why worry, time is of no concern. Or perhaps it should be. I could try for the record. After the second attempt possibly. Once I had my bearings. Not at all. I would amble. And with pendants and flags attached to the suitcases I could beg my grub and tobacco. Very minimum of money required. Neither broo nor social security. Just the self sufficiency of the sweetly self employed. I could be for the rest of my life. The Lands End to John O'Groats Man. That would very soon be my title. My name a byword – is not what is wanted otherwise these cunts from the media would be popping out from every bush crying This Is Your Life. No, anonymity is essential. Jesus it would be good. And far from impossible. I have often hitched about the place, many times. But hitching has to be banned or I may save time which is of course an absurdity. Pointless to hitch. Yet what difference will it make if I do save time because it will make no difference anyway. None whatsoever. Not at all. And if it takes six weeks a trip and the same back up I could average four return trips a year. If I am halfway through life just now ie a hundred and twenty return trips then in another hundred and twenty trips I would be dead. I can mark each trip on convenient milestones north and south. And when the reporters pop up I could simply say, I shall be calling a halt in 80 trips time. And I speak of returns my fine fellow. That would be twenty years hence by which time I would have become accustomed to fame. Although I could possibly fall down dead by then through fatigue or something. Hail rain shine. The dead of winter would be a challenge but could force me into shelter unless I acquire a passport and head out to sunnier climes, Australia for example to stave off the language problem yet speech would be no factor. No, impossible. I cannot leave The Great British Shores. Nor the Scottish one for that matter. Scotland is ideal. Straight around the Scottish Coast from the foot of Galloway right round to Berwick. Although Ayrshire is a worry. Hell of a boring coastline. But boredom is out of the question. Ayrshire will not be denied. So each return trip might involve say a four month slog if keeping rigidly to the coast on all minor roads particularly when you consider Kintyre for example or Morven by fuck and even I suppose Galloway to some extent. But that kind of thing is easily

resolved. I dont have to restrict myself to mapped out routes from which
the slightest deviation is frowned upon. On the contrary; that last minute
decision at the country crossroads can only enhance the affair. And
certain clothing items are already marked out as essential items. The
stout pair of boots and gnarled staff to ward off farmdogs and cows after
dusk. A hat and coat for wet weather. The Imitation Crombie may well
suffice. Though an anorak to cover the knees would no doubt reap
dividends. And after a few return trips – and being a circular route there
could be no such thing as returns ie I would be travelling on an arc, an arc
by christ o jesus and the farmfolk and country dwellers would know me
well, the goodwives leaving thick winter woollies by the side of the road,
flasks of oxtail soup under hedges. Shepherds perhaps offering shelter in
the remotest of bothies by the blazing log fires sipping hot toddies for the
wildest of nights, and the children crying, Mummy – here comes the
Scottish Coastroad Walker, and I would dispense homespun philosophies
and demonstrate how the daisy grows, the planet revolves etc. A stray
dog joining me having tagged along for a trip at a safe distance behind me
I at last turn and at my first grunt of encouragement it comes bounding
joyfully forwards showering me in wet noses and barked assurances to stick
by me through thick and thin and to eternally guard my last lowly grave
when I have at length fallen in mid-stride plumb tuckered out after many
many years viz twelve round trips at two years a trip. Yet it may be a
good bit shorter than that. On hot days in central summer busloads of
tourists to view me, pointed out by the driver as a Legend of the North,
the solitary trudging humpbacked figure with dog and gnarled staff
vanishing out of sight into the mist, Dont give him money Your Worship
you'll just hurt his feelings. Just a bit of your cheese piece and a saucer of
milk for the whelp. Group photographs with me peering suspiciously
from behind shoulders in the background or to the immediate fore
perhaps – it is rumoured the man was a Captain of Industry Your Grace,
been right round the Scottish Coastroad twenty eight times and known
from Galloway to Berwick as a friend to everyone. Yes, just a pinch of
your snuff and a packet of cigarette papers for chewing purposes only.
No sextants or compasses or any of that kind of shite but

James Lasdun

THE
SPOILING

JAMES LASDUN was born in 1958 and read English at Bristol University. He has worked in a restaurant, as an English language teacher and as a publisher's reader. He co-edits *Straight Lines* and has reviewed for *The Times Literary Supplement* and other journals.

When Ronald's wife left him, it was understood that the Boyce family flag would go on flying under his name. The friends they had appropriated during the ten years of their deteriorating marriage would, with the two children, the Volvo, and the large Kensington house, remain his property. Margaret, it was understood, would take herself altogether elsewhere to find an altogether new life. It was, after all, she who had wanted to bring an end to the business and, as Ronald reasoned in his special aggrieved-but-magnanimous voice, it was the least she could do to refrain from disrupting the children's upbringing by removing them from the home which had nurtured their healthy little bodies and minds with such abundance of love and prosperity.

From the start, Ronald had established himself as dictator of furnishings and family customs in the Boyce household. He had a natural instinct for covering and softening – quince wall-to-wall carpets throughout, lilac wallpaper covering every wall but those of the still bare hallway, a large and undistinguished collection of hunting and sporting prints covering the wallpaper in the drawing-room and, to his wife's perpetual embarrassment, a series of photographs of her as a naked toddler on Brighton beach, which Ronald had insisted on framing and hanging in a column beside the walnut cabinet in the drawing-room. Later on, he added pictures of his own children in similar circumstances and, finally, one of himself being presented to the Queen Mother at the opening ceremony of his company's new factory. Curiously, perhaps, he did not remove the pictures of his wife when she left him, and they hang there still, the first things to meet the eyes of the guests as they arrive at this, the eleventh of his annual New Year's Eve buffet parties.

The guests are a mixture. There are the business fraternity and their wives; they are the good solid friends who were so supportive when Ronald's wife left him: the managing director and his wife who are affable and fuss over the children, forever telling them what a clever man their daddy is, and how he will soon be on the board, Colin Porter, the firm accountant – a bachelor who takes himself rather seriously but, as Ronald has discovered, rather likes to be patronized – Gordon Cavendish, Bob Goldsmith, who now works for a rival company, Teddy Bantock – all good solid men with good solid wives. Then there is the motley collection of guests employed variously in or around the fringes of 'Art'. Ronald is doubly proud of this collection – first, as novelties from the glamorous world of culture to be paraded in front of his rather unglamorous business colleagues, and secondly, because they were originally friends of his wife and their presence here today both indicates a highly gratifying transference of affections and reconfirms his sense of his own righteousness.

The doorbell rings with increasing frequency. Ronald likes to make warm physical contact with each guest as he or she arrives; hand-shakes and back-patting for the men, kisses and hugs for the women. He has learnt the importance of the bold gesture – that most people will accept for real any posture you care to present them with, and that, while he might be tortured in private by a nagging sense of his own littleness, the world is prepared to accept him at face value, as a man who has suffered nobly and attained a certain grandeur. He is entitled to whatever intimacy he can extract. And indeed, in the faces of the guests as they enter, he discerns nothing but mute expressions of admiration and sympathy; mute, that is, until the rather brash Bella Suzman, who makes quilts, bursts in, flings her arms around Ronald, holds him away for a minute, gazing mournfully into his eyes, and then declaims what sounds like a set speech:

'Ronnie, you are marvellous, after all you've been through, how you have the guts and determination to soldier on as if nothing has happened, when we all know how difficult it must have been for you (here she pauses for breath), I simply cannot understand. And the children ...' (here she trails off) Ronald's head is tilted in humility, a resigned smile fixed on his handsome, lipless face:

'You're always so kind Bella – let me take your coat (peeling the fur from her back), I'm very philosophic about it all now, besides (laughing) your quilt was never quite big enough for the two of us, so perhaps it's just as well.' He places a glass of champagne in her hand, casts his eye over the room, which has begun to fill up, sees Colin Porter, the firm accountant, standing alone feigning interest in the design of his glass, and, ever the good host, takes Bella across the room to meet him.

'Colin, meet my old friend Bella – Bella's a designer ... Colin's our resident financial wizard, aren't you Colin old chap?'

There is something rather edgy in Ronald's style tonight, something a little off balance – the condescension towards Colin is not tempered with quite the usual dose of sugary warmth. However, Colin does not register this, and as Ronald drifts gracefully away from the pair, he catches the sound of Colin's monotone –

'Well, I wouldn't say wizard . . .'

The bell rings again, Ronald glides through the guests, turns deftly into the hall, and peeps through the eye-hole in the doorway. No, not yet. A shade of disappointment touches his face, but disappears as he opens the door –

'Hector, glad you made it. How's it going?'

Hector is a young painter; Ronald's wife spotted his paintings in a gallery a few years ago, and bought them in outright defiance of her husband, who had a healthy suspicion of Art whose market value was not properly established. Ronald's way of reconciling himself to the fact was to adopt Hector as a protégé – giving him a solid meal now and then, and introducing him to his moneyed friends. For his part, Hector knows the value of such men. He also knows that their alliance is an unholy one, that on both sides it is a matter purely of self-advancement. He feels a little compromised fraternizing in this way with one who is so clearly worthy of his contempt, but he has partially acquitted himself by adopting a tone of off-handedness bordering on surliness. When Ronald invites him round, he is never sure 'whether he can make it', though he usually does, albeit calculatedly late. What he has not reckoned on is the ability of London business society to reduce anything that threatens it to a plaything. And so his aggressive stance not only fails to upset Ronald, but actively delights him.

'Slowly,' is his mumbled reply to Ronald's question.

'As always, as always.'

Ronald wants to make some remark about 'we men of culture' finding it difficult to adjust to the world's hurried pace, but something is distracting him, and the pat phrase will not form itself. He leads Hector into the room, which is now alive with the sound of well-heeled Londoners engaging in conversation. The Christmas tree is still there, decorated with the usual Czechoslovakian glass baubles, and the picture frames are all hung with pieces of tinsel. The central heating is perhaps a little too high, though at the moment it is giving the guests that glow of protective comfort so conducive to an easy flow of chatter. As Ronald gazes around the room for someone to introduce Hector to, he hears Henrietta Cavendish telling her carrot story to the Costane boys –

'... well a young couple came rather late and said they were sorry but their daughter Patricia had been choking on a carrot – the hostess looked rather upset and said ...'

Ronald, who has always affected amusement at this story, the difficulty of doing so increasing each year, finds, as it is repeated for the eleventh time, that he is suddenly unendurably irritated by it. He suppresses an urge to say something very rude to Mrs Cavendish, but he leads Hector over there, and rather unceremoniously interrupts the threesome, so that the story's punch-line – '*Our* Patricia choked to *death* on a carrot ...' is lost in the general bustle.

'Henrietta, meet Hector, an artist friend of mine.'

Mrs Cavendish switches audience and conversation with a swiftness and composure that comes only with many years' experience of the minutiae of cocktail ritual.

'Oh, an artist ... what did you say your name was?'

'Hector – Hector Neil.'

(Pause.) 'Ahh. Where do you exhibit?'

Hector has been through this many times – the name asked, and met with the blankness of unfamiliarity, the circumventory demands for credentials to prove validity of title 'artist'. For 'where do you exhibit?' understand: 'Do you exhibit at all or are you just some jumped-up dauber claiming the title and status of "artist" without so much as a mention in *Harper's* to your name?' Hector tries to keep things light –

'Oh, here and there, I've just had a show at Mountjoy's,' he answers.

'Ah yes, I think I've heard ...' Mrs Cavendish now knows enough to pitch the tone of her conversation at the right point along the scale, running from rapture to contempt, which she adopts when talking to artists. Her husband Gordon is an investor and has put quite a bit of the firm's money into works of Art, so Mrs Cavendish knows a thing or two about the subject.

'I see things are taking a turn for the better in the art world,' she begins.

'In what way?' Hector is on his guard – he did not expect this woman to know about the 'art world'.

'Well, this return to figurative painting –'

Hector feels it befits him to adopt a certain jealous hostility with amateurs encroaching on his territory. Besides, he finds this particular subject particularly distasteful.

'What return to figurative painting?'

'Well surely you know what I mean – it's being talked about everywhere – abstract painting is finished. Nobody wants that kind of thing any more, ask my husband, he'll tell you.'

Hector stares at her angrily but makes no reply.

She goes on, 'Well you must admit it is salutary – I mean as an artist yourself, don't you think things have gone far enough? I've always thought that, to be truly great, art has to celebrate the human form. My husband agrees, and he knows about these things.'

Hector has spent the day painstakingly piecing together a decalcomania collage. He is a member of a group of painters concerned with developing certain forms of abstract painting. He knows very well what Mrs Cavendish is talking about, and he knows it to his cost, for his pictures are not selling, and the grants are drying up.

Among the fantasies that Hector entertains for the sake of protecting his sanity is the verbal reduction of one of his critics to a cowering wreck, preferably in public. And now, instead of taking Mrs Cavendish's words as an inescapable fact of current taste, he takes them as a personal affront and finds himself in the satisfying position of being able to make his fantasy come to life.

'I don't honestly give a damn about the human form, and I don't intend to waste my time discussing art with someone who gets all her opinions on the subject from magazines at the hairdresser.'

Mrs Cavendish makes a sour smile. She is not going to show herself ruffled by this blustering young man.

'No. Well you must talk to my husband. He knows more about these things than I do. *Gordon...*'

She catches her husband's attention and makes the 'rescue me' sign they have formed for awkward moments at such parties. Gordon comes over –

'Gordon, this is Hector – we were just discussing art. It seems I'm out of my depth.'

Hector catches her rolling her eyes up at her husband, in a gesture of contemptuous despair. He knows he is being insulted, and after a moment's reflection he is pleased to find that he is genuinely injured by the behaviour of this pair – sufficiently injured, in fact, to make a scene. Thus, without saying a word, he strides briskly out of the room and, slamming the front door behind him, leaves the house.

There is a moment's hush in the room. Ronald, immediately alerted to the source of attention, stares with barely concealed anger at Mrs Cavendish, who is making gestures of innocent wonder to those around her who witnessed Hector's exit. It is particularly important to Ronald that there should be no tensions tonight, and for the second time Mrs Cavendish has been a source of irritation. He begins to fear that the puppeteer's dexterity with which he normally manipulates his guests may be deserting him, and that his hold over the evening will slip. However, he reassumes his hostly smile, and moves across to Mrs Cavendish with the intention of apologizing for his young friend's irascibility. But the apology is never made – before Ronald reaches Mrs Cavendish, the doorbell rings again. He wheels about with something less than dignity. It can only be one person, the other guests have all arrived. Before opening the front door Ronald makes an effort to recover the suave composure that has once again deserted him. Discreetly looking at himself in the hall mirror, clenching his jaw muscles as he does so, he sleeks back his wavy brown hair and adjusts his collar so that his rather large Adam's apple is not left in such naked profile.

He looks through the peephole, prepares a solemn smile, and opens the door.

'Hilary, welcome, come in. And you've brought Marty too, good.'

He does not kiss Hilary, but he pats Marty, clumsily, on the head. The boy recoils slightly.

'Hello Ronald – I'm so sorry we're late, but Marty needed some persuading, didn't you dear? and I couldn't leave him on his own.'

'I should think not,' says Ronald, patting Marty again. 'He can help Lizzie and Robert pass round the dips and things if he likes – would you like to do that Marty?'

The boy stares up at Ronald through the thick lenses of a pair of round tortoiseshell glasses. His fair hair hangs lifelessly down the white cheeks of his expressionless face. He blinks and mutters:

'I don't mind.'

Hilary, thirty-seven, tired-looking, pointed but not unattractive features, a birdlike nervousness in her movements, does not seem the kind of woman to cause Ronald much anxiety. And were it not for the particular nature of her circumstances, in relation to those of Ronald, there might indeed be no cause for this embarrassed fidgetiness that seems to be afflicting both of them as they enter the drawing-room.

She was the best friend of Margaret – Ronald's ex-wife – since their days together at art school. Margaret, honouring the unspoken agreement with her husband to the last detail, or perhaps from a genuine desire for a complete break, visited Hilary for the last time six months ago, and made it clear that she would not be in touch again. The bewildered Hilary took the news as just another phase in the bad dream which had begun with her own husband's incipient alcoholism, and had become a nightmare with his death two years ago in a journalists' bar in Hanoi.

Since then Hilary has lived alone with her son in a flat in Stockwell. She has a part-time administrative job on the paper that used to employ her husband, and earns barely enough to support herself and Marty. The years have accustomed her to a life occupied, for the most part, with the dreary business of simply keeping things going, but they have not dulled in her any hope of a more comfortable kind of existence. She makes no attempt to conceal from herself the fact that, while she is able to cope on her own, a man who could support her as her husband once supported her would make life very much more tolerable. Such a man might also relieve the rather unhealthy closeness with her son which she has found herself being wedged into.

She is not unaware that mutual friends were plotting a match between herself and Ronald long before he and his wife finally divorced. Neither is she unaware that Ronald is attracted to her – the assiduous attention he began paying her when her husband started to collapse, the use of her bereavement as a licence to soft-talk her and to peer more than merely sympathetically into her eyes never escaped her. She was not exactly flattered, because there was something not exactly wholesome in Ronald's manner of flattery. But there was a shrewd aspect to her otherwise quite ingenuous personality which told her that, when all was said and done, Ronald was a good deal better than nothing; that in many ways he was in fact remarkably suitable.

Yet she never encouraged him. At first she hung back because the whole business of affairs with married men was too alien to the life she was brought up to for it to occur to her as a real possibility. But even afterwards, when there was no question of deception on either side, and Ronald's desire for her was plain for all to see, there was still something about Ronald which made the prospect of intimacy with him seem slightly repulsive.

The title 'best friend' became purely nominal after Margaret married Ronald, but Hilary was still able to witness the breakdown of that marriage – and the transformation of Margaret from a cheerful and talented young woman into the bitter woman who seemed to delight in embarrassing and humiliating her husband at every available opportunity – from a rather closer point of view than anybody else. And what she saw did not quite support the theory in general circulation that Margaret had wanted to be an artist, but through a failure of nerve had decided to marry young and raise a family instead, visiting the consequences of her frustration upon her patient husband. Hilary saw that things were by no means as simple as this, nor as one-sided. She had once called round on the couple, to be met with a frosty greeting from Ronald, and the sight of Margaret crumpled up on the sofa nursing a swollen lip and a bruised chin.

Years later, Margaret used to hint that she had given up painting because Ronald, jealous at the prospect of a wife who might become more successful than himself, had poured such incessant scorn on her efforts that her confidence had been completely shattered. However, by this time Margaret was so obviously soured by her marriage that Hilary could not quite believe what she said, or hinted at. Besides, she suspected that Margaret might be jealous of her, or at least determined that the man whom she was going to leave should not find happiness in another woman with any ease, especially when that other woman was supposed to be her own best friend. So while Hilary took great pains to show Margaret that she was innocent of any complicity with Ronald, she kept an open mind on the question of Ronald's real nature.

It is very much in her capacity as his wife's best friend that Ronald is attracted to Hilary. He finds the prospect of himself and Hilary lying naked and interlocked in a new intimacy, watched over by the hurt and demonically jealous figure of his former wife, a most appealing vision. In his darker moments his only regret is that, even if this vision were realized, the figure of Margaret would only ever be as palpable as his fantasy could make her.

Apart from the satisfaction to be had from seducing his wife's best friend, Ronald has a perfectly practical reason for wishing to wed Hilary; he finds life as a single father uncomfortable and lonely. Of course, he adores his two children, but a nine-year-old daughter and an eight-year-old son are more trouble than company, and a succession of au pairs have come and gone with an alarming rapidity.

Witnessing Hilary's self-sacrificing devotion to her sick husband gave Ronald ample proof of her wifely virtues, sufficient, indeed, for him to have conceived what he believes to be a real, passionate affection for her. Tonight, he has determined, will be the deciding night; he has designed the occasion as a showcase for the kind of life he has to offer Hilary – a life full of warmth, hospitality, geniality, stimulating conversation, good food, limitless hot water, in short, everything a reasonable woman could ask for. And Hilary, too, knows as she walks into the warm, crowded room, that tonight will be a night for certain decisions.

Ronald summons his children – 'Lizzie, Robert, come here.'

They come over, their little hands bearing dishes of crisps and Twiglets. Lizzie, the elder child, has pretty, but oddly unchildlike features, as if her face has reached adulthood before her body. And standing in her quaint, old-fashioned green velvet dress with frills around the collar and the wrists, a look of extreme alertness in her eyes, she makes a strong contrast of independent individuality against her brother who, from all appearances, could still be any little boy.

'Marty is going to help you pass the things around, but take him to the kitchen first, and give him some orange juice.'

They have met Marty before, so the extreme unwillingness to meet others of their kind that afflicts most children is somewhat alleviated. Nevertheless they have not reached the age when one's natural hostility to strangers, or near strangers, is automatically concealed, and the looks they give Marty are not friendly. Marty is unwilling to leave his mother's side, but the dislike of being thought of as wet makes him struggle against his inclination to stay by her, and he sullenly follows the other two into the kitchen, squirming out of the way of a final pat from Ronald as he does so.

In the centre of the large, tile-floored, formica-surfaced kitchen, stand two tables on which are arranged the plates and cutlery, and the various dishes to be consumed later tonight. A single lamp in a conical shade, suspended from the ceiling directly above the tables, is all that illuminates the room at the moment. It gives off a bright, but very localized beam, highlighting the tables but leaving the rest of the room quite dim. The effect is to intensify the various colours of the food to a dramatic pitch, and so to give the whole spread an ethereal quality, as if it were a glossy photograph from the food pages of a women's magazine, enlarged and made three dimensional. For a moment, Marty is transfixed by the sight of the dishes as they glisten from the tables. On one table are the savouries. Bowls of pink taramasalata, yoghurt and cucumber salad, a pale green avocado mousse, rice salad, olives, sliced tomatoes, and half eggs stuffed with a mixture of their own yolks, mayonnaise, and red cayenne pepper, are ranged next to two large flat dishes, one containing rows of thick slices of Parma ham, and the other, slices of cold roast beef graded from, at one end, a well-cooked grey-brown to, at the other end, a rare blood-red. And finally, there are two huge pudding basins, one of potato salad in a rich-looking mayonnaise dressing, its goldness set off by green flecks of chopped chives, and the other, of pieces of cold chicken cooked in tarragon, cream, cherries and burnt almonds. On the second table are the cheeses and the desserts – two more pudding basins, one containing a fresh fruit salad, and the other a mound of small, chocolate-coated, cream-filled profiteroles.

Marty acquired, with his father's encouragement, a sophisticated palate at an early age. In fact, it was due largely to the promise of such delicacies as he now beholds that his mother was able to persuade him to come tonight. And he is clearly not disappointed, although a habit of reserve limits his reaction to what he now sees to a long, expressionless stare, preventing any cry of glee that another child might have made. Despite this reserve, young Robert quickly observes that Marty is impressed with the food; he stands in front of Marty, picks up a profiterole, and pops it into his mouth, looking provocatively at Marty as he does so, as if to dare him to take one too. But before an impulse to take up the challenge can even begin to shape itself, Lizzie smacks her little brother on the hand:

'I'm telling daddy you took one of those,' she says smartly.

The boy's face puckers up into a tiny expression of fury – '*You* took one before,' he says, his high voice full of reproach.

'That's because daddy said I could for helping.'

'Well I've helped too.'

She ignores this remark and asks Marty if he would like some orange juice.

'No thanks,' is his muttered reply.

Robert breaks into a fit of laughter, half put-on, half genuine, and dances around the table singing, 'He doesn't want your orange juice, he doesn't want your orange juice' over and over until his sister smacks him sharply on the arm. This time the puckering face looks dangerously close to tears. Sensing trouble approaching, Lizzie quickly pops another profiterole into her brother's mouth in an attempt to pacify him, and then, with an instinct for sisterliness, takes one herself. For an instant, the boy stands still, uncertain which emotion to give way to – tearful anger or conspiratorial glee. To the relief of his sister, he decides on the latter.

'Now *you* have one,' he says to Marty, offering him one.

'No thanks,' says Marty again. He is not merely being unsociable; the fact is that he does not have an ordinary child's sweet tooth, and the thought of a sticky ball of chocolate, choux pastry and whipped cream does not particularly appeal to him. What he would accept, and what he is longing to be offered, is something from the other table – something with the savoury taste of *real* food. But no offer is made.

'Well I'll just have to eat it myself then,' says Robert, putting it into his mouth and turning to his sister with a slightly uncertain smile. She does not smile back. The key to the power she exerts over her younger brother is her unpredictability. Her seemingly irrational oscillations between sweet indulgence and high-handed intolerance have successfully baffled him into crediting her with the mysterious motives of a superior creature. He chews nervously on his profiterole, awaiting the unfolding of the significance of her cold expression.

'This time I really am telling daddy,' she says, and walks towards the door.

Robert catches her by the waist of her dress; there is a tearing sound, though no visible damage is done. She screams with anger and begins clawing at his arm to free herself – 'Let go you stupid idiot' – but the boy's desire not to be informed on lends him a tenaciousness which she cannot break. However, while he clings dumbly to her, his head and arms buried in the folds about her waist, she coolly assesses the situation, looks about her for a weapon, sees a wooden spoon on the shelf by her, grabs it, and briefly catching the eye of Marty who is looking on forlornly, brings it down on her brother's head. Robert lets go instantly, and lets out a howl of pain. Now it is his turn to try and seek refuge in a parent; he makes for the door, but Lizzie is standing in front of it, brandishing her wooden spoon.

'You can stop being a cry baby,' she tells him. 'Anyway it serves you right for tearing my dress.'

Robert's howls melt into whimpers of self-pity. He slumps down on a chair, nursing his bruised head.

'You wouldn't have done that if mummy was here,' he sobs.

'Well she isn't here is she?'

'Where is your mother?' asks Marty. The other children are rather startled at his sudden intrusion into their private quarrel; they stare at him a moment before Lizzie replies, 'She's gone away,' in a tone of profound significance.

'Why?' asks Marty.

Before Lizzie can answer, Robert interrupts sulkily, 'Daddy sent her away.'

'Oh Robert! don't tell lies!' says his sister, shocked.

'It's true. He sent her away because she was bad and made him cross, and if she was here now she'd punish you.'

'No she wouldn't. Daddy wouldn't let her. You know what he did last time she punished me.'

There is a pause.

'What did he do?' asks Marty, his curiosity aroused.

'He smacked her,' says Lizzie, with smug simplicity, to which Robert adds with venom:

'He hit her on the face till she bled and the next day her eye was all purple and puffed up.'

Marty's face hangs in horror – 'He hit her?'

'She was bad and he said if it wasn't for her always saying and doing the wrong thing he'd have been on the board years ago, and now she's gone, he'll probably be on the board very soon,' says Robert, hesitating a moment before he adds, 'Doesn't your father ever hit your mother?'

Lizzie stares at her brother, appalled; their father specifically warned them to make no mention of Marty's father, but the tactless question has been asked, and hangs unanswered for a moment in the silence of the dim room.

'My father's dead.'

There is no audible emotion in Marty's voice, but Robert knows he has blundered into something beyond his comprehension. He looks helplessly from Marty to his sister, as if to ask her for support. But she looks at him blankly, unwilling to be conscripted to his aid or perhaps simply as dumbstruck as himself. By a kind of crude, guileless logic, Robert's mind turns to the profiteroles again. He takes one out of the bowl and offers it to Marty –

'Go on, nobody'll notice.'

A glance at his sister tells him that she does not disapprove of this ploy. Again, Marty refuses.

'Why not? don't you like them?' asks Robert.

'No, not really.' Then, feeling he has somehow earned a privilege by virtue of having been asked the indelicate question about his dead father, Marty adds:

'But can we have some of the other stuff, from the other table?'

The other two children stare at him blankly. The thought of taking what they think of as adult food, to be consumed only at meals, has never entered their minds – it is not part of their game, and they are plainly at a loss to see why anybody could possibly want to take a slice of cold ham when they weren't supposed to.

'No, you can't do that,' says Lizzie coldly.

But Marty needs to hear no words to know that he has transgressed in some small, but fatal way; that any foothold he has made in the entrance to the private world of these children has been abruptly lost. And with an only child's hypersensitivity to the intricacies of other children's affections, he senses a feeling, long familiar to him, of being gently, but irredeemably, cast out.

The process of mutual withdrawing is undelayed; Marty relapses from his brief talkativeness back into sullen silence, and the other two, no longer interested in him, drift out of the room bearing replenished dishes of crisps, closing the door a little behind them.

Marty lingers in the room, feeling an uncomfortable mood of directionless resentment descending upon him. He gazes at the table of savouries, hesitating for a moment. Then, pursing his lips, he reaches forward, takes a stuffed egg, and crams it, whole, into his mouth. It tastes good. As he chews it he remembers a time, three years ago, when his father in one of the moods of complete benevolence that came to him less and less frequently as he approached his end, took him to a Greek restaurant in Soho. He filled Marty with delicacies from a table of hors d'oeuvres, till he could eat no more, all the time giving him little sips of wine so that the warm glow of the room seemed subsumed within his own temples. He finds it difficult to think of his father – such efforts as he makes to summon up the memory of the dead man are met, more often than not, with blankness. He was aware of a general sigh of relief breathed by the friends and relatives when his father died, but he knew that, for his mother, the relief nowhere near compensated for the loss, and whether by virtue of his constant closeness with his mother, or of some real, deep-rooted affection for the man, the feelings of the mother became the feelings of the son. So, while he finds it difficult to recreate the image of his father, he returns to the task again and again, struggling for the satisfaction of an occasional fleeting vision of the heavy, bearded man hunched over a typewriter that seemed ridiculously small beneath his large hands.

But now he cannot make the vision come. His concentration is diverted by something which has been vaguely hovering behind his thoughts all evening; something which began as an unaccountable sense of unease on seeing the tense formality of Ronald's greeting of his mother, and which was silently shaping itself into a distinct, attributable emotion during the scene, just passed, with Lizzie and Robert. It is a sense of why he and his mother are here tonight, and now, as the demands of this sense to come into the foreground of his mind force the small, pale boy to abandon his efforts to summon his father's spectre, Marty feels himself overwhelmed by the sudden and fearful awareness that he is going to have Ronald for a father, and Lizzie and Robert for brother and sister. In contrast to his mother's soul-searching hesitancy about this union, Marty's attitude to it comes with the utter clarity of unswerving instinct, and the instinct tells him very simply 'no'. But the certainty of this reaction brings with it only another, more painful sense; that of his complete incapability of averting the imposition of family bonds with people for whom he has less than no affection. With the feeling of panic that attends the knowledge that one is unavoidably going to be made unhappy, Marty quits the room, in search of his mother.

As he opens the living-room door he is met by a rush of heat which, if momentarily pleasant, quickly becomes uncomfortable. The guests are still standing, but are showing signs of weakening under the excessive warmth. Handkerchiefs are being wiped across moist foreheads, layers of clothing discarded, hands stretched out to convenient ledges for support. There are too many people for the hum of conversation ever to fade entirely, but as Marty looks about for his mother, he notices how, among some of the groups of adults poised as if in earnest conversation with each other, for all the shifts of facial expression and all the throat-clearing, nothing is actually said for long moments, until the phantom of silence that hovers over them flickers on to the next group.

Marty does not immediately see his mother. He peers about, but the moist heat of the room mists up the lenses of his glasses – cool from the unheated kitchen. He takes them off to wipe them. At once all edges lose their clarity; the people in the room blur into indistinct figures, remote and meaningless, their physical presence reduced for a moment to the same level of vague irrelevance to the certainties of Marty's world as that of their motley individualities. As he polishes the lenses, certain rearrangements of grouping occur in the room so that, on replacing the glasses, among the figures that shift back into focus are those of his mother and Ronald standing close together in the far left-hand corner, apparently rapt in conversation. He moves towards them, bluntly ignoring the well-intentioned smiles beamed down upon him by the guests through whom he weaves. But he hesitates before interrupting the couple. They do not appear to notice him, although Marty knows he is standing directly in Ronald's line of vision. He wonders whether perhaps he ought not to intrude, but the idea that he could possibly be in a position wherein approaching his mother would amount to 'intrusion' only increases his anxiety. And so, abandoning all scruples, he steps forward and gives his mother's sleeve a sharp tug.

For a moment she does not respond, and Ronald, taking no notice of the boy, continues to talk to her in a low, serious tone. Marty gives the sleeve another, sharper tug, his desire for attention growing in proportion to his sense of being ignored. This time his mother places her free hand on his, in a gesture of vague reassurance. But Marty needs more than this. He tugs the sleeve again and says in a voice shrill with angry impatience:

'Mum, look at me.'

She looks down at her son with an abstracted smile.

'What is it dear?' she asks, but in a tone that does not express much concern, and her son, feeling rebuffed, makes no answer. Seeing that Hilary has acknowledged Marty, Ronald does so too and, in a voice that is intended to be jolly, asks him why he isn't helping Lizzie and Robert with the crisps. Before Marty can reply, Hilary adds, with an insensitivity that is unusual for her:

'Yes dear, do go and help the other two, Ronald and I are having a talk.'

Marty is visibly shocked by this apparent callousness. That his mother and Ronald are not 'talking', but 'having a talk', confirms his dismayed sense of things going mightily awry, and he is barely able to suppress a surge of tears that rises inside him. He turns away from the pair and wanders rather aimlessly among the guests, his only care being to avoid the glance of Bella Suzman who, he fears, is rooting to make a fuss over him. There is a growing lassitude in the room; it is getting late, and the guests are impatient to eat. Ronald, normally so attentive at these functions has, for the last fifteen or twenty minutes, neglected to fill the empty glasses, or to reshuffle the guests, so that a slight sense of premature staleness seems to have descended on the company. Lizzie and Robert have retired, bored, to an upstairs bedroom. The plates of crisps they are supposed to be passing around are lying, abandoned, on the walnut cabinet.

Marty finds himself in front of this cabinet, and notices the photographs of the Boyce family aligned above it. He gazes sulkily at the gilt-framed pictures, automatically filling and refilling his mouth with crisps as he does so. He recognizes the figure of Ronald, his hair slicked back, standing stiffly in a row with other smartly dressed young men all

present. Bella Suzman confronts him with a huge grin, and is about to talk to him, but he shoves rudely past her, and walks out of the room before she can utter.

He stands in the cool quiet of the inner hall, wondering what to do. The large mirror throws back a reflection of him looking unnaturally white. He gazes at himself until the image blurs around its edges and seems almost to dissolve. It is a fancy he has, that certain select people have the power to transform matter, and that he is being taught the secrets of the process, prior to being initiated into this mysterious élite. It is always with slight trepidation that he tries to stare his own reflection into oblivion, the fear that he will undergo some terrifying metamorphosis contending with his rational scepticism about the whole business. A noise from the top of the staircase interrupts his efforts. He looks up and sees in the gloom Robert's face protruding between two of the banister railings on the second flight of stairs. The two boys look at each other in silence for a moment, then Robert's head recedes into the shadows and Marty hears him scuffling off.

Having left the drawing-room, Marty is loath to re-enter it. But he must occupy himself somehow. He walks up and down the hallway, rapping his knuckles sharply on the radiator casing, as if in such mindless hyperactivity he might find distraction from the confused and painful images that the evening has presented to him; images which, animated by the champagne, seem now to be jostling for precedence in his bewildered mind. But he quickly becomes tired of this particular diversion. The strange mixture of petulance and anxiety that possesses him soon makes the glaring whiteness of the hall, unrelieved except by the mirror reflecting only the white doorway opposite, unbearable in its monotony. Marty walks along the corridor, towards the back of the house. There is a door on the right, beyond the back of the drawing-room, which he guesses must be a second entrance into the kitchen. He opens it and walks in. There on the table, beneath the muted arc of the suspended lamp, the evening's food still stands, the content of each bowl and dish glowing with its pristine colour. Marty is drawn irresistibly towards it. In the hush of the room, and to the boy still half-drunk from his glassful of champagne, the food has all the power of attraction that an open coffer of Inca gold and jewels might have for the first traveller to penetrate its secret vault. And it is with something of the guilty delight of such a traveller that Marty begins to consume his treasure.

His intention, at first, is just to have a little taste; he will limit himself to one item, or perhaps two. The question is which two? After a moment's deliberation he settles on the beef and the potato salad. He selects a slice of beef from the bloodiest end of the dishful, and pushes it, whole, into his mouth. As he chews it, savouring the juice imparted from its fibres, he dips two fingers into the bowl of potato salad, and scoops out a big yellow mound of the stuff which, after he has swallowed the beef, he promptly crams into his mouth.

That dispensed with, and the taste of raw beef and mayonnaise lingering so pleasantly on his tongue, it occurs to Marty that nobody will know the difference if he has just a little taste of everything. Accordingly, he begins a gastronomic tour of the whole table. First he dips his fingers into the taramasalata, delighting in its fishy, oily, essence. Then he broaches the yoghurt and cucumber salad, finding it a little dull in comparison, so that he has to return for another taste of the taramasalata to restore that original delight. Next, in quick succession, a slice of dressed tomato, another stuffed egg, a fingerful of the delicate avocado mousse, the largest, thickest slice of ham, and the flesh of a green olive the size of a plum, all disappear down his throat. He pauses a moment to allow the mingled flavours time to release their aromas fully in his mouth. His enjoyment is marred a little by the anguish that still nags at him, and by a faint feeling of nausea that always follows when he drinks alcohol. But he concentrates on his business all the more purposefully, in an effort to dispel these distractions. He deems the rice salad too plain to be worth bothering with, so that all that remains for his attention is the bowl of cold chicken.

This poses a slight moral problem for Marty: the pieces of chicken are a little too large for his conscience to turn a blind eye to; moreover, they will produce evidence, in the form of gnawed bones, which will need to be removed. He tentatively dips a finger into the bowl, and tastes the sauce. The combination of cream, tarragon, black cherries, and burnt almonds, is altogether new to him, and its light, sweet freshness holds him, for a second, in utter possession. All his scruples about taking the chicken vanish immediately, and, selecting a piece of breast and wing, he proceeds to tear at the soft white meat, until there is nothing left but sinew and bones. These he places on the table, next to the olive stone, meaning to dispose of them in a minute.

First, however, he must have something more to drink. There are some uncorked bottles of what looks like red wine on the sideboard by the washing machine. Marty steps over, and picks one up. He takes a mouthful straight from the bottle, swallows half of it, but as the bitter flavour registers on his tongue, he is suddenly incapable of swallowing the rest, and in a spasm of disgust he spits it out. He looks in horror at the splattered red stain at his feet, but the desire to clear his mouth of the bitter taste of the retsina presses more urgently than the problem of clearing up the mess. He swills out his mouth with water, but the bitterness will not wash away. He returns to the table, thinking that the taste of something stronger than the wine might do the trick. A large scoop of the cucumber and yoghurt salad seems to make things better. But to make sure, Marty helps himself to another slice of ham, and very quickly he finds himself unable to resist making another tour of the table.

He is vaguely aware of somebody moving about in the next door room, the dining-room, that leads in turn to the drawing-room. But while he senses danger, he is too deeply engaged in his private orgy to retreat; it is as if he is bound to a task, the exact purpose of which he can only half comprehend, but which he knows to be connected with the feelings of jealousy and despair that the evening has stirred up within him. So there is something a little manic, this time, about the way in which Marty picks from dish to dish. The way he thrusts his hands into the food and back into his mouth seems exaggerated, as if he is investing each gesture with some passionate and private significance – and this suggestion is strengthened by the fact that he is muttering something as he eats. The actual words are unintelligible, lost in the grunts and gulps with which he consumes the food, but their tone is unmistakably malevolent. In fact, most of the muttering does not consist of words at all; Marty is losing himself in a private fantasy of denunciation against Ronald and his children, and the sounds he is making are, on the whole, no more than a kind of musical accompaniment to his mental maledictions. And these, too, have no articulate shape; the growing violence of the boy's reaction against his host has distilled itself into an antipathy that is too pure to need words for its expression.

The door from the dining-room opens.

Marty, his back to the door, and his concentration completely absorbed in wrapping a piece of avocado-mousse-coated beef around a chicken drumstick, does not hear the click of the handle. But he does hear, a moment later, a shocked voice cry out, 'Jesus Christ!' as Ronald takes in the sound and sight of the small boy muttering, and stooped over a buffet table covered in a debris of bones, olive stones, pieces of fat, half-eaten eggs, and unidentifiable blobs of dropped or discarded food.

Marty swings around and stares, terrified, into Ronald's face. But this face, unlike the face of Robert between the banister railings, does not disappear when stared at. Instead, it advances slowly towards Marty, fixing the boy's eyes with an expression of hopeless anger. Marty backs off to the other side of the table. The man approaches. He is breathing heavily, as if strangled by some violent seizure struggling within him. His prominent Adam's apple is jerking up and down in ugly spasms, and his eyes move slowly back and forth between the ruined feast and the culprit cowering on the other side of the table. And Marty gazes back in appalled fascination at this metamorphosed version of the suave Ronald from the drawing-room. Gazes at him, held to the table as if cornered, not by any physical boundary, but by the enthralled terror a victim has for its predator. Suddenly some tensile string, which seems to hold the two apart as much as it draws them together, snaps; Ronald shouts something abusive but indistinct at Marty, and flinging his hand up behind him, lunges it forward, aiming for the boy's head across the table. Marty dodges and escapes all but a flick of fingertip across his hair. But he gives a sharp, piercing yelp of shock as he does so. Ronald is infuriated by this evasion of his punishment. He seems bereft of all sense not only of propriety, but also of dignity, for now, instead of cooling off and sending the boy out with a sharp ticking off, he begins to stalk round the table after Marty. The boy contrives to stay on the opposite side of the table, but his normal pallor is now visibly increased by fear.

There is a sound of movement in the next-door room. Marty stops running and looks abruptly towards the door, but Ronald hears neither the sound of the movement nor the sound of the door opening. Nor, for an instant, does he see the incredulous faces of Hilary and the other half-dozen guests who have run to the source of the scream that pierced into the drawing-room, to be met by the spectacle of their host with his back to them, dodging from side to side in an effort to catch the little boy on the other side of the table. But Ronald quickly senses their presence, and turns about to face them. There is a moment of silence; the guests have still not quite comprehended the meaning of what they behold. Ronald, too, is trying to find a meaning for it, dazedly re-living the evening in search for a clue.

Briefly, a thought takes shape in his mind, offering itself as a kind of answer; it is that this horrible child, who apparently cares nothing for the consequences of his actions, will one day turn into a Hector, dining at the table of those whom he despises, and that Hector will one day turn into a version of him, Ronald, himself, and that they are all three inextricably linked together as different phases in the same process of atrophy. But the thought eludes him as he grasps it, and the actuality of the dim room, the guests silently staring at him, and the boy behind the table, once more impinges on his consciousness. For a moment he has a fancy that he can laugh the whole thing off – pretend that he and Marty were only fooling around. But a look at the boy quickly tells him that this exit has been closed. There is something very peculiar in Marty's expression; the sheer whiteness of his face is now touched with an ominous green. Ronald notices that he is swallowing compulsively, and with a twinge of disgust, the man realizes what is about to happen. He steps back, appalled, as Marty lurches forward, still looking intently at him, opens his mouth slowly as if making a huge, exaggerated smile, and then emits a miasma of yellow vomit that descends in a splatter across the dishes on the table.

There is a general gasp from the guests at the door, and Ronald turns away in despair from this final seal on the doom he has felt governing the evening from the beginning. He looks deflated and miserable, like a man who knows he has lost.

Hilary walks forward to her son and gently wipes around his mouth with a tissue.

'Come on dear, I'll take you home,' she says to him. And taking his hand, she leads him out of the room, bowing her head and murmuring an almost inaudible apology to Ronald as she passes him. At the doorway Marty, still holding his mother's hand, hangs back and turns around. He looks up at Ronald, his limp hair falling back behind his ears. A smile forms itself on his face, and, as he turns finally to go, he shifts his glasses up the bridge of his nose in a private, but unmistakable, gesture of victory.

Brian McCabe

TABLE D'HÔTE

BRIAN McCABE was born in 1951 in Edinburgh, where he now lives and works. He has published two collections of poetry, and his short stories and poems have appeared in various periodicals and anthologies. He was awarded a writer's bursary by the Scottish Arts Council in 1980.

1. Hors d'oeuvres

Maria sits opposite Eric, not drinking her wine.

She has raised her glass and now she holds it there, just a little below her chin. Soon she'll drink, or put the glass back down on the table, but not yet. For the moment she'll go on looking across the table at Eric, watch him as he fidgets with his glass, his serviette and his knife. He wishes to avoid Maria's blue, astonished eyes.

– *How did it happen? Be honest, Eric.*

Now the hand can resume its mission, tilting the glass as it carries it to the mouth. Maria's lips take the rim of the glass at last, the more eagerly for having been made to wait. She drinks.

Eric sits opposite Maria, not drinking his wine.

He is looking down into his glass. He tilts the glass from side to side, making his reflected face change shape. In the red wine his features loom and distort. Drunk – was that how it happened? He looks up at Maria, for a moment confronts that blue, candid stare. Be honest.

– *I met her. I kept meeting her, bumping into her.*

Eric's hands begin a restless, evasive gesture above the flowers, the little vase of flowers on the restaurant table. When Maria looks at the hands, the hands begin to feel foolish. They catch hold of one another, retreat behind the flowers – but no, they can't hide there. At length Eric knits the fingers of his two hands together and places them on his place-mat, where he'll endeavour to make them stay. His head is bowed, and all in all it looks very much as if Eric might be about to say grace. *For what we are about to receive* ... that's how it happened, those restless hands.

– *One night I met her at a party, a party at Frank's.*

Cleverly Eric pauses to let the name resonate. If he were to think aloud now he would say: *Frank – remember him, Maria? The one you said had hairy shoulders.* Instead he pauses, sniffs at the bouquet of the wine, takes a civilized sip, then throws his head back and drains the upturned glass.

Maria, meanwhile, watches his Adam's apple pulsate. It reminds her, oddly, of a fish – the opening and closing of gills. When Eric puts down his glass she sees the mouth – it pouts, smacks its lips, smiles. She finds herself addressing Eric's teeth:

– *How long ago was this?*

Eric's smile becomes less than a smile, then vanishes. The lips now form an O-shape, as if preparing themselves for that vowel:

– *Only a few weeks ago. When you were in London, and –*

And so Eric, wearily, recounts the events by which he and Lillian became lovers. How they met that night at Frank's party, danced for a time together, drank far too much wine, retired to the room being used for coats in order to smoke a little joint and talk about ... but what was it they talked about – relationships? Occasionally he glances at Maria, and from the sceptical look in her eyes it is clear that none of this explains how anything happened – but then how is he to convey it? The atmosphere of lust and romance, the tacit intimacy behind the sordid procedure. Especially in a restaurant and besides – how the memory dissembles! Because that night wasn't the night, not the night that he and Lillian.

Eric interrupts his narrative to pick at his teeth with a toothpick, though the hors d'oeuvres haven't yet arrived. He extricates a morsel of breakfast, examines it closely, then discards. To avoid Maria's eyes he stares into the alcove beyond her shoulder, where the ornamental mirrors on the wall slice his image into two disparate halves. By moving his head a little this way and that, he plays at making his face fragment and then reform. Best keep it simple.

– *Then I went back to her place for coffee. And.*

Eric's hands come to life again: one tugs a cigarette from the packet, while the other swoops for the bottle and, catching it, offers it up to

Maria. Maria's hand holds out her glass, while Eric's hand tilts the bottle
and pours. Maria's other hand lights the lighter and offers the flame to
Eric's other hand, the hand with the cigarette. His hand steadies hers as
he takes the light. Both watch with distrust the hands – which go on
serving one another regardless, parting and coming together, regardless
of how it happened.

Maria, exhaling two jets of blue smoke from her nostrils, begins to
examine her fingernails impatiently. Then, realizing that the story – this
tale of the unexpected: 'How Eric And Lillian Happened' – is lacking still
its dénouement, she decides to prompt the teller:

– *Is she good in bed?*

Eric spills a little wine as he puts down his glass. He studies his hands,
the cigarette, the red stain growing on the white tablecloth. He smiles
sorrowfully at his drink, not wishing to lie to Maria. Reluctant, also, to
be honest. His one-eyed reflection stares up at him from the wine, a
gloomy fish. Eric shrugs his shoulders.

– *Yes.*

Maria begins to suffer.

2. Main Course – a choice of EITHER:

Sooner or later someone will have to say something. The hors d'oeuvres,
indifferent though they were, have been eagerly consumed. The wine, too,
has come in useful, and Eric has already ordered a second bottle of the
same. And everything is going smoothly but for the fact that silence has
joined the two at table. On the one hand Maria ought to say something
since it is, strictly speaking, her turn. On the other hand Eric feels that he
ought to say something – if only to qualify that fateful *yes*. A little small-
talk is all that is required, yet neither Eric nor Maria are able, it seems, to
provide it. At the table adjacent quite the contrary situation has
developed: a young couple, having opted for the *à la carte* menu, now
discuss animatedly which dishes they ought to select. But then there are
so very many to choose from, and clearly there is so much to talk about,
that the young man calls to the waiter and orders a bottle of champagne
to be going on with. The young lady expresses her delight by blowing the
young man a little kiss over the table, and he responds by taking her hand
in his and squeezing it the way a hand ought to be squeezed – firmly but
gently, of course. Maria, reflecting upon the fact that she and Frank,

during their brief but exhilarating time together, dined out only once, decides to break the silence by asking Eric:

– *Eric, how often have you and Lillian.*

But Eric averts his eyes to see the waiter at his side, presenting the second bottle for inspection. Eric nods, smiles. Carefully then the waiter unpeels the seal, lays the bottle down upon the table, begins the slow ritual of uncorking the wine.

– *Everything all right sir?*

– *Uh huh.*

Easing the cork soundlessly from the bottle, with neither Eric nor Maria caring to disturb the silence, the waiter proceeds to refill each of the glasses. At length he lays the bottle down between them and, before he departs, makes a few small alterations to the arrangement of the objects on the table – the little vase of flowers a little more into the centre, the ashtray a little more to the side, the pepper and salt a little closer together. He makes a slight bow before he turns to depart. Eric nods, smiles. Alone together again, Eric and Maria pick up their glasses in unison and sample the second bottle. It tastes better than the first, and Eric looks at his glass appreciatively as he says:

– *Slept together? A few times, quite a few.*

He picks up his knife and tries to balance it on his finger, but it tilts this way and that precariously. He looks forgetfully at Maria, pities her – sipping with distaste her wine, frowning slightly, twisting a lock of her hair between two fingers. She appears so forlorn, suddenly, that within himself Eric feels an irresistible rush of affection and regret. Regrettably, his knife rebounds off the side-plate and clangs to the floor. The couple at the adjacent table look over, briefly, then look away. Eric dives, begins to search around Maria's feet. Retrieving his knife and on the way back up, he is stunned momentarily by the apparition, between skirt and stocking top, of one bright, corallaceous thigh.

Maria looks with pity at the bald spot on the crown of Eric's head as he surfaces with the knife. His face flushed, his breathing harsh, for a moment Eric looks old, exhausted. Maria finds herself offering him a cigarette, and though the question she asks is a difficult one, the tone of her voice is warm and consolatory:

– *Are you in love with her, Eric?*

Eric does not know, or is unwilling to state, the answer. He looks over his shoulder towards the kitchen – surely the main course must be on its way by now. He scratches his chin impatiently, rubs one of his eyes, makes the most of blowing his nose, but no – it still hasn't come. He picks up his knife, puts it down again, then hazards a kind of guess:

– *I'm fond of her. I don't know . . .*

His hand goes for the bottle, picks it up and waves it around a little – a gay gesture, but done with sorrow. Maria offers her empty glass, and as it is refilled her wrist begins to sag with the weight of the wine.

– *You make it sound like a misfortune.*

Eric manages to smile and frown simultaneously at this acute observation, but when the smile goes the frown remains, and it is with a bitter curl of the lips that he replies:

– *Isn't it?*

As if to reassure herself that love need not be a misfortune, Maria glances briefly at the couple adjacent. The conversation has paused, both being engrossed in their avocados, but somehow they give the impression that even silence is a kind of sharing. She turns to Eric, watches him smoke his cigarette – how he prevaricates even with that: worrying at the ashtray with it, rolling it around between his fingers, tapping his lips with the tip . . .

– *So what are you going to do?*

Eric's lips droop to the rim of the glass. As he gulps the wine a thin trickle escapes from the corner of his mouth and meanders down his chin. He dabs at his face with the paper serviette, shrugs his shoulders.

– *I'm not sure . . . what to do.*

Eric takes the paper serviette and begins to do some origami. He makes a triangular fold. Perhaps a little boat. His fingers fidget with the sail, tugging and pressing. When it is finished, he places it in the little harbour between his knife and his fork. Maria watches Eric's thoughtless finger push the little boat out of the harbour, around the salt-cellar lighthouse, out into the open table. Looking away, she sees that the waiter is now on his way to the table and yes, the main course has come at last. She waits until the waiter is present at the table before she addresses Eric:

– *Sooner or later, you'll have to decide . . .*

And as the waiter lays out the clean plates he once again inquires:

– *Everything all right sir?*

– *Uh huh.*

Eric begins to suffer.

3. Dessert OU fromage

Maria is very disappointed.

She has moved back from the table and now she sits almost sideways in her chair – her legs crossed away from Eric, her body averted. She sips at her wine, then holds the glass in her lap. When Maria looks down, her heavy hair swings over her face hiding her profile. She looks down now, frowning at her wine.

Eric is very disappointed.

The *boeuf bordelaise* lacked garlic, among other things, notably *boeuf*, and was really a kind of non-committal stew. Placing his knife and fork in the position that means it's finished, he now sets aside his plate and turns to the waiting trifle. He dips his spoon into the cream, moves it around a little, then leans towards Maria and pleads with the hair:
– *At least I've been honest with you.*
Maria looks up, but not at Eric. Her glance goes to the Ideal Couple, who are now beginning their steaks. Their conversation, less punctuated now by laughter, has obviously moved on to deeper, more serious topics: the young lady is listening intently, between mouthfuls of choice fillet, to what her escort is saying; the young man appears both elegant and sincere as he talks, and from his gestures alone it is possible to assume that he is well beyond all petty considerations and is already drawing analogies, guiding the discourse towards its proper and highly interesting conclusion. Maria drains her glass and puts it back down in her lap. She looks down, hides in the hair.
– *Maria, this is ridiculous.*
This time she does glance at Eric, but it is over her shoulder, virtually, and her eyes lack interest. She raises her eyebrows slightly:
– *Mm?*
When Eric throws his hands out to either side of his pudding, expressing his exasperation, his left wrist collides with the bottle. He watches in wonder as the wine blooms huge in the white linen, a beautiful blood-flower. His hand, acting on its own initiative, rights the bottle before it rolls off the edge of the table.
– *Christ, I'll order another.*
He pours the remaining inch of wine into his glass, then leans over the

chair-back and waves the empty bottle at the waiter. The waiter who isn't there. He turns back to face Maria, missing the table with his elbow.

– *I mean the way you're sitting, Maria. How can I talk to your profile?*

Reluctantly then Maria turns to face him, moves her chair forward a little, puts her empty glass on the table and begins to unwrap the little triangle of camembert which turned out to be the *fromage.* Her voice has become almost supernaturally quiet:

– *We can't afford another bottle.*

Dejectedly she collects the dirty cutlery and the plates, then lays them down over the red stain. They cover some of it, at least. She puts both her elbows on the table, presses her fingers into the roots of her hair, whispers:

– *Eric, don't you love me any more?*

Eric brings his glass down on top of the little glass ashtray. The glass against the glass makes an unfortunate noise, and the couple adjacent turn their heads and stare in unison. Eric tries an apologetic smile. They look away, resume their togetherness. Eric plays with his trifle and frowns as he considers this new riddle.

– *I think so . . . yes.*

A barely perceptible quiver passes over Maria's lips and chin, then a deeper tremor makes her cheeks shudder and her eyes close tightly. She raises her glass, holds it there – just a little below her chin. Evidently it is empty.

– *Maria, of course I—*

But of course it is too late: already she has bowed her head as the tears come, darting quickly from her eyes, racing one another down the cheeks, dripping from the curve of the chin. Grey spots appear here and there on the tablecloth as Maria, discreetly, weeps.

Eric offers her – oddly enough, still intact – his little paper boat.

– *Of course I do.*

He looks around to see who's looking. No one, apparently, has noticed and it is with a feeling of gratitude that Eric sends his hand over the table to pat Maria's bare arm. Of course he does, if the question should arise, love her.

Maria sniffs, dabs her face with the crumpled yacht, then sits up and pushes the hair back from her face. Seeing the waiter approach, she picks up her handbag and excuses herself from table.

– Coffee sir?
– Uh huh, please.

When the waiter collects the dirty dishes, Eric stutters an apology for the Red Sea underneath. The waiter makes a formal, polite comment to the effect that it is nothing, then departs. Unwilling to face his schizoid twin in the alcove, Eric goes to the gents.

4. Coffee (VAT not inclusive)

Maria has lost her self-respect.

Standing before the wash-hand basin, she searches for it in her bag. She finds a hairbrush, her mascara and the little rectangular mirror which, though too small for the job, might present her with a less literal self-portrait than the one she sees behind the taps. Even so she can see quite clearly that her eyelids are red-rimmed and swollen, and that the mascara has trailed down her cheeks. Wondering if she is still attractive, Maria stoops to the running water and cups it in her hands. After splashing her face with it, she starts work on the disguise.

Eric has lost his self-respect.

Washing his hands, he searches for it in the mirror. He tries on various expressions, eyes his image from a number of angles. He attempts a broad, confident grin and his image leers back at him quickly. Sincerity comes next, and this time Eric has to avert his eyes from the doleful countenance which reproves him. He tries on a few ugly faces: grotesque, gargoyle-like pouts; cross-eyed consternations; one doleful Frankenstein mask; demonic, wicked grins. Drying his fingers on a wet towel, he wonders if he is still an upright citizen. He zips up his flies.

Out in the restaurant, meanwhile, everything has been going on smoothly until now. The waiter has taken the opportunity, during Eric-and-Maria's absence, to clear up the debris they have strewn all over the table ... and already he has delivered the coffee, the bill. But now, suddenly, something dreadful is occurring at the table adjacent. The young man, his fork half-way to his mouth, can hardly believe that it is really happening ... but yes, it really is: she has stood up so abruptly that the chair has overturned. From her accent and appearance it is clear to the entire populace of the restaurant that she must be a well-brought-up, well-educated girl but ... all that has gone, suddenly, and she is banging her fist hard on the table and shouting, really shouting at the young man:

– *Bastard! You fucking ... swine!*

A unanimous silence. Then, perhaps because the swear-words were so well-pronounced, a snigger. Then a gasp from another table, and a low-toned comment from another. The young lady, having burst loudly into tears, refuses to be pacified by either the waiter or the bastard-swine. Another waiter appears with the coats, and it is clear that the young man is being requested to leave – after, of course, settling the bill. The young man says something quietly to his young lady as he takes out his wallet, but she won't wait another moment: breaking free from the hands which seek to hold and subdue her, she grabs her coat and her bag and marches adamantly out. The bastard-swine pays the bill and follows her, feeling the eyes on his back, sensing the theories being put forward at the tables around – though he and only he can know what exactly was the cause of such an unfortunate outburst.

It all happens so quickly that Eric and Maria, returning to their table from the toilets, are unaware that anything has gone wrong. Indeed, they are mystified by the waiter's apology. But gradually, by the general atmosphere and the scandalized chatter going on all around, they are able to surmise that something out of the ordinary has taken place at the adjacent table – though what it was, exactly, they can't imagine.

Eric takes out his cheque-book, turns the bill over and looks for the name of the restaurant. Underneath the name he notices that there is a brief, italicized message, which reads:

'*We hope you have enjoyed your meal. If you have, please come again soon ... and tell all your friends about it!*'

And as he writes the cheque Eric yawns repeatedly, and between the yawns there are fragments of a question:

– *Want to ... go to my place ... or yours?*

Maria's lips turn down at the corners with sincere disgust. She stirs the skin into her coffee, rattling the spoon in the cup.

– *How about both?*

Eric looks up from his half-made signature, puzzled for a moment.

Then, realizing what Maria means, he proceeds with the surname. As the waiter takes the bill away, she adds:

– *Or maybe you'd like to call on Lillian?*

Eric shakes his head and moves around uneasily in his seat, surprised that the suggestion has arisen, and impatient to leave the restaurant. And now that the bill has been paid, and though Eric and Maria may yet have much to discuss, there is really nothing else to do but leave. And clearly they will have to go somewhere.

Bernard Mac Laverty

LIFE
DRAWING

BERNARD MAC LAVERTY was born in Belfast in 1942. He worked for ten years as a medical laboratory technician at Queen's University, Belfast, before studying English at the same university. He then moved to Edinburgh to teach in a comprehensive school and he currently lives on the Isle of Islay, off the west coast of Scotland. He has also written *Lamb*, a novel; *Secrets and Other Stories*, which won a Scottish Arts Council Book Award in 1977; and a book for very young children, *A Man in Search of a Pet*, which he also illustrated.

After darkness fell and he could no longer watch the landscape from the train window, Liam Diamond began reading his book. He had to take his feet off the seat opposite and make do with a less comfortable position to let a woman sit down. She was equine and fifty and he didn't give her a second glance. To take his mind off what was to come he tried to concentrate. The book was a study of the Viennese painter Egon Schiele who, it seemed, had become so involved with his thirteen-year-old girl models that he ended up in jail. Augustus John came to mind – 'To paint someone you must first sleep with them' – and he smiled. Schiele's portraits, mostly of himself, exploded off the page beside the text, distracting him. All sinew and gristle and distortion. There was something decadent about them, like Soutine's pictures of hanging sides of beef.

Occasionally he would look up to see if he knew where he was but saw only the darkness and himself reflected from it. The street-lights of small towns showed more and more snow on the roads the farther north he got. To stretch he went to the toilet and noticed the faces as he passed between the seats. Like animals being transported. On his way back he saw a completely different set of faces but he knew they looked the same. He hated train journeys, seeing so many people, so many houses. It made him realize he was part of things whether he liked it or not. Seeing so many unknown people through their back windows, standing outside shops, walking the streets, moronically waving from level crossings – they grew amorphous and repulsive. They were going about their static lives while he had a sense of being on the move. And yet he knew he was not. At some stage any one of those people might travel past his flat on a train and see him in the act of pulling his curtains. The thought depressed him so much that he could no longer read. He leaned his head against the window and, although he had his eyes closed, he did not sleep.

The snow, thawed to slush and quickly re-frozen, crackled under his feet and made walking difficult. For a moment he was not sure which was the house. In the dark he had to remember it by number and shade his eyes against the yellow glare of the sodium street-lights to make out the figures on the small terrace doors. He saw 56 and walked three houses further along. The heavy wrought-iron knocker echoed in the hallway as it had always done. He waited, looking up at the semicircular fan light. Snow was beginning to fall again, tiny flakes swirling in the corona of light. He was about to knock again or look to see if they had got a bell when he heard shuffling from the other side of the door. It opened a few inches and a white-haired old woman peered out. Her hair was held in place by a hair-net a shade different from her own hair colour. It was one of the Miss Harts but for the life of him he couldn't remember which. She looked at him, not understanding.

'Yes?'

'I'm Liam,' he said.

'Oh thanks be to goodness for that. We're glad you could come.' Then she shouted over her shoulder, 'It's Liam.'

She shuffled backwards opening the door and admitting him. Inside she tremulously shook his hand, then took his bag and set it on the ground. Like a servant she took his coat and hung it on the hall-stand. It was still in the same place and the hallway was still a dark electric yellow.

'Bertha's up with him now. You'll forgive us sending the telegram to the College but we thought you would like to know,' said Miss Hart. If Bertha was up the stairs then she must be Maisie.

'Yes, yes you did the right thing,' said Liam. 'How is he?'

'Poorly. The doctor has just left – he had another call. He says he'll not last the night.'

'That's too bad.'

By now they were standing in the kitchen. The fireplace was black and empty. One bar of the dished electric fire took the chill off the room and no more.

'You must be tired,' said Miss Hart. 'It's such a journey. Would you like a cup of tea? I tell you what, just you go up now and I'll bring you your tea when it's ready. All right?'

'Yes thank you.'

When he reached the head of the stairs she called after him, 'And send Bertha down.'

Bertha met him on the landing. She was small and withered and her head reached to his chest. When she saw him she started to cry and reached out her arms to him saying, 'Liam, poor Liam.' She nuzzled against him weeping. 'The poor old soul,' she kept repeating. Liam was embarrassed, feeling the thin arms of this old woman he hardly knew about his hips.

'Maisie says you have to go down now,' he said, separating himself from her and patting her crooked back. He watched her go down the stairs, one tottering step at a time, gripping the banister, her rheumatic knuckles standing out like limpets.

He paused at the bedroom door and for some reason flexed his hands before he went in. He was shocked to see the state his father was in. He was now almost completely bald except for some fluffy hair above his ears. His cheeks were sunken, his mouth hanging open. His head was back on the pillow so that the strings of his neck stood out.

'Hello, it's me, Liam,' he said when he was at the bed. The old man opened his eyes flickeringly. He tried to speak. Liam had to lean over but failed to decipher what was said. He reached out and lifted his father's hand in a kind of wrong handshake.

'Want anything?'

His father signalled by a slight movement of his thumb that he needed something. A drink? Liam poured some water and put the glass to the old man's lips. Arcs of scum had formed at the corners of his sagging mouth. Some of the water spilled on to the sheet. It remained for a while in droplets before sinking into dark circles.

'Was that what you wanted?' The old man nodded no. Liam looked around the room trying to see what his father could want. It was exactly as he had remembered it. In twenty years he hadn't changed the wallpaper, yellow roses looping on an umber trellis. He lifted a straight-backed chair and drew it up close to the bed. He sat with his elbows on his knees, leaning forward.

'How do you feel?'

The old man made no response and the question echoed around and around the silence in Liam's head.

Maisie brought in tea on a tray, closing the door behind her with her elbow. Liam noticed that two red spots had come up on her cheeks. She spoke quickly in an embarrassed whisper, looking back and forth between the dying man and his son.

'We couldn't find where he kept the teapot so it's just a tea-bag in a cup. Is that all right? Will that be enough for you to eat? We sent out for a tin of ham, just in case. He had nothing in the house at all, God love him.'

'You've done very well,' said Liam. 'You shouldn't have gone to all this trouble.'

'If you couldn't do it for a neighbour like Mr Diamond – well? Forty-two years and there was never a cross word between us. A gentleman we always called him, Bertha and I. He kept himself to himself. Do you think he can hear us?' The old man did not move.

'How long has he been like this?' asked Liam.

'Just three days. He didn't bring in his milk one day and that's not like him, y'know. He'd left a key with Mrs Rankin, in case he'd ever lock himself out again – he did once, the wind blew the door shut – and she came in and found him like this in the chair downstairs. He was frozen, God love him. The doctor said it was a stroke.'

Liam nodded, looking at his father. He stood up and began edging the woman towards the bedroom door.

'I don't know how to thank you, Miss Hart. You've been more than good.'

'We got your address from your brother. Mrs Rankin phoned America on Tuesday.'

'Is he coming home?'

'He said he'd try. She said the line was as clear as a bell. It was like talking to next door. Yes, he said he'd try but he doubted it very much.' She had her hand on the door knob. 'Is that enough sandwiches?'

'Yes thanks, that's fine.' They stood looking at one another awkwardly. Liam fumbled in his pocket. 'Can I pay you for the ham ... and the telegram?'

'I wouldn't dream of it,' she said. 'Don't insult me now, Liam.'

He withdrew his hand from his pocket and smiled his thanks to her.

'It's late,' he said. 'Perhaps you should go now and I'll sit up with him.'

'Very good. The priest was here earlier and gave him ...' she groped for the word with her hands.

'Extreme Unction?'

'Yes. That's twice he has been in three days. Very attentive. Sometimes I think if our ministers were half as good...'

'Yes but he wasn't what you would call gospel greedy.'

'He was lately,' she said.

'Changed times.'

She half turned to go and said, almost coyly, 'I'd hardly have known you with the beard.' She looked up at him, nodding her head in disbelief. He was trying to make her go, standing close to her but she skirted round him and went over to the bed. She touched the old man's shoulder.

'I'm away now, Mr Diamond. Liam is here. I'll see you in the morning,' she shouted into his ear. Then she was away.

Liam heard the old ladies' voices in the hallway below, then the slam of the front door. He heard the crackling of their feet over the frozen slush beneath the window. He lifted the tray off the chest of drawers and on to his knee. He hadn't realized it but he was hungry. He ate the sandwiches and the piece of fruit-cake, conscious of the chewing noise he was making with his mouth in the silence of the bedroom. There was little his father could do about it now. They used to have the most terrible rows about it. You'd have thought it was a matter of life and death. At table he had sometimes trembled with rage at the boys' eating habits, at their greed as he called it. At the noises they made 'like cows getting out of muck'. After their mother had left them he took over the responsibility for everything. One night as he served sausages from the pan Liam, not realizing the filthy mood he was in, made a grab. His father in a sudden downward thrust jabbed the fork he had been using to cook the sausages into the back of Liam's hand.

'Control yourself.'

Four bright beads of blood appeared as Liam stared at them in disbelief.

'They'll remind you to use your fork in future.'

He was sixteen at the time.

The bedroom was cold and when he finally got round to drinking his tea it was tepid. He was annoyed that he couldn't heat it by pouring more. His feet were numb and felt damp. He went downstairs and put on his overcoat and brought the electric fire up to the bedroom, switching on both bars. He sat huddled over it, his fingers fanned out, trying to get warm. When the second bar was switched on there was a clicking noise and the smell of burning dust. He looked over at the bed but there was no movement.

'How do you feel?' he said again, not expecting an answer. For a long time he sat staring at the old man whose breathing was audible but quiet – a kind of soft whistling in his nose. The alarm clock, its face bisected with a crack, said twelve thirty. Liam checked it against the red figures of his digital watch. He stood up and went to the window. Outside the roofs tilted at white snow-covered angles. A faulty gutter hung spikes of icicles. There was no sound in the street but from the main road came the distant hum of a late car that faded into silence.

He went out on to the landing and into what was his own bedroom. There was no bulb when he switched the light on so he took one from the hall and screwed it into the shadeless socket. The bed was there in the corner with its mattress of blue stripes. The lino was the same with its square pock-marks showing other places the bed had been. The cheap green curtains that never quite met on their cord still did not meet.

He moved to the wall cupboard by the small fireplace and had to tug at the handle to get it open. Inside the surface of everything had gone opaque with dust. Two old radios, one with a fretwork face, the other more modern with a tuning dial showing such places as Hilversum, Luxembourg, Athlone; a Dansette record player with its lid missing and its arm bent back showing wires like severed nerves and blood vessels; the empty frame of the smashed glass picture was still there; several umbrellas, all broken. And there was his box of poster paints. He lifted it out and blew off the dust.

It was a large Quality Street tin; he eased the lid off, bracing it against his stomach muscles. The colours in the jars had shrunk to hard discs. Viridian Green, Vermillion, Jonquil Yellow. At the bottom of the box he found several sticks of charcoal, light in his fingers when he lifted them, warped. He dropped them into his pocket and put the tin back into the cupboard. There was a pile of magazines and papers and beneath that again he saw his large Windsor and Newton sketch-book. He eased it out and began to look through the work in it. Embarrassment was what he felt most turning the pages, looking at the work of this schoolboy. He could see little talent in it, yet he realized he must have been good. There were several drawings of hands in red pastel which had promise. The rest of the pages were blank. He set the sketch-book aside to take with him and closed the door.

Looking round the room it had the appearance of nakedness. He crouched and looked under the bed but there was nothing there. His fingers coming in contact with the freezing lino made him aware how cold he was. His jaw was tight and he knew that if he relaxed it he would shiver. He went back to his father's bedroom and sat down.

The old man had not changed his position. He had wanted him to be a lawyer or a doctor but Liam had insisted, although he had won a scholarship to the university, on going to art college. All that summer his father tried everything he knew to stop him. He tried to reason with him:

'*Be* something. And you can carry on doing your art. Art is OK as a sideline.'

But mostly he shouted at him, 'I've heard about these art students and what they get up to. Shameless bitches prancing about with nothing on. And what sort of a job are you going to get? Drawing on pavements?' He nagged him every moment they were together about other things. Lying late in bed, the length of his hair, his outrageous appearance. Why hadn't he been like the other lads and got himself a job for the summer? It wasn't too late because he would willingly pay him if he came in and helped out in the shop.

One night, just as he was going to bed, Liam found the old framed print of cattle drinking. He had taken out the glass and had begun to paint on the glass itself with small tins of Humbrol enamel paints left over from aeroplane kits he had never finished. They produced a strange and exciting texture which was even better when the paint was viewed from the other side of the pane of glass. He sat stripped to the waist in his pyjama trousers painting a self-portrait reflected from the mirror on the wardrobe door. The creamy opaque nature of the paint excited him. It slid on to the glass, it built up, in places it ran scalloping like cinema curtains and yet he could control it. He lost all track of time as he sat with his eyes focused on the face staring back at him and the painting he was trying to make of it. It became a face he had not known, the holes, the lines, the spots. He was in a new geography.

His brother and he used to play a game looking at each other's faces upside down. One lay on his back across the bed, his head flopped over the edge reddening as the blood flooded into it. The other sat in a chair and stared at him. After a time the horror of seeing the eyes where the mouth should be, the inverted nose, the forehead gashed with red lips, would drive him to cover his eyes with his hands. 'It's your turn now,' he would say and they would change places. It was like familiar words said over and over again until they became meaningless and once he ceased to have purchase on the meaning of a word it became terrifying, an incantation. In adolescence he had come to hate his brother, could not stand the physical presence of him just as when he was lying upside down on the bed. It was the same with his father. He could not bear to touch him and yet for one whole winter when he had a bad shoulder he had to stay up late to rub him with oil of wintergreen. The old boy would sit with one hip on the bed and Liam would stand behind him massaging the stinking stuff into the white flesh of his back. The smell, the way the blubbery skin moved under his fingers, made him want to be sick. No matter how many times he washed his hands, at school the next day he would still reek of oil of wintergreen.

It might have been the smell of the Humbrol paints or the strip of light under Liam's door – whatever it was his father came in and yelled that it was half past three in the morning and what the hell did he think he was doing sitting half-naked drawing at this hour of the morning. He had smacked him full force with the flat of his hand on his bare back and, stung by the pain of it, Liam had leapt to retaliate. Then his father had started to laugh, a cold snickering laugh. 'Would you? Would you? Would you indeed?' he kept repeating with a smile pulled on his mouth and his fists bunched to knuckles in front of him. Liam retreated to the bed and his father turned on his heel and left. Thinking the incident was over Liam gritted his teeth and fists and cursed his father. He looked over his shoulder into the mirror and saw the primitive daub of his father's hand, splayed fingers outlined across his back. He heard him on the stairs and when he came back into the bedroom with the poker in his hand he felt his insides turn to water. But his father looked away from him with a sneer and smashed the painting to shards with one stroke. As he went out the door he said, 'Watch your feet in the morning.'

He had never really 'left home'. It was more a matter of going to art college in London and not bothering to come back. Almost as soon as he was away from the house his hatred for his father eased. He simply stopped thinking about him. Of late he had wondered if he was alive or dead – if he still had the shop. The only communication they had had over the years was when Liam sent him, not without a touch of vindictiveness, an invitation to some of the openings of his exhibitions.

Liam sat with his fingertips joined, staring at the old man. It was going to be a long night. He looked at his watch and it was only after two. He paced up and down the room listening to the tick of snow on the window pane. When he stopped to look down he saw it flurrying through the haloes of the street-lamps. He went into his own bedroom and brought back the sketch-book. He moved his chair to the other side of the bed so that the light fell on his page. Balancing the book on his knee he began to draw his father's head with the stick of charcoal. It made a light hiss each time a line appeared on the cartridge paper. When drawing he always thought of himself as a wary animal drinking, the way he looked up and down, up and down, at his subject. The old man had failed badly. His head scarcely dented the pillows, his cheeks were hollow and he had not been shaved for some days. Earlier when he had held his hand it had been clean and dry and light like the hand of a girl. The bedside light deepened the shadows of his face and highlighted the rivulets of veins on his temple. It was a long time since he had used charcoal and he became engrossed in the way it had to be handled and the different subleties of line he could get out of it. He loved to watch a drawing develop before his eyes.

His work had been well received and among the small Dublin art world he was much admired – justly he thought. But some critics had scorned his work as 'cold' and 'formalist' – one had written 'Like Mondrian except that he can't draw a straight line' – and this annoyed him because it was precisely what he was trying to do. He felt it unfair to be criticized for succeeding in his aims.

His father began to cough – a low, wet, bubbling sound. Liam leaned forward and touched the back of his hand gently. Was this man to blame in any way? Or had he only himself to blame for the shambles of his life? He had married once and lived with two other women. At present he was on his own. Each relationship had ended in hate and bitterness, not because of drink or lack of money or any of the usual reasons but because of a mutual nauseating dislike.

He turned the page and began to draw the old man again. The variations in tone from jet black to pale grey depending on the pressure he used fascinated him. The hooded lids of the old man's eyes, the fuzz of hair sprouting from the ear next the light, the darkness of the partially open mouth. Liam drew several more drawings, absorbed, working slowly, refining the line of each until it was to his satisfaction. He was pleased with what he had done. At art school he had loved the life class better than any other. It never ceased to amaze him how sometimes it could come just right, better than he had hoped for; the feeling that something was working through him to produce a better work than at first envisaged.

Then outside he heard the sound of an engine followed by the clinking of milk bottles. When he looked at his watch he was amazed to see that it was five thirty. He leaned over to speak to his father.

'Are you all right?'

His breathing was not audible and when Liam touched his arm it was cold. His face was cold as well. He felt for his heart, slipping his hand inside his pyjama jacket, but could feel nothing. He was dead. His father. He was dead, and the slackness of his dropped jaw disturbed his son. In the light of the lamp his dead face looked like the open-mouthed moon. Liam wondered if he should tie it up before it set. In a Pasolini film he had seen Herod's jaw being trussed and he wondered if he was capable of doing it for his father.

Then he saw himself in his hesitation, saw the lack of any emotion in his approach to the problem. He was aware of the deadness inside himself and felt helpless to do anything about it. It was why all his women had left him. One of them accused him of making love the way other people rodded drains.

He knelt down beside the bed and tried to think of something good from the time he had spent with his father. Anger and sneers and nagging was all that he could picture. He knew he was grateful for his rearing but he could not *feel* it. If his father had not been there somebody else would have done it. And yet it could not have been easy – a man left with two boys and a business to run. He had worked himself to a sinew in his tobacconist's, opening at seven in the morning to catch the workers and closing at ten at night. Was it for his boys that he worked so hard? The man was in the habit of earning and yet he never spent. He had even opened for three hours on Christmas Day.

Liam stared at the dead drained face and suddenly the mouth held in that shape reminded him of something pleasant. It was the only joke his father had ever told and to make up for the smallness of his repertoire he had told it many times, of two ships passing in mid-Atlantic. He always megaphoned his hands to tell the story.

'Where are you bound for?' shouts one captain.

'Rio – de – Janeir – o. Where are you bound for?' ·

And the other captain not to be outdone outdone yells back, 'Cork – a – lork – a – lor – io.'

When he had finished the joke he always repeated the punch-line, laughing and nodding in disbelief that something could be so funny.

'Cork – a – lork – a – lorio.'

Liam found that his eyes had filled with tears. He tried to keep them coming but they would not. In the end he had to close his eyes and a tear spilled from his left eye on to his cheek. It was small and he wiped it away with a crooked index finger.

He stood up from the kneeling position and closed the sketch-book that was lying open on the bed. He might work on them later. Perhaps a charcoal series. He walked to the window. Dawn would not be up for hours yet. In America it would be daylight and his brother would be in shirt-sleeves. He would have to wait until Mrs Rankin was up before he could phone him – and the doctor would be needed for a death certificate. There was nothing he could do at the moment, except perhaps tie up the jaw. The Miss Harts when they arrived would know everything that ought to be done.

Adam Mars-Jones

STRUCTURAL ANTHROP-OLOGY

ADAM MARS-JONES was born in 1954 and educated at Westminster, Cambridge and Virginia.

S tructural anthropology is psychoanalysis on a basis broader than the individual. Both techniques seek to discover the workings of the human mind by examining its unconscious productions, but while psychoanalysis studies patterns inside a single skull, awake or asleep, structural anthropology concentrates on the communal dream that is ritual behaviour. Then, too, psychoanalysis confines itself by and large to its own culture, while anthropology operates by preference at a distance conducive to objectivity, among tribes whose conscious carapace offers relatively little resistance to the anthropologist's scientific tools. But these are self-imposed limits, and a degree of overlap is common enough; though based in Vienna, Freud felt free to discuss the mental workings of his contemporary, Woodrow Wilson, distant in space, of his European neighbour, Leonardo da Vinci, distant in time, and of course of Oedipus, at a considerable remove of both time and space. In the same way, the techniques of structural anthropology pioneered by Lévi-Strauss can uncover much that is startling in our own culture, if applied with care and thoroughness.

But let us pass from introduction to example. Nurses in a provincial hospital recently took charge of a man who had been bizarrely punished by his wife for infidelity. She had returned unexpectedly to the family home, and could hear him misbehaving. He was engaged in sexual congress that was both noisy and enthusiastic, characteristics which had been missing for some time from his dealings with his wife. She herself made no noise, let herself out of the flat, and returned at her usual time. She cooked a fine dinner, taking care to grind up some sleeping-pills and include them in the mashed potatoes. Her husband retired early to bed, pleading tiredness, and a little later on she stripped him as he slept, and stuck his hand to his penis with Super Glue.

The doctors and nurses faced the problem of separating manual and genital flesh from their tangle, and they had moreover to improvise an arrangement to enable the patient to urinate; plastic surgery was eventually required to restore the appearance of the parts.

And there it is, a little sordid, a little amusing, a story of no great distinction, promising no great yield of insight. But this story moves faster than any story can on its own merits, it *travels* at high speed, and suddenly it is everywhere; it satisfies a need that runs unexpectedly deep, and someone can even be heard claiming it was current years ago, in another town. It is therefore a myth, even if it happened, and can be guaranteed to explain itself if asked the right questions. But its music will remain mysterious until it is struck with the subtle mallet of structural anthropology, which gives resonances priority over mere sound.

·1. Nature/Culture

The crucial opposition, as ever, is nature/culture. Sexuality is *wild*, *tamed* in marriage, revealed as *wild* all along in adultery. The dangerous animal is transformed into a social adhesive, but breaks loose again. The animal parts boiled down into glue threaten no such resurrection; hence the woman's choice of instrument for her revenge. The actual composition of glue in modern times is rarely organic, but the collective unconscious always is; it refers to the constants of human experience, and not to mere life 'as it is lived'. The collective unconscious exists independently of chronological sequence, and doesn't keep pace with developments in glue technology. Nor for that matter is a man excused by his ignorance of Greek mythology from desiring his father's death and his mother's body.

2. Limp/Stiff

The secondary axis of oppositions in our chosen myth is limp/stiff; the married man undertakes to be *stiff* with his wife, *limp* in all other contexts. Impotence in the marriage-bed and tumescence elsewhere are symmetrical threats to social order and the next generation. But here, the adulterer is punished for his criminal stiffness with *more*, with a stiffness he cannot control, for it is precisely his lack of control which is stigmatized. The betrayed woman betrays *him* to the castrating laughter of the world by parodying his virility, source of his transgression; the permanent erection she gives him nevertheless shows him to be impotent. Hardness and softness are equally laughable, equally disgusting, when they are constant pathological states, unmediated by contract and by alternation.

3. Food/Drug

The married man sacrifices excitement and variety, distraction and unpredictability, in the interests of a higher set of values; he enters an economy of duties and pleasures. He signs a contract to stop playing the field, and to start cultivating it; he must reduce his erotic options to one before he can reproduce himself in the next generation. Energy invested in marriage accrues as capital; in promiscuity it is dissipated and comes to nothing. The married man renounces sex as a drug and binds himself to a life of intimate affection, of sex as food; from this point on, his hunger will be satisfied rather than stimulated. But the adulterous husband violates the metabolism of marriage by continuing to demand excitement instead of sustenance. Very well then; the woman whose power to satisfy appetite he has scorned will retaliate by *drugging his food*. And she will make use of drugs in their narcotic rather than stimulant aspect; instead of excitement she will deliver sedation, and helplessness instead of a heightened awareness. For her, adultery is, like alcohol, a 'sedative hypnotic with paradoxical stimulation', a down that only masquerades as an up; and her revenge necessarily dramatizes her attitudes to betrayal.

4. Private/Public

When two people combine as husband and wife, and no longer define themselves as their parents' children, their changed status must be marked by a ritual; as they move from separate establishments into a shared household they pass through a kind of sacred corridor, which irreversibly differentiates the past from the future. Although they are private individuals making a private decision, they must declare it in public, and though they are drastically loosening their ties with their parents, their wedding is traditionally attended by all the people from whom they are, in effect, receding.

Whether they choose to be married in church or opt for the ceremonial minimum in front of a Registrar, their act is no less ritual, and as such it cannot simply be dropped and not mentioned again. It must be renounced; a formula must be found which symbolically inverts the ritual of binding. Even though the magic has died, the spell must be said backwards for the release of the participants. Their disenchantment must be fully enacted.

And we can see this process at work in our myth. The original ritual impels the couple through a solemn public space and towards the marriage-bed; the counter-ritual starts in that same bed, now a trap for the sinner and not a nest, and expels the guilty party towards a public space purged of all solemnity. The husband drugged in the marriage-bed is already paying the price for his transgression; having preferred excitement to security, he must abide by his choice, and forfeits safety absolutely. But there is more in store for him.

His wife's selection, for her symbolic inverse of a *church*, of a *hospital*, is a masterstroke on the part of the collective unconscious. They are respectively the homes of a mystery resistant to analysis and an analysis resistant to mystery; a suggestive darkness, and an inescapable light.

We may add in passing that only structural anthropology increases mystery in the process of explaining it. Here at last science and religion marry and settle down.

And there is a further excellence to the patterning, in that a man who has spurned his chosen bed and sought sex elsewhere, is immobilized in a bed he hasn't chosen; a bed in which the body is examined and treated clinically, without a moment's consideration for the sensual component he has rated so highly. He occupies an asexual bed, then, lying there in limbo, defined by no relationships, and sharing the premises with other transients who at least have the prospect of returning to their interrupted lives. He, however, has sought to combine freedom of action with the security of the hearth, and has been brusquely deprived of both.

5. Comedy/Tragedy

In our study of structural elements we have so far considered the glue, the sleeping-pills, the bed, and the hospital. There remain the hand and the penis. By her sarcastic conjunction of these two organs the wife insists on the comic rather than the tragic aspects of her predicament; she makes the dissolution of her marriage a matter for public laughter rather than private heartbreak. She represents her husband as caught in the act, but the act itself is ironically diminished; his posture convicts him not of adultery but self-abuse. The enforced junction of hand and penis yokes man's highest ambitions and his betraying weakness.

(It is obviously his dominant hand that she so mockingly cements in place; impossible to imagine her spoiling the symbolism by insulting the left hand of a right-hander. That would be quite foreign to the exhaustive brilliance of a mind that doesn't even know it is operating!)

She juxtaposes the opposable thumb, which was such an achievement of evolution, with the third leg – those guilty tissues which threaten to slide Man back into the swamp of undifferentiation. The woman declares the marital atrocity simply waste, the crime against herself mere self-indulgence.

In her construction of a counter-ritual the woman has developed a persona whose trademark is *the ironic fulfilment of wishes*; she has metamorphosed from one folk-tale character into another, from Captive Maiden into Witch. Her husband wants to be stiff elsewhere than in her bed? She can arrange it. He wants an adventure? She will see what she can do.

With her glue she ensures their separation, with the hardness she contrives for him she parodies his virility. But her final coup is her magical ability to use others to work her revenge; there is a superficial mercy to her actions with the tube of glue, but the surgeons must exercise their skills unstintingly. The way in which these members of the community seem to carry out the betrayed woman's commands gives the punishment an air of impersonality; the woman herself refrains from the knife, but hands him over to her agents for surgery. They collaborate in his humiliation.

The knife is in fact being used to repair damage, but this is not apparent to the victim, except at that lowermost level where words mean two opposite things (compare Freud on the binary meanings of basic words). The patient's hand *cleaves* to his penis, the doctors must *cleave* them apart again.

But the women in the Hospital are essentially more important than the men. The surgeons are predominantly male, the nurses by and large female, and it is the nurses who make up the hospital community as perceived by the patient. The doctors pay visits, but the nurses seem to live on the wards. And so the final phase of the adulterer's punishment is accomplished. With her woman's laughter his wife hands him over to the laughter of women who re-enact the transformation of the female from subservient employee to ambiguous manipulator: women who touch him without tenderness, who are intimate with him but not interested, who tend without establishing a relationship with the man in their care; who confirm his exile from a world where the female can be taken for granted, and who may even be laughing behind their hands.

What remains of our original story? Certainly nothing of the sordid or trivial; these elements have been absorbed into their opposites. And simplicity too has yielded the complex, without losing its shape. For just below the surface of story, like the succulent separate threads beneath the skin of a perfectly-cooked vegetable-spaghetti, lies the tangled richness of myth.

Salman Rushdie

THE
FREE
RADIO

SALMAN RUSHDIE was born in Bombay in June 1947 and now lives in London. He has written two novels, *Grimus* and *Midnight's Children*, which won the Booker McConnell Prize for 1981.

We all knew nothing good would happen to him while the thief's widow had her claws dug into his flesh, but the boy was an innocent, a real goof, you can't teach such people. That boy could have had a good life. God had blessed him with God's own looks, and his father had gone to the grave for him, but didn't he leave the boy a brand new first-class bicycle rickshaw with plastic-covered seats and all? Looks he had, his own trade he had, there would have been a good wife in time, he should just have taken out some years to save some rupees, but no, he must fall for a thief's widow before the hairs had time to come out on his chin, before his milk-teeth had split, one might say. We felt bad for him, but who listens to the wisdom of the old today? I say who listens? Exactly, nobody, certainly not a stone-head like Ramani the rickshaw-wallah. But I blame the widow. I saw it happen, you know, I saw most of it until I couldn't stand any more, I sat under this very banyan smoking this same hookah and not much escaped my notice. And at one stage I tried to save him from his fate but it was no go ... the widow was certainly attractive, no point denying, in a sort of hard vicious way she was all right, but it was her mentality that was rotten. Ten years older than Ramani she must have been, five children alive and two dead, what that thief did besides robbing and making babies God only knows, but he left her not one new paisa, so of course she would be interested in Ramani. I'm not saying a rickshaw-wallah makes much in this town but two mouthfuls are better to eat than wind. And not many people will look twice at the widow of a good-for-nothing.

They met right here. One day he rode into this street without a passenger, but grinning as usual as if someone had given him a ten-chip tip, singing some playback music from the radio, his hair greased like for a wedding. He was not such a fool he didn't know the girls watched him all the time. The thief's widow had gone to the bania shop to buy some three grains of dal and I won't say where the money came from, but people saw men at night near her rutputty shack, even the bania himself they were telling me but I will not comment. She had all her five brats with her and suddenly, cool as a fan, she called out, 'Hey! Rickshaaa!' Loud, you know, like a truly cheap type. Showing us she can afford to ride in rickshaws, as if anyone was interested, her children must have gone hungry to pay for the ride but in my opinion it was investment for her, because she had decided already to put her hooks into Ramani. So they all poured into the rickshaw and he took her away, and with the five children as well as the widow there was quite a weight, so he was puffing and veins were standing out on his legs, and I thought, Careful my son, or you will have this burden to pull for all of your life. But after that Ramani and the thief's widow were seen everywhere, shamelessly, in public places, and I was glad his mother was dead because if she saw this her face would have fallen off from shame.

Sometimes in those days Ramani came into this street in the evening to meet some friends, and they thought they were very smart because they would go into the back room of the Irani's canteen and drink illegal liquor, only of course everybody knew, but who would do anything, if boys ruin their lives let their parents worry. I was sad to see Ramani fall into this bad company, his parents were known to me before they died, but when I told Ramani he grinned like a sheep and said I was wrong, nothing bad was taking place. Let it go, I thought, I knew those cronies of his, they all wore the armbands of the new Youth Movement, this was the time of the state of emergency you understand, and these friends were not peaceful persons, there were stories of beatings-up, so I sat quiet under my tree. Ramani wore no armband but he went with them because they impressed him, the fool.

These armband youths were always flattering Ramani. Such a handsome chap, they told him, compared to you Dev Anand and Shashi Kapoor are like lepers only, you should go to Bombay and be put in the talkie pictures. They flattered him with dreams because they knew they could take money from him at cards and he would buy them drink while they did it, though he was no richer than they. So now Ramani's head became filled with these dreams, because it had nothing else inside to take up any space, and this is another reason why I blame the widow woman, because she had more years and should have had more sense, in two ticks she could have made him forget all about it, but no, I heard her telling him one day for all to hear, 'Truly you have the looks of Lord Krishna himself, except you are not blue all over.' In the street! So all would know they were lovers! From that day on I was sure a disaster would happen.

The next time the thief's widow came into the street to visit the bania shop I decided to act. Not for my sake but for the boy's dead parents I risked being shamed by a … no, I will not call her the name, she is elsewhere now and they will know what she is like.

'Thief's widow!' I called out. She stopped dead as if I had hit her with a whip, jerking her face in an ugly way. 'Come here and speak,' I told her. Now she could not refuse because I am not without importance in the town and maybe she thought that if people saw us talking they would stop ignoring her in the street, so she came as I knew she would.

'I have to say this thing only,' I told her with dignity. 'Ramani the rickshaw boy is dear to me, and you must find some person of your own age, or better still, go to the widows' hostel in Banaras and spend the rest of your life in holy prayer, thanking God that widow-burning is now illegal.'

So now she tried to shame me by screaming and calling me curses and saying I was a poisonous old man who should have died years ago, and then she said, 'Let me tell you, mister *retired* teacher sahib, that your Ramani has asked to marry me and I have said No, because I wish no more children, and he is a young man and should have his own. So tell that to the whole world and stop your cobra poison.'

For a time after that I closed my eyes to this affair of Ramani and the thief's widow, because I had done all I could and there were many other things in the town to interest a person like myself. For instance the local health officer had brought a big white caravan into the street and had permission to park it out of the way under the banyan tree; and every night men were taken into this van for a while and things were done to them – I did not care to be around at these times, because the youths with armbands were always in attendance, so I took my hookah and sat in another place. I heard rumours of what was happening in the caravan but I closed my ears. There are things it is better not to know if one wishes to avoid putting a strain on the heart.

But it was while the caravan, which smelt of ether, was in town that the extent of the widow's wickedness became plain because at this time Ramani suddenly began to talk about his new fantasy, telling everyone he could find that very shortly he was to receive a highly special and personalized gift from the government in Delhi itself, and this gift was to be a brand new first-class battery-operated transistor radio.

Because we had always believed that Ramani was a little soft in the head, with his notions of being a film-star and what not, most of us just nodded tolerantly and said Yes, Ram, that is nice for you, and What a fine generous government it is that gives radios to persons who are so keen on popular music. But Ramani insisted it was true, and seemed happier than at any point in his life, a happiness which could not be explained simply by the imminence of the transistor.

Soon after the dream radio was first mentioned, Ramani and the thief's widow were married, and then I understood everything. I did not attend the nuptials, it was a poor affair by all accounts, but afterwards I spoke to Ram as he came past the banyan with an empty rickshaw one day. He came to sit by me and I asked, 'My child, did you go to the caravan? What have you let them do to you?'

'Don't worry,' he said, 'Everything is tremendously wonderful. I am in love, teacher sahib, and I have made it possible for me to marry my woman.'

I confess I became angry, I almost wept as I realized that Ramani had gone voluntarily to subject himself to a humiliation which was being forced upon the other men who were taken to the caravan. I scolded him bitterly, 'My idiot child, you have let that woman deprive you of your manhood!'

'It is not so bad,' Ram said, 'It does not stop love-making – forgive me, teacher sahib – or anything. It stops babies only and my woman did not want children any more, so now all is tip-top. Also it is in national interest,' he confided, 'And soon the free radio will arrive.'

'The free radio,' I repeated.

'Yes, remember, teacher sahib,' Ram said confidentially, 'Some years back when the tailor had this operation? In no time the radio arrived and from all over town people gathered to listen to it. It is how the government says thank you. It will be excellent to have.'

'Go away, get away from me,' I told him in despair, and did not have the heart to tell him what everyone else in the country already knew, which was that the free radio scheme had been *funtoosh* for years.

After these events the thief's widow who was now Ram's wife did not come into town very often, being no doubt too ashamed of what she had made him do, but Ramani worked longer hours than ever before, and every time he saw any of the dozens of people he'd told about the radio he would put one hand up to his ear as if he were already holding the thing in it, and he would mimic broadcasts with a certain energetic skill. '*Yé Akashvani hai*,' he announced to the streets, '*This is All-India Radio. Here is the news. A government spokesman today announced that Ramani rickshaw-wallah's radio was on its way and would be delivered at any moment. And now some playback music*,' after which he would sing songs by Asha Puthli or Lata Mangeshkar in a high, ridiculous falsetto. Ram always had the rare quality of total belief in his dreams, and there were moments when his faith in the imaginary radio almost took us in, so that we half-believed it was indeed on its way, or even that it was there, cupped invisibly against his ear as he rode his rickshaw around the streets of the town. We began to expect to hear Ramani, around a corner or at the far end of a street, ringing his bell and yelling cheerfully, 'All-India Radio! This is All-India Radio!'

Time passed. Ram continued to carry the invisible radio around town. One year passed. Still his caricatures of the radio channel filled the air in the streets. But when I saw him now there was a new thing in his face, a strained thing, as if he were having to make some phenomenal effort, which was much more tiring than driving a rickshaw, more tiring even than a rickshaw containing a thief's widow and her five living children and the ghosts of two dead ones, as if his whole being were having to work to keep up the myth of the radio, as if all the energy of his young body was being poured into that fictional space between his ear and his hand, and he was trying to bring the radio into existence by a mighty, and possibly fatal, act of will. I felt most helpless, I can tell you, because I had divined that into the idea of the radio Ramani had poured all his worries and regrets about what he had done, and that if the dream were to die he would realize the full extent of his crime against his body and understand that the thief's widow had turned him, before she married him, into a thief of a more terrible kind, because she had made him rob himself.

And then the white caravan came back to its place under the banyan tree and I knew there was nothing to be done any more, because Ram would certainly come to get his gift. He did not come for one day, then for two, and I learned afterwards that he had not wished to seem greedy, he didn't want the health officer to think he was desperate for the radio, and besides he was half-hoping they would come and give it to him, perhaps with some kind of formal presentation ceremony. A fool is a fool and there is no accounting for his notions.

On the third day he came. Ringing his bicycle bell and imitating weather forecasts, ear cupped as usual, he arrived at the caravan. And in the rickshaw sat the thief's widow, the witch, who had not been able to resist coming along to watch her companion's destruction.

It did not take very long. Ram went into the caravan gaily, waving at his armbanded cronies who were guarding it against the anger of the people, and I am told (for I had left the scene to spare myself the pain) that his hair was well-oiled and his clothes were starched. The thief's widow did not move from the rickshaw, but sat there with a black sari pulled over her head, clutching at her children as if they were straws. After a few moments there were sounds of disagreement inside the caravan, and then louder noises still, and finally the youths in armbands went in to see what was becoming, and after that Ram was frog-marched out by his drinking-chums, and his hair-grease was smudged on to his face and there was blood coming from his mouth. His hand was no longer cupped by his ear; and still, they tell me, the thief's black widow did not move from her place in the rickshaw, although they dumped her husband in the dust.

Yes, I know, I'm an old man, my ideas are wrinkled with age, ideas of the old school, and these days they tell me sterilization and god knows what is necessary, and maybe I'm wrong to blame the widow as well, why not, maybe all the views of the old can be discounted now, and if that's so, let it be. But I'm telling this story and I haven't finished yet. Some days after the incident at the caravan I saw Ramani selling his rickshaw to the old Muslim crook who runs the bicycle-repair shop. When he saw me watching, Ram came to me and said, 'Goodbye, teacher sahib, I am off to Bombay, where I will become a bigger film star than Dev Anand or Shashi Kapoor even.'

'*I* am off?' I asked him. 'You are going alone?'

He stiffened. The thief's widow had already taught him not to be humble in the presence of elders.

'My wife and children will come also,' he said. It was the last time we spoke. They left that same day on the bus.

After some months had passed I got his first letter, which was not written by himself of course since how could he know how to write? He had paid a professional letter-writer, which must have cost him many rupees, because everything in life costs money and in Bombay it costs twice as much. Don't ask why he wrote to *me*, but he did, I have the letters and can give you proof positive, so maybe there are some uses for old people still, or maybe I was the only one who'd be interested, but anyway the letters were full of his new career, they told me how he'd been discovered at once, a big studio had given him a test, now they were grooming him for stardom, he spent his days at the Sun'n'Sand hotel at Juhu beach in the company of top lady stars such as Sadhana and Sonia, he was buying a big house on Malabar Hill built in the split-level mode, the thief's widow was well and happy and getting fat, and life was filled with light and success and a little legal alcohol; they were wonderful letters, brimming with happiness and confidence, but whenever I read them, and sometimes I read them still, I remember the expression which came into his face in the days just before he learned the truth about his radio, and the huge mad energy which he had poured into the act of conjuring reality, by an act of magnificent faith, out of the hot thin air between his cupped hand and his ear.

Victor Sage

THE
FESTIVAL
EDITION

VICTOR SAGE was born in Shropshire in 1942. He was educated at the universities of Durham, Birmingham and East Anglia, where he now teaches literature. His stories have been published in *The New Review*, *The Magazine of Fantasy and Science Fiction* and *Straight Lines*. He has recently completed a collection of shorter fiction, and is at present working on a book on the horror tradition.

'Mount Pleasant',
Richmond,
July 13th '53.

It seems as though I shall have to go to Ireland. I had a long letter this morning from Dampmartin (headed the Minute Press). The deadlines for the Editions are all put forward: the Festival Series must be completed in something like (I calculate) one quarter the time the original contract stated. I never heard of such a thing. Dispatched a letter of protest, copy to my agent Walters. Some kind of prelude to going bust, no doubt. There's no telling with these small firms. I haven't said a thing to Pauline, of course. This morning she went into one of her good-for-nothing-parasite-intellectual speeches. An argument followed, in which she supported the book-burning activities of Hitler. It seems I belong to a class of people who 'do' nothing. Photocopy of A arrived through the post.

'Mount Pleasant',
Richmond,
July 15th '53.

Charming letter from Doyle (headed Kildare St). As I suspected, Dampmartin has been on to him. He invites me to come over and do the collation in his own library at Malahide. What a prospect. I spent a long time toying with my egg this morning, hovering on the edge of telling Pauline. But the conditions weren't right. Pauline carries a hanky in her sleeve. Merely an old-fashioned habit, I used to think. Until I realized it was a sign she had a headache. 'Sign' is wrong, strictly speaking. The habit has a utilitarian origin: while she is in this condition, her tear-ducts moisten and she needs to wipe her eyes. To *me* it's a sign, not to her. Pauline wears dark clothing when she has her period. That too is a sign, not strictly speaking: she bleeds a great deal, and fears she will leave a stain wherever she sits. This morning, the conditions were not right: Pauline was wearing a handkerchief tucked into her sleeve *and* her black skirt.

> 'Mount Pleasant',
> Richmond,
> July 16th '53.

I've written back to Doyle, accepting his invitation. Shades of 'La Mancha' and the Boswell papers. Dampmartin telephoned this morning (isn't that a coincidence!). Urgency is required. It is now, Pauline informs me urgently, sixty-seven days since we made love. What is the matter with me? To this question, which she asks me daily, she has a slender variety of answers. There are signs in my behaviour of premature senility. I am passive. I take her for granted. At least she plays tennis and keeps her figure. What is the matter with me? Of course, I know it's useless to present her with the truth. It merely enrages her. Why *will* I therefore hoard my little victories to bursting point? I can hear the kind inquiries echoing down the years: is it *just* laziness? Has she not invested in me to the extent of having my two lovely children? Do I not owe it to her, morally, to say nothing of the more practical forms of obligation, to keep her informed of my intentions? Am I even *listening*? No, conditions not right.

> 'Mount Pleasant',
> Richmond,
> July 17th '53.

I've been looking over A this morning: pristine foul papers. No wonder everyone else has printed the test from A. B is a nuisance: the truth of the matter always is. Then supposing they are right *and* B is a nuisance. The Festival Edition will just go the conventional primrose path I suppose. No telling till I get to B. It's all, no doubt, somebody else's financial whim. How does one ever know about the economics of publishing? Knowing Dampmartin, I should imagine the whole series is a front for something else. Transfer of capital. Oil, I expect. Other people's oil. What a fate, to be the chimera of a Shaftesbury Avenue bank-book! But the intellectual problem remains, whether the means of expressing it is a whim of the market or not, isn't that a fact? 'No bold, or resolute, piece of thinking is ever out of date.' Went off into a long daydream at the thought of lingering over the collation of A and B, the sound of wood-pigeons clear and cool outside the window of Doyle's private library. Woken by a bloodcurdling yell outside my study door: Jason had hit Gregory on the nose with a tennis racket. On inspection, it proved to be broken. Pauline fainted, reminding me strongly of Lady Macbeth. I drove them all to the hospital. The rest of the day was consumed in comforting Pauline. Gregory is suitably proud of his plastered-up nose. To Jason's disgust, he performs the perfect Indian accent. A pity: I was going to tell Pauline about the Irish trip today.

'Mount Pleasant',
Richmond,
July 19th '53.

Just out of – no, *more* than curiosity – I looked in my diary today of three years ago. Apparently, there was a local election. Pauline and I went down to the Guildhall together to vote. We scoffed in unison at the Tory canvassers outside the door. We walked in, gave our numbers to the clerk, and received our voting slips. We entered our adjacent booths. Pauline peeped round the partition, pretending to look at my slip. I laughed, covered it up with my hand, and put a cross against the Tory candidate. It gave me an unaccountable glow of pleasure secretly to have cancelled Pauline's vote. Electorally speaking, things were exactly the same when we came out of the town hall as when we had gone in. But the pair of spectacles through which I viewed the world – not to speak of Pauline – had assumed a rosy diffusion. We commiserated with one another that evening when we learnt that the Tory had got in. Even so, said Pauline, toasting me in cooking sherry, our two votes had helped narrow the gap. Morally, I appear to have regressed since then.

'Mount Pleasant',
Richmond,
July 20th '53.

Philips telephoned today. I arranged to have lunch with him. Pauline
wanted to know who it was. She never opens my letters. She never picks
up the extension. But she always asks. I told her it was someone wanting
a book. At lunch, Philips adopted the tone of an outraged headmaster:
was I aware that my overdraft had 'achieved four figures'. I pretended to
consult him about the Festival Edition, portraying it, as diffidently as I
could manage, as the nemesis of debt. They wanted to violate my
contract. I should be able to take advantage of the penalty clause.
Dampmartin had already said as much. I should be getting considerably
more than I had anticipated. There would be the royalties from schools
and libraries which, as he well knew, would be obliged to take the book.
Plus I had not – he should bear this in mind too – had the second half of
the advance. Philips talked on, admonishing, buying drinks. I couldn't
help wondering what sort of a man Doyle is. In order to write that article
in HLQ, Miss Burgeon must have been over to see this man. She must
have inspected B at Malahide personally in the man's own library. Does
Doyle know what she's printed, as a result? An article suggesting – no
less – that *none* of the corrections in B are authorial. Apart from anything
else, it devalues B completely, if he ever wants to sell it. I bet she didn't
show it to him before publication. Has the man thought of this, or is he
interested merely in objective scholarship. My attention was recalled by
Philips's parting shot: he hoped the Festival Edition wasn't going to be
'another Maypole'. Philips's idea of a Parthian shaft. Whan I got home,
my heart sank: there was a new washing-machine sitting in its cardboard
carton in the hall. On top of it lay a note from Pauline: she had gone to
the hospital in a taxi. Gregory had put a fork through Jason's foot.

'Mount Pleasant',
Richmond,
July 22nd '53

An uneventful, and therefore successful, day. First the reply from Doyle.
He will meet me off the boat (personal attention from the great man) if I
can confirm when I'm coming. Pauline was exhausted after yesterday and

had a lie in. When I woke her with a cup of tea, she took a long time to come to, murmuring that she felt 'cut off'. Jason, the cause of this defence mechanism, was in bed. I changed the dressing on his foot, then down to the travel agents'. Took Gregory with me, and left him in the car. Then to the post office to telegram Doyle I shall be arriving on the 31st.

'Mount Pleasant',
Richmond,
July 23rd '53.

Conversation at the moment is a positive tissue of signs. Not just signs: signs of signs. It is possible, even necessary perhaps, to inflict wounds without wounding. The law being what it is. To tiptoe behind the victim of the moment with the knife that is not a knife and plunge it, harmlessly, into the back that is not a back. I wonder how many people acknowledge this to themselves. I met Marshall today. I told him about the new terms for the Festival Edition, adding that I hoped it wouldn't be 'another Maypole'. He laughed knowingly. Thus I had my little victory over Philips and deceived Marshall into thinking this 'witticism' was mine into the bargain. Marshall, not to be put down, asked me how Pauline was. I frowned and answered that she was feeling 'cut off'. By the way, I asked, How is Alice? It was then that I remembered that Alice Marshall had just recovered from a mastectomy. The words resounded in my mind, Does she feel 'cut off' too? This kind of thing is vulgar and unfortunate – it interferes with the system. Marshall was looking at me hard, as well he might. I could see he was wondering what association had conjured up the vision of his ailing wife in my mind. In the end, he settled for the banal connection 'wife'. Poorly, he said, in the tone of an undertaker. When I got home, Pauline was sitting up in bed. She was crying. What's the matter dear, I said, almost without thinking, Feeling 'poorly'?

'Mount Pleasant',
Richmond,
July 27th '53.

Since time is running out, I decided to broach Matters Hibernian. Last night, I suggested the boys go down to Lympne to their grandmother for the day. Drove them to Waterloo this morning. Jason appears to have made a remarkable recovery, though he limps theatrically and his brogues have an extra row of holes across the front. Pauline was still in bed when I got back. Lapsang Souchong, her favourite. She was touched. Throughout our love-making, I could hear Reynolds next door trying to start his mower. It was obvious to me that the carburettor was blocked. Later, while she lay with a dreamy expression on her face, I began my exposition, neatly reversing the order of events in favour of their priority. Philips had been hounding me recently. The new washing-machine stepped out of line here. Then I began to stage the drama of Dampmartin's unheard-of change of contract. It was a complex point in law whether he could achieve such a thing. In any case, I needed to complete my work quickly. So that we could go away for a holiday? Without the children? I told her of my correspondence with Doyle, carefully adding a summary of the MSS. Why didn't you tell me this before, said Pauline. I didn't want to worry her. Pauline's eyes filled with tears. Stupid MSS, she cried, I wish they were all at the bottom of the ocean. What was the matter with me? As usual, Nothing. She smiled. When would we be going, she asked, bucking up. Here was a difficulty. *I* should be going. But don't you want me with you, asked Pauline. I replied with a variety of arguments, some of them not as judicious as I could have wished. I stressed the need for peace and quiet. Finally I confessed I had already booked a return on the *Munster* from Liverpool on the 30th. Here, all my good work stood on the brink of ruins. She drew back, her eyes burning with suspicion. Pauline is a tremendous, a *towering* sulker; her tear-ducts began to leak, her cheeks ripple like a rice-pudding fresh out of the oven, her mouth – the type that novelists refer to as 'generous' – pinches itself into an absolute parsimony of the spirit. I knew now that nothing I did would avail, including doing nothing. I went into my study and listened for some time, to the silence, staring at the words: '*Intrat* Frier [sic] with lanthorne'. It struck me that the stage direction was in Latin. Quilley's edition didn't say whether he had taken it from A or B. But if the *author* revised A, why would he have changed the stage directions to Latin? Inspection of B may well clear this up. Later, the phone rang: it was Gregory from Waterloo. Jason had got out of the train somewhere between Lympne and Waterloo to get an ice-cream and the train had gone without him. One up to Gregory.

'Mount Pleasant',
Richmond,
July 29th '53.

The expected storm-clouds arrived, and broke, this morning. For two days virtually, the house has been a place where people pass each other on the stairs or in the hall, eyes fixed on a highly desirable, far-off place. Pauline has been cold, tossing me the occasional scorpion. At breakfast Jason, who appears to thrive on getting mislaid, upset his cornflakes over Pauline's new skirt. Ugh, she said, burying her face in her hands, Why don't you all burn in hell? We looked at one another, puzzled. Upstairs, she went into one of her lightning, thumb-nail character-assassinations. I think of these as caricatures by Rowlandson or Hogarth. Even as she was talking, the captions slipped up before my eyes. 'Hue and Cry' as she pursues me into the bathroom, 'The Vanity of Human Wishes' as, razor aloft, I stare at her in the bathroom mirror; 'Marriage à la Mode', as we dash, necks out like geese escaping the axe, back into the bedroom.

'Bracken',
Malahide,
July 31st '53.

Why on earth did she let them bring their cameras? They crouched down, kneeling on the platform, grossly parodic of sports photographers, snapping me climbing into the train. Pauline looked on, like any mother. That is to say, she looked away. That look is the ultimate sign of the proprietary. Cats do it with mice. I retired from the window and entered the first compartment. The elderly couple looked at me with distaste. I took off my mac and sat down. The tattooed man opposite leaned forward and tapped me on the leg: Pauline had come to the window. The train pulled off at walking pace. She walked with it, looking in at me, frowning a 'meaning'. Her lips almost touched the glass, as she started to mouth the words I pretended not to understand. I looked up at the luggage-rack, feeling awful. I think she's trying to tell you something, said the old man, Your Wife. Pauline was running sideways. Have you got your BRAN? *Have* you? She was sprinting now, periodically falling behind like a figure in a film with parallax problems, but then catching up again. She winced

at the effort. Your B–R–A–N? I smiled and stabbed my index finger at
the travelling bag in my hand, while I contemplated the image of the
unlabelled brown carton, sitting where I had left it, on the pantry shelf.
At Crewe, I thought of her, letting the children out of the car, making a
bee-line for the shelf. I must love her, must I not, if I can forget about my
own haemorrhoids like this? The crossing was uneventful. The sea as
calm as a mirror. Very few passengers. This morning, we were bobbing at
North Wall. I spent a bad night. I dreamt I was dancing with Miss
Burgeon. As we danced, her arms got tighter and tighter. Soon all
pretence of dancing was lost, and I was simply being crushed to pulp. I
woke with the sound of my ribs cracking in my ears, like a good fire. She
looked like a photo of Pauline I carry in my wallet. It was taken in Italy
during the war. She's sitting astride a bicycle, smiling broadly, wearing
her WAAC sergeant-major's uniform. Behind her, strung across the
road, is a banner which reads:

DEATH IS *SO* PERMANENT

As I stood on the quay, looking round for Doyle, I was approached by a
greasy-haired man with one arm. He introduced himself as 'Christie, Mr
Doyle's man'. His breath smelt of alcohol. We climbed into a donkey and
trap and set off at a tremendous clip along the coast road. It was a
hazardous affair: every time we went past a church, his arm shot out and
dumped the reins firmly in my lap. He needed the arm to cross himself. I
had forgotten this custom amongst the devout of this country. When I
inquired about his injury, he replied curtly that it had been 'bit off be
d'pig'. Lunch was ready when we arrived here, but still no sign of Doyle. I
am itching to work. Spent the afternoon restraining the itch and
exploring the town. Much like a Sussex resort; but more decayed than
genteel. There's one hotel, The Grand, the pink stucco peeling off the
facade like a skin disease. This house is the emblem of the whole place: a
Georgian mansion with cumbersome Victorian Gothic restoration. At
one time the home of a prosperous Anglo-Irish family. There's a
gatehouse, where Christie and his wife live. Signs of a way of life that has
disappeared: a tennis-court covered in mess, a kitchen garden with
vestiges of lavender. The whole surrounded by enormous elms. It looks as
if rooks, not wood-pigeons, will accompny my idyll. I must ask Christie
about the thing in the garden. It looks like a genuine round tower from
the early medieval period. It all has a damp, unkempt air. But my room,

overlooking the garden on the first floor is large and airy. A large bay window and *two* beds. Mrs Christie says Doyle hardly ever comes here. I'm not surprised.

'Bracken',
Malahide,
Aug. 1st '53.

The differences between A and B start at the title page. A, the 1602–3 printing, introduces the play: 'As it hath been often presented at St Paules', whereas B, the 1642 edition, reads:

The Feaste of Tyme
A Tragedie
As it hath been divers tymes Acted
with Applause

Being much corrected and amended

by the Author
Before his death

London
Printed by GC for Richard Wagstaffe
1642

There's no point in contesting the obvious; Gascoigne, it has been well-established, is the author. But whether the corrections are his, as claimed on the title page, is another matter. Fawcett and Quilley in their editions both accepted that they were substantially authorial. I dissent: even a preliminary examination of B makes me suspect they are wrong. Its going to be a hard job proving this.

'Bracken',
Malahide,
Aug. 2nd '53.

I had a postcard from Pauline this morning, in which she informs me that I have left my bran behind. She urges me to buy more. Perhaps she's right. My curse very bad this morning. A is well-printed and retains the characteristics of an author's MS, rather than a transcript. A cast list, for example, appears before each scene, indicating that the author was laying out his characters. Even Miss Burgeon accepts this. But in B, the printing is untidy. There are several pieces where effects are duplicated. One feature is reproduced from A and the other added for what looks like dramatic propriety. I, iv, 23ff., for example, where Isabella is writing her reply to Bruno, the stage directions read simply: 'Sound a lute'; this is reproduced in B, but there are also in addition twenty lines of banal prattle for three musicians. B therefore derives from A, but probably from a copy corrected by reference to a MS. Of course, one cannot rule out the interference of the compositor. There are also, however, places where B is superior to A, as if the transcriber of A could not read a word in his author's MS, but the corrector of B has guessed it (notably 'loins' for A's puzzling 'lions' at II, vii, 48–9). Corrector of B therefore has a certain competence. He's a thorough worker. Of course, he would be if he were the author! But I have a feeling he's not. There's someone else there.

'Bracken',
Malahide,
Aug. 3rd '53.

A letter from Doyle this morning, Dublin postmark. He apologizes for his absence and hopes I've settled in well. He says, rather vaguely, that he 'hopes to meet me soon'. I think I can establish that the MS used to correct A was a prompt-book. There are several signs of this: the most obvious is the practical distribution of stage properties which occurs only in B: 'with a bawble', 'with a boke' and 'Tapers behind the Aras' at II, i, 48. A prologue and epilogue have been added in B, the former of which can be accurately placed, by internal evidence, in 1635. Someone therefore corrected A from the prompt-book used in the revival of the play in 1635 and that corrected text became B. This is like trying to reconstruct the plan of a maze that has overgrown. The problem seems insoluble: in order to find the centre, I must reconstruct the plan, otherwise I may stumble on it unawares. But in order to reconstruct the plan, I must find the centre, because all the paths look alike.

'Bracken',
Malahide,
Aug. 5th '53.

A bad night. My curse troubling me. I lay in bed this morning for a while, watching the rookery in the elms. The birds circulate constantly; whenever one lands, another takes off. Shift-work? I must watch to see if they take it in turns. The rational itch is discomforting, it makes one feel 'cut off'. Another postcard from Pauline this morning with additions from the boys. Their collective scrawl is like chain-link fencing: I have to look through it to the meaning. Then they wonder why I haven't written to them. After a few hours, my eyes started to hurt, so I locked up the library and walked down to the sea. The light here is soothing. Staring at the sea, I began to feel as if I were not there.

> 'Bracken',
> Malahide,
> Aug. 6th '53.

No external evidence exists, except Miss Burgeon's. The *Feaste* was the only full-length book which 'GC' and Wagstaffe published in 1642. From this and a whole lot of other facts, mostly irrelevant, she comes to the conclusion that *all* the corrections are by another hand and Gascoigne had nothing to do with B at all. There's a general habit of following her. Orr declares that 'the triviality of the revisions shows that the Corrector knew little, and cared less, about the meaning of the text he was working on. A mere theatre hack ...'; Fawcett, sounding more like Gypsy Rose Lee than a reputable scholar, goes further: 'I see some stripling stage-manager, anxious at his first assignment to reduce this incomprehensible old play to immediate theatrical sense. He fidgets with it ...'; Quilley is even more unconvincing. He believes Gascoigne himself made the corrections, but when the powers of his mind were in decline, a speculation based solely on the belief that the author was a personal messenger of Queen Elizabeth to Paris and contracted syphilis, a belief for which there is not a scrap of evidence. Some of the corrections are like the late manner of Gascoigne. So, although some kinds of correction are banal, the 'theatre hack' idea is not good enough: this man can write. Of course, everyone is assuming that all the corrections come from a single source. The truth must be something like this: someone revised the MS of A; someone else (my man) corrected *that* for the printer of B; the compositor of B was lazy and couldn't read the MS well. My Someone is, according to my investigations, only Someone No. 3 in the chain. But do I conclude from this that the situation is hopeless and revert to A as my authoritative text? All previous commentators have done precisely that. But I still feel that one hand is responsible for all the important corrections. I asked Christie about the folly. He says it is ancient, but that Doyle had it bricked up. He speaks of Doyle with exaggerated respect.

'Bracken',
Malahide,
Aug. 7th '53.

Such a man was no hack. He *was* a man of the theatre. He knew Gascoigne's work intimately. He could write like him. He probably had his permission to correct. This looks like a *reductio ad absurdum* of my argument: the qualities I need for my Not-Gascoigne can only be found, it seems, in Gascoigne himself. I've reached the crucial point in the maze where mere exploration will no longer suffice. Having postulated my Not-Gascoigne, I must now produce him, or go back. This afternoon I went for a long ramble over towards Donabate. There are many of these round towers. I'm reading Dr Joyce on their origin. They've apparently been the object of much scholarly disputation, fuelled by political and religious opposition between the disputants. Are they Christian or Pagan? This region is where the original struggle took place: 'Fine Gael', or, as it is now called, 'Fingal': the 'territory of the strangers'. Apparently a section of the 'firbolgs' landed here. This is also where St Patrick began his campaign to convert the inhabitants of this country. There's a legend that St Columba died in one of these towers, transcribing a MS of the Bible.

'Bracken',
Malahide,
Aug. 8th '53.

Not-Gascoigne puzzles me. There are times when he adds to no apparent purpose. Some of these could be survivals of original corrections made by Gascoigne. For instance III, v. Bruno and his pages Cinthio and Julio are in an orchard. Here, in a beautifully contrived piece of formal banter, they agree to exchange sonnets. Then there follows an added scene in which Bruno, pretending to paint Cinthio, while Julio looks on, delivers the following hyperbole:

> Thy qualities are like unto a lake
> That tidelesse keeps a summe of constancie,
> Through all its eager lappings at the marge.
> Restlesse, it swelleth; yet surcease is there none;
> It shrinketh in winter like a frightened girle
> Naked to the gaze of a casual swain,
> Yet sets at nought the rapine of the land ...

Unseen at the window, Isabella, wife of Aracchino the Duke's Steward, falls in love with Bruno's words, applying them in a rather crude conceit to herself:

> O now methinks I have the armes of night
> That yearneth for the coming of the sable moon:
> Such words do strike upon my willing ear
> Like showres of seedes cast on the fertil earth;
> Sure he must be a very Gabriel
> This man, and I the Mary of his choice,
> Blessed with magnificat of heav'nlie joye ...

The elegant, sexually ambiguous scene of A is converted into blasphemous operatic farce. Likewise in IV, vii, while Bruno and Isabella consummate their adultery, a long exchange between the Friar and the Duke appearing above has been added. It discourses, in clumsy and indifferent verse, on the dangers of necromancy and the power of ghosts. Similarly the last act, magnificent tragedy in A, has been converted in B into melodrama. Aracchino, Isabella's jealous husband, kills the two pages and throws the blame on to her by posing as an 'apparition' in a dream and speaking through a hole in the wall of Bruno's bedchamber. Enraged, Bruno kills her. Then Aracchino enters and reveals all, gloating over the damnation of both adulterers. Bruno rejects this magnificently in A, claiming that he and Isabella and the two boys are a constellation of stars which no idea of sin could blemish or alter. In B, the force of his speech is travestied by correction. Plus a final scene has been added in B, in which the Duke and Friar arrest Aracchino for the murder of the pages and gloat over Bruno. In A, he's merely taken off by soldiers.

I think I can trace different levels of motivation in these corrections. First, the need to use theatrical resources: the corrector's theatre almost certainly possessed a balcony, and some of these additions were made in order to take advantage of it. Second, a taste for melodrama and blood-boltering. Third, an element of sectarian propaganda. The additions have the effect of making the Duke and the Friar the controllers of the play's action. The play in B's version affirms the power of Church and State over the individual. All Bruno's magnificent speeches against damnation are converted into 'confessions' as a result of this new structure. Since the play is set in Italy, the Protestant audience would immediately recognize the corruption of Catholicism at work. But they must not be allowed to identify with the heroic figure of Bruno too much, as they would in the A version perhaps, because his occult reasons for rejecting the Church's judgement amount in themselves to subversiveness and heresy. Had A been performed in the 1630s, the Friar's and Duke's responses to the hero would have been so feeble as to have had the effect of virtually endorsing papism.

'Bracken',
Malahide,
Aug. 9th '53.

Today at last, I've done it! The centre of the maze. Dashed down my spoon at breakfast, and went into the library. I remembered that in an appendix somewhere Fawcett referred to a suggestion by Theobald that a possible candidate for a corrector for *The Feaste* might be the actor/theatre-manager Robert Daniels. I think I only remembered because he has the same surname as myself. Daniels was a friend of Gascoigne's and worked with him in the theatre. What is more, he aspired to writing plays himself. Doyle's library has a copy of the only edition of his plays (Pease, 1846). Heavy influence of Gascoigne in the verse. But – more strikingly – all the stage directions are in Latin! I *think* I've made a discovery. I went for a long walk this afternoon to try and quell my excitement. Failed. My Not-Gascoigne *is* Daniels. I feel sure.

'Bracken',
Malahide,
Aug. 10th '53.

This morning, when I looked out of my window, I thought I was seeing things for a moment. A man was in the garden, lying horizontally on a white cloud, apparently asleep. When I looked closer, I saw that the garden bench was completely enveloped in mist, so that he appeared from a distance to be levitating about a foot and a half off the ground. An old tramp, by the looks of him. Looked most odd. He was there for most of the day; I could see him through the library window, asleep, supported by the bench, the mist having disappeared. He was not there in the evening.

'Bracken',
Malahide,
Aug. 11th '53.

I've written to tell Pauline I shall be home soon. Christie tells me that Mr Doyle is coming down from Dublin on the 16th. I've grown quite curious about this mysterious patron of scholarship. In the meantime, I press on with the work. I've almost finished now. The more I go on, the more sure I am that I've made a breakthrough. I've been checking the previous editions of *The Feaste* today. Doyle has an exhaustive collection. He must have been thinking of editing it himself some day. Dilke's edition was based on A. Fawcett and Quilley both use A and record, inaccurately, B's variants. So it looks as if my theory of the text is unique. Looked out the window in the library, as I was working. The tramp was there again. I asked Christie about him. He said they often get 'travellers' and I should pay no attention to the man.

'Bracken',
Malahide,
Aug. 13th '53.

Spent this morning making notes from the Pease ed. of Daniels's plays. I hadn't bothered to look at it before, but the frontispiece is arresting. It's going to be quite a *coup* to reprint it in the Festival Edition as visual evidence. It's a large face, but not a handsome one. The nose is hooked and the lips thin. He must have made a marvellous Iago. It looks as if he's in costume for Bruno in *The Feaste*. I went for a ramble this afternoon, when I got back, I found the tinker or whatever he is peering in at the library window. I tiptoed behind him, but, unfortunately, I must have made a noise because he fled. Otherwise, I'd have caught him red-handed. I came from the garden, so perhaps he saw my face reflected in the window. He's obviously up to no good.

'Bracken',
Malahide,
Aug. 14th '53.

Mostly odds and ends now. Most of the work can be done when I get back to Richmond. The tramp was still there today, prowling openly about the garden. In the end, I was so distracted I went out and hailed him. A man in a sorry state. He was covered in grass and leaves and dressed in old rags. When I asked him, he said he'd come from 'nowhere'. He referred to it as if it were somewhere. I asked him if he'd been sleeping in the garden and he nodded, his teeth chattering. Christie came out and shouted that there was a telephone call from Doyle. I told the tramp to wait. On the telephone, I must have sounded a bit abstracted because Doyle passed a remark about my manner. He will be delayed until the nineteenth, apparently. When I got back to the bench, I found the man still sitting there. Is it food you need, I asked, and a bed for the night? I delved in my pocket and fetched out two pounds, all I had on me. Euphoria about the edition, I suppose; charity is disgusting and meaningless to me. He will no doubt make for the nearest public house. It relieved some of my feelings, I think. He has a few days growth of beard, but there's something about the eyes and nose that seems familiar to me. My good deed for the month accomplished anyway.

'Bracken',
Malahide,
Aug. 15th '53.

This really *is* too much. The fellow was there again this morning. I tried to ignore him and get on with my work, but it proved impossible for me to concentrate. I kept seeing him out of the corner of my eye, roaming about in the garden. Then he came right up to the library window and stared insolently in at me. I waved him away, but he wouldn't go. In the end, I was so angry I went outside and asked him what on earth he wanted. Why didn't he be off on his way? He looked at me as if I had insulted him. It had rained during the night and his clothes were in an even worse state than before. His breath smelt of alcohol. I rebuked him for using my money to buy drink with. I told him he would get nothing

else out of me and if he didn't stop making a nuisance of himself, I should
be forced to call the police. He muttered something I didn't catch and
shook his fist at me. Gratitude!

'Bracken',
Malahide,
Aug. 17th '53.

An unnerving day. It began this morning, when he came again to the
library window. I rushed outside, but couldn't find him. When I got back,
he was sitting in my chair, leafing through my papers. He refused to
move. When I asked who he was and what he wanted, he shrugged. Then
he started speaking in a curious, nasal tone. Not an Irish accent. A long,
rambling affair I couldn't make head or tail of. Without warning, he
picked up my papers, including the MS of B, and strewed them over the
floor. How was my work progressing, he asked. When I told him to mind
his own business, he replied that it *was* his business. On the contrary, he
said, *I* should have minded *mine*. But it was 'too late now'. He was there.
What was I going to do about it? When I asked him what he was talking
about, he repeated that I was obliged to do something about him; I told
him I didn't understand. For answer, I received a passionate, largely
unintelligible, oration on the subject of Time, during which he picked up
more of my papers and threw them angrily on the floor. I was outraged, but determined to control myself. Of course, I realized by now that
this was no ordinary vagabond, but a person of some education, quite
severely deranged. I decided at that point, since he looks given to
violence, to humour the man until I could find out what institution he has
escaped from. I took him upstairs and ran him a bath (he stank
unimaginably) and dressed him in some of my spare clothes. He was
violently hungry. He said he couldn't remember when he had last eaten. I
went down to the kitchen and fetched up a loaf of bread and half a
Stilton, all of which he wolfed down very convincingly. This afternoon, I
probed him again and received another jumble of high-sounding,
accusatory nonsense. Despite what appears an almost total unhingement,
the man's powers of eloquence seem curiously unimpaired. While he
talked, I was distracted again by the feeling that I had seen his face
somewhere before. I remembered: it was the woodcut of Daniels. There

is a *distinct* resemblance. Sometimes the mind behaves peculiarly under stress, one must take that into account. He started throwing out mysterious appeals; he asked me to 'put myself in his shoes'. Since at the time, he was wearing a spare pair of mine, I took a rather dim view of this metaphor. He insisted that I was obliged to look after him. In vain I protested that I had never seen him before (except in a woodcut); that I am a stranger in this country (so is he, he says); that charity is against my principles (it was not charity, he declared, that Adam asked of God). I laughed aloud at the audacity of this image and the cool manner in which it was deployed. It seems, when I can make any sense at all of what he says, that I am responsible for him. By this is meant, not just his local welfare ('a groatsworth of appeasement' as he puts it) but, fantastically, his *whole existence*. The man appears to have imagination and cunning in equal proportions. He claims to have been perfectly happy slumbering away somewhere in Moorgate Fields, when some 'arrant fool' (i.e. myself) began to 'meddle' with him. He seems very ill, declining at this point into absolute ravings and rambling on about the vision of a face – *my* face – looking down at him, as if he were lying at the bottom of a deep well. Then he felt as if he were about to wake up. When he tried to turn over in bed, he felt as if something was there preventing him. It turned out to be the back of a bench in a garden. *This* garden. Where did he get his clothes from, I asked disingenuously, trying to humour him. He says that he scouted round and found them in a hut in the garden. There's never a moment's hesitation in his replies. At this point, I began to wonder if I was using the right approach, trying to humour him in this way. It didn't seem to be leading anywhere. All my attempts to get information out of him were met with some variation of this basic tale, interspersed with diatribes about my irresponsibility. Then he fell asleep and started to snore. I was in a quandary. I went downstairs, rather haphazardly, wondering what to do. After all, it's not my house. It's hardly my place to give casual accommodation to escaped lunatics, even if their fantasies do centre on me. Christie was in the kitchen, drinking tea and talking to his wife. I told them I'd taken in the man who was in the garden, and asked their advice. They looked at each other. He claims to be a ghost, I said, laughing. This was obviously the wrong way of putting it. Instead of straining their credulity, my story appears to have had the opposite effect. Mrs Christie asked me how tall he was, whether he had crossed the threshold 'unbidden', or whether I had invited him in. When supper came, she solemly laid out an extra portion of stew 'for the one above', and insisted on leaving it on the landing outside my room. When I tried to explain to her that the man only *thought* he was a ghost, she tapped her nose with her finger and smiled. I didn't realize the degree of superstition that prevails amongst these people. The 'ghost', having again eaten vast quantities of real food and briefly treated me to some more of his visions, has fallen asleep and is lying in the other bed, as I write, snoring some very material snores.

'Bracken'
Malahide,
Aug. 18th '53.

This morning when I got up, he followed me into the bathroom and stood there looking at me in the mirror while I cleaned my teeth and shaved. He looked as if he'd never seen a mirror in his life before. At breakfast, since he insisted on coming down with me, we sat side by side. Rather inconsistently after yesterday, Mrs Christie didn't seem to want to serve us both at first. But after I had persuaded her to put out an extra bowl of porridge for our friend and set an extra place, he decided he wasn't hungry after all and suddenly went out into the garden. As I went out into the hall, I heard Christie talking to someone on the telephone. From the respectful tone, I think it was Doyle. Christie was saying 'yes' and 'yesterday' (or was it yes and today? – I can't tell the days apart in his accent.) I followed the man out into the garden. He was standing looking at the folly. I asked him if he was going to make any sense today. Where had he come from? At this he got very angry and started to shout at me. He shouted that I had no business not believing his story when I myself was responsible for it. He took me by the collar, the spittle running out over his lips, and shouted, his face close to mine, When you *deduced* me, you bastard. At this, I decided that confrontation was a fairly useless tactic. It was obviously going to be a longer job than I thought and I had better resign myself. Alright, I said, Why are you impersonating Daniels? The question seemed to have the desired effect. He stopped in his tracks and snorted like a bull. Impersonating nothing, he said, I *am* Daniels. Of course, he was. There was something that puzzled me, though. Why would a seventeenth-century incubus want to travel all this time and distance? At this point, my mind was racing ahead. I had to humour him until such time as I could sneak away and telephone the Garda. I therefore asked, since he *was* Daniels, what he had actually done to the B text of *The Feaste of Time*. Well, your theory is obviously correct, he replied. He gave a bitter laugh. Otherwise, I wouldn't be here, would I? I granted him the logic of this. I steered him back towards the house, hardly listening to the lecture he'd started to deliver on Tudor and Stuart history and the shortcomings of my editorial practice. On the face of it, it's astounding that he knows so much about the subject. But if he's been sneaking into the library every day and reading over my papers, what can I expect? But how on earth can he have done this, when I have the key? I got him upstairs, without listening to his doubtless fascinating peroration. I excused myself, without really needing to, and went down into the hall. I tried to get Christie to telephone the Garda, but he refused. What can Sean O'Riordan do against a spirit, he asked. I explained that I saw his point, that the duties of rural policemen were prescribed within certain limits, but that, happily, if he would just listen to me, this fell within them. He is not a spirit, I said, He is a man who *thinks* he's a spirit. It was a distinction he didn't seem prepared to admit. I spelt it out: The man is insane; he has escaped from a local mental institution and it is our (yours and mine) bounden duty to restore him to his keepers as soon as possible. Otherwise, I couldn't answer for the consequences. He was immoveable. Eventually, I rang the Garda myself. After a considerable amount of very unenlightening argument, in which I failed utterly to make myself clear, a voice said that Mr O'Riordan would arrive in about two hours. When I got back to my room, 'Daniels' was gone. I searched the house and grounds, but he was nowhere to be seen. I appealed to Christie to come with me. To my surprise, he denied that he had ever seen him. When I asked him who he thought I was talking to on the bench the other day, he said that 'it wasn't for him to say'. I insisted that he come with me. Just as we were coming round the shrubbery for the third time, the CG arrived on a bicycle. It was evident from the opening words and the expression on the face, that he found difficulty in accommodating himself to the simplest of mental operations. However, I decided to persevere. I told him about the man 'Daniels'. He nodded, his face riddled with blankness, and licked his pencil tip. Christie and he, babbling in the local patois, became animated. Then we went upstairs. I had to confess the man had disappeared. But I showed him the soiled bed. Apparently, none of the local institutions had patients missing. Mr O'Riordan laboriously made one or two brief notes, then went away. I went back up to my room. As I opened the door 'Daniels' clambered out of the wardrobe, laughing. He realized that I hadn't been listening and that I intended to put the Garda on to him, so he had hidden away amongst the boots and shoes. Since then, we have progressed no further. As I write, he's sleeping in the other bed. What puzzles me is that he really does seem to know as much as I do about the subject of my work. Having seen that the ethics of confrontation are liable to produce violence, I went further in the opposite direction this evening. We proceeded to have a 'conversation' – on the assumption that he was a survival from the seventeenth century. In other circumstances (as a sort of mock-dialogue, perhaps) it would have been entertaining and amusing, even interesting, perhaps, to some. We talked Tudor history and the policy of Lord Grey in Ireland. He quoted my favourite passage of Edmund Spenser on the flies over the Bog of Allen. I remarked that I had always thought it a paradox that Spenser, our supreme poet of love, should have been able to write a pamphlet on the extermination of the Irish. Not if you knew Mrs Spenser, he replied. He quoted all my favourite passages from Raleigh's hymn to Cynthia and narrated, as an eye-witness, the story of Raleigh's exile to Ireland, a subject about which I've been reading before falling asleep at night. I asked him – laughingly conscious of my role as 'interviewer' – whether it was true or not that Spenser was trying to help Raleigh regain favour with Queen Elizabeth. Not only Spenser, he replied, but Gascoigne too. It's a pity he's so mad, because the man is really interesting. Of course, I know what books he's read, because I've read them all myself. I can tell when he's fantasizing and when he's merely repeating some standard text. Half of his 'personal reminiscences' are verbatim quotations from *The School of Night* by Muriel Bradbrook. I happen to have just been re-reading it and so can check them. He insists, of course, that he isn't talking about history at all. It's only history for me, he says.

'Bracken',
Malahide,
Aug. 19th '53.

Mr Doyle arrived at last from Dublin. His visit was almost ruined by the presence of this absurd interloper. We went to lunch at Doyle's club in Raheny. Over lunch (quantities of pink gin and Dover sole) I explained my findings to him. Afterwards, we strolled in the little cypress garden behind the clubhouse, continuing to argue, in a friendly way, over Daniels's authorship of the variants in B. Doyle, I must say, is a highly intelligent man and put up some pretty fierce opposition. As we passed down the row of cypresses, I saw 'Daniels' step out from behind one of the trees and fall in step with us. He must have overheard us talking this morning when Doyle arrived at the house and stowed away in the car. He was walking on the other side of Doyle, trying to attract his attention. Fortunately Doyle ignored him. But the longer Doyle's head was turned towards me, the more importunate 'Daniels' became. I continued to expound my theory as best I could. The effort to keep Doyle's attention made me more and more animated. Each time I paused for breath I found that 'Daniels' had carried on – in his totally personalizing, anectodal style – where I had left off and had actually succeeded in engaging Doyle's attention. I had to struggle, almost fainting with the effort, to regain it. At last, they started to draw ahead of me, Doyle nodding vigorously, and I had to run to catch up. Panting, I caught Doyle by the shoulder and spun him round. I told him not to listen. If I were honest, I said, I had not found the real Daniels by deduction anyway, but by an inspired form of guesswork plus a little mundane reasoning. Precisely, said Doyle, That is what you have been expounding to me for the last two hours, is it not? But this one, *this* 'Daniels' is an imposter, I insisted, pointing at the smiling figure behind him. Doyle looked over his shoulder at 'Daniels', then back at me. Are you now telling me, said Doyle, After all that rigmarole, that you *doubt your own conclusions*? I did think he looked like the woodcut, I admitted, but he can't really be like it, or its just a meaningless coincidence. He's just been copying my findings. Doyle turned. 'Daniels' started speaking rapidly to him. He told Doyle that the reason I was able to deduce him was that he lived in series-time. He started to say wild things. He said that Gascoigne, unknown to scholars, had been a member of the School of Night. He plotted with Spenser and Raleigh against Shakespeare. He claimed that Gascoigne wrote a pamphlet called 'Necromancie, his time', which no one can now find. Doyle seemed to listen but, quite rightly, didn't know what to make of this jumble of nonsense. You see, I said, You see what I mean. Doyle nodded and took me by the arm. We all three went back into the clubhouse and sat down. It was obvious, to my great relief, that the credibility of 'Daniels' had finally been impugned. Doyle ordered me a cup of coffee and ignored him. We spent the rest of the day, almost within his earshot, discussing what to do about the situation.

'Bracken'
Malahide,
Aug. 20th '53.

Another long session with Doyle this morning. He's put my mind at rest a little. He suggests that perhaps I should change my attitude towards Daniels. Why not, if he claims to have access to such knowledge, take advantage of him? He urged me to write up my findings and take Daniels back to England with me. The two of us, he said smiling, should work on the Edition. He laughed. He is, after all, he said, The Living Proof. A joke I can appreciate. Throughout our conversation, Daniels insisted on sitting with us in the library. He had his back turned to us. He didn't seem to mind Doyle's insulting suggestion. Doyle didn't look at him, but said that he would take my word for his feelings on the matter. I must say this man Doyle does seem a thoughtful type. We agreed on tomorrow. In the meantime, I wrote to Pauline, informing her that I was bringing a 'guest' (I nearly wrote 'ghost'!) back from Ireland with me.

'Mount Pleasant',
Richmond,
Aug. 21st '53.

Rode to North Wall this morning in Doyle's car. Daniels insisted on having luggage, so I had to dash round yesterday buying extra suitcases for him. Fortunately, he's the same size as I am, so he could be sent out to buy his own clothes. Embarcation was embarrassing. Doyle shook me by the hand, but ignored Daniels. I was pleased. The man on the boat made a fuss about Daniels's ticket, of course. I managed to negotiate that by slipping him a fiver. I've never seen a man more reluctant to accept a bribe. I'm getting quite used to fusses. The crossing was rough. I was alright, spending the time in the bar, but Daniels seemed ill and retired to his berth. I had a little time to reflect on this whole business. I pay no attention to the nonsense he talks about Time, but he has acquired, from wherever, a detailed knowledge of my work. Almost as detailed, it seems from questioning him, as my own. This makes him an asset, as Doyle has suggested, because he can actually help me, but also a danger, because if he talked to Fawcett or Quilley or Miss Burgeon (particularly Miss Burgeon) my Festival Edition would be obsolete before it came out. When we docked at Liverpool, I went down to his cabin. To my astonishment, he was drunk. I had to get a porter to carry his bags. He must have slipped away to one of the bars on the lower decks. At customs I sent him on ahead and pretended his bags were mine. I didn't want any altercation with the authorities after the ticket problem. Unfortunately they insisted on opening them. They turned out to be full of Irish whiskey. He must have bought it with the money I sent him out to buy clothes with. There was a terrible fuss, throughout all of which I could see him going on before through the 'Nothing to declare' alley. I was detained in a small, unpleasant room, stripped, and forced to pay exhorbitant duty. Pauline and the children were at Euston when we eventually arrived. They had been waiting for hours. I was very annoyed: despite my specific instructions to the contrary, they had brought their cameras again. I got down from the train. Where's the visitor, said Pauline, Let's have a look at him. We all waited for him to come out, but he didn't appear. I got his bags down from the luggage rack in the compartment we'd been in. It was empty. Perhaps he was being tactful, I thought. I'm worried. He knows my address, of course. What can I do? I took the hated baggage home. This evening I rang Doyle to tell him what had happened, but couldn't get through. I got Pauline to make up the spare bed and leave the front door open, in case he arrives later.

The Railway Hotel,
Glasgow,
Aug. 22nd '53.

A troubled night. Pauline tossing and turning. I couldn't stop thinking about Daniels. Having already spent some time by letter preparing Pauline for what Daniels is like, he's had the effrontery to disappear. You said he was a ghost, she said this evening. No, I said he *thought* he was a ghost. Then I realized she's misread my handwriting. Actually, he's an actor. It sounded so lame. How can she believe in him at all, if he's obviously not there. Unpredictably, she seems quite unperturbed. She said she didn't want the house 'cluttered up with actors'. I went into the spare room this morning out of some vain desire that he might have crept in during the night. The boys were in there, wrecking the bed. This caused me unaccountable anger. As I entered my study, preparing to deal with some of my correspondence, a thought struck me. Supposing Daniels paid a visit to Fawcett or Quilley, or communicated with Miss Burgeon by transatlantic telephone. The impact, if not the validity, of my work could be in jeopardy. I immediately ran outside and leapt into a passing taxi. At Victoria, I got on a train to Brighton. On the way down, I became more firmly convinced of Daniels's game. He was doing this to all the editors in turn. Extorting money from them all, each one not knowing he had made deals with the others until too late. For some reason, I was the last in the chain. Fawcett greeted me at the door. He denied that Daniels was there. I went through the house like a whirlwind. There was a dreadful scene in the garden. I saw red. Fawcett had brought out his wife as testimony to the fact that Daniels had never been there. He was hiding behind her, literally and metaphorically. I ferreted him out, literally, and took him by the lapels. You paid him a mint, I shouted. His wife ran indoors and Fawcett started to threaten me with the police. Back to Victoria. By this time I was frantic. I telephoned Pauline to see if Daniels had come home in the meantime. Then the full thought struck me: Daniels could be an agent of Fawcett, Quilley, or Miss Burgeon, or the whole lot, sent out to spy on me. But that is far too simple an explanation. That way paranoia lies. I decided after I must be more calm about the affair. Pauline urged me to get out to Kelvinside tomorrow early. It is probable that Fawcett is lying to me. Methinks he doth protest too much. But it's obvious violence will get me nowhere. I must be more circumspect with Quilley. If Daniels is an agent, Quilley is hardly going to tell me. But supposing Daniels is an agent, and is *also* blackmailing his employers in turn. A double agent. The cliché, after all, of this cold war.

'Mount Pleasant',
Richmond,
Aug. 23rd '53.

Quilley found me early this morning in his garden. He didn't seem surprised to see me and opened the french window of his study and invited me in. I assume Fawcett telephoned him after yesterday. I asked him, with point-blank disingenuousness, if Daniels had been there, touting for money. Quilley laughed. He said that the only Daniels that ever 'crossed his threshold' was myself. I was immediately convinced that he was lying. I didn't tell him Daniels was posing as a ghost, so how did he know what to make an allusion to in his little joke about crossing the threshold? He tried to probe me about my findings. He mentioned that Miss Burgeon is about to publish another article in HLQ on the editorial problem of *The Feaste*, he had it from the editor himself. Could Daniels have been in touch with her, said Quilley. I smiled back. All things are possible, I said. In the middle of this conversation, Pauline rang up. She sounded strange. She revealed that Daniels had turned up in Richmond. I asked to speak to him, but she said he 'wasn't there at the moment'. Until I see him, I thought, I can be sure of no one. She was waiting for me at Euston with a strange man in tow. No sign of Daniels. Where is he, I hissed. Pauline introduced the man as a 'medical friend'. He started to talk immediately, ninety to the dozen, about his hospital. His talk was full of obscurity. Something about some experiments he was doing for the National Health Service which he wanted me to help him with. Just when this man was beginning to bore and distress me with his talk of experiments, Daniels appeared from behind a concrete pillar and took my bag off me, nice as pie. When I asked him where he had been, he replied that he'd been having a look round London, not having seen it for two hundred and fifty years. Of course, I said, And what did he think of the 'new' Houses of Parliament? He said he didn't understand all that levelling talk, but he thought the building was in a 'right Romish spirit'. It could be amusing, this kind of double-talk, if the circumstances were different. Pauline and her medical friend walked behind us. When we got to the car, the medical friend left. I told him to give me a ring sometime soon about the experiments and he said he would. Now Daniels is back, I mustn't let him out of my sight until the Edition is finished.

'Mount Pleasant',
Richmond,
Aug. 24th '53.

Spent the whole day in the study, Daniels in the chair next to me, going over the notes to the Edition. He can be extremely diverting on scholastic matters, converting everything historical to personal experience, giving me the 'low-down' on the first night of the revival performance of *The*

Feaste, showing how he played Bruno's lines, what expression he put into them, etc., talking of the scuffle in St Martin's Lane after the performance over the papist elements in the play, and so on. Some of this is checkable and usable in the Edition. I laughed and joked, drawing him out, pretending to write *everything* down religiously. Once, when I went out to get us some more whiskey (his own Irish), I found Pauline lurking in the hall, like a servant in a Victorian novelette. My aim now is to try and integrate him into the family. I think this constant antagonism is counter-productive. He seems to like the boys (little monsters). At least, he spends a lot of time talking to them, looking at their drawings of aeroplanes. I have to join in, purely as a public relations exercise. This afternoon, I ran round the garden playing football with them two against two. Daniels had to be 'taught' the game, of course; he seemed to learn with far too much alacrity. Pauline he ignores. She seems to spend a lot of time on the telephone at the moment. This evening, while Daniels and the boys were watching TV in the lounge, I went upstairs and found her weeping on the bed. She told me she was worried about me. It was not me, I assured her, she needed to worry about. Not him, she said, You. The man I married. Then she added bitterly, *supposedly*. I assured her there was no question about the legality of her marriage. I tried to explain the situation. I said it was imperative for me to keep Daniels quiet until I could finish the Edition. I begged her to help me, in any way she could. She kept crying and asking me 'what I meant'. There are limits, I said, I didn't mean you had to go *that* far. But a lot was at stake. He was obviously unscrupulous. She could see that from his behaviour already. All this disappearing business. I confessed to her that he had started to blackmail me. That I had decided to comply with him until the work was finished. Soon I could pay him off and we could take a holiday with the children in the Bahamas. Her response to this was extraordinary. Does it have to be the Bahamas? She agreed eventually to the Isle of Wight, on one condition. That tomorrow night, her medical friend come to supper. I warned her that if I had to start helping this Dr Saul with his National Health project, I should not be able to go to the Isle of Wight as well, so she'd better get her priorities straight. She seemed to see the point, saying she was sure 'something could be arranged'. I agreed, on one condition. That we find a way of getting rid of Daniels for the evening. Not only would he be an embarrassment, but I was spending all day with him and was bored stiff by evening time. But Pauline was again quite unpredictable: she said that, since Dr Saul had been there at Euston and knew therefore that Daniels was our resident guest (resident *ghost*, I quipped) wouldn't it be stranger if Daniels was not there than if he was? Dr Saul had said he was interested in meeting him. I agreed, but rather reluctantly.

'Mount Pleasant',
Richmond,
Aug. 25th '53.

Work goes forward. Daniels has the most odd theories, I grant him that. He told me that Gascoigne had told him that the astronomical speeches in the play are plagiarized from Bruno the Nolan's *De Umbris Idearum*. A magnificent idea, quite unprovable as far as I can see, since the 'astronomy' in question is a version of Plotinus's one-and-many theory and has no empirical status. Still, the A text does have references to heavenly bodies which could be construed as implying a heliocentric model. Daniels claims to have been employed to adjust some of the references to stars in B, so that they would be understood as Ptolemaic. In fact, Daniels says, Gascoigne was a Copernican and the play in its A text was in danger of constituting heresy. By a few corrections, however, it could be made to seem that Bruno was the heretic, not the author. Hence he could be burnt, like his historical namesake, and the Catholic hierarchy be confirmed in their power. The Protestant audience, unstable about their own relation to papism, would be duly inflamed and horrified. A good standard Lutheran trick. At supper a terrible argument occurred between Daniels and the doctor about astral bodies. I caught Pauline's eye. Hadn't I warned her? In the end Daniels denounced Dr Saul, as dapper a Jew as one could ever hope to meet, as 'a Papist and a bigot'. The doctor retired drunk and defeated. Pauline was inconsolable. She talked with him for a long time out in the front drive. I calmed Daniels down in the study with a glass of Irish.

'Mount Pleasant',
Richmond,
Aug. 26th '53.

When I took him down to the bank with me this morning, they refused to honour my cheque. I could see him through the window, browsing through some leaflets. He didn't seem to notice. I knew if he did notice, there was a likelihood he would disappear again. We went home immediately. I made an excuse to slip back out, bribing the boys to engage his attention with my last few bits of change. Philips was unsympathetic to begin with. But then I told him all about Daniels and the situation of the Edition. I used all my powers of eloquence on him. In the end, he relented, saying that it was not really his policy, as a bank manager, to support blackmail, but he could 'see my problem, and it was rather a special one'. It's lucky he's sweet on Pauline. When I got home, I found the boys hot and flushed, sword-fighting with Daniels. They had certain articles of clothing removed. Pauline seemed to have gone out. I joined in and, after a bit, took off some of my clothes, in order to make Daniels think I approved of this kind of thing. In reality, I was frightened of the gleam that had come into his eye. Afterwards, when he was dressing, I went over to Jason and started to explain to him what he should do if Daniels ever tried to put his hand on his thigh, or anything of that order. To illustrate, I put my hand on Jason's thigh. I told him it could be dangerous to resist a man like Daniels and the safest thing to do was to lie back and wait. Jason started to whimper. Daniels smiled when he saw what was going on. I heard him quoting under his breath Bruno's hyperbole:

> Thy qualities are like unto a lake ...

Pauline came to the top of the stairs and started screaming and throwing crockery. What on earth was she doing upstairs with the crockery? I couldn't help thinking it was a pity she didn't know the play.

'Mount Pleasant',
Richmond,
Aug. 27th '53.

This doctor seems to be paying a lot of attention to Pauline. She tells me she's going out to tea with him the day after tomorrow. Is he an old flame, I wonder? Or is he just anxious to get my help on his project? Worked all day in the study with Daniels. Afterwards I paid him. He insists on payment after every session like a psychiatrist. Later he went to Leicester Square and started to comb the passers-by for whores. I stood on the corner watching. He was quite unsuccessful, but in the end *I* was

moved on by a policeman who told me that if I didn't watch it I would
'blot my copybook'. At night, Daniels drank a great deal of whiskey and
started quoting long speeches from the play, reaming off all Bruno's
soliloquies from the first three acts until I was bored stiff and Pauline
came in and told him to stop shouting because he had woken the boys.

'Mount Pleasant',
Richmond,
Aug. 28th '53.

I'm now almost ready to send the Edition, together with Daniels's new
additions, to Dampmartin. Daniels is very restless. He craves, of all
things, to see a *play*.

'Mount Pleasant',
Richmond,
Aug. 29th '53.

Tonight we went to a production of *The White Devil* at the Old Vic.
Daniels snorted throughout. He kept shouting that Webster was a 'lackey
of Rome, and the dogs of the Lord'. Pauline shepherded the boys outside
while I stayed to cope with him. He seems to know the play off by heart
and kept shouting their speeches in unison with the actors in a tone of
disgust. I managed to help two or three of them eject him. Afterwards I
came home with him in a taxi, Pauline having taken the car. We stopped
at most of the pubs in Waterloo. In the end we were quite drunk. I
admitted that I was seeing double, but Daniels insisted to the taxi driver
that he was sober enough to pay the fare himself and threw it, as a result,
all over the floor of the cab.

'Mount Pleasant',
Richmond,
Aug. 30th '53.

I've suddenly realized that Daniels has changed his tactics completely. He
still demands money, of course. But he's much less active now. He
doesn't seem to want to go out. There's no danger of losing him now.
Quite the opposite, if I don't watch it we shan't be able to get rid of him.

His manner is servile. He has started to pay attention to Pauline, helping her in small domestic chores, chattering trivially, etc. He must have realized that, the Edition almost finished, his hold on me will slacken completely overnight.

> 'Mount Pleasant',
> Richmond,
> Aug. 31st '53.

Pauline's doctor friend came today and spent a long time talking to Daniels. I felt quite jealous. They were turned away from me, so I couldn't catch everything they said. The man is very naïve for a scientist. He apparently takes quite seriously Daniels's claim to be a seventeenth-century 'phenomenon' translated into the twentieth century by my act of unconscious 'conjuring'. He wants to 'study' him. As soon as Daniels was down the far end of the room, conducting one of his newly conceived 'charming' speeches to Pauline, I took the opportunity of enlightening Dr Saul. I assured him that Daniels was not even a seventeenth-century actor, let alone an incubus. He was a twentieth-century impostor, plain and simple, who was blackmailing me and whom I had decided to appease, for the sake of the Edition. This seemed to convince him, though he must be quite stupid, I think. I couldn't restrain myself from suggesting, as he was leaving, that perhaps he would like to enlist the help of Daniels rather than myself in his National Health project. I caught Pauline's arm. My wife and I were going for a well-deserved rest on the Isle of Wight.

> 'Mount Pleasant',
> Richmond,
> Sept. 1st '53.

The new tactic continues. It disturbs me. He seems almost given over to flattery at the moment, spending every moment he can with Pauline and the boys. I hear his voice everywhere, feverishly discussing some detail or other of domestic life. The boys seem in awe of him. I shall have to speak to Pauline about this. After the other night at the play, I'm beginning to wonder what his new scheme is, now that the Edition is finished. He constantly makes reference to *The Feaste*, often phrasing his speech so that it is a half-quotation, an echo; as if his behaviour were only an allusion to something else.

Johns Hotel,
Paddington,
Sept. 2nd '53.

The Edition finally finished and posted off. I couldn't believe it. Rang Dampmartin to tell him, in a state of euphoria. He seemed not to share it. He said, casually, that he thought I had 'plenty of time left'. I was stunned. If that was the situation, why hadn't he let me know? How could I take advantage of the penalty clause, if the Edition was not now to be completed ahead of time. Time, said Dampmartin glibly, Is relative. Other contributors to the Festival Series were going to be late, so the board had decided to put back the dates of publication to the original terms of contract. I came off the phone, not knowing where I was. I went upstairs to tell Pauline. She was in bed, reading a book. I sat down in despair on the edge of the bed and took off my shoes and socks. I glanced in the wardrobe mirror. The bedclothes were very ruffled at the bottom and, to my astonishment, there was an *extra pair of naked feet* sticking out. I tore away the bedclothes and stared at them, the naked lovers, caught *in flagrante delicto*. Daniels wound his arms round Pauline, serpent-like, smiling and murmuring Bruno's speech from III, ii, 48ff. Pauline recoiled from me in horror and pushed Daniels away, screaming. This then was the purpose of his recent blandishments. I was bitter, but I couldn't help, even in the height of bitterness, noticing that I myself was echoing Aracchino's renunciation of Isabella in IV, i, 21ff. I saw the joke. D'you know in what jeopardy you have placed your immortal soul? She had the effrontery to protest her innocence: Pauline has no knowledge of the play. She told me she *hadn't noticed him* in bed with her! Death, I said to the mirror, Is *so* permanent. I swept out and drove here.

'Mount Pleasant',
Richmond,
Sept. 3rd '53.

Walking down Charing Cross Road this morning, I saw a sign in a booksellers that jolted me back to reality. It was an advertisement for the forthcoming Festival Series from the Minute Press. The list of plays was in the form of a playbill, stippled all over with minute cap-and-bells motifs. As I looked at it, I realized that *The Feaste of Time* was missing. It couldn't be that I was late, because Dampmartin told me yesterday that I am earlier than all the other contributors. A printer's error, perhaps. Not very likely. Then the truth began to click like the tumblers in a lock. The reason why the Edition doesn't appear on the list is that the play no longer exists. Or, more strictly, has not yet come into being. The bundle of papers I have sent to Dampmartin is quite meaningless. Far from being a reconstruction of what happened in 1635, it is a shadowy projection of what is about to happen – what is already happening – in 1953. The final trick of the theatre-manager: to find out what Daniels is going to do next, all I have to do is *consult the plot of the play* (the B text, of course). I have been cast as Aracchino, the jealous husband. Pauline, God bless her, is Isabella. Jason and Gregory are playing Cinthio and Julio. And Bruno? Daniels himself, of course. This is why he's been paying so much attention to my family all of a sudden. When I arrived home, there was a curt note from 'the adultress'. She and the boys have gone to Lympne to her mother's. Daniels is nowhere to be seen. It's incredible that I haven't seen this before. He's been acting the part of a blackmailer all along, impersonating a double-agent for the other editors in order to get me to write out his insane play script in full. He's a life-manager, not a theatre-manager. He depends on me, of course, for the next stage in the plot. If I refuse to kill the boys, he cannot then kill Pauline. I sat and laughed. Perhaps I should go to the Bahamas and leave them all stuck down in Lympne like a set of marionettes with cut strings. It was tempting for a moment. If I do that, I shall never have the satisfaction of catching him and exorcizing him. I can't get him out of hiding until I at least pretend to kill the boys and throw the blame for the deed on Pauline, as the play demands. She has in fact become jealous of Daniels's attentions to the boys, so the monomaniac has already advanced that little part of the plot. Poor Pauline. Poor Isabella.

'Lilac Cottage',
Lympne,
Sept. 4th '53.

Bought some retractable toy daggers this morning from a joke shop.

Spent the whole afternoon at the abattoir waiting to buy from the suspicious foreman a couple of bladders of ox-blood. He said he 'drew the line at bladders'. Fortunately, I had some party balloons which could stand in. This thing has to be done properly. I've realized at last what is at stake. Not the Edition, which is now a mere instrument. But my whole family. What a fool I've been not to be able to see this litter of signs. When I boarded the train at Waterloo, I thought I saw Daniels get on too, several coaches away. I couldn't be sure I wasn't starting to see things. The strain of this business has been considerable. It was a corridorless local, so I had to wait until we got to Westernhanger halt. I wasn't seeing things. He got off on the other side of the train and pretended to be tapping the wheel. I could see his feet under the carriage. It's not in the play: I shall take him to task for that. I shall turn his own inquisition scene on him. I walked without looking back up the road. When I reached here, Pauline and Audrey were sitting in front of the fire, Jason and Gregory had already been put to bed. I went up and sat on their bed, poor little pages, while they slept. At supper, I tried to humour Pauline and Audrey, but they wouldn't be drawn. As I went to draw the curtains, I burst into uncontrollable laughter: reflected in the window was the image of Daniels, dressed as a Kentish farmer. At last we all went to bed. I lay awake, listening. Pauline seemed very restless: I could tell from her breathing she was not properly asleep. I had to risk it. I went downstairs and put the back door off the latch. Then back to bed to wait. After what seemed half the night I heard a scrabbling noise and some heavy breathing. He seemed to be climbing up the drainpipe. Then I realized that he had to do the thing properly. He couldn't afford to acknowledge any 'invitation' of mine, like the back door ... I heard the landing window slide open and a thud as he dropped in on to the floor. I slipped into the boys' room and quickly slid the 'bladders' under the sheets. I could see his shape watching in the doorway. I 'stabbed' them both repeatedly. They brought the house down. Pauline came rushing in, saw the daggers and the bed full of spreading stains and started to scream. The ox-blood balloons worked very nicely. Daniels came in, I slipped behind the wardrobe. Bruno confronted Isabella with the crime of having killed his beloved pages. He began the alternating *basso* of his accusation speech. Audrey tried to rush in, but he swept her aside, taking from his pocket a silk scarf. This he wrapped slowly around Isabella's neck and pulled tight, intoning:

> Out, Fading Candle: the deed is almost done,
> And I can pledge these broken epigrams
> In blood, swallow all signs at last ...

I must say, he had some difficulty getting this out above the screams of the boys. At this point, I stepped out from behind the wardrobe and began Aracchino's gloating recitative with the dying Isabella:

> Sing now, Siren: let's see thee dash
> This ruffian Galley on the rocks of hell:
> In thy lap's stead have I dug his tomb
> And quit his manhood with thy woman's sleight.
> Lap, lap up thy adulterous vomit ...

I think Daniels has finally realized what he has set in motion.

> 'Mount Pleasant',
> Richmond,
> Sept. 9th '53.

It only remains now for the finale. The Duke and Friar need to come in and cap the gloating Aracchino in his own wretched morality-play sentiments. Drove here this morning with the 'corpses' of the boys in the back, They kept shouting and throwing things at one another. Pauline lapsed from time to time into hysteria. Poor thing, she's very tired. I explained to her about the final scene. Its all going to be quite easy to set up. I suggested she ring her friend Dr Saul and see if he's interested in coming. Then I rang the local police and suggested that probably the best place for them to station themselves would be the attic. I'll have to make copies of speeches for everybody. The local Anglican vicar can stand in for the Friar, though this will infuriate Daniels. I'm afraid at this late hour we shall have to make shift as best we can. All set then. Tomorrow at ten.

Clive Sinclair

AMERICA

CLIVE SINCLAIR was born in 1948 and educated at the universities of East Anglia and California at Santa Cruz. His stories, interviews and travel pieces have been published in *Encounter, New Review, London Magazine, Penthouse, Quarto* and *Transatlantic Review*. He has also written a novel, *Bibliosexuality*, and a collection of short stories, *Hearts of Gold*, and he is currently writing a book about Isaac Bashevis Singer and his novelist brother I. J. Singer. He was awarded the Bicentennial Arts Fellowship for 1980 and won the Somerset Maugham Award for 1981 with *Hearts of Gold*.

When I was little I thought *merica* was an English noun, always preceded by what my tutor called the indefinite article. Although I never heard it referred to in the plural I imagined that somewhere on Florianska Street there was a shop that specialized in selling a scintillating variety of *mericas*, which I visualized as enormous crystalline balls cunningly worked so that when struck by light they emitted countless golden rays. I was afraid of the dark and inclined to weep for my mother's eternal absence whenever she left me alone, but I never doubted the existence of that store. However, for such a sickly child the trip to Florianska Street (if made alone) was the equivalent of an expedition to the ends of the earth. Nevertheless, it remained my dream. I believed that my mother's brothers shared that dream, for it was they who uttered the magic word most frequently, but they never once offered to lead me to my childhood paradise. Instead, they looked upon it as their sacred duty to make me sturdy. Uncle Konrad would accompany me to the meadows beside the Vistula where we flew a kite. 'See how it wriggles in the sky,' Uncle Konrad cried, 'like bacteria under my microscope.' Uncle Konrad was a biologist (killed during a cholera epidemic, coincidentally, by the bacteria my kite most resembled). Actually, as it was sucked further and further away it reminded me more of the loathsome lozenges I was required to dissolve in my mouth every time I contracted a sore throat. Uncle Kazimir was an entomologist. He took

me scrambling in the scrub that proliferated along the Route of the
Eagles' Nests. Here he pointed out the manifold varieties of insect life. All
of which disgusted me. Poor Uncle Kazimir. He died of fever in Ceylon,
on a futile expedition. He travelled to the tropical isle with a group of
fellow enthusiasts, only to be fatally discouraged by the local authorities,
who explained that the beetles could not possibly be killed since they
might be the reincarnation of someone's grandmother. Sure enough,
Uncle Kazimir's name is now carried by a green beetle which inhabits the
swampy region of the Danube delta. We preserved his collection of shiny
bugs in glass cabinets like campaign medals. Only Uncle Lucian kept me
entertained. He was a photographer. My greatest delight was to be
smuggled into his studio and hidden behind the velvet drapes, where I
pretended that I was snuggled beneath my mother's voluminous skirts,
while he went about obtaining the portrait of a fine lady. Out of gratitude
I determined to buy a *merica* for Uncle Lucian.

I lacked the courage for such an adventure, and detested my cowardice.
I fell sick. The family doctor said it was nerves and prescribed a tonic. My
mother fretted; my father was unsympathetic. I got no stronger. One day
the smelly Jewish girl who scrubbed our floors came to my room secretly
with a silver amulet which she told me to put under my pillow. I held my
nose as she knelt beside me to explain the curious symbols that were
engraved upon it. She said that the bird, a comical creature the like of
which I had never seen even at the zoological gardens in Warsaw,
represented life. 'Why?' I asked. 'Don't argue,' she replied, 'the rabbi said
so.' But this did not satisfy me; I simply could not grasp how a bird could
be the symbol of life, when the only birds I had seen at close quarters
were destined to be plucked, cooked and devoured. Pullets, pigeons
(delicious in squab pie), pheasants, partridges, songbirds, even a wood-
cock. It was true that Uncle Kazimir kept an owl in his study, but that
creature dealt out death, not life. I never saw the owl without a dead
mouse on the floor of its cage, its wicked beak clacking in anticipation.
Then I remembered a word that I had heard at school many times,
especially in Bible classes; this bird was a *sacrifice*! Like all the others it
would die that I might live. 'Foolish boy,' clucked the Jewess, 'listen and
don't ask questions. The first words mean "perfect healing". This word –
semerpad – is a secret name for God. The next lines are a quotation from
Genesis, "Joseph is a fruitful vine by a fountain; its branches run over the
wall."' 'But my name is not Joseph,' I protested. 'My biggest boy is also

not called Joseph,' she replied, 'but this charm still cured him of scarlet fever. Now he is as strong as an ox, *kine-ahora*. Please God, you will soon be just as healthy.' It was a good game, I decided, so I put the amulet beneath my pillow. I wanted to say something nice to the Jewess. 'You have a magnificent bosom,' I said, 'it is a crime to keep it so well concealed.' Her reaction was frightening; she blushed like a schoolgirl and raised her hand as if to strike me. Yet the same words, spoken by Uncle Lucian to his clients, were always received with such gratitude. When I recovered the doctor claimed all the credit. But I knew whom to thank. To celebrate my return to the dining-table my mother ordered the cook to kill our fattest goose.

The dinner was a splendid occasion; not only were my parents and all my uncles and aunts present but also many friends and celebrated acquaintances. Because of the number of guests there were long delays between the abundant courses, so my mother permitted me to play in my hideout beneath the tablecloth. Consequently, I knew it was not clumsiness that caused the Jewess to spill soup upon my Aunt Amelia's shoulder but a squeeze on her calf from Uncle Lucian. I also knew whose shiny boot was rubbing against whose shapely ankle, though I could think of no reason for such activity. However, I had learned to keep my mouth shut; my indiscretion with the Jewess had taught me that adult behaviour was not as simple as it seemed. Now that I was better the jaunts with my uncles were resumed, and once again I made up my mind to find a *merica* for my favourite. But this time I had a plan. 'I am going on a journey,' I told the Jewess, 'can your rabbi make a talisman to protect me?' She laughed. 'So now you believe in them?' she said. I recognized the question as rhetorical and did not answer. A few days afterwards the Jewess produced a second silver amulet. 'What does it say?' I asked. 'This one is more complicated,' said the Jewess. 'It begins with two four-letter names for God entwined, then it lists the angels who will watch over you – Gabriel, Michael, Badriel. The rest is written in code to deceive the evil eye.' With that in my pocket I felt confident enough to walk unaccompanied through Planty Park.

It was early October and the park was alive with children collecting horse chestnuts. Nannies sat upon the benches casting benevolent glances in the direction of their charges, though they seemed more interested in the bold soldiers who sauntered past. Feeling carefree I also stooped to gather the newly fallen chestnuts, even then touched by the transience of their beauty. And with that thought came a glimmer of comprehension for Uncle Lucian's professional passion, and I could guess why so many women came to see him. In a secluded corner of the park, when the Town Hall was already in sight, a young lout suddenly appeared. I called upon my guardian angels to protect me, whereupon a passing dove emptied its bowels upon the ruffian's head. And so I came safely into Rynek Główny, the Market Square. Fashionable women swirling parasols to deflect the heat of the autumn sun strolled through the Sukiennice, admiring the silks and laces on display, while their maids bartered with the peasants who had come in from the country to sell their produce. Since winter was inevitably approaching many carts were full of firewood. 'Ready for delivery!' promised the drivers, as they prodded their old nags into life. Among all this bustle I recognized a familiar figure. His head was concealed beneath the black cloth of his camera, but Ignacy Krieger was unmistakable. There he stood like the man behind a Punch and Judy show, but he was the audience and the whole world was his stage. 'Hello, young man!' he shouted. 'What are you doing so far from home?' 'Shopping,' I replied grandly. 'Look what I have just purchased,' he said proudly as he gestured toward his glowing mahogany camera with its gleaming brass lens, 'a brand new Thornton Pickard, all the way from England. Just what I need for my street scenes. I'm afraid that your uncle is going to be very jealous.' Ignacy Krieger was one of Uncle Lucian's greatest rivals. 'Now that you are such a man-about-town,' he continued, 'you must visit my studio.' Ignacy Krieger's famous studio! His obnoxious son Nathan, one of my classmates, never tired of boasting about his father's glorious studio with its ingenious gadgets. I was determined to strike a blow for my uncle. 'Not today,' I said, 'I am going to find a *merica* for Uncle Lucian.'

The sun illuminated Florianska Street, gilding the pedestrians and burnishing the shops. In the dazzling light the contents of each window looked like booty in a treasure chest. I saw diamonds, emeralds, rubies, silver cups, golden chains; I saw glossy furs, patent leather boots, and a host of wonderful trinkets – but I saw no sign of a *merica*. At the end of the street I had to hold back my tears of disappointment. But I refused to give up the search: I knew that my uncle's main supplier, Fotografia

Polska, was situated not far away on Krupnicza Street. Perhaps they would be able to help. The shop was full of familiar objects; bellows, lenses, tripods, cameras; all the paraphernalia Uncle Lucian adored. There were several glass discs, some concave, others convex, which slightly resembled what I had in mind. I approached the counter. 'What do you want, sonny?' said the supercilious salesman (I would report his lack of courtesy to Uncle Lucian, I thought). I looked him straight in the eye. 'I want a *merica*,' I said. 'So do we all,' he said, 'so do we all.' 'I want a *merica*,' I repeated. 'Do you know what America is?' he asked. I was angry, but I told him. 'You fool,' he guffawed, 'America is a country on the other side of the world.' Utterly humiliated, my dream shattered, I left Fotografia Polska. Blinded with tears I began to run along Krupnicza Street, until the sun went down and the only light came from the gas lamps. My imagination tried to frighten me with wild possibilities, but I no longer believed in it. Even so, I did not dare walk back through Planty Park after dark; there may not have been any witches or goblins, but I was pretty sure there were bandits and kidnappers. Who could help me now? Only Gabriel, Badriel, and Michael. Thanks to them I remembered that Awit Szubert, another of Uncle Lucian's rivals, had a studio at Number 7 Krupnicza Street. The door was not locked, so I ran up the stairs (carpeted, he was a successful man) and entered the studio just as the magnesium let rip. A small girl in a nightshirt was reclining on a settee opposite the camera; something about her pose made my hands tingle. 'Good heavens!' exclaimed Awit Szubert. 'What are you doing here?' Yet again I wept. 'Play for a while, my pet,' said Awit Szubert, 'I must take this little gentleman home.' My mother was shocked by my unorthodox arrival in a cab. Awit Szubert explained the circumstances. 'My poor boy,' cried my mother, 'weren't you afraid?' 'No,' I said, 'I was protected.' I showed her my amulet, with its Hebrew inscriptions and prominent Star of David. 'Where did you get this?' my mother demanded. She looked annoyed. It was too much for me, after the day's disappointment. 'From Hannah, the Jewess,' I wailed. Then, with marvellous dexterity, Uncle Lucian (who seemed remarkably un-comfortable) saved the situation by jumbling the letters of AMERICA to form an ungrammatical English anagram that was also his auto-biography, 'I CAMERA.' Even Awit Szubert laughed.

Years later I remember that afternoon with perfect clarity. Why not?

America turned out to be my future also. Oh yes, I found America in the end. Look at me now in a pisspot on the sleazy side of Hollywood Boulevard, my floor littered with empty Kodak film containers. My shutters are always closed. I have no desire to see the filthy posters nor read the flickering neon promises that lick the skies every night; instead I linger over the eloquent images that are windows on my past. This is the photograph Ignacy Krieger took that day in Rynek Glówny, the cabs forever awaiting their fashionable passengers, who still promenade while their servants haggle, even though all the firewood has long since been burnt to ashes; and there in the foreground stands a lovely boy (myself) embarked upon his great adventure. This is my father taken by Awit Szubert (he hated his brothers-in-law, especially Uncle Lucian), his jacket buttoned to the throat in the manner of the time, parting to reveal a gold collar-stud, not a wrinkle on his fleshy face, his moustache finely pointed, his mutton-chop whiskers beautifully trimmed, his receding hair neatly combed (he did not live long enough to go bald), and such hope in his eyes. Ah – my beautiful mother! See how she clings to the polished oak banisters at the bottom of our great staircase, as if she would otherwise float away, her feet hidden by the wooden gryphon which now guards some other boy as he sleeps above. I recall how hard Awit Szubert (why not Uncle Lucian?) worked to make her smile, but all she could give him was a sorrowful gaze out of melancholy eyes (what was on her mind?). Her hair is parted in the middle and piled high upon the crown of her head. She wears rings and bracelets and holds a rose. The rest of her body is concealed by her dark constricting dress. I try to recapture the scent of the perfume she wore that day, but it is a hopeless task. Here are some spectacular landscapes Awit Szubert took on our expedition to the Tatra Mountains. And this – which I dare not look at too frequently. A nude study, by Uncle Lucian, of Hannah. I am still grateful for the way she tried to comfort me after Awit Szubert had brought me home, and my mother had put me to bed. She came quietly into my room. What was she doing in the house at that hour? 'You are not the only person America has made a fool of,' she said. 'The biggest fool of all was Christopher Columbus. He thought it was India or Japan. Do you know he had a Jewish interpreter with him? Luis de Torres. Well Louie goes up to the Red Indians and starts talking to them in Hebrew. He thinks he's in the East, you see? What a *schlemiel*! But at least he found gold in the *goldeneh medina*. Unlike my husband. Now there's a real *shmendrick* for you. A fool's paradise, that's all the *goldeneh medina* is to him. He can't even save enough to send for me. So how can he expect me to resist a *shmoozer* like your Uncle Lucian?' She pinched my cheek. 'You're a naughty boy, too,' she said. 'All that talk of bosoms. When you're bigger you'll be a real Casanova. The world will be at your feet.' She should see me now.

I do not wish to speak ill of the Jews after all they have been through (Hannah included), but there is no doubt that they are responsible for my lamentable condition. By *they* I mean the Jewish moguls who control Hollywood. Perhaps they will remember me as the young man (young, alas, no longer) who used to deliver stills of the latest productions to their opulent offices. At that time I worked for one of the top production photographers in Hollywood. Since then we have all passed a good deal of water, as Mr Goldwyn put it. And I would be famous now, if not for *them*. I had accumulated a wonderful collection of photographs of all the biggest stars which I was planning to publish. It would have made my name. But my agent got a phone call from a shyster lawyer warning him that I had infringed every copyright rule in the book. He dropped me like a hot potato. Next thing I knew my house had been burgled and all my negatives had vanished. Why such persecution? Because of one night of madness with Errol Flynn, that's why! I met him at a big party up in Laurel Canyon. Errol's ribs were still sore from his notorious fight with John Huston so he was boozing rather than whoring. He needed to be somewhere else so I offered to give him a ride (he was in no condition to drive). He tossed me the keys to his car. 'Take mine,' he said. We ended up in an unspeakable dive off Sunset Strip frequented by low life, actors, and gossip columnists, where we joined some of his German cronies. Consider my position. I had come all the way to Los Angeles from Poland only to discover that the City of Angels was not populated with the likes of Gabriel, Michael, and Badriel, but with puffed-up Jewish pedlars whose cousins I could have seen any day of the week on Szeroka Street. Only now I was taking orders from *them*! Is it any wonder I cheered when Errol jumped on a table and did an impersonation of Adolf Hitler (in my opinion he was a much better actor than people said)? '*Daloy gramotniye!*' I yelled, echoing the old war-cry of the Black Hundreds (coined for them by the Tsarist secret police for use during pogroms).

Unfortunately, I forgot that most of the producers were Poles and that some of them were literate enough to know that the literates I wanted to do away with were Jews. The incident made the papers, pictures and all. Check the photo library of the *Los Angeles Times* if you don't believe me.

When it was too late we went back to my place. I lived in a modest house on Holly Drive, connected to the road by a steep flight of steps cut into the canyon wall. Errol staggered up them, miraculously keeping his balance, while hanging on to bottles of vodka and wine and a pot of caviar (which he had taken from a cache in his car). We drank, we ate, we told obscene stories (only Errol's were true). Soon the Germans were snoring. I felt wonderful. For a whole evening I had forgotten my lowly station in life; once more I was as bold as that boy who had gone in search of America. Drink had turned me into a sentimental fool. I showed Errol the photograph of my mother. 'A beautiful woman,' he agreed. Then I gave him Hannah. She was three-quarters towards the camera, so that although her breasts and body hair were fully exposed, there seemed to be some reluctance in their display. She was bending slightly, allowing her full breasts to hang, so emphasizing their nakedness. The sepia tone, the angle which revealed her shape so well, all gave this image of Hannah a three-dimensional effect which was not lost on Errol Flynn. He unbuttoned his flies and took out his famous instrument. 'This lady is about to be accorded a unique privilege,' he said. Whereupon he began to flick his penis lightly with the photograph. You must understand that the *cartes-de-visite* produced by Uncle Lucian and his contemporaries were not the flimsy things you get at drugstores nowadays but proper pieces of card. So Errol did not have any trouble producing an erection, nor in maintaining it. Poor Hannah took a beating that night. Luckily Errol Flynn's semen overshot her and landed upon my carpet. He left me to wipe it up, the animal. Next day I was on the black-list.

Some job I found! Every night I tramp around the restaurants on Hollywood and Sunset with a camera supplied by my employer (not the Leica I demanded). 'Heil Hitler,' I say to the fat Jewish customers who are dining with their gaudy wives or cheap mistresses (they hear, 'Smile mister'). How I despise them! So greasy is their hair that drops of oil collect on the tips like obscene ornaments. Oh where are my mother's antimacassars? The women make a mockery of her discreet elegance with their vulgar display of valuable jewellery. Of course they are delighted to have their picture taken, their eyes send messages to mine ('Make me beautiful'), while their diamonds contact the light meter that turns the lens of my camera into a rhinestone monocle. And so I press the button and the shutter opens letting in an image that will leave its contaminating stain upon my memory (among many others). I hand them my company's card. 'When will the print be ready?' they ask. 'Tomorrow,' I say. But the night continues. Some restaurants are large enough to contain dance-halls. It is here that I meet my nemesis (again and again). High above my head a large ball spins suspended from the ceiling; covered with hundreds of tiny mirrors it sends scintillas of silver light cascading down through the smoke. Everyone longs for the brief feel of the spotlight. Except me. For the shaft misses my face and stabs me through the heart. My America! Why? Why?

Why did I ever leave Poland? When Uncle Lucian gave me my first camera on my fifteenth birthday I had no inkling that it would be the last birthday I was to spend in the company of my family. Indeed, my joy knew no bounds when my father informed me that I would be able to use my camera on Awit Szubert's next expedition to the Tatras. Awit Szubert had made an annual pilgrimage to the Tatra Mountains from the time dry bromide plates were first available in Poland a quarter of a century before. Now, to mark his twenty-fifth visit, he had invited all his fellow photographers and their families to accompany him. It needed a whole carriage on the Cracow to Zakopane train to accommodate us all. The journey was exceedingly slow due to the excessive number of curves and steep inclines the engine had to climb, but we didn't care as we gorged ourselves upon the contents of our delicious hampers. At last the train gathered speed as it steamed through the valley towards Nowy Targ, the final station before Zakopane itself. After Nowy Targ the train began the ascent up the long gradient into Zakopane. As we traversed the terraced fields the highlanders (still unselfconscious) in embroidered shirts, white felt trousers, broad belts, and black hats, downed their tools to cheer, while their wives and children waved from the lofts of their wooden chalets, a spectacle which greatly excited Ignacy Krieger (who was planning the series on the traditional costumes of Poland which was to win him a gold medal at the Vienna exposition). In those days the mountains were pretty wild; the hidden valleys were well stocked with game – including wolves, bears, and boars – and in the caves – so it was rumoured – were bands of brigands. Naturally, I pressed my face to the window in the hope of catching sight of the one or the other (without success). At our destination the Mayor himself opened our carriage door and greeted Awit Szubert as if he were King of the Tatras. A pretty girl almost swooned when he kissed her on the cheek as she handed him a posy of wild flowers. A brass band struck up a melody of local tunes. The town was exuberant, and slightly pompous, for the people believed what foolish anthropologists had told them; that the Tatras were the birthplace of Polish civilization, and the cradle of a new independent Poland. 'Bah,' said Uncle Lucian. Whenever I look at Awit Szubert's photographs memories of those first exhilarating days in the mountains come flooding back. There are six figures picked out against the snow in his study of Zawrat Mountain: I am closest to the camera; besides me is my father; ahead of us are Uncle Lucian, Ignacy Krieger, Nathan Krieger, and our guide Jan (who claimed to have been a bandit in his youth). We didn't realize it at the time but we were carefully positioned to lead the viewer's eye toward the centre of the composition. A few minutes later my father and Uncle Lucian, who never liked one another, began to argue (maybe Uncle Lucian was upset because my father had commissioned Awit Szubert to take the family portraits). 'Please,' insisted Jan, 'you must never raise your voices in the mountains. The danger of avalanches is very great.'

My favourite excursion was to Morskie Oko, the Eye of the Sea. Legend had it that this beautiful lake was connected by underground tunnel to the sea some fifteen hundred metres below (but I didn't credit legend). Over-laden with lunch packs and photographic equipment, we scrambled over the last rocky outcrops and gratefully flung ourselves down the shingle to its shores. Here we basked. As the sun rose higher in the sky the lake changed colour from blue to brilliant green, until it did indeed resemble a giant lens. 'Photography is no longer merely nature's pencil,' said Awit Szubert as he assembled his camera upon its tripod, 'now with the help of an accurate lens and light sensitive plates I am able to reconstruct photographic images according to the rules of pictorial composition. I have become an artist.' So saying he shooed us out of sight so that we did not disturb the serene atmosphere with our lack of divinity. There are no boats on Morskie Oko in his photograph. But immediately afterwards the glassy calm of the lake was shattered by the launching of a dozen small dinghies. I found room on board with the Kriegers, while my father was left with only Uncle Lucian for company. We drifted around, overawed by the surrounding circle of mountains, until our reveries were scattered by an outbreak of hostilities between my father and my mother's brother. Although it was mainly commotion odd words were carried across the lake to our boat. 'He is old enough ... He must be told ... Never ... I am his father.' Of course it was impossible to be sure who was saying what.

'Christopher,' said my father, 'what do you think of your Uncle Lucian?' 'I love him,' I replied. 'And me?' he asked. 'You are my father,' I said. He continued his preparations without another word, nothing was going to spoil his big day. He had been looking forward to the hunt from the moment we arrived at Zakopane (it had long been his ambition to shoot a wild boar and hang its head over the fireplace in his smoking room). But as it turned out, it was a lucky day for boars. At first everything went according to plan. We slipped quietly into the forest below the Black Pond (where Awit Szubert was busy with another of his studies), searching the snow for footprints, watching the saplings and bushes for any slight movement that might betray the presence of a wild animal. Having selected promising areas the hunt began in earnest. 'Each of you has a horn,' said our guide. 'You must blow upon it as soon as you spot a boar. In no circumstance shoot until we are all accounted for. I want no accidents.' Soon we were scattered in all parts of the forest. What occurred next is confused in my mind, and I am grateful that there are no photographs to settle the matter. It appeared that there were two figures in the distance gesticulating wildly; or perhaps one was waving his arms frantically, while the other was pointing a gun at him. Certainly we heard what sounded like shots, but they could have been the prelude to the louder crack that brought the snow toppling off the mountain peak. The image disintegrated. The air was filled with a million ice crystals, as though all the dots that combine to make up a photograph had exploded. Blinded and deafened, we were no longer witnesses. Thereafter, when we regrouped in a clearing, we deduced that the two figures must have been my father and Uncle Lucian. This was finally confirmed when Uncle Lucian was seen staggering towards us. Unfortunately my father was never seen again. What had happened? 'A terrible accident,' was all we could get from Uncle Lucian. So that was the story we told my mother; that my father had been buried alive in a sudden avalanche. At least we were spared the funeral.

To tell you the truth, my father's permanent absence made little difference to his former household (of which I was now the head). However, the realization of my new status seemed to come as a shock to all concerned. My mother appeared more than usually preoccupied. (Surely she was not still mourning for my father?) As for Uncle Lucian, his moods were inexplicable and his behaviour incomprehensible. Time after time I would enter a room and find him deep in some intense conversation with my mother, only for him to draw away as soon as he saw me coming. I took to opening doors quietly in the hope of overhearing snatches of their dialogue, but all I caught were meaningless phrases. However, I was able to identify several instances of an 'either . . . or' construction associated with threats. And once (I swear) I heard my mother utter the word 'Blackmail'. After many weeks the disharmony subsided and was replaced by a duet, the key word of which seemed to be 'America'. Nevertheless, my mother did not recover her previous cheerful disposition. On account of Uncle Lucian's strange behaviour since the accident my visits to his studio had become more and more infrequent, until I stopped going there completely. But I resolved to make one more call, to confront Uncle Lucian man-to-man, if only for my mother's sake. His studio door was never locked during working hours (in the hope, I suppose, that a customer turned away by Awit Szubert or Ignacy Krieger might find their way to his establishment) which was to my advantage as I wished to catch him unawares. Since he was busy with a client I slipped behind the velvet drapes where my childish counterpart had hidden so many times before. Fool that I was, I couldn't resist a peep. Standing on a pedestal where my uncle had placed her, Hannah completed the movement until she was facing the camera. She was naked. I was astounded. I did not believe that women ever allowed men to see them in such a condition. And yet here I was, opposite Hannah, able to examine all her most secret parts. 'You must promise never to show that photograph to anyone,' she said. Uncle Lucian laughed. He put his hand between her legs. 'Not today,' she said, 'I am fertile.' 'Very well,' said Uncle Lucian, 'kneel.' Hannah knelt. She unbuttoned Uncle Lucian's trousers. He gasped. Hannah couldn't speak, her mouth was full. My own hands began to tingle, as they had at Awit Szubert's studio, and I

imagined that Hannah's lips were pressed to my penis. Then imagination
became reality as my hands forced Hannah's head against me, harder,
harder ('Harder! Harder!' echoed Uncle Lucian), until my pants were
oozing. Hannah quivered, as if with disgust, then wiped her mouth.
'What will become of him?' she asked. 'Christopher?' said Uncle Lucian.
'Our son,' replied Hannah. 'He is to start a new life,' said Uncle Lucian,
'in America.'

A new life indeed! And now it is nearly over. I am an old man, too
decrepit to attract a woman. Hence my weekly visit to Mrs Klopstok's
brothel (which has moved out to Santa Monica). You know all there is to
know about me, so perhaps you would care to accompany me here too? 'I
have a new girl for you tonight,' says Mrs Klopstok. 'You will find her in
the "New Deal" room.' Mrs Klopstok likes me, she thinks we have
similar backgrounds; at any rate, we have aged together. The whore
wears a wrap that she has not bothered to button, so that I can glimpse
her nakedness beneath. Her body is not bad. Her face is also acceptable,
though it shows the beginnings of a beard. 'I am Erica,' she says. As I fuck
her I make a pun (to myself, of course), 'This is my life in an Erica.'
Perhaps I will leave her my beautiful photographs, to decorate her room.

Jonathan Steffen

FORMICA

J ONATHAN STEFFEN was born in London in 1958 and grew up in Leeds. He was educated at Solihull School and at King's College, Cambridge, where he read English. In 1981 he was awarded the Harper-Wood Travelling Studentship for English Poetry and Literature by St John's College, Cambridge. His work has previously appeared in the *New Edinburgh Review*.

The table had a formica top to it – a dubious mottled pink punctuated with cigarette burns. A green aluminium ashtray, quietly choking on cigarette ends, an untouched bar of chocolate, a battered copy of *Gone with the Wind* and a tube of antiseptic cream – half-used – distinguished the table from the ten or so others in the antiseptic room. And three pairs of elbows. The three pairs of eyes belonging to the three pairs of elbows bored a hole in the expiring ashtray.

'You are still taking your pills though, dear?'

'Yes, Mother.'

'Because you must take them you know.'

'I know, Mother.'

'Your pills.'

'Mother, I am still taking my pills. I am taking my pills with a vengeance. I am putting all the energy, all the youthful vigour of my twenty-one years into taking my pills. I am taking the taking of my pills very seriously, Mother.'

'There's no need to talk to your mother like that, Neil', said his father, evenly.

'No, there's no need to talk to me like that, Neil,' said his mother.

Silence reasserted itself again, pressing the elbows into the table, the eyes into the ashtray. Slices of conversations found their way across the room from the other tables. Mrs Pritchard's bunions, apparently, were no better, it must be her time of life, Chelsea hadn't deserved to win the FA Cup in 1970, load of fairies anyway, someone hoped someone else liked carnations, and didn't they match the tables perfectly how nice, it's the darkness, yes, the garden's lovely.

'The Vicar sends his love and blessings, Neil,' his mother remembered. 'And I saw Mark the other day outside the butcher's, he says he'll try and come along sometime next week to see you.'

'Mark?'

'Yes, dear – it is Mark, isn't it?'

'Mike, Mother, Mike, I know no one called Mark, Mike you mean.'

'Yes, dear – the boy with the large buttocks.'

'You have an unerring eye for detail, Mother.'

Neil's father lit a cigarette. In his large, powerful hand the white cylinder looked curiously insubstantial, almost vulnerable. Neil waited for the words to come – the lawn or the dog?

'The lawn's looking marvellous, anyway. Mum and I have had a good go at it this weekend.'

The lawn. Of course the lawn.

'We wanted to get the garden looking nice for next week when you come home,' his mother almost apologized.

Searching for a reply, Neil shifted his elbows on the formica, picked up the chocolate between his finger and thumb, balanced it upright on the paperback – thus obscuring Clark Gable's nose and half his face, an improvement, he thought – and became acutely interested in the tinfoil wrapping. 'Yes, it's nice when the lawn is nice,' he managed. This observation seemed agreeable to all.

'Tea?' a voice threatened. And again, louder this time: 'Tea?' A trolley rumbled and clanked its way in a slightly wounded fashion across the linoleum, attached to a woman in a pink overall and very low-heeled shoes. China wobbled.

'It's coming this way,' thought Neil, and started to study the screw-on cap of the tube of antiseptic cream as his mother began to smile in a general manner.

'Tea?'

'Tea, Neil!' exclaimed his mother, attempting to suggest surprised delight, as if the trolley and its accomplice were a new invention. 'Would you like some tea? Yes, let's have some tea, thank you very much, we'd love some.'

The tea was deposited rather than poured into three anonymous white china cups and the trolley lurched off.

They sipped.

Eventually: 'Dr Anderson said you were almost ready to come out this week, Neil,' said his father, 'but we all agreed it was best for you to stay the extra week.'

'To make sure you're quite recovered,' clarified his mother.

'Yes, to make sure you're quite recovered. You mustn't rush these things. He seems a very reasonable bloke to me, this Dr Anderson?'

'He stinks,' said Neil, with heavy precision.

'Neil!' his mother exclaimed, looking about her whilst trying to reassemble her general smile, 'how dare you speak like that about Dr Anderson who's helped you so much. You've always been so rude!' And then in case this last sentence had been loud enough to catch the ears of another table: 'Fruit and nut is your favourite, isn't it?'

Neil said, 'Yes it is. Thank you very much.' And meant it.

The ashtray again.

Chairs started to complain on the linoleum, handbags clipped shut, keys jingled as the other visitors started to take their leave. See you next week then, and the roses of course, love to Jack, no, it was last Tuesday, well then. Slowly the rest of the pink formica reassumed control of the room.

'Well then,' Neil's father suggested.

'We must be off now, Neil,' said his mother, confidentially. 'Now you will take your pills like Dr Anderson said?'

'Yes, Mother.'

'And not flush them down the toilet again?'

'No, Mother.'

'And do get enough sleep, dear.'

'I shall, Mother.'

They got up, as one. Neil's father held out one statuesque hand. Neil shook it, in silence.

'Is there anything else you want, then?'

'No, Dad.'

'Well, take care of yourself now. And we'll be here on Friday to collect you.' Suddenly he seemed to Neil very pale, very light. 'What time are we supposed to be here?'

'Between two and three.'

'Good. Well, goodbye.' He turned and moved towards the door. Somewhere along the corridor the tea-trolley gave a final despairing clatter. Neil's mother looked at her son, looked at the floor, looked at the table and threw her arms around him.

'Oh, Neil, it will be nice to have you home again.' To Neil this moment seemed to last a long time.

She let him go, sniffed once and started to pull on a glove. 'After all,' she said to him, pulling on the glove and suddenly noticing, suddenly concentrating very hard on a grease-mark on the third finger, 'After all.'

And she left, thinking about nothing, about nothing.

Graham Swift

THE
WATCH

Tell me, what is more magical, more sinister, more malign yet
consoling, more expressive of the constancy – and fickleness – of
fate than a clock? Think of the clock which is ticking now,
behind you, above you, peeping from your cuff. Think of the watches
which chirp blithely on the wrists of the newly dead. Think of those clocks
which are prayed to so that their hands might never register some
moment of doom – but they jerk forward nonetheless; or, conversely, of
those clocks which are begged to hasten their movement so that some
span of misery might reach its end, but they stubbornly refuse to budge.
Think of those clocks, gently chiming on mantelpieces, which soothe one
man and attack the nerves of another. And think of that clock, renowned
in song, which when its old master died, stopped also, like a faithful
mastiff, never to go again. Is it so remarkable to imagine – as savages
once did on first seeing them – that in these whirring, clicking
mechanisms there lives a spirit, a power, a demon?

My family is – was – a family of clockmakers. Three generations ago,
driven by political turmoils, they fled to England from the Polish city of
Lublin – a city famous for its baroque buildings, for its cunning artefacts,
for clocks. For two centuries the Krepskis fashioned the clocks of Lublin.
But Krepski, it is claimed, is only a corruption of the German Krepf, and
trace back further my family line and you will find connections with the

great horologers of Nuremburg and Prague. For my forefathers were no mere craftsmen, no mere technicians. Pale, myopic men they may have been, sitting in dim workshops, counting the money they made by keeping the local gentry punctual; but they were also sorcerers, men of mission. They shared a primitive but unshakeable faith that clocks and watches not only recorded time, but contained it – they spun it with their loom-like motion. That clocks, indeed, were the *cause* of time. That without their assiduous tick-tocking, present and future would never meet, oblivion would reign and the world would vanish down its own gullet in some self-annihilating instant.

The man who regards his watch every so often, who thinks of time as something fixed and arranged, like a railway timetable, and not as a thing to which is owed the very beating of his heart, may easily scoff. My family's faith is not to be communicated by appeals to reason. And yet in our case there is one unique and clinching item of evidence, one undeniable and sacred repository of material proof ...

No one can say why, of all my worthy ancestors, my great-grandfather Stanislaw should have been singled out. No one can determine what mysterious conjunction of influences, what gatherings of instinct, knowledge and skill made the moment propitious. But on a September day, in Lublin, in 1809, my great-grandfather made the breakthrough which to the clockmaker is as the elixir to the alchemist. He created a clock which would not only function perpetually without winding, but from which time itself, that invisible yet palpable essence, could actually be gleaned – by contact, by proximity – like some form of magnetic charge. So, at least, it proved. The properties of this clock – or large pocket-watch to be precise, for its benefits necessitated that it be easily carried – were not immediately observable. My great-grandfather had only an uncanny intuition. In his diary for that September day he writes cryptically, 'The new watch – I know, feel it in my blood – it is the *one.*' Thereafter, at weekly intervals, the same entry: 'The new watch – not yet wound.' The weekly interval lapses into a monthly one. Then, on September 3rd 1810 – the exact anniversary of the watch's birth – the entry, 'The Watch – a whole year without winding,' to which is added the mystical statement, 'We shall live for ever.'

But this is not all. I write now in the 1970s. In 1809 my great-grandfather was forty-two. Simple arithmetic will indicate that we are dealing here with extraordinary longevity. My great-grandfather died in

1900 – a man of one hundred and thirty-three, by this time an established and industrious clockmaker in one of the immigrant quarters of London. He was then, as a faded daguerreotype testifies, a man certainly old in appearance but not decrepit (you would have judged him perhaps a hale seventy), still on his feet and still busy at his trade; and he died not from senility but from being struck by an ill-managed horse-drawn omnibus while attempting one July day to cross Ludgate Hill. From this it will be seen that my great-grandfather's watch did not confer immortality. It gave to those who had access to it a perhaps indefinite store of years; it was proof against age and against all those processes by which we are able to say that a man's time runs out, but it was not proof against external accident. Witness the death of Juliusz, my great-grandfather's first-born, killed by a Russian musket-ball in 1807. And Josef, the second-born, who came to a violent end in the troubles which caused my great-grandfather to flee his country.

To come closer home. In 1900 my grandfather, Feliks (my great-grandfather's third son) was a mere stripling of ninety-two. Born in 1808, and therefore receiving almost immediate benefit from my great-grandfather's watch, he was even sounder in limb, relatively speaking, than his father. I can vouch for this because (though, in 1900, I was yet to be conceived) I am now speaking of a man whom I have known intimately for the greater part of my own life and who, indeed, reared me almost from birth.

In every respect my grandfather was the disciple and image of my great-grandfather. He worked long and hard at the workshop in East London where he and Stanislaw, though blessed among mortals, still laboured at the daily business of our family. As he grew older – and still older – he acquired the solemn, vigilant and somewhat miserly looks of my great-grandfather. In 1900 he was the only remaining son and heir – for Stanislaw, by wondrous self-discipline, given his length of years, had refrained from begetting further children, having foreseen the jealousies and divisions that the watch might arouse in a large family.

Feliks thus became the guardian of the watch which had now ticked away unwound for little short of a century. Its power was undiminished. Feliks lived on to the age of one hundred and sixty-one. He met his death, in brazen and spectacular fashion, but a few years ago, from a bolt of lightning, whilst walking in a violent storm in the Sussex downs. I myself can bear witness to his vigour, both of body and mind, at that more-than-ripe old age. For I myself watched him tramp off defiantly on that August night. I myself pleaded with him to heed the fury of the weather. And, after he failed to return, it was I who discovered his rain-soaked body, at the foot of a split tree, and pulled from his waistcoat pocket, on the end of its gold chain, the Great Watch – still ticking.

But what of my father? Where was he while my grandfather took me in charge? That is another story – which we shall come to shortly. One of perversity and rebellion, and one, so my grandfather was never slow to remind me, which cast a shadow on our family honour and pride.

You will note that I have made no mention of the womenfolk of our family. Furthermore, I have said that Stanislaw took what must be considered some pains to limit his progeny. Increase in years, you might suppose, would lead to increase in issue. But this was not so – and Great-grandfather's feat was, perhaps, not so formidable. Consider the position of a man who has the prospect before him of an extraordinary length of years and who looks back at his own past as other men look at history books. The limits of his being, his 'place in time', as the phrase goes, the fact of his perishability begin to fade and he begins not to interest himself in those means by which other men seek to prolong their existence. And of these, what is more universal than the begetting of children, the passing on of one's own blood?

Because they were little moved by the breeding instinct my great-grandfather and my grandfather were little moved by women. The wives they had – both of them got through three – followed very much the oriental pattern where women are little more than the property of their husbands. Chosen neither for their beauty nor fecundity but more for blind docility, they were kept apart from the masculine mysteries of clockmaking and were only acquainted with the Great Watch on a sort of concessionary basis. If the only one of them I knew myself – my grandfather's last wife Eleanor – is anything to go by, they were slavish, silent, timid creatures, living in a kind of bemused remoteness from their husbands (who, after all, might be more than twice their age).

I remember my grandfather once expatiating on the reasons for this subjection and exclusion of women. 'Women, you see,' he warned, 'have no sense of time, they do not appreciate the urgency of things – that is what puts them in their place' – an explanation which I found unpersuasive then, perhaps because I was a young man and not un-interested in young women. But the years have confirmed the – painful – truth of my grandfather's judgement. Show me a woman who has the same urgency as a man. Show me a woman who cares as much about the impending deadline, the ticking seconds, the vanishing hours. Ah yes, you will say, this is masculine humbug. Ah yes, I betray all the prejudice and contempt which ruined my brief marriage – which has ruined my life. But look at the matter on a broader plane. In the natural order of things it is women who are the longer lived. Why is this? Is it not precisely because they lack urgency – that urgency which preoccupies men, which drives them to unnatural subterfuges and desperate acts, which exhausts them and ushers them to an early death?

But urgency – despite his words – was not something that showed much in my grandfather's face. Understandably. For endowed with a theoretically infinite stock of time, what cause did he have for urgency? I have spoken of my elders' miserly and watchful looks. But this miserliness was not the miserliness of restless and rapacious greed; it was the contented, vacant miserliness of the miser who sits happily on a vast hoard of money which he has no intention of spending. And the watchfulness was not a sentry-like alertness; it was more the smug superciliousness of a man who knows he occupies a unique vantage point. In fact it is true to say, the longer my forefathers lived, the less animated they became. The more they immersed themselves in their obsession with time, the more they sank in their actions into mechanical and unvarying routine, tick-tocking their lives out like the miraculous instrument that enabled them to do so.

They did not want excitement, these Methuselahs, they dreamt no dreams. Nothing characterizes more my life with my grandfather than the memory of countless monotonous evenings in the house he had at Highgate – evenings in which my guardian (that man who was born before Waterloo) would sit after dinner, intent, so it would seem, on nothing other than the process of his own digestion, while my grandmother would batten herself down in some inoffensive wifely task – darning socks, sewing buttons – and the silence, the heavy, aching silence (how the memory of certain silences can weigh upon you), would be punctuated only – by the tick of clocks.

Once I dared to break this silence, to challenge this leaden oppression of Time. I was a healthy, well-fed boy of thirteen. At such an age – who can deny it? – there is freshness. The moments slip by and you do not stop to count them. It was a summer evening and Highgate had, in those days, a verdant, even pastoral air. My grandfather was expounding (picture a boy of thirteen, a man of a hundred and twenty) upon his only subject when I interrupted him to ask, 'But isn't it best when we forget time?'

I am sure that with these ingenuous words there rose in me – only to hold brief sway – the spirit of my rebellious and dead father. I was not aware of the depths of my heresy. My grandfather's face took on the look of those fathers who are in the habit of removing their belts and applying them to their sons' hides. He did not remove his belt. Instead, I received the lashings of a terrible diatribe upon the folly of a world – of which my words were a very motto – which dared to believe that Time could take care of itself; followed by an invocation of the toils of my ancestors; followed, inevitably, by a calling down upon my head of the sins of my father. As I cringed before all this I acknowledged the indissoluble, if irrational link between age and authority. Youth must bow to age. This was the god-like fury of one hundred and twenty years beating down on me and I had no choice but to prostrate myself. And yet, simultaneously – as the fugitive summer twilight still flickered from the garden – I pondered on the awesome loneliness of being my grandfather's age – the loneliness (can you conceive it?) of having *no* contemporaries. And I took stock of the fact that seldom, if ever, had I seen my grandfather – this man of guarded and scrupulous mien – roused by such passion. Only once, indeed, did I see him so roused again – that day of his death, when, despite my efforts to dissuade him, he strode out into the gathering storm.

The sins of my father? What was my father's sin but to seek some other means of outwitting Time than that held out to him? The means of adventure, of hazard and daring, the means of a short life but a full, a memorable one. Was he really impelled by motives so different from those of his own father and his father's father?

Perhaps every third generation is a misfit. Born in 1895, my father would have become the third beneficiary of the Great Watch. From the earliest age, like every true Krepski male-child, he was reared on the staple diet of clocks and chronometry. But, even as a boy, he showed distinct and sometimes hysterical signs of not wishing to assume the family mantle. Grandfather Feliks has told me that he sometimes feared that little Stefan actually plotted to steal the Watch (which he ought to have regarded as the Gift of Gifts) in order to smash it or hide it or simply hurl it away somewhere. My grandfather consequently kept it always on his person and even wore it about his neck, on a locked chain at night – which cannot have aided his sleep.

These were times of great anguish. Stefan was growing up into one of those psychopathic children who wish to wreak merciless destruction on all that their fathers hold dearest. His revolt, unprecedented in the family annals, may seem inexplicable. But I think I understand it. When Feliks was born his own father Stanislaw was thirty-nine, an unexceptional state of affairs. When Stefan grew out of mindless infancy, his father was on the brink of his first hundred. Who can say how a ten-year-old reacts to a centenarian father?

And what was Stefan's final solution to paternal oppression? It was a well-tried one, even a hackneyed one, but one never attempted before in our family from land-locked Lublin. At the age of fifteen, in 1910, he ran away to sea, to the beckoning embraces of risk, fortune, fame – or oblivion. It was thought that no more would be seen of him. But this intrepid father of mine, not content with his runaway defiance or with braving the rough world he had pitched himself into, returned, after three years, for the pleasure of staring fixedly into my grandfather's face. He was then a youth of eighteen. But three years' voyaging – to Shanghai, Yokohama, Valparaiso . . . – had toughened his skin and packed into his young frame more resourcefulness than my hundred-year-old grandfather had ever known, bent over his cogs and pendula.

My grandfather realized that he faced a man. That weather-beaten stare was a match for his hundred nominal years. The result of this sailor's return was reconciliation, a rare balance between father and son – enhanced rather than marred by the fact that only a month or so afterwards Stefan took up with a woman of dubious character – the widow of a music-hall manager (perhaps it is significant that she was twelve years *older* than my father) – got her with child and married her. Thus I arrived on the scene.

My grandfather showed remarkable forbearance. He even stooped for a while to taste the transitory delights of variety artists and buxom singers. It seemed that he would not object – whether it was fitting or not – to Stefan and his lineage partaking of the Watch. It was even possible that

Stefan – the only Krepski not to have done so in the way that fish take to swimming and birds to flight – might come round at last to the trade of clockmaking.

But all this was not to be. In 1914 – the year of my birth – Stefan once more took to the sea, this time in the service of his country (for he was the first Krepski to be born on British soil). Once more there were heated confrontations, but my grandfather could not prevail. Perhaps he knew that even without the pretext of war Stefan would have sooner or later felt stirred again by the life of daring and adventure. Feliks, at last, swallowing his anger and disappointment before the parting warrior, held out the prospect of the Watch as a father to a son, even if he could not hold it out as a master clockmaker to a faithful apprentice. Perhaps Stefan might indeed have returned in 1918, a salty hero, ready to settle down and receive its benison. Perhaps he too might have lived to a ripe one hundred, and another hundred more – were it not for the German shell which sent him and the rest of his gallant ship's crew to the bottom at the battle of Jutland.

So it was that I, who knew so well my grandfather whose own memories stretched back to Napoleonic times, and would doubtless have known – were it not for that fool of an omnibus driver – my great-grandfather, born while America was still a British colony, have no memories of my father at all. For when the great guns were booming at Jutland and my father's ship was raising its churning propellors to the sky, I was asleep in my cot in Bethnal Green, watched over by my equally unwitting mother. She was to die too, but six months later, of a mixture of grief and influenza. And I passed, at the age of two, into my grandfather's hands, and so into the ghostly hands of my venerable ancestors. From merest infancy I was destined to be a clockmaker, one of the solemn priesthood of Time, and whenever I erred in my noviceship, as on that beguiling evening in Highgate, to have set before me the warning example of my father – dead (though his name lives in glory – you will see it on the memorial at Chatham, the only Krepski amongst all those Jones and Wilsons) at the laughable age of twenty-one.

But this is not a story about my father, nor even about clockmaking. All these lengthy preliminaries are only a way of explaining how on a certain day, a week ago, in a room on the second floor of a delapidated but (as shall be seen) illustrious Victorian building, I, Adam Krepski, sat, pressing in my hand till the sweat oozed from my palm, the Watch made by my great-grandfather, which for over one hundred and seventy years had neither stopped nor ever been wound. The day, as it happens, was my wedding anniversary. A cause for remembrance, but not for celebration. It is nearly thirty years since my wife left me.

And what was making me clutch so tightly that precious mechanism?

It was the cries. The cries coming up the dismal, echoing staircase; the cries from the room on the landing below, which for several weeks I had heard at sporadic intervals, but which now had reached a new, intense note and came with ever-increasing frequency. The cries of a woman, feline, inarticulate – at least to my ears, for I knew them to be the cries of an Asian woman – an Indian, a Pakistani – expressive first of outrage and grief (they had been mixed in those first days with the shouts of a man), but now of pain, of terror, of – it was this that tightened my grip so fervently on that Watch – of unmistakable *urgency*.

My wedding anniversary. Now I consider it, time has played more than one trick on me . . .

And what was I doing in that gloomy and half-derelict building, I, a Krepski clockmaker? That is a long and ravelled tale – one which begins perhaps on that fateful day in July 1957, when I married.

My grandfather (who in that same year reached one hundred and fifty) was against it from the outset. The eve of my wedding was another of those humbling moments in my life when he invoked the folly of my father. Not that Deborah had any of the questionable credentials of the widow of a music-hall manager. She was a thirty-five-year-old primary-school teacher, and I, after all, was forty-three. But – now my grandfather was midway through his second century – the misogynist bent of our family had reached in him a heightened, indiscriminate pitch. On the death of his third wife, in 1948, he had ceased to play the hypocrite and got himself a housekeeper, not a fourth wife. The disadvantage of this decision, so he sometimes complained to me, was that housekeepers had to be paid. His position towards womankind was entrenched. He saw my marriage-to-be as a hopeless backsliding into the mire of vain biological yearnings and the fraudulent permanence of procreation.

He was wrong. I did not marry to beget children (that fact was to be my undoing) nor to sell my soul to Time. I married simply to have another human being to talk to other than my grandfather.

Do not mistake me. I did not wish to abandon him. I had no intention of giving up my place beside him in the Krepski workshop or of forfeiting my share in the Watch. But consider the weight of his hundred and fifty years on my forty-odd. Consider that since the age of three, not having known my father and, barely, my mother, I had been brought up by this prodigy who even at my birth was over a hundred. Might I not feel, in watered-down form, the oppressions and frustrations of my father? At twenty-five I had already grown tired of my grandfather's somehow hollow accounts of the Polish uprisings of 1830, of exiled life in Paris, of the London of the 1850s and 60s. I had begun to perceive that mixed with his blatant misogyny was a more general, brooding misanthropy – a contempt for the common run of men who lived out their meagre three score and ten. His eyes (one of which was permanently out of true from the constant use of a clockmaker's eye-piece) had developed a dull, sanctimonious stare. About his person there hung, like some sick-room smell infesting his clothes, an air of stagnancy, ill-humour, isolation, and even, to judge from his frayed jackets and the disrepair of his Highgate home, relative penury.

For what had become of 'Krepski and Krepski, Clock and Watchmakers of Repute', in the course of my lifetime? It was no longer the thriving East End workshop, employing six skilled craftsmen and three apprentices, it had been at the turn of the century. Economic changes had dealt it blows. The mass-production of wrist-watches which were now two-a-penny and cheap electrical (electrical!) clocks had squeezed out the small business. On top of this was my grandfather's ever-increasing suspiciousness of nature. For, even if lack of money had not forced him to do so, he would have gradually dismissed his faithful workmen for fear they might discover the secret of the Watch and betray it to the world. That watch could prolong human life but not the life of commercial enterprise. By the 1950s Krepski and Krepski was no more than one of those grimy, tiny, Dickensian-looking shops one can still see on the fringes of the City, signboarded 'Watch and Clock Repairers' but looking more like a rundown pawnbroker's, to which aged customers would, very occasionally, bring the odd ancient mechanism for a 'seeing-to'.

Grandfather was a hundred and fifty. He looked like a sour-minded but able-bodied man of half that age. Had he retired at the customary time (that is, some time during the 1860s or 70s) he would have known the satisfaction of passing on a business at the peak of its success and of enjoying a comfortable 'old age'. In the 1950s, still a fit man, he had no choice but to continue at the grinding task of scraping a living. Even had he retired and I had managed to support him, he would have returned, surely enough, to the shop in Goswell Road, like a stray dog to its kennel.

Imagine the companionship of this man – in our poky, draughty place of work which vibrated ceaselessly to the rumblings of the City traffic outside; in the Highgate house with its flaking paintwork, damp walls and cracked crockery, and only the growlings of Mrs Murdoch, the housekeeper, to break the monotony. Was I to be blamed for flying with relief from this entombment to the arms of an impulsive, bright-minded, plumply attractive schoolteacher who – at thirty-five – was actually perturbed by the way the years were passing her by?

Ah, but in that last fact lay the seeds of marital catastrophe. Grandfather was right. A true Krepski, a true guardian of the Watch, should marry, if he is to marry at all, a plain, stupid and barren wife. Deborah was none of these things: she was that volatile phenomenon, a woman at what for women is a dangerous age, suddenly blessed with the prospect of womanhood fulfilled. Shall I describe our union as merely connubial? Shall I offer the picture of myself as the sober, steady, semi-paternal figure (I was eight years her elder) taking under my sheltering wing this slightly delicate, slightly frightened creature? No. Those first months were a whirlwind, a vortex into which I was sucked, gently at first and then with accelerating and uninhibited voracity. The walls of our first-floor flat shook to the onslaughts of female passion; they echoed to Deborah's screams (for at the height of ecstasy Deborah would scream, at an ear-splitting pitch). And I, an, at first, unwitting and passive instrument to all this, a clay figure into which life was rapidly pummelled and breathed, suddenly woke to the fact that for thirty years my life had been measured by clocks; that for people who are not Krepskis, Time is not a servant but an old and pitiless adversary. They have only so long on this earth and they want only to live, to have lived. And when the opportunity comes it is seized with predatory fury.

Deborah, how easy the choice might have been if I had not been a Krepski. Sometimes, in those early days, I would wake up, nestled by my wife's ever-willing flesh, and those years in Goswell Road would seem eclipsed: I was once more a boy – as on that audacious summer evening in

Highgate – seduced by the world's caress. But then, in an instant, I would remember my grandfather, waiting already at his work-bench, the Great Watch ticking in his pocket, the clock-making, time-enslaving blood that flowed in his and my veins.

How easy the choice if passion were boundless and endless. But it is not, that is the rub; it must be preserved before it perishes and put in some permanent form. All men must make their pact with history. The spring-tide of marriage ebbs, takes on slower, saner, more effectual rhythms; the white-heat cools, diffuses, but is not lost. All this is natural, and has its natural and rightful object. But it was here that Deborah and I came to the dividing of the ways. I watched my wife through the rusting iron railings of the playground of the primary school where sometimes I met her at lunch-time. There was a delicate, wholesome bloom on her cheeks. Who could have guessed where that bloom came from? Who could have imagined what wild abandon could seize this eminently respectable figure behind closed doors and drawn curtains? Yet that abandon was no longer indulged; it was withheld, denied (I had come to relish it) and would only be offered freely again in exchange for a more lasting gift. And who could mistake what that gift must be, watching her in the playground, her teacher's whistle round her neck, in the midst of those squealing infants, fully aware that my eyes were on her; patting on the head, as though to make the point unmistakable, now a pugnacious boy with grazed knees, now a Jamaican girl with pigtails?

Had I told her, in all this time, about the Great Watch? Had I told her that I might outlive her by perhaps a century and that our life together – all in all to her – might become (so, alas, it has) a mere oasis in the sands of memory? Had I told her that my grandfather, whom she thought a doughty man of seventy-five, was really twice that age? And had I told her that in us Krepskis the spirit of fatherhood is dead? We do not need children to carry our image into the future, to provide us with that over-used bulwark against extinction.

No. I had told her none of these things. I held my tongue in the vain – the wishful? – belief that I might pass in her eyes for an ordinary mortal. If I told her, I assured myself, would she not think I was mad? And, then again, why should I not (was it so great a thing?) flout the scruples which were part of my heritage and give a child to this woman with whom, for a brief period at least, I had explored the timeless realm of passion?

Our marriage entered its fourth year. She approached the ominous age of forty. I was forty-seven, a point at which other men might recognize the signs of age but at which I felt only the protective armour of the Watch tighten around me, the immunity of Krepski-hood squeeze me like an iron maiden. Dear Father Stefan, I prayed in hope. But no answering voice came from the cold depths of the Skaggerak or the Heligoland Bight. Instead I imagined a ghostly sigh from far-off Poland – and an angry murmuring, perhaps, closer to hand, as Great-grandfather Stanislaw turned in his Highgate grave. And I looked each day into the tacitly retributive eyes of my grandfather.

Deborah and I waged war. We bickered, we quarrelled, we made threats. And then at last, abandoning all subterfuge, I told her. She did not think I was mad. Something in my voice, my manner told her that this was not madness. If it had been madness, perhaps, it would have been easier to endure. Her face turned white. In one fell stroke her universe was upturned. Her stock of love, her hungry flesh, her empty womb were mocked and belittled. She looked at me as if I might have been a monster with two heads or a fish's tail. The next day she fled – 'left me' is too mild a term – and, rather than co-exist another hour with my indefinite lease of life, returned to her mother, who – poor soul – was ailing, in need of nursing, and shortly to die.

Tick-tock, tick-tock. The invalid clocks clanked and wheezed on the shelves in Goswell Road. Grandfather showed tact. He did not rub salt in the wound. Our reunion even had, too, its brief honeymoon. The night of Deborah's departure I sat up with him in the house at Highgate and he recalled, not with the usual dry deliberateness but with tender spontaneity, the lost Poland of his youth. Yet this very tenderness was an ill omen. Men of fantastic age are not given to nostalgia. It is the brevity of life, the rapid passage of finite years, that gives rise to sentiment and regret. During my interlude with Deborah a change had crept over my grandfather. The air of stagnancy, the fixation in the eyes were still there but what was new was that he himself seemed aware of these things as he had not before. Sorrow shadowed his face, and weariness, weariness.

The shop was on its last legs. Anyone could see there was no future in it; and yet for Grandfather, for me, there was, always, future. We pottered away, in the musty workroom, ekeing out what scant business came our way. The Great Watch, that symbol of Time conquered, ticking remorselessly in Grandfather's waistcoat, had become, we knew, our

master. Sometimes I dreamt wildly of destroying it, of taking a hammer
to its invulnerable mechanism. But how could I have committed an act so
sacrilegious, and one which, for all I knew, might have reduced my
grandfather, in an instant, to dust?

We worked on. I remember the hollow mood – neither relief nor
reluctance but some empty reflex between the two – with which we shut
the shop each night at six and made our journey home. How we would
sit, like two creatures sealed in a bubble, as our number 43 trundled up
the Holloway Road, watching the fretfulness of the evening rush (how
frenzied the activity of others when one's own pace is slow and
interminable) with a cold reptilean stare.

Ah, happy restless world, with oblivion waiting to solve its cares.

Ah, lost Deborah, placing gladioli on the grave of her mother.

The sons, and grandsons, of the ordinary world do their duty by their
sires. They look after them in their twilight years. But what if twilight
never falls?

By the summer of my grandfather's hundred and sixty-second year I
could endure no more. With the last dregs of my feeble savings I rented a
cottage in the Sussex downs. My aim was to do what necessity urged: to
sell up the shop; to find myself a job with a steady income by which I
might support Grandfather and myself. Admittedly, I was now fifty-five,
but my knowledge of clocks might find me a place with an antique
dealer's or as sub-curator in some obscure museum of horology. In order
to attempt all this, Grandfather had first to be lured to a safe distance.

This is not to say that the cottage was merely an – expensive –
expedient. One part of me sincerely wished my grandfather to stop
peering into the dusty orbs of clocks and to peer out again at the World –
even the tame, parochial world of Sussex. Ever lurking in my mind was
the notion that age ripens, mellows and brings its own, placid
contentments. Why had not his unique length of years afforded my
grandfather more opportunity to enjoy, to savour, to contemplate the
world? Why should he not enter now an era of meditative tranquillity, of
god-like congruence with Nature? Youth should bow to age not only in
duty but in veneration. Perhaps I had always been ashamed – perhaps it
was a source of secret despair for my own future – that my grandfather's
years had only produced in him the crabbed, cantankerous creature I
knew. Perhaps I hoped that extraordinary age might have instilled in him
extraordinary sagacity. Perhaps I saw him – wild, impossible vision –

turning in his country hermitage into some hallowed figure, a Sussex shaman, a Wise Man of the Downs, an oracle to whom the young and foolish world might flock for succour.

Or perhaps my motive was simpler than this. Perhaps it was no more than that of those plausible, burdened sons and daughters who, with well-meaning looks and at no small cost, place their parents in Homes, in order to have them out of sight and mind – in order, that is, to have them safely murdered.

My clinching argument was that, though all that would be left of Krepski and Krepski would be the Great Watch, yet that all would be all-in-all. And as a preliminary concession I agreed to spend a first experimental weekend with him at the cottage.

We travelled down on a Friday afternoon. It was one of those close, sullen high-summer days which make the flesh crawl and seem to bring out from nowhere swarms of flying insects. Grandfather sat in his seat in the railway carriage and hid his face behind a newspaper. This, like the weather, was a bad sign. Normally, he regarded papers with disdain. What did the news of 1977 mean to a man born in 1808? Almost by definition, papers were tokens of man's subjection to time; their business was ephemerality. Yet recently, so I had noticed, he had begun to buy them and to read them almost with avidity; and what his eyes went to first were reports of accidents and disasters, sudden violent deaths.

Now and then, as we passed through the Surrey suburbs, he came out from behind his screen. His face was not the face of a man travelling towards rejuvenating horizons. It was the petrified face of a man whom no novelty can touch.

The Sussex downs, an hour from London, still retain their quiet nooks and folds. Our cottage – one of a pair let by some palm-rubbing local speculator as weekend retreats – stood at one end of the village and at the foot of one of those characteristic, peculiarly female eminences of the Downs, referred to in the Ordnance Survey map as a Beacon. In spite of the sticky heat, I proposed this as the object of a walk the day after our arrival. The place was a noted viewpoint. Let us look down, I thought, us immortals, at the world.

Grandfather was less enthusiastic. His reluctance had nothing to do with his strength of limb. The climb was steep, but Grandfather, despite his years, was as fit as a man of forty. His unwillingness lay in a scarcely concealed desire to sabotage and deride this enterprise of mine. He had spent the first hours after arrival shambling round the cottage, not bothering to unpack his things, inspecting the oak timbers, the 'traditional fireplace' and the 'charming cottage garden' with an air of acid distaste, and finally settling heavily into a chair in just the same hunched manner in which he settled into his habitual chair in Highgate or his work stool at the shop. Long life ought to elicit a capacity for change. But it is the opposite (I know it well). Longevity encourages intransigence, conservatism. It teaches you to revert to type.

The sultry weather had not freshened. Half-way up the slope of the beacon we gave up our ascent, both of us in a muck-sweat. Even at this relative height no breezes challenged the leaden atmosphere, and the famous view, northwards to the Weald of Kent, was lost in grey curtains of haze and the shadows of black, greasy clouds. We sat on the tussocked grass, recovering our breath, Grandfather a little to one side and below me, mute as boulders. The silence hanging between us was like an epitaph upon my futile hopes: Give up this doomed exercise.

And yet, not silence. That is, not *our* silence, but the silence in which we sat. A silence which, as our gasps for breath subsided, became gradually palpable, audible, insistent. We sat, listening, on the warm grass, ears pricked like alert rabbits. We forgot our abortive climb. When had we last heard such silence, used to the throbbing traffic of the Goswell Road? And what a full, what a tumultuous silence. Under the humid pressure of the atmosphere the earth was opening up its pores and the silence was a compound of its numberless exhalations. The Downs themselves – those great feminine curves of flesh – were tingling, oozing. And what were all the components of this massive silence – the furious hatching of insects, the sighing of the grass, the trill of larks, the far-off bleat of sheep – but the issue of that swelling pregnancy? What, in turn, was that pregnancy, pressing, even as we sat, into our puny backsides, but the pregnancy of Time?

Old, they say, as the hills. Grandfather sat motionless, his face turned away from me. For a moment, I imagined the tough, chalk-scented grass spreading over him, rising round him to make of him no more than a turf cairn. On the Ordnance Survey maps were the acne-marks of neolithic barrows and iron-age earthworks.

Silence. And the only noise, the only man-made obtrusion into that overpowering silence was the tick of Great-grandfather's Watch.

We began to descend. Grandfather's face wore a look of gloom; of humility, of pride, of remorse, contrition – despair.

The night was quick in coming, hastened by the louring clouds. And it brought the appropriate conditions – a drop in temperature, a clash of air currents – to release the pent-up explosion. As the electricity in the atmosphere accumulated so Grandfather grew increasingly restless. He began to pace about the cottage, face twitching, darting black scowls in my direction. Twice, he got out the Watch, looked at it as if on the verge of some dreadful decision, then with an agonized expression returned it to his pocket. I was afraid of him. Thunder clattered and lightning flashed in the distance. And then, as if an invisible giant had taken a vast stride, a wind tore at the elm trees in the lane, half a dozen unfamiliar doors and windows banged in the cottage, and the bolts from heaven seemed suddenly aimed at a point over our heads. Grandfather's agitation intensified accordingly. His lips worked at themselves. I expected them to froth. Another whirlwind outside. I went upstairs to fasten one of the banging windows. When I returned he was standing by the front door, buttoning his raincoat.

'Don't try to stop me!'

But I could not have stopped him if I had dared. His mania cast an uncrossable barrier around him. I watched him pass out into the frenzied air. Barely half a minute after his exit the skies opened and rain lashed down.

I was not so obtuse as to imagine that my grandfather had gone for a mere stroll. But something kept me from pursuing him. I sat in a rocking chair by the 'traditional fireplace', waiting and (discern my motive if you will) even smiling, fixedly, while the thunder volleyed outside. Something about the drama of the moment, something about this invasion of the elements into our lives I could not help but find (like the man who grins idiotically at his executioner) gratifying.

And then I acted. The Beacon: that was the best place for storm watching. For defying – or inviting – the wrath of the skies. I reached for my own waterproof and walking shoes and strode out into the tumult.

During a thunderstorm, in Thuringia, so the story goes, Martin Luther broke down, fell to his knees, begged the Almighty for forgiveness and swore to become a monk. I am not a religious man – had I not been brought up to regard a certain timepiece as the only object of worship? – but that night I feared for my soul; that night I believed a God was at work, directing my steps to the scene of divine revenge. The thunder beat its drums. By the intermittent flashes of lightning I found my way to the slopes of the Beacon; but, once there, it seemed I did not need a guide to point my course – I did not need to reach the top and stand there like some demented weathercock. The Downs are bald, bold formations and in the magnesium-glare of lightning any features could be picked out. Clinging to the incline was a solitary clump of trees, of the kind which, on the Downs, are said to have a druidical significance. I needed to go no further. One of the trees had been split and felled by a scimitar of lightning. Grandfather lay lifeless beside its twisted wreckage, an anguished grimace frozen on his face. And in his waistcoat pocket, beneath his sodden coat and jacket, the Great Watch, its tiny, perfect, mechanical brain ignorant of storms, of drama, of human catastrophe, still ticked indifferently.

Help me, powers that be! Help me, Father Time! I stood in the crematorium, the last of the Krepskis, the Great Watch ticking in my pocket. Flames completed on Grandfather the work of the lightning, and reduced, in a matter of seconds, his one-hundred-and-sixty-year-old body to cinders. That day, a day so different – a tranquil, golden August day – from that night of death, I could have walked away and become a new man. I could have traced my steps – only a short distance – to the school playground where Deborah still stood among her frolicking brood, and asked to be reconciled. Her mother; my grandfather. The chastening bonds of bereavement.

I could have flung the Watch away. Indeed, I considered having it incinerated with Grandfather's corpse – but the rules of crematoria are strict on such matters. And did I not, that same afternoon, having attended the perfunctory reading of a barren will at a solicitor's in Chancery Lane, walk on the Thames Embankment, under the plane trees, holding the Watch in my sweating hand and daring myself to throw it? Twice I drew back my arm and twice let it fall. From the glinting river the waterborne voice of my father said, Why not? Why not? But I thought of Grandfather's ashes, still warm and active in their urn (surely when one lives the best part of two centuries one does not die so quickly?). I thought of Great-grandfather Stanislaw, and of his forebears, whose names I knew like a litany – Stanislaw senior, Kasimierz, Ignacy,

Tadeusz. In the curving reaches of the Thames I saw what I had never seen: the baroque spires of Lublin; the outstretched plains of Poland.

It is true what the psychologists say: our ancestors are our first and only gods. It is from them we get our guilt, our duty, our sin – our destiny. A few claps of thunder had awed me, a few celestial firecrackers had given me a passing scare. I gripped the Watch. I did not go back to the infants' school that afternoon, nor even, at first, to the house in Highgate. I went – all the way on foot, like a devout pilgrim – to the street in Whitechapel where my great-grandfather, a flourishing clock-maker in his hundred and twelfth year had set up home in the 1870s. In the 1870s there were fine houses as well as slums in Whitechapel. The street was still there. And so was the old home – its crumbling stucco, its cracked and boarded-up windows, its litter-strewn front steps a mockery of the former building which had once boasted two maids and a cook. I stared at it. By some prompting of fate, by some inevitable reflex on my part, I knocked on the door. The face of an Asian woman; timid, soulful. Someone had told me there was a room to let in this house. Yes, it was true – on the second floor.

So I did not throw away the Watch: I found a shrine in which to place it. And I did not return – save to dispose of its meagre contents and arrange its sale – to the house in Highgate. I refashioned my world, on a hermit's terms, out of an ancestral room in Whitechapel. Time, as even the ignorant will tell you and every clock-face will demonstrate, is circular. The longer you live, the more you long to go back, to go back. I closed my eyes on that old charlatan, the future. And Deborah remained for ever in her playground, whistling at her children, like someone vainly whistling for a runaway dog which already lies dead at the side of the road.

Thus I came to be sitting, a week ago, in that same room in Whitechapel, clutching, as I had that day by the Thames, the Watch in my itching palm. And still they came, the cries, desolate and unappeasable, from the floor below.

What was the meaning of these cries? I knew (I who had renounced such things to live in perpetual marriage with the Watch) they were the cries that come from the interminglings of men and women, the cries of heart-break, of vain desire. I knew they were the cries of that same Asian woman who had opened the door for me that day of Grandfather's cremation. A Mrs – or Miss? – Matharu. The husband (lover?) had come and gone at varying times. A shift-worker of some sort. Sometimes I met him on the stairs. An exchange of nods; a word. But I did not seek more. I burrowed in my ancestral lair. And even when the shouting began – his ferocious, rapid, hers like some ruffled, clucking bird – I did not intervene. Thunderstorms pass. Clocks tick on. The shouts were followed by screams, blows, the noise of slamming doors – sobs. Still I sat tight. Then one day the door slammed with the unmistakable tone of finality (ah, Deborah); and the sobs that followed were not the sobs that still beg and plead, but solitary sobs, whimpering and dirge-like – the sobs of the lonely lingering out the empty hours.

Did I go down the stairs? Did I give a gentle knock to the door and ask softly, 'Can I help?' No. The world is full of snares.

Time heals. Soon these whimperings would cease. And so they did. Or, rather, faded into almost-silence, as the music fades before some giant coda, only to build up again into new crescendos of anguish.

I gripped my ticking talisman, as the sick and dying cling, in their hour of need, to pitiful trinkets. Do not imagine that these female cries merely assailed my peace and did not bring to me, as to their utterer, real suffering. For I recognized that they emanated from a region ungoverned by time, and were therefore as poisonous, as lethal to us Krepskis as fresh air to a fish.

We were alone in the building, this wailing woman and I. The house – the whole street – lay under the ultimatum of a compulsory purchase. The notices had been issued. Already the other rooms were vacated. And already, beyond my window, walls were tumbling, bulldozers were sending clouds of dust into the air. The house of Krepski must fall soon; as had fallen already the one-time houses of Jewish tailors, Dutch goldsmiths, Russian furriers – a whole neighbourhood of immigrant tradesmen, stepping off the ships at London docks and bringing with them the strands of their far-flung pasts. How could it be that all this history had been reduced, before my eyes, to a few heaps of flattened rubble and a few grey demarcations of corrugated fencing?

Another rending cry, like the tearing of flesh itself. I stood up; I clutched my forehead; sat down; stood up again. I descended the stairs. But I did not loosen my grip on the Watch.

She lay – beneath a tangled heap of bedclothes, on a mattress in the large, draughty room which I imagined had once been my great-grandfather's 'drawing-room', but which now served as living-room, kitchen and bedroom – in the obvious grip not so much of grief as of illness. Clearly, she had been unable to answer my knock at the door, which was unlocked, and perhaps had been for weeks. Sweat beaded her face. Her eyes burned. And even as I stood over her she drew a constricted gasp of pain and her body shuddered beneath the heaped bedclothes which I suspected had been pulled rapidly about her as I entered.

Circumstances conspire. This woman, as I knew from the dozen words we had exchanged in little more than a year, spoke scarcely any English. She could not describe her plight; I could not inquire. No language was needed to tell me I should fetch a doctor, but as I bent over her, with the caution with which any Krepski bends over a woman, she suddenly gripped my arm, no less fiercely than my free hand gripped the Watch. When I signalled my intention, mouthing the word 'doctor' several times, she gripped it tighter still, and an extra dimension of torment seemed to enter her face. It struck me that had I been a younger man (I was sixty-three, but little did she know that in Krepski terms I was still callow) her grip on my arm might have been less ready. Even so, fear as much as importunacy knotted her face. More than one layer of shame seemed present in her eyes as she let out another uncontrollable moan and her body strained beneath the bedclothes.

'What's wrong? What's wrong?'

You will doubtless think me foolish and colossally ignorant for not recognizing before this point the symptoms of child-birth. For such they were. I, a Krepski who held in my hand the power to live so long and whose forefathers had lived so long before him, did not recognize the beginnings of life, and did not know what a woman in labour is like. But, once the knowledge dawned, I understood not only the fact but its implications and the reasons for this woman's mingled terror and entreaty. The child was the child of a fugitive father. Daddy was far away, ignorant perhaps of this fruit of his dalliance, just as my father Stefan, far away on the North Sea, was ignorant of my mother stooping over my cot. Daddy, perhaps, was no Daddy by law; and who could say whether by *law* either Daddy or Mummy were rightful immigrants. That might explain the hand gripping me so tightly as I turned for professional help. Add to all this that I was an Englishman and I bent over this woman – whose mother had perhaps worn a veil in some village by the Ganges – as she suffered the most intimate female distress ... You will see the position was vexed.

And I had no choice but to be the witness – the midwife – to this hopeless issue.

I understood that the moment was near. Her black-olive eyes fixed me from above the tangled sheets, in which, as if obeying some ancient instinct, she tried to hide her mouth. The point must soon come when she must abandon all modesty – and I all squeamishness – and I could see her weighing this terrible candour against the fact that I was her only help.

But as we stared at each other a strange thing happened. In the little half-oval of face which she showed me I seemed to see, as if her eyes were equipped with some extraordinary ultra-optical lens, the huge hinterlands of her native Asia and the endless nut-brown faces of her ancestors. At the same time, marshalled within myself, assembling from the distant margins of Poland, were the ranks of my Krepski sires. What a strange thing that our lives should collide, here where neither had its origins. How strange that they should collide at all. What a strange and extraordinary thing that I should be born a Krepski, she a Matharu. What an impossible concatenation of chances goes to the making of any birth.

I must have smiled at these thoughts – or at least lent to my face some expression which infected hers. For her look suddenly softened – her black irises melted – then immediately hardened again. She screwed her eyes shut, let out a scream, and with a gesture of submission – as she might have submitted to that brute of a husband – pulled back the bedclothes from the lower part of her body, drew up her legs, and, clutching at the bedhead with her hands, began to strain mightily.

Her eyes were shut; I think they remained shut throughout the whole ensuing procedure. But mine opened, wider and wider, at what perhaps no Krepski had seen, or at least *viewed* with such privileged and terrified intentness. The mother – for this is what she was now indubitably becoming – arched her spine, heaved her monstrous belly, seemed to offer her whole body to be cleaved from between the legs upwards, and those expanding eyes of mine saw a glistening, wet, purple-mottled object, like some wrinkled marble pebble, appear where the split began.

This pebble grew – and grew – growing impossibly large for the narrow opening in which it seemed intent on jamming itself. For a whole minute, indeed, it stuck there, as if this were its final resting place, while the mother screamed. And then suddenly it ceased to be a pebble. It was a lump of clenched, unformed flesh, suffused with blood, aware that its position was critical. The mother gasped; it became a head, a gnarled, battered, Punch-and-Judy head. The mother gasped again, this time with an audible relief and exultation; and it was no longer a head, but a whole *creature*, with arms and legs and little groping hands; and it was no longer caught in that awesome constriction but suddenly spilling out with slippery ease, like something poured from a pickle jar, a slithery brine accompanying it. But this was not all. As if it were not remarkable enough that so large a thing should emerge from so small a hole, there followed it, rapidly, an indescribable mass of multicoloured effluents, the texture and hue of liquid coral, gelatine, stewed blackberries . . .

From what a ragout is a human life concocted.

What was I doing throughout this spectacular performance? My eyes were popping, my knees were giving; I was clutching the Great Watch, fit to crush it, in my right hand. But now, with the little being writhing in slow motion on the gory sheets and the mother's moans of relief beginning to mingle with a new anguish, I knew that I had my own unavoidable part to play in this drama. Once, on Grandfather's television at Highgate, I had watched (disgusted but fascinated) a programme about child-delivery. I knew that much pertained to the fleshy tube which even now snaked and coiled between mother and baby. The mother understood it too; for with her last reserves of energy she was gesturing to a chest of drawers on the far side of the room. In one of the drawers I found a pair of kitchen scissors . . .

With the instant of birth begins the possibility of manslaughter. My untutored hands did what they could while my stomach fought down surging tides – not just of nausea but of strange, welling fear. Like the TV surgeon, I held up the slippery creature and, with an irresolute hand, slapped it. It grimaced feebly and made the sound – a sound of choking pain – which they say means life has taken hold. But it looked wretched and sick to me. I put it down on the mattress close to the mother's side, as if some maternal fluence could do the trick I could not. We looked at each other, she and I, with the imploring looks of actual lovers, actual cogenitors who have pooled their flesh in a single hope.

Deborah ... with your playground whistle.

I had heard the expression 'life hangs in the balance'. I knew that it applied to tense moments in operating theatres and in condemned cells when a reprieve may still come, but I never knew – used to life as an ambling affair that might span centuries – what it meant. And only now do I know what enormous concentrations of time, what huge counter-forces of piled-up years, decades, centuries, go into those moments when the balance might swing, one way or the other.

We looked at the pitiful child. Its blind face was creased; its fingers worked. Its breaths were clearly numbered. The mother began to blubber, adding yet more drops to her other, nameless outpourings; and I felt my ticking, clockmaker's heart swell inside me. A silent, involuntary prayer escaped me.

And suddenly they were there again. Stanislaw and Feliks and Stefan; winging towards me by some uncanny process, bringing with them the mysterious essence of the elements that had received them and de-composed them. Great-grandfather from his Highgate grave, Grandfather from his urn, Father (was he the first to arrive?) from the grey depths where the fishes had nibbled him and the currents long since corroded and dispersed him. Earth, fire, water. They flocked out of the bowels of Nature. And with them came Stanislaw senior, Kasimierz, Tadeusz; and all the others whose names I forget; and even the mythical Krepfs of Nuremburg and Prague.

My hand was on the magic, genie-summoning Watch. In that moment I knew that Time is not something that exists, like territory to be annexed, outside us. What are we all but the distillation of all time? What is each one of us but the sum of all the time before him?

The little baby chest was trembling feebly; the hands still groped; the wrinkled face was turning blue. I held out the Great Watch of Stanislaw. I let it swing gently on its gold chain over the miniscule fingers of this new-born child. They say the first instinct a baby has is to grasp. It touched the ticking masterpiece fashioned in Lublin in the days of the Grand Duchy of Warsaw. A tiny forefinger and thumb clasped with the force of feathers the delicately chased gold casing and the thick, yellowed glass. A second – an eternity passed. And then – the almost motionless chest began to heave vigorously. The face knotted itself up to emit a harsh, stuttering wail, in the timbre of which there seemed the rudiments of a chuckle. The mother's tearful eyes brightened. At the same time I felt inside me a renewed flutter of fear. No, not of fear exactly: a draining away of something; a stripping away of some imposture, as if I had no right to be where I was.

The diminutive fingers still gripped the Watch. Through the gold chain I felt the faintest hint of a baby tug. And a miraculous thing – as miraculous as this infant's resurgence of life – happened. I set it down now as a fact worthy to be engraved in record. At 6.30 p.m. on a July day scarcely a week ago, the hand of a baby (what titanic power must have been in those fingers, what pent-up equivalent of years and years of accumulated time?) stopped my great-grandfather's Watch, which had ticked, without requiring the hand of man to wind it, since September 1809.

The fear – the sensation of being assailed from within – clutched me more intently. This room, in the house of my great-grandfather – in which my ancestors themselves had invisibly mustered (had they fled already, exorcized ghosts?) – was no longer my sanctuary but the centre of a desert. Weighing upon me with a force to equal that which had kept this child alive, was the desolation of my future, growing older and older, but never old enough, and growing every day, more puny, more shrivelled, more insectile.

I released my grip on the chain. I pressed the Great Watch into the hands of an infant. I got up from my position squatting by the mattress. I looked at the mother. How could I have explained, even if I had her language? The baby was breathing; it would live. The mother would pull through. I knew this better than any doctor. I turned to the door and made my exit. Things grew indistinct around me. I stumbled down the flight of stairs to the street door.

Outside, I found a phone-box and, giving the barest particulars, called an ambulance to the mother and child. Then I blundered on. No, not if you are thinking this, in the direction of Deborah. Nor in the direction of the Thames, to hurl, not the Watch, but myself into the murky stream and join my sea-changed father.

Not in any direction. No direction was necessary. For in the historic streets of Whitechapel, minutes later, I was struck, not by an omnibus, not by an arrow of lightning, nor by a shell from one of the Kaiser's iron-clads, but by an internal blow, mysterious and devastating, a blow by which not physical trees but family trees are toppled and torn up by their roots.

Another ambulance wailed down Stepney Way, not for a mother and child, but for me.

And now *I* lie beneath fevered bedclothes. And now I can tell – from the disinterested if baffled faces of doctors (who no doubt have a different way of gauging time from clockmakers), from the looks of buxom nurses (ah – Deborah) who bend over my bed, lift my limp wrist and eye their regulation-issue watches – that my own breaths are numbered.

William Trevor

SINNED AGAINST AND SINNING

WILLIAM TREVOR was born in Mitchelstown, Co. Cork, in 1928, and spent his childhood in provincial Ireland. He attended a number of Irish schools and later Trinity College, Dublin. His books include *Mrs Eckdorf in O'Neill's Hotel*, *The Ballroom of Romance*, *Angels at the Ritz*, which won The Royal Society of Literature Award, *The Children of Dynmouth*, which won the Whitbread Award, *Lovers of their Time* and *Other People's Worlds*. In 1976 Mr Trevor received the Allied Irish Banks' Prize and in 1977 was awarded the CBE in recognition of his valuable services to literature.

Neither Julia nor James could remember a time when Mags had not been there. She was part of the family, although neither a relation nor a connection. Long before either of them had been born she'd been, at school, their mother's best friend.

They were grown up now and had children of their own; the Memory Lane they travelled down at Mags's funeral was long; it was impossible not to recall the past there'd been with her. 'Our dear sister,' the clergyman in the crematorium murmured, and quite abruptly Julia's most vivid memory was of being on the beach at Rustington playing 'Mags's Game', a kind of Grandmother's Footsteps; and James remembered how Mags had interceded when his crime of taking unripe grapes from the greenhouse had been discovered. Imposing no character of its own upon the mourners, the crematorium filled easily with such moments, with summer jaunts and treats in teashops, with talk and stories and dressing up for nursery plays, with Mags's voice for ever reading the adventures of the Swallows and the Amazons.

Cicily, whose friend at school she'd been, remembered Miss Harper being harsh, accusing Mags of sloth and untidiness, and making Mags cry. There'd been a day when everyone had been made to learn 'The Voice and the Peak' and Miss Harper, because of her down on Mags, had made it seem that Mags had brought this communal punishment about by being the final straw in her ignorance of the verb *craindre*. There'd been, quite a few years later, Mags's ill-judged love affair with Robert Blakley, the callousness of Robert's eventual rejection of her, and Mags's scar as a result: her life-long fear of ever again getting her fingers burnt in the same way. In 1948, when Cicily was having James, Mags had come to stay, to help and in particular to look after Julia, who was just beginning to toddle. That had been the beginning of helping with the children; in 1955 she'd moved in after a series of au pair girls had proved in various ways to be less than satisfactory. She'd taken over the garden; her coffee cake became a family favourite.

Cosmo, Cicily's husband, father of James and Julia, recalled at Mags's funeral his first meeting with her. He'd heard about her – rather a lot about her – ever since he'd known Cicily. The unfairness that had been meted out to Mags at school was something he had nodded sympathetic-ally over; as well as over her ill-treatment at the hands of Robert Blakley, and the sudden and unexpected death of her mother, to whom she'd always been so devoted, and with whom, after the Robert Blakley affair, she had determined to make her life, her father having died when she was three. 'This is Mags,' Cicily had said one day in the Trocadero, where they were all to lunch together, celebrating Cicily's and Cosmo's engagement. 'Hullo, Cosmo,' Mags had said, holding out a hand for him to shake. She did not much care for men, he'd thought, gripping the hand and moving it slightly in a handshake. She was tall and rather angular, with a bony face and black untidy hair and unplucked eyebrows. Her lips were a little chapped; she wore no make-up. It was because of Robert Blakley, he'd thought, that she did not take to men. 'I've heard an awful lot about you, Mags,' he said, laughing. She declined a drink, falling instead into excited chat with Cicily, whose cheeks had pinkened with pleasure at the reunion. They talked about girls they'd known, and the dreadful Miss Harper, and Miss Roforth the headmis-tress. At Mags's funeral he remembered that surreptitiously he had asked the waiter to bring him another gin and tonic.

They were a noticeably good-looking family. Cosmo and Cicily, in their middle fifties, were grey-haired but stylishly so, and both of them retained the spare figures of their youth. Cosmo's pale blue eyes and his chiselled face had been bequeathed to his son; and Cicily's smile, her slightly slanting mouth and perfect nose had come to Julia. They all looked a little similar, the men of a certain height, the two women complementing it, the same fair colouring in all four. There was a lack of awkwardness in their movements, a natural easiness that had often caused strangers to wonder where Mags came in.

The coffin began to move, sliding towards beige curtains, which obediently parted. Flames would devour it, they all four thought simultaneously, Mags would become a handful of dust: a part of the family had been torn away. How, Julia wondered, would her parents manage now? To be on their own after so long would surely be a little strange.

They returned to Tudors, the house near Maidenhead where the family had always lived. It was a pleasant house, half-timbered, black and white, more or less in the country. Cosmo had been left it by an aunt at just the right moment, when he'd been at the beginning of his career in the rare books world; Julia and James had been born there. Seeing Tudors for the first time, Mags had said she'd fallen in love with it.

After the funeral service they stood around in the long low-ceilinged sitting-room, glad that it was over. They didn't say much, and soon moved off in two directions, the men to the garden, Cicily and Julia to the room that had been Mags's bedroom. In an efficiently drawn-up will some of her jewellery had been left to Julia and an eighteenth-century clock to James. There'd been bequests for Cicily and Cosmo too, and some clothes and money for Mrs Forde, the daily woman at Tudors.

'Her mother had that,' Cicily said, picking up an amber brooch, a dragon with a gold setting. 'I think it's rather valuable.'

Julia held it in the palm of her hand, gazing at it. 'It's lovely,' she said. It had been Mags's favourite piece, worn only on special occasions. Julia could remember it on a blue blouse polka-dotted with white. It seemed unfair that Mags, the same age as her mother, should have died; Mags who had done no harm to anyone. Having never been married or known children of her own, it seemed that the least she deserved was a longer life.

'Poor old Mags,' her mother said, as if divining these thoughts.

'You'll miss her terribly.'

'Yes, we shall.'

In the garden Cosmo walked with his son, who happened in that moment to be saying the same thing.

'Yes, Cicily'll miss her,' Cosmo replied. 'Dreadfully.'

'So'll you, Father.'

'Yes, I shall too.'

The garden was as pleasant as the house, running down to the river, with japonica and escallonia now in bloom on a meadow bank. It was without herbaceous borders, sheltered by high stone walls. Magnolias and acers added colour to the slope of grass that stretched from wall to wall. Later there'd be roses and laburnum. It was Mags who had planned the arrangement of all these shrubs, who had organized the removal of some cherry trees that weren't to her liking, and had every week in summer cut the grass with her Flymo. It was generally agreed that her good taste had given the garden character.

'There'd been some man, hadn't there?' James asked his father as they stood on the bank of the river, watching pleasure boats go by.

'Robert Blakley. Oh, a long time ago.'

'But it left a mark?'

'Yes, it left a mark.'

In the room that had been Mags's bedroom Cicily said:

'Misfortune came easily to her. It somehow seemed quite expected that Robert Blakley should let her down.'

'What did he do?'

'Just said he'd made a mistake and walked away.'

'Perhaps it was as well if he was like that.'

'I never liked him.'

It seemed to Cicily, and always had, that though misfortune had come easily to her friend it had never been deserved. The world had sinned against her without allowing her the joy of sinning. Ready-made a victim, she'd been supplied with no weapons that Cicily could see as useful in her own defence. The nicest thing that had ever happened in Mags's life might well have been their long friendship and Mags's involvement with the family.

Before lunch they all had a glass or two of sherry because they felt they needed it. It cheered them up, as the lunch itself did. But even so, as Julia said goodbye to her parents, she wondered again how well they'd manage now. She said as much to James as they drove away together in his car, the French clock carefully propped on the back seat, the jewellery in Julia's handbag. When all these years there'd been a triangular quality about conversation in Tudors, how would conversation now continue?

It would not continue, Cosmo thought. There would be silences in Tudors, for already he could feel them gathering. On summer weekends he would start the Flymo for Cicily; they would go as usual to the Borders in July. But as they perused the menu in the bar of the Glenview

Hotel they'd dread the moment when the waiter took it from them, when they could put off no longer the conversation that eluded them. At Christmas it would be all right because, as usual, Julia and James and all the children would come to Tudors, but in the bleak hours after they'd left the emptiness would have an awful edge. Mags had chattered so.

Changing out of the sober clothes she'd worn for the funeral, Cicily recalled a visit with Mags to Fenwick's. It was she who had suggested it, 1969 it must have been. 'I insist,' she'd said. 'Absolutely no arguments.' The fact was, Mags hadn't bought herself so much as a new scarf for years. As a girl, she'd always done her best, but living in Tudors, spending most of her day in the garden, she'd stopped bothering. 'And if Fenwick's haven't anything then we go to Jaeger's,' Cicily had insisted. 'We're going to spend the whole day sorting you out.' Mags of course had protested, but in the end had agreed. She was quite well off, having inherited a useful income from her mother; she could easily afford to splash out.

But in the event she didn't. In Fenwick's the saleswoman was rude. She shook her head repeatedly when Mags stood in front of a looking-glass, first in yellow and then in blue. 'Not entirely madam's style,' she decreed. 'More yours, madam,' she suggested to Cicily. In the end they'd left the shop without anything and instead of going on to Jaeger's went to Dickins and Jones for coffee. Mags wept, not noisily, not making a fuss. She cried with her head bent forward so that people wouldn't see. She apologized and then confessed that she hated shopping for clothes: it was always the same, it always went wrong. Saleswomen sighed when they saw her coming. Almost before she could open her mouth she became the victim of their tired feet.

They went to D. H. Evans that day and bought a dreary wool dress in a shade of granite. It made Mags look like an old age pensioner. 'Really nice,' the saleswoman assured them. 'Really suits the lady.'

That was the trouble, Cicily reflected as she hung up the coat she'd worn for the funeral: Mags had never had the confidence to fight back. She should have pointed out to the saleswoman in Fenwick's that the choice was hers, that she didn't need to be told what her style was. She should have protested that Miss Harper was being unfair. She should have told Robert Blakley to go to hell. Mags had been far better-looking than she'd ever known. With decent make-up and decent clothes she could have been quite striking in her way.

Cicily brushed her hair, glancing at her own face in her dressing-table looking-glass. No saleswoman had ever dared to patronize her; her beauty saw to that. It was all so wretchedly unfair.

Later that day Cosmo sat in the small room he called his study, its walls lined with old books. He had drawn the curtains and turned on the green-shaded desk light. In the kitchen Cicily was preparing their supper, cold ham and salad, and a vegetable soup to cheer it up. He'd passed the kitchen door and seen her at it, 'Any Questions' on the wireless. It was his fault; he knew it was; for twenty-seven years, ever since Mags had become part of the family, it had been his fault. He should have had the wisdom to know: he should have said over his dead body or something strong like that. 'I don't care who she is or how she's suffered,' he should have insisted, 'she's not going to come and live with us.' But of course it hadn't been like that, because Mags had just drifted into the family. Anyone would have thought him mad if he'd suggested that with the passing years she'd consume his marriage.

'Cosmo. Supper.'

He called back, saying he was coming, already putting the moment off. He turned the desk light out but when he left his study he didn't go directly to the kitchen. 'I'm making up the fire,' he announced from the sitting-room, pouring himself a glass of whisky and quickly drinking it.

'Julia seemed well,' Cicily said, pushing the wooden bowl of salad across the kitchen table at him.

'Yes, she did.' It was singular in a way, he thought, that he and Cicily should have taken to their hearts a person who was, physically, so very much the opposite of them. Mags had been like a cuckoo in the midst of the handsome family, and he wondered if she'd ever noticed it, if she'd ever said to herself that it was typical of her tendency to misfortune to find herself so dramatically shown up. He wanted to talk to Cicily about that. They had to talk about everything. They had to clear the air; certainly they had to agree that they were at a beginning, that they could not just go on.

'I suppose it was her looks,' he said, aware that he was putting it clumsily, 'that in the end didn't appeal to Robert Blakley. I mean, not as much as he'd imagined.'

'Oh, he was a horrid man.'

'No, but I mean, Cicily – '

'I don't want to talk about Robert Blakley.'

Neatly she arranged ham and salad on her fork. Any time she wanted to, he thought, she could pick up an affair. Men still found her as worth a second look as they always had: you could see it at cocktail parties and on trains, or even walking with her on the street. He felt proud of her, and glad that she hadn't let herself go.

'No, I meant she wasn't much to look at ever,' he said.

'Poor Mags had far more than looks. Let's not dwell on this, Cosmo.'

'I think we have to, dear.'

'She's dead. Nothing we can say will bring her back.'

'It's not that kind of thing we have to talk about.'

'She wanted her clothes to go to Oxfam. Except what she left to Mrs Forde. I'll see to that tonight.'

When, seven years ago, Cosmo had had an affair with a girl in his office the guilt he might have felt had failed to come about. His unfaithfulness – the only occasion of it in his marriage – had not caused him remorse and heart-searching, as he'd expected it would. He did not return to Tudors after an afternoon with the girl to find himself wanting at once to confess to Cicily. Nor did he walk into a room and find Cicily seeming to be forlorn because she was being wronged and did not know it. He did not think of her, alone and even lonely, while he was with the girl. Such thoughts were unnecessary because Cicily was always all right, because there was always Mags. It had even occasionally seemed to him that she had Mags and he the girl.

Cosmo had never in any way objected to the presence of Mags in his house. She had made things easier all round, it was a mutually satisfactory arrangement. Even at the time of his office affair it had not occurred to him that her presence could possibly be designated as an error; and in all honesty she had never been a source of irritation to him. It was her death, her absence, that had brought the facts to light.

'We have to talk, you know,' he said, still eating ham and salad. 'There are all sorts of things to come to terms with.'

'Talk, Cosmo? What things? What do you mean?'

'We could have made a mistake, you know, having Mags here all these years.'

She frowned. She shook her head, more in bewilderment than denial. He said, 'I think we need to talk about it now.'

But Cicily wanted to be quiet. Immediately after supper she'd go through the clothes, arranging them for Oxfam, keeping back the things for Mrs Forde. She wanted to get all that done as soon as possible. She remembered being in the sanatorium one time with Mags, both of them with measles. They'd talked for hours about what they'd like to do with their lives. She herself had at that time wanted to be a nurse. 'I want to have babies', Mags had said. 'I want to marry a decent kind of man and have a house in the country somewhere and bring up children.'

'You see,' Cosmo was saying, 'there'll be a certain adjustment.'

She nodded, not really listening. Half of Mags's desire had come about: at least she'd lived in a house in the country and at least she'd brought up children, even if the children weren't her own. There still was a school photograph, she and Mags and a girl called Evie Hopegood sitting in the sun outside the library. Just after it had been taken Miss Harper had come along and given Mags a row for sprawling in her chair.

'Incidentally,' Cicily said, 'the man's coming to mend that window-sash tomorrow.'

Cosmo didn't reply. Perhaps this wasn't the right moment to pursue the matter. Perhaps in a day or two, when she'd become more used to the empty house, he should try again.

They finished their meal. He helped her to wash up, something that hadn't been necessary in the past. She went upstairs, he watched the television in the sitting-room.

Young men and girls were playing a game with tractor tyres. They were dressed in running shorts and singlets, one team's red, the other's yellow. Points were scored, a man with a pork-pie hat grimaced into the camera and announced the score. Another man breezed up, trailing a microphone. He placed an arm around the first man's shoulders and said that things were really hotting up. Huge inflated ducks appeared, the beginning of another game. Cosmo turned the television off.

He poured himself another drink. He was aware that he wanted to be drunk, which was, in other circumstances, a condition he avoided. He knew that in a day or two the conversation he wished to have would be equally difficult. He'd go on trying to have it and every effort would fail. He drank steadily, walking up and down the long, low-ceiling sitting-room, glancing out into the garden, where dusk was already gathering. He turned the television on again and found the young men and girls playing a game with buckets of coloured water. He changed the channel. 'I can't help being a lotus-eater,' a man was saying, while an elderly woman wept. Elsewhere Shipham's paste was being promoted.

'It's no good putting it off,' Cosmo said, standing in the doorway of the room that had been Mags's. He had filled his glass almost to the brim and then had added a spurt of soda water. 'We have to talk about our marriage, Cicily.'

She dropped a tweed skirt on to Mrs Forde's pile on the floor. She frowned, thinking she must have misheard. It was unlike him to drink after supper, or indeed before. He'd brought a strong smell of alcohol into the room, which for some reason offended her.

'Our marriage,' he repeated.

'What about it?'

'I've been trying to say, Cicily. I want to talk about it. Now that Mags is dead.'

'Whatever had poor Mags to do with it? And now that she *is* dead, how on earth – ?'

'Actually she consumed it.'

He knew he was not sober, but he knew as well that he was telling the truth. He had a feeling that had been trying to surface for days, which finally had succeeded in doing so while he was watching the athletes with the tractor tyres: deprived of a marriage herself, Mags had lived off theirs. Had she also, he wondered, avenged herself for all sorts of things, even for being the kind of person she was?

These feelings about Mags had intensified since he'd been watching the television show, and it now seemed to Cosmo that everything had been turned inside out by her death. He wondered if James and Julia, looking back one day on their parents' marriage, would agree that the presence of Mags in the house had been a mistake; he wondered if Cicily ever would.

'Consumed?' Cicily said. 'I wasn't aware – '

'We were neither of us aware.'

'I don't know why you're drinking whisky.'

'Cicily, I want to tell you: I had an affair with a girl seven years ago.'

She stared at him, her lips slightly parted, her eyes unblinking. She looked like a statue, and then she puckered up her forehead, frowning again.

'You never told me,' she said, feeling the protest to be absurd as soon as she'd made it.

'I have to tell you now, Cicily.'

She sat down on the bed that had been her friend's. His voice went on speaking, saying something about Mags always being there, mentioning the Glenview Hotel for some reason, mentioning Robert Blakley and saying that Mags had probably intended no ill-will.

'But you liked her,' she whispered. 'You liked her and what on earth had poor Mags – '

'I'm trying to say I'm sorry, Cicily.'

'Sorry?'

'I'm sorry for being unfaithful.'

'But how could I not know? How could you go off with someone else and I not notice anything?'

'I think because Mags was here.'

She closed her eyes, not wanting to see him, in the doorway with his whisky. It didn't make sense what he was saying. Mags was their friend; Mags had never in her life said a thing against him. It was unfair to bring Mags into it. It was ludicrous and silly, like trying to find an excuse.

'The whole thing,' he said, 'from start to finish is all my fault. I shouldn't have allowed Mags to be here, I should have known.'

She opened her eyes and looked across the room at him. He was standing exactly as he had been before, wretchedness in his face. 'You're making this up,' she said, believing that he must be, believing that for some reason he'd been jealous of Mags all these years and now was trying to revenge himself by inventing a relationship with some girl. He was not the kind to go after girls; he wasn't the kind to hurt people.

'No,' he said. 'I'm making nothing up.' The girl had wept when, in the end, he'd decreed that for her there was too little in it to justify their continuing the association. He'd felt about the girl the way he'd wanted to feel about being unfaithful to Cicily: guilty and ashamed and miserable.

'I can't believe it of you,' Cicily whispered, weeping as the girl had wept. 'I feel I'm in an awful nightmare.'

'I'm sorry.'

'My God, what use is saying you're sorry? We had a perfectly good marriage, we were a happy family – '

'My dear, I'm not denying that. All I'm saying – '

'All you're saying,' she cried out bitterly, 'is that none of it meant anything to you. Did you hate me? Did I repel you? Was she marvellous, this girl? Did she make you feel young again? My God, you hypocrite!'

She picked up from the bed a summer dress that had been Mags's, a pattern of checks in several shades of blue. She twisted it between her hands, but Cosmo knew that the action was involuntary, that she was venting her misery on the first thing that came to hand.

'It's the usual thing,' she said more quietly, 'for men in middle age.'

'Cicily – '

'Girls are like prizes at a fun-fair. You shoot a row of ducks and there's your girl with her child's complexion still, and her rosebud lips and eager breasts – '

'Please, Cicily – '

'Why shouldn't she have eager breasts, for God's sake? At least don't deny her her breasts or her milky throat, or her eyes that melted with love. Like a creature in a Sunday supplement, was she? Advertising vodka or tipped cigarettes, discovering herself with an older man. You fell in love with all that and you manage to blame a woman who's dead. Why not blame yourself, Cosmo? Why not simply say you wanted a change?'

'I do blame myself. I've told you I do.'

'Why didn't you marry your girl? Because James and Julia would have despised you? Because she wouldn't have you?'

He didn't reply, and a reply wasn't really expected. She was right when she mentioned their children. He'd known at the time of the affair that they would have despised him for making what they'd have considered to be a fool of himself, going off with a girl who was young enough to be his daughter.

'I want you to understand about Mags,' he said. 'There's something we have to talk about, it's all connected, Cicily. I should have felt sorry for you, but there was always you and Mags, chatting. I kept saying you were all right because you had Mags. I couldn't help it, Cicily.'

'Mags has nothing to do with it. Mags was always blamed by people, ill-used behind her back – '

'I know. I'm sorry. It simply appears to be true, it's hard to understand.'

She sobbed, seeming not to have heard him, still twisting the dress between her fingers. She whispered something but he couldn't hear what it was. He said:

'I'm telling you because I love you, Cicily. Because it can't be between us.'

But even as he spoke he wasn't certain that he still loved Cicily. There was something stale in their relationship, even a whiff of tedium. A happy ending would be that Cicily would find another man and he a girl as different from Cicily as the girl in his office had been. Why should they sit for the rest of their days in Tudors or the bar of the Glenview Hotel trying to make bricks without straw? What was the point, in middle age, of such a dreary effort?

In the room that had been Mags's the weeping of Cicily grew louder and eventually she flung her head on to the pillow and pressed her face into its softness in an effort to stifle her sobs. He looked around at the familiar clothes – dresses and coats and skirts and blouses, pairs of shoes lined up on the floor. At this age happy endings with other people weren't two a penny, and for a moment he wondered if perhaps they had the strength and the patience to blow life into a marriage with which they had lost touch. He shook his head, still standing by the door while Cicily wept. It was asking too much of her: how could she suddenly look back at every cut knee Mags had bandaged, every cake she'd baked, every word she'd spoken, and see them differently? How could she come to consider that he'd been right, that day in the Trocadero, to recognize that Mags didn't care for men? Of course, he thought as well, he could be wrong: like Miss Harper, he might be placing blame where blame did not belong; like Robert Blakley, he might be treating a victim to a victim's due.

It didn't matter. In innocence or otherwise the damage had been done. They would try for a bit because that was what people did; for companionship of a kind they might stay together, or they might not. Whatever happened, Mags would remain triumphant in their marriage, sinned against while he had done the sinning.